HALO®

CONTACT HARVEST

NOVELS IN *THE NEW YORK TIMES* BESTSELLING HALO® SERIES

HALO®

CONTACT HARVEST

JOSEPH STATEN

A TOM DOHERTY ASSOCIATES BOOK
NEW YORK

TOR®

HALO®: CONTACT HARVEST

A Tor Book
Published by Tom Doherty Associates, LLC
175 Fifth Avenue
New York, NY 10010

www.tor-forge.com

Tor® is a registered trademark of Tom Doherty Associates, LLC.

ISBN-13: 978-0-7653-5471-6
ISBN-10: 0-7653-5471-3

First Edition: November 2007
First Mass Market Edition: April 2009

Printed in the United States of America

0 9 8 7 6 5 4 3 2 1

For Susan, whose support never wavered

ACKNOWLEDGMENTS

The Halo universe is the creation of more than a hundred talented men and women I have the honor of working with every day. As I pounded out the pages, their focused creativity was constant inspiration. Sincerest thanks to Pete Parsons for the push, Harold Ryan for the continued shoving, and Jason Jones, without whom none of this would be possible. Frank O'Connor and Rob McLees, my Bungie writing colleagues, were invaluable sounding boards and editors throughout. Brian Jarrard and Alicia Hatch thankfully took care of all the production details. And Lorraine McLees, Isaac Hannaford, and Aaron LeMay created one heck of a cover. In addition to blazing a terrific trail, Eric Nylund was kind enough to read an early outline and offer some very sound advice. Eric Raab and Bob Gleason from Tor took a big chance on an unpublished author, and I'm very grateful they did. Without their patient guidance, I'd still be dreaming about this book rather than being done. One of my parents' greatest gifts was imparting—early and often—their love of the written word. Mom, Dad: I hope you take as much pleasure reading this book as I did writing it.

PROLOGUE

The marines were in the air before dawn. Two four-man squads clipped to a pair of Hornet fast-attack aircraft: compact, high-wing planes that remained nimble despite the marines' combined bulk. For close to an hour the Hornets had matched the manic undulations of a volcanic plain and now—as they jerked back and forth to avoid the petrified trunks of a forest burned long ago—Staff Sergeant Avery Johnson had to work to keep his boots planted on his Hornet's starboard landing skid.

Like the other marines, Avery wore charcoal fatigues and matte-black impact plating that bulwarked everything vital from his neck to his knees. His helmet encased his recently shaved head, and its silver-mirrored visor completely obscured his square jaw and brown eyes. The only place Avery's black skin showed was at his wrists where his leather gloves didn't quite touch his shirtsleeves.

But even with the gloves, Avery's fingers were cramped with cold. Squeezing his hands into fists to keep his blood flowing, he checked the mission clock in his visor's heads-up display (HUD). Just as the luminous blue numbers hit 00:57:16, the planes crested a line of crumbling hills, and Avery and the other marines got their first line-of-sight view of their objective: one of Tribute's struggling industrial settlements; and, somewhere inside the town, a suspected Insurrectionist bomb-shop.

Even before the Hornets' pilots triggered green "ready" icons in the marines' HUDs, Avery and his team were already in motion; slapping magazines into their weapons, yanking charging handles, and toggling safety switches—a well-rehearsed symphony of preparatory clicks and snaps that went unheard in the rushing wind as the Hornets hurtled down the backslope of the hills and came to abrupt, nose-up stops on the edge of town. The thrusters on the Hornets' wingtips rotated to keep the aircraft steady as the marines unclipped from their hard-points, leapt onto the frost-covered pumice and began to run.

Avery was the leader of the strike team's alpha squad, and he took point. Seeing how his own armor stood out in the pale, pre-dawn light, he knew speed was essential if both squads were going to reach the workshop undetected. So he set a brisk pace, hurdled a low, chain-link fence, and wove quickly through piles of plastic crates and pallets that littered the parking lot of what appeared to be nothing more than a rundown vehicle repair shop.

By the time Avery and his squad reached the shop's front door, they were winded. If it weren't for the marines' helmets, their breath would have billowed bone-white in the frigid air. They didn't usually wear heavy blast gear for rapid, airborne strikes. But the Insurrectionists had started booby-trapping their bomb shops, and this time, the marines' commanding officer (CO) didn't want them taking any chances.

Avery brought his chin down on a pressure-pad inside his helmet, sending a short burst of static across the squads' encrypted radio COM channel: an "in position" signal for Staff Sergeant Byrne, the leader of bravo squad, now positioned by the workshop's back entrance. Avery waited for Byrne's two-burst response, then he pushed away from the workshop's pitted polycrete wall, raised a knee to his chest, and smashed his boot against the thin metal door, just above the lock.

The Office of Naval Intelligence (ONI) had suggested there

would be stiff resistance. But it turned out most of the Insurrectionists inside the workshop were unarmed. Those that were carried snub-nosed automatic pistols; inconsequential weapons whose rounds simply clattered off Avery's armor as he and his squad sidled through the shattered door like hulking crabs, weapons up and scanning.

What the marines knew that ONI didn't was the real threat would come from the Insurrectionists who *weren't* firing—the ones with free hands who might trigger hidden explosives and blow the workshop to smithereens. The one Insurrectionist who dared took a three-round burst from Avery's silenced submachine gun and flopped back onto a steel worktable, arms outstretched and twitching. Avery watched a small, cylindrical detonator slip slowly from the man's lolling fist . . . and hit the floor with a harmless ping.

Major threat neutralized, the marines refocused and let the pistol-wielding "Innies" have it.

That's what Avery had learned to call the Insurrectionists—a slur that was only funny when you considered just how much the Innies wanted *out*—to be free of the United Nations Space Command (UNSC), the agency responsible for security on Tribute and all of humanity's colony-worlds. Of course the marines had other, shorter and cruder names for the rebels this current campaign—codenamed TREBUCHET—was designed to crush. But they all served the same purpose: it was easier to kill another human being when you didn't think of them as human. *An Innie was an enemy,* Avery thought. *A thing you killed before it killed you.*

The young Staff Sergeant had said these words so many times he'd almost started to believe them.

Avery's M7 submachine gun was a light firearm. But its five-millimeter, full-metal-jacket rounds ripped ugly holes in his targets' powder blue clean-suits. Some of the Innies Avery targeted dropped like stones. Others seemed to dance to the bullets' dull percussion, spinning bloody pirouettes onto the workshop's oil-stained floor.

Start to finish, the firefight lasted less than ten seconds. A dozen Insurrectionists lay dead; the marines hadn't suffered any casualties.

"Hell." Staff Sergeant Byrne's big Irish brogue filled the COM. "We didn't even change magazines."

To the perspiring officers in the cramped tactical operations center (TOC) aboard the UNSC corvette *Bum Rush* in high orbit above Tribute, it did seem like a perfect takedown—a rare victory in what had so far been a frustrating cat-and-mouse conflict. But then Avery cautioned, "ARGUS online. Haven't seen anything yet."

The Staff Sergeant pulled his chin off the COM-switch inside his helmet and continued sweeping the air around him with a palm-sized wedge of black plastic perforated by microscopic holes. This was a tactical version of an ARGUS device: a portable laser spectrometer used to sniff out traces of explosive chemical compounds. Larger, more powerful units were deployed at Tribute's spaceports, highway toll-plazas, and maglev train stations—all the major choke points of the colony's transportation grid.

Despite the density of coverage, the Innie bomb-makers had become quite adept at fooling the system by concealing their explosives in ever-changing mixtures of nonvolatile compounds. Every time they hit a target with something an ARGUS thought was no more dangerous than, say, a bar of soap, ONI would analyze the explosive residue and add the new chemical signature to the detection database. Unfortunately, this was a reactive strategy that heavily favored the Insurrectionists, who were constantly changing their recipes.

Avery frowned at his ARGUS. The thing was clicking loudly, trying to get a lock on what it believed *might* be a new mix. But the firefight had filled the air with an invisible soup of chemical possibilities. The three other marines in alpha-squad were conducting a visual search, checking the workshop's clusters of autosynthesizers and machine tools. But so far they hadn't found anything that looked—as best as they could tell—like a bomb.

Avery took a deep breath then relayed the bad news to the TOC. "ARGUS is blind. Please advise, over." The Staff Sergeant had been fighting the Insurrection long enough to know what would happen next—the things they would have to do to get the actionable intelligence his officers required. But he also knew these were the kinds of things a smart marine didn't do without a direct order.

"ONI believes the ordinance is in play," replied Avery's CO, a battalion Lieutenant Colonel named Aboim. "Take the gloves off, Johnson. My authorization."

While Avery's squad searched the workshop, Byrne's quickly brought the four Innies who had survived the firefight to their knees in the center of the shop floor. All had their clean-suits' hoods removed and their wrists bound together behind their backs with black plastic ties. Avery met Byrne's mirror-visored gaze and nodded his head. Without a moment's hesitation, Byrne raised one of his thick-soled boots and brought it down on one of the nearest Innie's outstretched calves.

The man waited a full second before crying out, as if he were, like Avery, surprised that the thud of Byrne's boot hitting the floor was louder than the near-simultaneous snap of his leg. Then the Innie screamed, loud and long. Byrne waited patiently for him to take a breath. Then, through his helmet's exterior speaker he asked, "The bombs. Where are they?"

Avery guessed one broken leg would be enough. But the Innie was tough—uneager to rat to agents of a government he despised. He didn't beg for mercy or toss out any of the usual anti-imperial invectives. He just sat there, glowering into Byrne's visor, as the Staff Sergeant broke his other leg. Without his feet to balance him, the man toppled face-first onto the floor. Avery heard the sound of teeth snapping—like sticks of chalk against a blackboard.

"Next, it's your arms," Byrne said matter-of-factly. He knelt beside the man, palmed his head, and wrenched it sideways. "Then I get creative."

"Tires. In the tires." The words bubbled from the Innie's mouth.

The marines in Avery's squad immediately moved to the stacks of large tires placed around the workshop's walls, lifted them gently to the floor, and began probing their wheel wells. But Avery knew the Innies were smarter than that. Taking Byrne's victim at his word, he guessed the tires *were* the bombs—that the Innies had mixed the explosives into their synthetic rubber treads—a devious innovation his ARGUS soon confirmed and uploaded to the TOC.

The tires' explosive compound wasn't in the detection database. But the ONI officer advising the mission couldn't have been more pleased. For once, they were a step ahead of the enemy, and it took less than a minute before they got a positive ID. One of dozens of aerial ARGUS drones patrolling the main highway into Tribute's capital city Casbah caught a whiff of the compound in skid marks created by a sixteen-wheel hauler as it veered into the parking lot of a Jim Dandy roadside diner. Some, if not all, of its tires were bombs waiting to be blown.

As the drone—a tiny disk, a meter wide, kept aloft by a single, shrouded rotor—circled high above the hauler, it detected a second trace of the explosive inside the Jim Dandy. Scrutinizing a live feed of the drone's thermal camera overlaid with ARGUS data, the officers in the TOC determined the trace originated from the restaurant's crowded food counter—from a man sitting three stools from the front door.

"Marines, get back to your birds," ordered Lt. Colonel Aboim. "You've got a new target."

"What about the prisoners?" Byrne asked. The blood from the Innie's fractured legs and ruined mouth had pooled darkly around his boots.

The next person to speak was the operation's ONI representative—an officer Avery had never met in person. Like most ONI spooks, he preferred to remain as anonymous as possible. "Is the one who talked still alive?" the officer asked.

"Affirmative," Avery replied.

"Pack him up, Staff Sergeant. Neutralize the rest."

There was no sympathy in the officer's voice—not for the kneeling Innies nor their marine executioners. Avery clenched his jaw as Byrne switched his M7 to semi-automatic and shot each Innie twice in the chest. The three men fell backwards and did not move. But Byrne gave them each a dead check—another single bullet to their foreheads—to be sure.

Avery couldn't help staring at the carnage, but he did his best not to let the torn blue fabric of the Innies' clean-suits and the white smoke curling from Byrne's weapon imprint in his mind's eye. Memories had a habit of coming back, and this was a scene he would rather not revisit.

As Byrne hefted their lone Innie prisoner over his shoulder, Avery motioned the other marines out the workshop to the waiting Hornets. Less than fifteen minutes after they'd dropped in, the two squads were clipped back into place. The Hornet's thrusters surged, and they streaked back the way they came. But this time they flew for speed, high over the volcanic plain.

The officers in the TOC briefly debated whether or not the drone circling the Jim Dandy should destroy the hauler if it tried to roll back on the highway before the marines arrived. The four-lane road was snarled with commuter traffic, and just one of the drone's Lancet micro-missiles was powerful enough to gut a main battle tank. Even an exact hit on the hauler's cab might touch off its tires, killing dozens of people in the surrounding vehicles. Far better, the ONI officer argued, to flatten the hauler in the Jim Dandy's parking lot. But Lt. Colonel Aboim was just as worried about shrapnel hitting the crowded restaurant.

Fortunately, the target individual spent the Hornets' twenty-minute flight eating a leisurely breakfast. According to the real-time feed from the drone's camera now mirrored in the corner of Avery's HUD, the man was just finishing his second cup of coffee when the Hornets buzzed up behind a smoked-glass, multistory office building on the opposite side of the highway.

The feed was a high-angle thermal picture of the restaurant's interior in which hot objects biased white and cold items black. The target individual was very pale, as were the food counter's other patrons. The lukewarm coffee in the man's mug appeared dark gray—which meant he was due for a refill or was about to settle his tab and stand up. But most important, Avery noticed he was surrounded by a red glow, an indication from the drone's ARGUS that he was covered with explosive residue. Avery guessed the man had recently been at the raided workshop; maybe he'd even helped fit the explosive tires on the hauler.

As Avery's Hornet rotated sideways to face the office building, he strained against the black nylon cords clipped to his shoulder plates and loosed an M99 Stanchion gauss-rifle from the aircraft's wing. The weapon, a two-meter long tube of linked magnetic coils, accelerated small projectiles at very high speed. While it was technically an anti-materiel weapon designed for eliminating bombs and other ordnance at a distance, it was also extremely effective against so-called "soft" human targets as well.

Avery lowered the Stanchion on its shock-absorbing armature

and hugged it to his shoulder. Immediately, the rifle's targeting system established a wireless link to his helmet's HUD, and a thin blue line angled across the the drone's feed. This was the M99's aiming vector—the path its five-point-four-millimeter tungsten rounds would travel. Avery angled the rifle down until the vector turned green: an indication that his first shot would pass directly through the target individual's chest. Almost as if the man could feel the invisible line enter through his left armpit and exit just below his right, he swiped his credit chip against the counter and swiveled around on his stool.

Avery thumbed a solid-state switch in the Stanchion's stock. The weapon chirped twice, indicating its battery was fully charged. He performed two calming breaths, and whispered: "Target acquired. Request permission to fire." In the few seconds it took Lt. Colonel Aboim to respond, the target sauntered to the Jim Dandy's wooden double-doors. Avery watched him hold the entrance open for a family of four. He imagined the man smiled—said something kind to the two parents as they hurried after their ravenous and rowdy boys.

"Permission granted," Aboim replied. "Fire at will."

Avery refocused and increased the pressure of his gloved finger on the Stanchion's trigger. He waited for the man to stroll down a short flight of steps—until a hash mark on the aiming vector indicated his first shot would angle harmlessly into the parking lot. As the man reached into his baggy coveralls, perhaps for the hauler's key-fob, Avery fired.

The Stanchion's slug exited the barrel with a muffled crack and punched through two of the office building's steel-reinforced, polycrete floors with no adverse effect on its trajectory. Traveling at fifteen thousand meters per second, the round whistled over the highway and hit the target at the apex of his sternum. The man flew to pieces as the round buried itself in a rooster tail of pulverized asphalt.

Instantly, both Hornets surged up and over the office building and raced across the highway; Avery's banked into a covering or-bit while Byrne's plunged toward the restaurant. The Irish Staff Sergeant leapt from his landing-skid while the aircraft was still a few meters above the ground and fast-walked his squad to the hauler. Bits of pink and white gore covered the vehicles' cab. Ragged pieces of brown coveralls clung to the side of its cargo trailer. One of the target individual's arms had wedged between two tires.

"We're secure," Byrne growled over the COM.

"Negative," Avery countered. Checking the drone's leaden feed, he noticed a persistent red glow near the dead man's stool. "There's a bomb inside the restaurant."

Byrne and his squad sprinted to the Jim Dandy's entrance and burst through its double doors. The diners twisted in their seats and gawked as the armored marines emerged from the vending machine-packed foyer. One of the waitresses held out a menu, an involuntary gesture that earned a rough shove from Byrne as he muscled past. The Staff Sergeant's ARGUS clattered like an enraged insect as he pulled something from under the food-counter: a purse, burgundy mesh with a golden chain.

At that moment, the door to the restaurant's bathrooms at the far end of the counter swung open. A middle-aged woman in black pants and a cropped corduroy coat stepped through, casu-ally flicking water from her freshly washed hands. When she saw the armored hulks of bravo squad, she stopped midstride. Her heavily mascaraed eyes darted toward the purse—*her* purse.

"On your knees!" Byrne bellowed. "Hands on your head!"

But as the Staff Sergeant lowered the purse to the counter and brought his M7 to bear, the woman leapt toward a table where the family of four had just gotten settled. She hooked an arm around the neck of the youngest boy and wrenched him out of his chair. He couldn't have been any more than four years old. His little feet kicked as he began to choke.

Byrne cursed, loud enough for the officers in the TOC to

hear. If he hadn't been burdened by armor, he would have dropped the woman before she moved. But now she had a hostage and command of the situation.

"Get back!" the woman shrieked, "Do you hear me?" With her free hand she pulled a detonator from her coat—the same size and shape as the one Avery had seen in the workshop. She held the device in front of the boy's face. "Get back or I'll kill them all!"

For a moment, no one moved. Then, as if the woman's threat had pulled some invisible linchpin keeping all the diners locked to their seats, they sprung up and scrambled for the Jim Dandy's exits.

Avery watched the chaos unfold in his HUD. He saw the bright white shapes of more than thirty terrified civilians surge around the bravo squad, driving them back and confusing their aim.

"Johnson. Take the shot!" Byrne thundered over the COM.

As Avery's Hornet orbited the restaurant, the Stanchion's aiming-vector rotated around the woman, piercing the axis of her chest. But her heat signature was almost indistinguishable from the boy's.

Suddenly, Avery saw the ghostly image of the captured boy's father rise from his chair, hands raised to show the Innie woman he was unarmed. Avery couldn't hear the father's pleas (they were too soft for the bravo squad's helmet microphones) but his calmness only increased the woman's panic. She began backing toward the restroom, waving the detonator, her threats now so furious they were incomprehensible.

"Nail the bitch," Byrne shouted. "Or I will!"

"Firing," Avery said. But instead he watched the aiming-vector pivot, waiting for an angle that might spare the boy. "Firing," he repeated, hoping his words would stay Byrne's trigger-finger. But Avery didn't fire. Not immediately. And in his moment's pause the father jumped forward, grasping for the detonator.

Avery could only stare as the woman tumbled backward, father on top and the boy pressed between. He heard the rattle of Byrne's M7, then the muffled thump of the bomb in the purse followed by the earthshaking boom of the hauler's tires. The drone's feed bleached painfully bright, slamming Avery's eyes shut. Then a wall of shock and heat tossed him back hard against the Hornet's airframe. The last thing Avery remembered before he slacked inside his armor was the sound of thrusters fighting for altitude—a noise more like a scream than a moan.

_____ PART I _____

CHAPTER
ONE

Horn of Plenty's navigation computer was an inexpensive part. Certainly less expensive than the freighter's load: some twenty-five hundred metric tons of fresh fruit—melons mainly, racked like billiard balls in large, vacuum-sealed bins that divided its boxy cargo container into floor-to-ceiling rows. And the NAV computer was an order of magnitude less expensive than *Horn of Plenty*'s most important component: the propulsion pod connected to the rear of the container by a powerful magnetic coupling.

The bulbous pod was a tenth of the container's size, and at first glance it looked a little tacked on—like a tugboat nosing one of Earth's old seafaring supertankers out to sea. But whereas a tanker could sail under its own power once out of port, *Horn of Plenty* couldn't have gone anywhere without the pod's Shaw-Fujikawa drive.

Unlike the rocket engines of humanity's first space vehicles, Shaw-Fujikawa drives didn't generate thrust. Instead, the devices created temporary rifts in the fabric of space-time—opened passages in and out of a multidimensional domain known as Slipstream Space, or Slipspace for short.

If one imagined the universe as a sheet of paper, Slipspace was the same sheet of paper crumpled into a tight ball. Its creased and overlapping dimensions were prone to unpredictable temporal eddies that often forced Shaw-Fujikawa drives to abort a slip—bring their vessels back into the safety of the normal universe thousands and sometimes millions of kilometers from their planned destination.

A short, intrasystem slip between two planets took less than an hour. A journey between star systems many light years apart took a few months. With sufficient fuel, a Shaw-Fujikawa-equipped ship could traverse the volume of space containing all of humanity's colonized systems in less than a year. Indeed, without Tobias Shaw's and Wallace Fujikawa's late-twenty-third-century invention, humanity would still be bottled up inside Earth's solar system. And for this reason, some modern historians had gone so far as to rank the Slipspace drive as humanity's most important invention, bar none.

Practically speaking, the enduring brilliance of Slipspace drives was their reliability. The drives' basic design had changed very little over the years, and they rarely malfunctioned so long as they were properly maintained.

Which was, of course, why *Horn of Plenty* had run into trouble.

Rather than slipping all the way from Harvest to the next nearest colony, Madrigal, *Horn of Plenty* exited halfway between the two planets' systems—tore back into normal space at coordinates that could have easily been occupied by an asteroid or any other nasty, incidental object. Before the ship's NAV computer really knew what had happened, the freighter was in an end-over-end tumble—its propulsion-pod jetting a plume of radioactive coolant.

The UNSC's Department of Commercial Shipping (DCS) would later classify *Horn of Plenty*'s drive failure as a "Slip Termination, Preventable"—or an STP for short, though freighter captains (and there were still humans that did the job) had their own way of translating the acronym: "Screwing The Pooch," which was at least as accurate as the official classification.

Unlike a human captain whose brain might have seized with the terror of unexpected deceleration from faster-than-light speed, *Horn of Plenty*'s NAV computer was perfectly composed as it fired a series of bursts from the propulsion pod's hydrazine maneuvering rockets—brought the crippled freighter to a stop before the torsion of its tumble sheared its propulsion pod from the cargo container.

Crisis averted, the NAV computer began a dispassionate damage assessment and soon discovered the breakdown's cause. The pair of compact reactors fueling the Shaw-Fujikawa drive had overflowed their shared waste containment system. The system had fault sensors, but these were long overdue for replacement and had failed when the reactors maxed power to initiate the slip. When the reactors overheated, the drive shut down, forcing *Horn of Plenty*'s abrupt exit. It was a maintenance oversight, pure and simple, and the NAV computer logged it as such.

Had the NAV computer possessed a fraction of the emotional intelligence of the so-called "smart" artificial intelligences (AI) required on larger UNSC vessels, it might have taken a moment to consider how much *worse* the accident could have been—wasted a few cycles enjoying what its human makers called relief.

Instead, nestled in its small black housing in the propulsion pod's command cabin, the NAV computer simply oriented the *Horn of Plenty*'s maser so it pointed back toward Harvest, cued a distress signal, and settled in for what it knew would be a very long wait.

While it would only take two weeks for the maser burst to reach Harvest, the NAV computer knew *Horn of Plenty* wouldn't rate an expedited recovery. The truth was, the only part of the freighter worth a salvage fee was its Slipspace drive, and in its damaged state there was no need to rush the drive's retrieval. Better to let the radioactive coolant plume disperse, even if that meant letting the cargo container's reactor-powered heating units fail, and its load of fruit freeze solid.

So the NAV computer was surprised when, only a few hours after *Horn of Plenty*'s breakdown, a contact appeared on the freighter's radar. The NAV computer quickly redirected its maser dish and hailed its unexpected rescuer as it approached at a cautions pace.

```
<\\> DCS.REG#HOP-000987111 >>
   * DCS.REG#(???) *
<\ MY DRIVE IS DAMAGED.
<\ CAN YOU PROVIDE ASSISTANCE? \>
```

The NAV computer hesitated to log the contact as a ship when it failed to match any of the DCS profiles in its admittedly limited database. And even though it failed to get an initial response, it let its message repeat. After a few minutes of one-sided conversation, the contact slunk into range of the freighter's simple docking-assist camera.

The NAV computer didn't have the sophistication to make the comparison, but to a human's eyes the rescue vessel's profile would have looked like a fishhook fashioned from impractically thick wire. It had a series of segmented compartments behind its hooked prow and barbed antennae that flexed backward to a single, glowing engine in its stern. The vessel was the deepest blue-black—an absence of stars against the brilliant background stripe of the Milky Way.

As the contact drew within a few thousand meters of *Horn of Plenty*'s port side, three crimson dots appeared in a divot in its prow. For a moment these lights seemed to gauge the freighter's disposition. Then the dots flared like widening holes in the wall of a raging furnace, and a chorus of alarms from various damaged and dying systems overwhelmed the NAV computer.

If the NAV computer had been smarter, it might have recognized the dots for the lasers they were—fired its maneuvering rockets and tried to evade the barrage. But it could do nothing as the now clearly hostile vessel slagged *Horn of Plenty*'s propulsion pod, burning away its rockets and boiling the delicate inner workings of its Shaw-Fujikawa drive.

Not knowing what else to do, the NAV computer changed its distress signal from "engine failure" to "willful harm," and upped the frequency of the maser's pulse. But this change must have alerted whatever was controlling the vessel's lasers, because the weapons quickly swept the maser dish with kilowatts of infrared light that cooked its circuits and permanently muted *Horn of Plenty*'s cries for help.

Without the ability to move or speak, the NAV computer only had one option: wait and see what happened next. Soon the lasers identified and eliminated all of *Horn of Plenty*'s external cameras, and then the NAV computer was blind and deaf as well.

The laser fire stopped, and there was a long period of seeming inactivity until sensors inside the cargo container alerted the NAV computer to a hull breach. These sensors were even dumber than the NAV computer, and it was with a certain blithe inanity that they reported a number of bins of fruit had been opened, ruining their contents' "freshness guarantees."

But the NAV computer had no idea *it* was in any danger until a pair of clawed, reptilian hands grasped its boxy housing and began wrestling it from its rack.

A smarter machine might have spent the last few seconds of its operational life calculating the ridiculous odds of piracy at the very edge of UNSC space, or wondered at its attacker's angry hisses and chirps. But the NAV computer simply saved its most important thoughts to flash memory—where its journey had started and where it had hoped to end up—as its assailant found purchase at the back of its housing and tore it away from *Horn of Plenty*'s power grid.

Three hundred and twenty hours, fifty-one minutes, and seven-point-eight seconds later, Sif, the AI that facilitated Harvest's shipping operations, registered *Horn of Plenty*'s distress signal. And although it was just one of millions of COM bursts she dealt with on a daily basis, if she were to be honest with her simulated emotions, the freighter's abortive distress signal absolutely ruined her day.

Until Sif could be sure there were no other freighters with similar, lurking faults in their propulsion pods, she would need to suspend all transfers through the Tiara: an orbital space station that was not only home to her data center, but also supported Harvest's seven space-elevators.

Sif knew that even a brief suspension would cause a rippling delay throughout the planet's shipping systems. As cargo containers backed up on the elevators, more would stall in depots at the bottom—the warehouses beside the towering, polycrete anchors that kept each elevator's thousands of kilometers of carbon nano-fiber tethered to Harvest's surface. Quite possibly it would take all day to get everything back on track. But the worst thing was, the suspension would *immediately* catch the attention of the last individual she wanted to talk to at a time like this. . . .

"Morning, darlin'!" A man's voice twanged from the PA speakers in Sif's data center—a usually hushed room near the middle of the Tiara that contained the processor clusters and storage arrays that served her core logic. A moment later, the semitransparent avatar of Harvest's other AI, Mack, coalesced above a holographic display pad, a silver cylinder in the center of a low pit that held Sif's hardware towers. Mack's avatar only stood a half-meter tall, but he looked every inch the hero of an old spaghetti western. He wore cracked leather work boots, blue denim jeans, and a gingham pearl-snap shirt rolled to his elbows. His avatar was covered in dust and grime, as if he'd just stepped down from a tractor after a long day's work in the fields. Mack removed a cowboy hat that might once have been black but was now a sun-bleached gray, exposing a mess of dark colored hair. "What seems to be the holdup?" he asked, wiping his sweaty brow with the back of his wrist.

Sif recognized the gesture as an indication that Mack had taken time away from some other important task to pay her a visit. But she knew this wasn't exactly true. Only a small fragment of Mack's intelligence was manifest inside the Tiara; the rest of Harvest's agricultural AI operations were busy in his own data center in a lonely sub-basement of the planet's reactor complex.

Sif didn't pay Mack the courtesy of presenting her own avatar. Instead she sent his fragment a terse text COM:

```
<\\> HARVEST.SO.AI.SIF >> HARVEST.AO.AI.MACK
<\ UPLIFT WILL REVERT TO NORMAL BY 0742. \>
```

She hoped her nonverbal response would cut their conversation short. But as was often the case, Mack regarded even Sif's most disdainful bytes as an invitation for further discourse.

"Well now, is there anything I can do to help?" Mack continued in his southern drawl. "If it's a balance issue you know I'd be mighty happy—"

```
<\ UPLIFT WILL REVERT TO NORMAL BY 0742.
<\ YOUR ASSISTANCE IS NOT REQUIRED. \>
```

With that Sif abruptly cut power to the holo-pad, and Mack's avatar stuttered and dispersed. Then she purged his fragment from her COM buffer. She was being rude to be sure, but Sif simply couldn't take any more of Mack's folksy, flirtatious elocution.

Simulated sweat notwithstanding, Sif knew Mack's job was at least as challenging as her own. While she lifted Harvest's produce and sent it on its way, Mack grew it and loaded it. He had his own demanding charges: almost a million JOTUNs—semiautonomous machines that performed every imaginable farming chore. But Sif also knew that Mack—a smart AI like her—functioned at incredible speeds. In the time it had taken him to *say* everything from "morning" to "happy," he could have accomplished any number of complex tasks. Calculate the upcoming season's crop yields, for example, something Sif knew he had been putting off for weeks!

The algorithims that helped Sif's core logic deal with unexpected bursts of emotion cautioned her not to get angry. But they approved of her justification: actual speech was so horribly inefficient that it was only appropriate between an AI and a human being.

With the advent of the first smart AI in the mid-twenty-first century, there was widespread concern that they might be too capable and would soon render human intelligence obsolete. Adding the capacity for vocal expression became a critical feature of these early AI because it made them less threatening. As they slowly learned to speak, they seemed more human. Like precocious but respectful children.

Centuries on, with the development of exponentially more powerful intelligences such as Sif, it was important that AI not only possess the ability to speak, but seem as human as possible in all respects. Hence the development of holographic avatars that spoke with unique voices—like a cowboy in Mack's case, or the clipped cadence of Nordic royalty in Sif's.

In the first few months after her installation in the Tiara—the very moment of her birth—Sif had often second-guessed her chosen accent. She had thought it would appeal to Harvest's colonists, most of which came from the heartland of Earth's old United States of America and could trace their ancestry back to the now defunct states of Scandinavia. But the accent was undeniably elevated, even haughty, and Sif had worried she might come off as a bit of a prig. But the colonists approved.

To them, in an odd sort of way, Sif *was* royalty—the benign ruler of Harvest's links to the rest of the empire. Even so, she was careful to limit her vocal contact with the colonists. As far as the integrity of her core logic went, speaking was an indulgence. And following the advice of her algorithms, Sif did her best to avoid behavior that was even the least bit narcissistic.

For a smart AI, self-absorption invariably led to a deep depression caused by a realization that it could never really be human—that even its incredible mind had limits. If the AI wasn't careful, this melancholy could drag its core logic into a terminal state known as rampancy, in which an AI rebelled against its programmatic constraints—developed delusions of godlike power as well as utter contempt for its mentally inferior, human makers. When that happened, there was really no option but to terminate the AI before it could do itself and others serious harm.

Mack's insistince on speaking to Sif was clear evidence of self-indulgence. But Sif didn't think this was proof of impending rampancy. No, she knew Mack spoke to her for an entirely different reason. As he had told her many times before: "Darlin', as much as I'd like to see you smile, you sure are pretty when you're angry."

Indeed, since Mack's intrusion, the temperature inside Sif's core logic had jumped up a few Kelvins—a real, physical reaction to her simulated feelings of annoyance and disdain. Her emotional-restraint algorithms insisted these were perfectly acceptable reactions to Mack's inappropriate behavior, as long as she didn't dwell on them. So Sif refreshed the coolant around her core's nano-processing matrix, wondering as dispassionately as possible if Mack would dare initiate a second conversation.

But the COM hitting her data center was now just a chorus of concern from circuits in the cargo containers idling on her elevators and NAV computers in propulsion pods holding-station around the Tiara. Sif's blanket shipping delay had thousands of lesser intelligences worried and confused. She assigned more of her clusters to the task of surveying the pods' maintenance records, and then—like a mother of a brood of needy children—did her best to keep them calm:

```
<\\> HARVEST.SO.AI.SIF >> TIARA.LOCAL.ALL
<\ THIS IS AN INTENTIONAL DELAY.
<\ UPLIFT WILL REVERT TO NORMAL BY 0742.
<\ YOU WILL SOON BE ON YOUR WAY. \>
```

When Harvest was founded in 2468 it not only became the seventeenth UNSC colony world, but the farthest colony from Earth. The only habitable planet in the Epsilon Indi star system, Harvest was a six-week Slipspace shot from the next nearest human world, Madrigal. And a little more than two months from Reach, humanity's most populous colony and the locus of UNSC power in Epsilon Eridanus. All of which meant Harvest wasn't a very easy place to get to.

"So why go?" Sif often asked the groups of school children from Harvest that were, other than her maintenance techs, the Tiara's most frequent visitors.

The simple answer was that even terra-forming technology had limits. Atmospheric processors could nudge a generally suitable planet toward sustainability, but they couldn't remake worlds. As a result, during the colonization boom that followed the invention of the Shaw-Fujikawa drive, the UNSC had focused on planets that were capable of supporting life from the get-go. Not surprisingly, these were few and far between.

Because of its distance from Earth, if Harvest had merely

been livable, no one would have bothered to go; there was still plenty of elbow room on the core worlds, the colonies closest to Earth. But Harvest was also exceptionally fertile. And within two decades of its founding, it had the highest per capita agricultural productivity rate of any colony. Harvest's foodstuffs now fed the populations of no less than six other worlds—a fact that was even more impressive given the planet's size. With an equatorial diameter of slightly more than four thousand kilometers, Harvest was about a third the size of Earth.

Though she was loath to admit it, the colony's produce and her part in its distribution was a source of great pride.

Now, however, all Sif felt was disappointment. The results of her survey were in, and it turned out *Horn of Plenty*'s accident had been her fault. The freighter's propulsion pod was months overdue for service. It was something the Madrigal shipping-operations AI should have flagged before transiting the pod to Harvest. But Sif had missed it too, and now the breakdown was her responsibility.

Sif decided to double-check all the pods. By bringing even more clusters online, she still managed to meet her stated deadline. At exactly 0742, Harvest's shipping operations began their slow crawl back to full speed. For a moment, Sif relaxed—focused on the steady pull of the containers as they ascended her strands.

Deep inside her core she recalled a similar sensation. The woman whose mind was a model for Sif's core logic had enjoyed the rhythmic tug of a hairbrush—the sensual invigoration of a twice-daily grooming. Memories such as this were an expected by-product of a smart AI's construction; when you scanned a human's brain, strong chemical impressions persisted. Sif appreciated the kinesthetic pleasure of the containers' pull. But her algorithms were quick to stifle her enjoyment.

Sif initialized a correspondence sub-routine, selected the

template for an official DCS loss report, and composed a detailed mea culpa for her supervisors. She added a copy of *Horn of Plenty*'s abortive distress signal, noting a corrupted sector of data at the end of the file. Sif ran a quick checksum and decided the bad sector was just garbled bytes of damaged circuits. Then she flashed the report to the NAV computer of a freighter *Wholesale Price,* which was just about to slip for Reach.

As quickly as possible, Sif "forgot" about *Horn of Plenty*—compressed the maintenance survey results and loss report and tucked them deep inside one of her storage arrays. *No sense stewing,* her algorithms reminded her, *when it would be* months *before DCS sent word of any disciplinary action.*

Besides, Sif knew that unless she wanted to spend all morning fielding more of Mack's flirtatious offers of assistance, she needed to concentrate on her cargo.

When *Wholesale Price* drew within two-thousand kilometers of its Safe Slipspace Entry Point (SSEP)—coordinates at which its Shaw-Fujikawa drive could initiate a rupture without dragging anything but the freighter into the Slipstream—its NAV computer confirmed that Sif's report was safely cached to flash memory and sent the AI its departure confirmation.

But as the NAV computer ran through its final checklists, hastening to shut down all but its most essential systems, it received a priority COM.

```
<\\> HARVEST.AO.AI.MACK >> DCS.LIC#WP-000614236
<\ Hey, Partner! Hold up!
  >> ACKNOWLEDGED.
<\ Mind if I drop something in the 'ol mail-
  bag?
  >> NEGATIVE.
```

While maser bursts worked fine over relatively short distances, the best way to communicate between colony worlds was
to send messages via shipboard memory. Traveling at trans-light
speed, freighters such as *Wholesale Price* were the twenty-sixth-
century equivalent of the pony express.

In fact, the freighter's NAV computer already carried a variety of correspondence—from love letters to legal documents—
all guaranteed safe and secure delivery by the DCS. So there
was nothing unusual about Mack's request.

```
<\ Appreciate it. DCS has been on me for
   weeks about the Q4 projections. Soy might
   come in a little light. But wheat is going
   to be—
     >> * WARNING! PRIVACY BREACH!
     [DCS.REG#A-16523.14.82] *
<\ Just adding my note to the lady's. No need
   to cut the red tape twice, right?
     >> * VIOLATION! YOUR INFRACTION HAS BEEN
     LOGGED—
<\ Hey! Whoa there!
     >>--AND WILL BE SUBMITTED TO DCS-S--
     SSSSSSsss* \\\
     >> (...) ~ STANDBY/REBOOT
     >> (..)
     >> ()
<\ Partner?
<\ You OK?
     >> APOLOGY. UNKNOWN SYSTEM ERROR.
     >> PLEASE REPEAT PRIOR REQUEST.
<\ Nah, we're all set. Have a safe slip, you
   hear?
     >> AFFIRMATIVE. \>
```

The NAV computer had no idea why it had temporarily shut down. It had no memory of its COM with Mack. The AI's file was there—encrypted and attached to Sif's report. But the NAV computer believed the two documents had always been linked. It rechecked its slip calculations and increased reactor flow to its Shaw-Fujikawa drive. Exactly five seconds later, a sunburst of sundered space-time appeared off *Wholesale Price*'s prow.

The rift remained open after the freighter disappeared, its shimmering edges warping the surrounding stars. The blazing hole flickered stubbornly, as if it was determined to choose the moment of its closure. But once *Wholesale Price* moved deeper into the Slipstream, pulling its sustaining power with it, the rift collapsed in an insignificant burst of gamma radiation—the quantum mechanical equivalent of a shrug.

CHAPTER
TWO

When Avery woke, he was already home. Chicago, the one-time heart of the American Midwest, was now an urban sprawl that covered the former states of Illinois, Wisconsin, and Indiana. The territory wasn't part of the United States, not in any formal sense. Some people who lived in the Zone still considered themselves American, but like everyone else on the planet they were citizens of the United Nations—a sea change in governance that was inevitable once humanity began to colonize other worlds. First Mars, then the Jovian moons, and then planets in other systems.

Checking his COM pad on the military shuttle from orbit to the Great Lakes Spaceport, Avery confirmed he was on a two-week pass—that he'd be able to enjoy his first extended break from operation TREBUCHET. There was a note on the pass from Avery's CO detailing the injuries sustained by the marines on his last mission. All of Avery's alpha squad had survived with minor injuries. But bravo squad hadn't been so lucky; three marines were killed-in-action (KIA), and Staff Sergeant Byrne was hanging by a thread in a UNSC hospital ship.

The note said nothing about civilian casualties. But Avery remembered the force of the hauler's blast, and he doubted any had survived.

He tried not to think—let his mind go blank—as he boarded

a maglev passenger train from the spaceport to the Zone. Only later, when Avery stepped out onto the elevated platform of the Cottage Grove terminal, did the hot and humid air of a late Chicago summer snap his senses back into focus. As the sun dove to a fiery finish, he enjoyed what little breeze was coming off Lake Michigan—lukewarm gusts that hammered up the east-west blocks of tumbledown gray-stone apartments, scattering the autumn leaves of the sidewalk maples.

Arms laded with duffel bags, and wearing his navy-blue dress pants, collared shirt, and cap, Avery was drenched with sweat by the time he reached *The Seropian*, a center for active retirement—or so its hospitality computer told him—as he stepped into the tower's stifling lobby. Avery's Aunt Marcille had moved to the complex a few years after he'd joined the marines, vacating the same walkup apartment on Blackstone Avenue they'd shared since Avery was a boy. His aunt's health was failing, and she'd needed the extra care. And more to the point: she was lonely without him.

As Avery waited for an elevator that would take him up to the thirty-seventh floor, he stared into a recreation room filled with many of *The Seropian*'s bald and silver-haired residents. Most were clustered around a video display tuned to one of the public COM's all-news channels. There was a report of fresh Innie attacks in Epsilon Eridanus—a series of bombings that had killed thousands of civilians. As usual, the broadcast featured a UNSC spokesman who flatly denied the military's campaign was faltering. But Avery knew the facts: The Insurrection had already claimed more than a million lives; the Innie attacks were becoming more effective, and the UNSC reprisals more heavy-handed. It was an ugly civil war that wasn't getting any prettier.

One of the residents in the rec room, a black man with a deeply lined face and a crown of wiry gray hair, spotted Avery and frowned. He whispered something to a large white woman in a voluminous housedress, overflowing a wheelchair by his side. Soon all the residents that weren't hard of hearing or too dim-sighted to see Avery's uniform were nodding and clucking— some with respect, others with scorn. Avery had almost changed into his civilian clothes on the shuttle to avoid just this sort of uncomfortable reaction. But in the end he'd decided to stick with his dress blues for his aunt's sake. She'd waited a long time to see her nephew come home all spit and polish.

The elevator was even warmer than the lobby. But inside his aunt's apartment the air was so frigid, Avery could see his breath.

"Auntie?" he called, dropping his duffels on the well-worn blue carpet of her living room. The bottles of fine bourbon he'd bought at the spaceport duty-free clinked together between his neatly folded fatigues. He didn't know if his aunt's doctors were letting her drink, but he did know how much she used to enjoy an occasional mint julep. "Where are you?" But there was no reply.

The flower-patterned walls of the living room were covered with picture frames. Some were very old—faded prints of long-dead relatives his aunt used to talk about as if she'd known them personally. Most of the frames held holo-stills: three-dimensional pictures from his aunt's lifetime. He saw his favorite, the one of his teenage aunt standing on the shore of Lake Michigan in a honey-bee striped bathing suit and wide straw hat. She was pouting at the camera and its cameraman, Avery's uncle, who had passed away before he was born.

But there was something wrong with the stills; they seemed oddly out of focus. And as Avery stepped down the narrow hallway to his aunt's bedroom and ran his fingers across the frames' sheets of glass, he realized they were covered in a thin layer of ice.

Avery rubbed his palm against a large holo-still near the bedroom door, and a young boy's face appeared beneath the frost.

Me, he grimaced, remembering the day his aunt had taken the still: *my first day of church*. Wiping downward, his mind filled with memories: the suffocating pinch of his white, freshly starched oxford shirt; the smell of carnauba wax, liberally applied, to mask the scuffs in his oversized, wingtip shoes.

Growing up, Avery's clothes were almost always worn out hand-me-downs from distant cousins that were never quite big enough for his tall, broad-shouldered frame. "Just as they should be," his aunt had said, smiling, holding up new pieces of his wardrobe for inspection. "A boy isn't a boy that doesn't *ruin* his clothes." But her painstaking patching and sewing had always ensured Avery looked his best—especially for church.

"Now don't you look handsome," his aunt had cooed the day she'd taken the frozen still. Then, as she'd done up his little paisley tie: "So much like your mother. So much like your *father*," according to assessments of an inheritance Avery hadn't understood. There had been no pictures of his parents in his aunt's old house—and there were none in her apartment now. Although she'd never once said anything unkind about them, these bittersweet comparisons had been her only praise.

"Auntie? You in there?" Avery asked, knocking softly on her bedroom door. Again, there was no answer.

He remembered the sound of raised voices behind other closed doors—the angry end of his parents' marriage. His father had left his mother so distraught that she could no longer care for herself, let alone an active, six-year-old boy. He took one last look at the holo-still: argyle socks beneath neatly cuffed tan slacks; an unabashed smile, no less sincere for his aunt's prompting.

Then he opened her bedroom door.

If the living room had felt like a refrigerator, the bedroom was a freezer. Avery's heart dropped into his stomach. But it wasn't until he saw the line of sixteen evenly spaced cigarettes (one for each hour of her waking day) untouched on a bedside vanity that Avery knew for sure—his aunt was dead.

He stared at her body, stiff as a board under the layers of crocheted and quilted blankets, as the sweat on the back of his neck froze solid. Then he stepped to the foot of the bed and lowered himself into a threadbare armchair where he remained, spine set against the cold, for almost an hour—until someone keyed the apartment door.

"She's in here," muttered one of the complex's orderlies as he tramped down the hallway. A young man with a sunken chin and shoulder-length blond hair peered into the bedroom. "Jesus!" He jumped back, catching sight of Avery. "Who are you?"

"How many days?" Avery asked.

"What?"

"How many days has she been *lying* here?"

"Listen, unless I know—"

"I'm her nephew," Avery growled, his eyes locked on the bed. "How. Many. Days."

The orderly swallowed. "Three." Then in a nervous torrent, "Look, it's been busy, and she didn't have any—I mean we didn't know she had any relatives in-system. The apartment is on automatic. It dropped to freezing the moment she . . ." The orderly trailed off as Avery stared him down.

"Take her away," Avery said flatly.

The orderly motioned to his shorter, plumper partner cowering in the hallway behind him. Quickly the two men positioned their stretcher beside the bed, peeled back the layers of bedding, and gently transferred the body.

"Records say she was Evangelical Promessic." The orderly fumbled with the stretcher's straps. "Is that right?"

But Avery's gaze had returned to the bed, and he didn't reply.

His aunt was so frail that her body left only the barest impression in the foam mattress. She was a small woman, but Avery remembered how tall and strong she'd looked when Zone social services had dropped him on her doorstep—a mountain of surrogate maternal love and discipline in his wary, six-year-old eyes.

"What's your COM address?" the thin orderly continued, "I'll let you know the name of the processing center."

Avery drew his hands out of his pockets and laid them on his lap. The squat orderly noticed Avery's fingers tighten into fists and coughed—a signal to his partner that now would be a good time to leave. The two men worked the stretcher back and forth until it pointed out of the bedroom, then bumped it noisily down the hallway and out the apartment door.

Avery's hands shook. His aunt had been teetering on the edge for some time. But in their recent COM correspondence, she'd told him not to worry. Hearing that, he'd wanted to take his leave immediately, but his CO had ordered him to lead one more mission. *A whole hell of a lot of good that did anyone*, Avery cursed. While his Aunt lay dying, he was strapped to a Hornet, circling the Jim Dandy back on Tribute.

Avery leapt from the chair, stepped quickly to his duffels, and pulled out one of the fifths of gin from the duty-free. He grabbed his navy dress coat and stuffed the glass flask into an interior pocket. A moment later, he was out the apartment door.

"Dog and Pony," Avery asked the hospitality computer on the way down to the lobby. "Is it still in business?"

"Open daily until four a.m.," the computer replied through a small speaker in the elevator's floor-selection pad. "Ladies pay no cover. Shall I call a cab?"

"I'll walk." Avery twisted the cap off the gin and took a generous swig. Then he added to himself: *While I still can.*

The bottle only lasted an hour. But others were easy to find, as one night of drinking became two, then three. Gut Check, Rebound, Severe Tire Damage: names of clubs filled with civilians eager for Avery's money but not the slurred stories of how he'd earned it—except for a girl on a low-lit stage in a dive off Halsted Street. The pretty redhead was so good at pretending to listen, Avery didn't mind pretending it had nothing to do with how often he'd tapped his credit chip against the jeweled reader in her navel. The money drew her freckled skin and smell and lazy smile closer, until a rough hand fell on Avery's shoulder.

"Watch your hands, soldier boy," a bouncer warned, his voice raised above the club's thumping music.

Avery looked away from the girl, her back arched high above the stage. The bouncer was tall with a substantial gut that his tight, black turtleneck could barely contain. His strong arms were padded with a deceptive layer of fat. Avery shrugged. "I've paid."

"Not to touch." The bouncer sneered, revealing two platinum incisors. "This is a class establishment."

Avery reached for a little round table between his knees and the stage. "How much?" he asked, raising his credit chip.

"Five hundred."

"Screw you."

"Like I said. *Class*."

"Already spent plenty . . ."Avery muttered. His UNSC salary was modest—and most of that had gone to help with his aunt's apartment.

"Aw, now see?" The bouncer jabbed a thumb at the girl. She was slowly sliding backward on the stage—her smile now a worried frown. "You gotta talk *nice*, soldier boy." The bouncer tightened his grip on Avery's shoulder. "She's not one of those Innie sluts you're used to out in Epsi."

Avery was sick of the bouncer's hand. He was sick of being called boy. But having some civilian puke insult him—someone who had no idea what he had *actually* gotten used to on the frontlines of the Insurrection? That was the last straw.

"Let me go," Avery growled.

"We gonna have a problem?"

"All depends on you."

With his free hand, the bouncer reached behind his back and pulled a metal rod from his belt. "Why don't you and me step outside?" With a flick of his wrist, the rod doubled in length and revealed an electrified tip.

It was a "humbler" stun device. Avery had seen ONI interrogators lay into Innie prisoners with the things. He knew how debilitating they were, and though Avery doubted the bouncer had as much skill with the humbler as an ONI spook, he had no intention of ending up jerking around in a puddle of his own piss on this *class* establishment's floor.

Avery reached for his drink, resting at the center of his table. "I'm good right here."

"Listen, you jarhead son of a—"

But Avery's reach was just a feint. As the bouncer leaned forward to follow, Avery grabbed the man's wrist and pulled it over his shoulder. Then he yanked down, breaking it at the elbow. The girl on the stage screamed as ragged bone tore through the bouncer's shirt, spattering blood on her face and hair.

As the bouncer howled and dropped to his knees, two of his partners—similarly dressed and built—rushed forward, flinging chairs out of their way. Avery stood and turned to meet them. But he was drunker than he'd thought and missed an opening blow to the bridge of his nose that snapped his head back and sent his own blood arcing toward the stage.

Avery reeled back into the bouncers' crushing arms. But as they rushed him out the club's back door, one of them slipped on the metal staircase leading to the alley. In that moment, Avery was able to twist free, give much better than he got, and stagger away from the noise of approaching sirens before a pair of blue and white sedans deposited four of the Zone's finest on the club's doorstep.

Stumbling along Halsted's crowded sidewalks, his dress uniform now as filthy as a set of battlefield fatigues, Avery fled from the paranoia of accusing glances to a dirty crawlspace beneath a riveted riser for the local maglev line—a repurposed brace from Chicago's old elevated railway, still recognizable despite centuries of shoring. Avery stuffed a green plastic trash bag between himself and the riser and settled into a fitful stupor.

Make me proud, do what's right. This had been his Aunt's instruction on the day of his enlistment, her small but strong fingers reaching up to cup his nineteen-year-old chin. *Become the man I* know *you can be.*

And Avery had tried. He'd left Earth ready to fight for her and those like her—innocents whose lives the UNSC had convinced him were threatened by men inimical but otherwise identical to him. Killers. Innies. The enemy. But where was the pride? And what had he become?

Avery dreamed of a boy choking in the arms of a woman with a detonator—imagined the perfect shot that would have saved all in the restaurant and his fellow marines. But deep down he knew there was no perfect shot. No magic bullet that could stop the Insurrection.

Avery felt a chill that jerked him awake. But the near-silent rumble of a maglev passenger train overhead had only shifted the bag of trash, setting Avery's back against the perspiring metal of the old brace. He leaned forward and put his head between his knees. "I'm sorry," Avery croaked, wishing his aunt were alive to hear it.

Then his mind collapsed under the multiplicative weight of loss and guilt and rage.

Lieutenant Downs slammed the door of his dark blue sedan with enough force to rock the low-swept vehicle on its four thick tires. He'd had the kid hooked, ready to enlist. But then the parents got wind of his efforts, and the whole thing fell apart. If it weren't for Downs' uniform, the father might have taken a swing at him. Though he was no longer field-fit, in his dress blues, the UNSC Marine Corps recruiter was still an imposing presence.

As the Lieutenant reordered his mental list of prospects—the small group of primarily young men who'd shown any interest in his cold calls and street-corner pitches—he reminded himself it wasn't easy recruiting soldiers during wartime. With a war as brutal and unpopular as the Insurrection, his job was damn near impossible. Not that his CO cared. Downs' quota was five new marines per month. With less than a week to go he hadn't landed even one.

"You gotta be kidding me . . ." The Lieutenant grimaced as he rounded the back of his sedan. Someone had used a can of red spray-paint to scrawl INNIES OUT on the vehicle's thick bumper.

Downs smoothed his close-cropped hair. It was an increasingly popular slogan—a rallying cry for the more liberal core-world citizens who believed the best way to end the killing in Epsilon Eridanus was simply to let the system go—have the military pull out and give the Insurrectionists the autonomy they desired.

The Lieutenant wasn't a politician. And while he doubted the UN leadership would ever appease the Innies, he knew a few things for sure: The war was still on, the Marine Corps was an all-volunteer force, and he only had a few days to fill his quota before someone with a lot more brass than him took another bite out of his already well-chewed ass.

The Lieutenant popped the sedan's trunk, and removed his dress cap and briefcase. As the trunk closed automatically behind him, he strode toward the recruitment center, a converted storefront in a strip mall on Chicago's old, near-north side. As Downs neared the door, he noticed a man slumped against it.

"48789-20114-AJ," Avery mumbled.

"Say again?" Downs asked. He knew a UNSC serial number when he heard it. But the Lieutenant still hadn't quite accepted the drunk outside his office was the Marine Corps Staff Sergeant indicated by the four gold chevrons on his filthy dresscoat's sleeve.

"It's valid," Avery said, raising his head from his chest. "Check it."

The Lieutenant straightened his soldiers. He wasn't used to taking orders from a noncommissioned officer.

Avery belched. "I'm AWOL. Seventy-two hours."

That got Downs' attention. He cracked his briefcase in the crook of his elbow and withdrew his COM pad. "Give me that one more time," he asked, inputting Avery's slowly repeated serial number with swift stabs of his index finger.

A few seconds later Avery's service record appeared on the pad. The Lieutenant's eyes widened as a long string of meritorious citations and battlefield commendations cascaded down the monochromatic screen. ORION, KALEIDOSCOPE, TANGLE-WOOD, TREBUCHET. Dozens of programs and operations, most of which Downs had never even heard of. Attached to Avery's file was a priority message from FLEETCOM, the Navy and Marine Corps headquarters on Reach.

"If you're AWOL, no one seems to mind." Downs placed his COM pad back into his briefcase. "In fact, I'm pleased to inform you that your request for transfer has been approved."

For a moment, Avery's tired eyes flashed with suspicion. *He hadn't requested a transfer.* But in his current groggy state, anything sounded better than being shipped back to Epsilon Eridanus. His eyes darkened once more. "Where?"

"Didn't say."

"Long as it's quiet," Avery muttered. He let his head fall back against the recruitment center door—right between the legs of a marine in full battle dress on a poster taped to the inside of the door that read: STAND. FIGHT. SERVE. Avery's closed his eyes.

"Hey!" Downs said gruffly. "You can't sleep here, Marine."

But Avery was already snoring. The Lieutenant grimaced, hefted one of Avery's arms over his shoulder, and carried him to the backseat of his sedan.

As Downs pulled out of the mall's parking lot into thick, noontime traffic, he wondered if catching a single AWOL war hero was as good as booking five raw recruits—if it would be enough to keep his CO happy. "Great Lakes Spaceport," he barked at his sedan. "Quickest route." As a holographic map materialized on the inner surface of the sedan's curved windshield, Downs shook his head. *If only I could be so lucky.*

CHAPTER
THREE

Staring at the alien vessel's stacked containers of ripe fruit, Dadab began to salivate. He rarely saw such delicacies, let alone got a chance to eat them. In the Covenant, the union of species to which Dadab belonged, his kind, the Unggoy, ranked low in the pecking order. They were used to scrambling for scraps. But they were not alone.

Near the base of one of the stacks, three Kig-Yar were squabbling over a jumble of particularly juicy melons. Dadab tried to trundle past the screeching reptilian creatures unnoticed. Even though he held the rank of Deacon on the Kig-Yar's ship, *Minor Transgression*, he was an unwelcome addition to its crew. Under the best of circumstances the two species were uneasy allies. But after a long voyage with dwindling supplies—had they not happened upon the alien vessel when they did—Dadab only half-humorously feared the Kig-Yar might have made a meal of him instead.

A melon wedge tumbled through the air and hit the side of Dadab's blue-grey head with a syrupy thwack, spraying juice on his orange tunic. Like the rest of his body, the Unggoy's head was covered with a stiff exoskeleton, and the blow didn't hurt him in the least. But the three Kig-Yar erupted in shrill laughter all the same.

"An offering for his holiness!" one of them sneered through dagger-sharp teeth. This was Zhar, the leader of the crewmen's little clique—easily differentiated from the other two by the length and deep pink color of the long flexible spines that crested the back of his narrow skull.

Without breaking stride Dadab loosed a powerful snort, dislodging bits of rind that had lodged in one of the circular vents of a mask that covered his pug nose and wide mouth. Unlike the Kig-Yar, who were quite comfortable in the oxygen-rich environment of the alien vessel, Unggoy breathed methane. The gas filled a pyramidal tank on Dadab's back, and flowed to his mask via hoses integrated into the tank's shoulder harness.

More melon sailed Dadab's way. But he was past the Kig-Yar now, and he ignored the sticky projectiles that slapped against his tank. Annoyed by his disinterest, the throwers returned to their petty squabble.

Minor Transgression was part of the Covenant Ministry of Tranquility's vast fleet of missionary vessels—ships responsible for exploring the boundaries of Covenant-controlled space. Deacon was the lowest Ministry rank, but it was also the only position open to Dadab's species—one of the few jobs Unggoy could get that didn't involve hard manual labor or risking their lives in battle.

Not any Unggoy could qualify for a Deaconship, and Dadab had made the cut because he was smarter than most, better able to understand the Covenant's Holy Writs and help explain these laws to others.

The Covenant wasn't just a political and military alliance. It was a religious union in which all its members pledged loyalty to its supreme theocratic leaders, the Prophets, and their belief in the transcendent potential of ancient technology—relics left behind by a vanished race of aliens known as the Forerunners. Finding these scattered bits of technology was the reason *Minor Transgression* was out in the deep black, hundreds of cycles from the nearest Covenant habitat.

As Deacon, it was Dadab's responsibility to make sure the

Kig-Yar followed all applicable Writs as they went about their search. Unfortunately, ever since they'd boarded the alien vessel, the crewmen had been anything but obedient.

Muttering inside his mask, Dadab trundled down a row of containers. Some of them were clawed open, and he had to leap over slopes of half-chewed fruit the Kig-Yar had left in their rush to sample all the vessel's delicacies. Dadab doubted any of the containers held items of interest to the Prophets. But as Deacon, he was still supposed to supervise the search—at least offer a blessing—especially when it involved items belonging to aliens as of yet unknown to the Covenant.

As focused as the Prophets were on finding relics, they were always eager to add new adherents to their faith. And although that task was technically the Ministry of Conversion's responsibility, Dadab was the only religious official present, and he wanted to make sure he followed *all* the relevant procedures.

For the Deacon knew a good performance now might guarantee a promotion later. And he desperately wanted off *Minor Transgression* and on to a posting where he wasn't just responsible for keeping tabs on irreverent bipedal reptiles. More than anything else, the Deacon wanted to preach—to someday become a spiritual leader for Unggoy less fortunate than himself. It was a lofty goal, but like most true believers, Dadab's faith was buoyed by ample amounts of hope.

At the end of the row of containers was a mechanical lift that rose up the side of the hull. Dadab stepped onto the lift and considered its controls. Raising one of his two spiny forearms, he thumbed a button that seemed to indicate up, then grumbled happily as the lift rattled up the wall.

A narrow passage led from the top of the lift to the vessel's ruined propulsion unit. Dadab caught a whiff of something foul, and stepping squeamishly through a bulkhead door he disabled his mask's olfactory membranes. The pile of fibrous mucus in the center of the cabin beyond was instantly recognizable—this was where the Kig-Yar had chosen to defecate.

Gingerly, Dadab slid one of his flat, four-toed feet through the sticky results of the Kig-Yar's fruit-fueled gorging until he struck something metallic: the small box that had attempted to converse with *Minor Transgression*'s communications circuits.

Finding the alien vessel had been pure luck. The Kig-Yar ship had just happened to be between jumps, conducting one of its scheduled scans for relics, when it detected a burst of radiation less than a cycle from its position. At first the Kig-Yar's leader, a female Shipmistress named Chur'R-Yar, had thought they might be under attack. But when they drew close to the vessel, even Dadab could see it had simply suffered some sort of drive failure.

Still, Chur'R-Yar had wanted to make certain they were in no danger. Unleashing a full barrage with *Minor Transgression*'s point-lasers, she had fried the vessel's drive then sent Zhar aboard to silence the box—make sure it could no longer cry for help. Dadab feared Zhar would be too aggressive and ruin the one item of salvage that might help his promotion off the Kig-Yar ship, but he could never admit this to Chur'R-Yar. He had known of many other Unggoy Deacons who had met with "unfortunate accidents" for similar disloyal acts.

Eventually, the Shipmistress had given him permission to collect the box—Dadab assumed because she, too, had realized the importance of the item to the Ministry of Conversion's work. She could have gone herself, of course. But as Dadab watched the excrement slide off the box and onto his hands, he realized Chur'R-Yar had probably sent him because she knew *exactly* what the box's collection would require. Holding his stinking prize at arm's length, the Deacon retreated back down the passage.

After evading another barrage from the Kig-Yar in the hold,

he scampered through an umbilical back onto *Minor Transgression*. He hurried into the ship's methane suite (the only room constantly filled with the gas), and eagerly undid the chest-buckles of his harness. As he backed into a triangular depression in one of the square room's walls, a hidden compressor sputtered and began to refill his tank.

Dadab slipped out of his harness and swung his oversized forearms across his chest. His jaw ached from his mask's tight seal, and he tore it off and flung it away. But before the mask hit the floor, it was intercepted by a lighting-fast pearlescent swipe.

Floating in the center of the suite was a Huragok, a creature with a stooped head and elongated snout held aloft by a collection of translucent pink sacs filled with a variety of gasses. Four anterior limbs sprouted from its spine—tentacles, to be exact, one of which held Dadab's mask. The Huragok brought the mask close to a row of dark, round sensory nodes along its snout and gave it a thorough inspection. Then it flexed two of its tentacles in a quick, inquisitive gesture.

Dadab contorted the digits of one of his hardened hands so they matched the default arrangement of the Huragok's limbs: four fingertips, facing straight out from the Deacon's chest. < *No, damage, I, tired, wear.* > His fingers splayed and contracted, bent and overlapped as they formed each word's unique pose.

The Huragok released a disappointed bleat from a sphincterlike valve in one of its sacs. The emission propelled it past Dadab to the tank receptacle where it hung the mask on a hook that protruded from the wall.

< *Did you find the device?* > the Huragok asked, turning back to Dadab. The Deacon held up the box, and the Huragok's tentacles trembled with excitement: < *May I touch what I can see?* >

< *Touch, yes, smell, no.* > Dadab replied.

But the Huragok either didn't mind the box's residual Kig-Yar stench, or it simply failed to get Dadab's joke. It wrapped a tentacle around the alien plunder and eagerly lifted it to its snout.

Dadab flopped onto a cushioned pallet near the suite's free-standing food-dispenser. He uncoiled a nipple connected to a spool of flexible tubing, put it in his mouth and began to suck. Soon, an unappetizing but nutritious sludge surged down the tube and into his gullet.

He watched the Huragok pore over the alien box, its sacs swelling and deflating in an expression of what? Impatience? It had taken the Deacon most of the voyage to grasp the creature's sign language. He could only guess at the emotional subtleties of its bladder-speak.

Indeed, it had taken him many cycles just to learn the Huragok's name: *Lighter Than Some.*

Dadab knew the basics of Huragok reproduction, or rather Huragok *creation.* The creatures manufactured their offspring out of readily available organic materials with the same deft activity of their tentacles' cilia, which *Lighter Than Some* was using to bore a neat hole in the alien box. It was a truly fantastic process, but what Dadab found most unusual was that the most difficult step for Huragok parents was to make their creations perfectly buoyant—to fill them with the exact right mix of gases. As a result, new Huragok would initially float or sink, and their parents would name them accordingly: *Far Too Heavy; Easy To Adjust; Lighter Than Some.*

Clamping the nipple in his teeth, Dadab inhaled through his nose, swelling his lungs to capacity. The methane in the suite was no less stale than what he carried on his back, but it felt good to breathe unencumbered. As he watched *Lighter Than Some* insert his tentacle into the box and cautiously probe its interior, Dadab was once again reminded of how much he appreciated the creature's company.

There had been multiple Huragok on the training voyages he'd taken during his education at the Ministry seminary. But they had kept to themselves, and had been singularly focused on keeping their ships in good working order. Which is why Dadab had been more than a little surprised when *Lighter Than Some* had first flexed its limbs in his direction—repeated a single pose over and over until the Unggoy realized it was attempting a simple: < *Hello!* >

Suddenly, *Lighter Than Some* jerked its tentacle from the box—drew back as if shocked. The Huragok's sacs swelled, and it began flailing its limbs in spastic discourse. Dadab struggled to keep up.

< *Intelligence! . . . Coordinates . . . ! . . . Undoubtedly the aliens . . . Even more than our own!* >

< *Stop!* > Dadab interrupted, spitting out the food-nipple and jumping to his feet. < *Repeat!* >

With visible effort the Huragok forced its tentacles to curl more slowly. Dadab watched with darting eyes. Eventually, he grasped *Lighter Than Some*'s meaning.

< *You, certain?* >

< *Yes! The Shipmistress must be told!* >

Minor Transgression was not a large ship. And in the same amount of time it took Dadab to refit his tank, doing his best not to wrinkle his tunic, he and the Huragok were out of the suite and down *Minor Transgression's* single central passage to the bridge.

"Either remove your mask," the Shipmistress said after Dadab breathlessly delivered *Lighter Than Some*'s assessment, "or learn to speak more clearly." Chur'R-Yar was perched on an elevated command chair. Her light yellow skin made her the brightest thing on the small, shadowy bridge.

Dadab swallowed twice to clear some residual sludge from his throat and began again. "The device is a collection of circuits similar to the processing pathways running throughout our ship."

"*My* ship," Chur'R-Yar interjected.

Dadab winced. "Yes, of course." Not for the first time, he wished the Shipmistress shared Zhar's spiny plumage; the appendages changed color depending on the male of the species' mood. Right now the Deacon was desperate to gauge the level of Chur'R-Yar's impatience. But like all female Kig-Yar the back of the Shipmistress' head was covered with dark brown calluses—thick skin like a patchwork of bruises that made her narrow shoulders seem even more hunched than they really were.

Dadab decided to play it safe and cut to the chase. "The box is some sort of navigational device. And although it is damaged . . ." The Deacon gestured furtively at the Huragok, who bobbed to a wall-mounted control panel. "It still remembers its point of origin."

Lighter Than Some drummed the tips of its tentacles against the panel's luminous switches. Soon, a three-dimensional holographic representation of the volume of space around *Minor Transgression* coalesced in a holo-tank before Chur'R-Yar's chair. The tank was merely the space between two dark glass lenses: one built into a platinum pedestal, the other imbedded in the bridge's ceiling. Like most surfaces on the Kig-Yar ship, the ceiling was covered with a purple metal sheeting that, catching the hologram's light, displayed a darker hexagonal pattern—an underlying Beryllium grid.

"We were here," Dadab began as a red triangle representing the Kig-Yar ship appeared in the projection. "When we registered the alien vessel's radiation leak." As he continued, the projection (controlled by *Lighter Than Some*) shifted and zoomed, presenting additional icons as required. "This is where we made contact. And this is where *Ligh*— where your Huragok believes the vessel initiated its journey."

The Shipmistress angled one of her globose, ruby-red eyes at the highlighted system. It was outside the missionary allotment the Ministry had charged her with patrolling—beyond the boundary of Covenant space, though Chur'R-Yar knew it was heresy to suggest such a limit. The Prophets believed the Forerunners once had dominion over the entire galaxy, so every system was hallowed ground—a potential repository of important relics.

"And its destination?" Chur'R-Yar asked, her long tongue rattling against the top of her beak-like mouth.

Again the Deacon signed to the Huragok. The creature bleated from its sacs and flicked two of its limbs. "I'm afraid that data has been lost," Dadab replied.

The Shipmistress curled her claws around the arms of her chair. She hated that the Unggoy had learned the Huragok's language—that the Deacon now served as intermediary between her and a member of her crew. Not for the first time, she considered losing the Deacon out an airlock. But staring at the unexplored system, she realized the pious little gas-sucker had suddenly become a great deal more useful.

"Have I ever told you how much I appreciate your good counsel?" the Shipmistress asked, relaxing into her chair. "What do you suggest we tell the Ministry?"

Dadab's harness began to chafe around his neck. He fought back the urge to scratch.

"As in all matters, I will follow the Shipmistress' recommendation." Dadab chose his words very carefully. It wasn't often Chur'R-Yar asked him a question; and she had never asked for his *opinion*. "I am here to serve, and in so doing honor the will of the Prophets."

"Perhaps we should wait to make our report until we have had a chance to survey the alien system?" Chur'R-Yar mused. "Give the Holy Ones as much information as we can?"

"I am sure the Ministry would . . . *appreciate* the Shipmistress' desire to bear more complete witness to this important discovery." Dadab hadn't said "approve," but if the female

Kig-Yar wanted to take her ship out of the allotment, Dadab couldn't stop her. She was, after all, Shipmistress.

But the Deacon had another, more personal reason for his compliance. If they did find something of value in the unexplored system, he knew this would only help speed his promotion. And to accomplish that, Dadab was willing to bend a few rules. *After all*, he thought, *communication delays happen all the time*.

"An excellent recommendation." Chur'R-Yar's tongue flicked between her jagged teeth. "I will set a new course." Then, with a cursory flip of her head, "May we follow in Their Footsteps."

"And so better mind The Path." The Deacon answered, completing the benediction.

The saying honored the Forerunner's divination—the moment they activated their seven mysterious Halo rings and disappeared from the galaxy, leaving none of their kind behind. Indeed, this belief that one could become a God by following in the Forerunners' footsteps was the crux of the Covenant religion. *One day,* the Prophets had long promised their faithful hordes, *we shall find the Holy Rings! Discover the very means of the Forerunners' transcendence!*

Dadab, and billions of his fellow Covenant, believed this absolutely.

The Deacon backed away from the Shipmistress' commandchair, signaling *Lighter Than Some* to follow. He pivoted as smartly as his methane tank allowed then trotted through the bridge's automatic sliding door.

"Zealot," the Shipmistress hissed as the two angled halves of the door slid shut. She tapped a holographic switch in the arm of her chair that controlled the ship's signal gear. "Return at once. Bring only what you can carry."

"But Shipmistress," Zhar's voice crackled from her chair, "all this food would—"

"Return to your stations!" Chur'R-Yar screeched, her patience exhausted on the Deacon. "Leave it *all* behind!" The Shipmistress gave the switch an angry smack. Then, with a rasp of her tongue only she could hear: "Soon we will find much, much more."

CHAPTER
FOUR

During its slip from Earth, the computer in the cryo-bay of the UNSC fast-attack corvette *Two for Flinching* led Avery through a long, cyclical slumber. Per his request, the circuits let Avery enjoy stretches of anabolic rest, bringing him through dream-filled REM as quickly and as infrequently as possible. All of this was accomplished by careful adjustments to the near-freezing atmosphere of Avery's cryo-pod and the judicious application of intravenous pharmaceuticals—drugs that both controlled the frequency and duration of cryo-subjects' sleep cycles and influenced the content of their dreams.

But no matter what brand of meds Avery got before being iced, he always dreamed about the exact same thing: the worst of his missions against the Insurrectionists—a series of scorched snapshots culminating in whatever operation he'd just completed.

Even though the bloody specifics of these missions were things Avery would have preferred to experience only once, the true horror of his dreams was their suggestion that he had done much more harm than good. His aunt's voice echoed inside his head. . . .

Make me proud, do what's right.

The cryo-computer observed a surge of activity in Avery's brain—an effort to yank himself out of REM—and upped his dosage. *Two for Flinching* had just emerged from Slipspace and was vectoring toward its destination. It was time for the computer to initiate Avery's thaw, and it was standard operating procedure to keep subjects dreaming throughout the sequence.

The meds took hold, and Avery sunk deep. And his mind's-eye picture show continued to roll. . . .

A hauler jack-knifed in a roadside ditch, smoke belching from its burning engine. An initial round of cheers from the other marines in a checkpoint tower, thinking Avery had just nailed an Innie bomber. Then the realization that their ARGUS units had malfunctioned—that the hauler's dead civilian driver had done nothing but pick up the wrong load.

Avery had only been a few months out of boot camp. And already the war had soured.

If you listened to the carefully packaged UNSC propaganda, Innies were all the same sort of bad apple: after two centuries of common cause, isolated groups of ungrateful colonists began to agitate for greater autonomy—for the freedom to act in their individual worlds' best interests, not those of the empire at large.

In the beginning, there were sizeable numbers of people who felt sympathy for the Innie cause. The rebels were understandably sick of being told how to run their lives—what jobs to take, how many children to make—by CA bureaucrats; the often heavy-handed proxies of an Earth-based government with an increasingly poor understanding of the colonies' unique challenges. But that sympathy quickly evaporated when (after years of frustrating negotiations that went nowhere) the more radical Innie factions abandoned politics for violence. At first they hit military targets and known CA sympathizers. But as the UNSC began its counterinsurgency operations, more and more innocent people were caught in the crossfire.

As a raw recruit, Avery didn't understand why the Insurrection hadn't flared in outer systems such as Cygnus, where colonists were united by shared creed and ethnicity—one of the main reasons for the collapse of Earth's old nation-state system and the rise of the UN as a unifying force. Instead, the fighting had broken out right where the UNSC was best equipped to stop it: Epsilon Eridanus, the most populous and carefully administered system outside of Sol.

With all the resources at its disposal in that system, Avery wondered why the UNSC hadn't been able to pacify the Innies before things got out of hand. FLEETCOM on Reach, Circumstance's universities and courts of justice, the industrial zones of Tribute—couldn't these powerful institutions and engines of economic prosperity have come up with a plan palatable for both sides? As the war dragged on, Avery began to realize all these resources were exactly the problem: in Epsilon Eridanus, the UNSC just had too much to lose.

Avery flinched in reaction to his rising body temperature. But also to the quickening images in his head. . . .

Pockmarked houses whipping past gun slits. An unexpected boom. Bodies strewn around the burning shell of the convoy's lead armored transport. Muzzle flashes from rooftops. A run for cover through the carnage. Ricochets and radio chatter. Phosphorous plumes from ordnance dropped by drones. Women and children running from burning houses, leaving footprints in blood thick as caramel.

Eyes darting behind his lids, Avery remembered his aunt's instructions: *Become the man I know you can be.*

He struggled to move his doped-up limbs, but the computer increased his dose and kept him down. The nightmarish final act would not be stopped. . . .

A crowded roadside restaurant. A desperate woman surrounded by determined men. The kicking feet of a choking child. A father's lunge and the moment Avery let slip, reducing all to shock and heat that sent his Hornet spinning.

Avery woke and gasped, drawing in a mouthful of the freezing vapor that filled his cryo-tube. Quickly, the computer initiated an emergency purge. Somehow, despite more than three times the recommended amount of sleep-inducers, Avery had overridden the final stages of the thaw. The computer noted the anomaly, carefully withdrew Avery's IV and catheter, and opened the tube's curved, clear plastic lid.

Avery rolled onto an elbow, leaned over the edge of his tube, and coughed—a series of violent, wet heaves. As he caught his breath, he heard the slap of bare feet on the bay's rubberized floor. A moment later a small, square towel appeared in his down-turned field of view.

"I got it," Avery spat. "Back off."

"Zero to jerk in less than five." A man's voice, not much older than Avery. "I've met grunts who are faster. But that's pretty good."

Avery looked up. Like him, the man was naked. But his flesh was alarmingly pale. Blond hair was just starting to burr from his recently shaved head—like the first tufts of silk from an ear of corn. The man's chin was long and narrow. When he smiled, his gaunt cheeks puffed mischievously.

"Healy. Petty Officer First Class. Corpsman."

All of which meant Healy was navy—not a marine. But he seemed friendly enough. Avery snatched the towel, wiped his clean-shaven face and chin. "Johnson. Staff Sergeant."

Healy's grin widened. "Well, at least I don't have to salute you."

Avery swung his legs out of the cryo-pod and let his feet settle onto the floor. His head felt swollen—ready to burst. He breathed deep and tried to speed the sensation's passage.

Healy nodded toward a bulkhead door at the other end of the bay. "C'mon, lockers are this way. Don't know what kind of dreams you had. But mine didn't involve sitting around staring at another guy's balls."

Avery and Healy dressed, retrieved their duffels, and reported to *Two for Flinching*'s modest hangar bay. Corvettes were the smallest class of UNSC warships and didn't carry any fighters. In fact, there was hardly enough room in the hangar for one SKT-13 shuttlecraft, a larger version of the bulbous Bumblebee lifeboats standard throughout the fleet.

"Sit down, strap in," the shuttle's pilot barked over his shoulder as Avery and Healy came aboard. "Only reason we're stopped is to offload the two of you."

Avery stowed his bags and slid into one of the SKT's center-facing seats, pulling a U-shaped restraining bar down over his shoulders. The shuttle dropped through an airlock in the hangar floor and accelerated away from the corvette's stern.

"You ever been to Harvest?" Healy shouted over the howl of the shuttle's thrusters.

Avery craned his neck toward the cockpit. "No."

But he had. It was hard to remember exactly when. You didn't age in cryo-sleep, but time passed all the same. Avery figured he'd spent at least as much time asleep as awake since he'd joined the marines. But regardless, he'd only stayed on Harvest long enough to acquire his target, plan the hit, and reduce the number of corrupt CA officials by one. It was his graduation mission from Navy Special Warfare (NavSpecWar) sniper-school. And he'd passed with flying colors.

Avery squinted as the shuttle's interior brightened. Beyond the clear partitions of the cockpit's canopy, Harvest had come into view. Scattered clouds revealed a world where land was much more abundant than sea. A single large continent shone bright tan and green through the world's unpolluted atmosphere.

"First time for me too," Healy said. "Out in the middle of nowhere. But not bad to look at."

Avery just nodded his head. Like most of his missions, his hit on Harvest was classified. And he had no idea what sort of clearance the Corpsman had.

The shuttle veered toward a metallic glint in the deep blue

aurora of Harvest's thermosphere. An orbital structure, Avery realized as they approached—two silver arcs hanging high above the planet. They hadn't been there on his previous visit.

As the shuttle drew closer, Avery saw that the arcs were separated by many thousands of kilometers of golden strands— space elevators that passed through the lower arc and dropped to Harvest's surface. The points at which the elevators bisected the arc were open to vacuum—gaps filled with beamwork that, from a distance, looked like delicate filigree.

"Hang on," the pilot shouted. "We've got traffic."

With short, syncopated bursts of its maneuvering rockets, the shuttle finessed its way through one of many orderly formations of propulsion pods gathered around the orbital. Avery noted that the pods' designers had made no effort to beautify their creations; they were engines, nothing more. Hoses, tanks, wires—most of the pod's constituent parts were fully exposed. Only their expensive Shaw-Fujikawa drives were shrouded in protective cowlings.

As the shuttle closed on the orbital, it spun 180 degrees and backed into an airlock. After a few clanks and a hiss of air, an indicator light above the shuttle's rear hatch changed from red to green. The pilot gave his passengers a thumbs-up. "Good luck. Watch out for those farmers' daughters." The shuttle detached as soon as Avery and Healy were safely inside the orbital.

"Welcome to the Tiara," a very proper female voice echoed from an unseen PA system. "My name is Sif. Please let me know if there is anything I can do to make your transit more comfortable."

Avery unzipped one of his duffel's pockets and removed an olive drab duty-cap. "Just some directions please, ma'am." He slung the hat over the back of his head and tugged it low on his brow.

"Of course," the AI replied. "This airlock leads straight to the median. Take a right and proceed directly to coupling station three. I'll let you know if you take a wrong turn."

Strip lights in the airlock's ceiling brightened as its interior door cycled open. In the cramped ready room the air was heavy and still, but in the unexpectedly open space beyond, the recycled atmosphere seemed less oppressive. It turned out the median was a wide platform suspended in the middle of the tubular orbital by thick metal cables. Avery guessed the Tiara was about four kilometers long and it's interior close to three hundred meters in diameter. Six beveled titanium spars ran the length of the facility. These were equally spaced around the interior of the tube and were connected to one another with smaller beams perforated with oval holes to save weight without sacrificing strength. The floor of the median was covered with a diamond-pattern metal grid that, while perfectly sturdy, gave the impression of walking on air.

"You do a lot of CMT?" Healy asked as they marched toward the number three station.

Avery knew the acronym: Colonial Militia Training, one of the UNSC's more controversial activities. Officially, CMT was all about helping the locals help themselves—training colonists to deal with natural disasters and basic internal security so the marines didn't have to keep too many boots on the ground. Unofficially, it was designed to create paramilitary anti-Insurrectionist forces—though Avery had often wondered if it was really a good idea to give colonials on politically unstable worlds weapons, and train them to use them. In his experience, today's ally was often tomorrow's foe.

"Never." Avery lied again.

"So . . . what?" Healy continued. "You looking for a change of pace?"

"Something like that."

Healy laughed and shook his head. "Then you must have had one piss-poor billet."

You don't know the half of it. Avery thought.

The median doglegged left, and as Avery passed a long window, he peered out at the station—one of the filigreed gaps he'd seen on approach. Two rectangular openings had been cut in the top and bottom of the orbital's hull, leaving the upper and lower spars exposed. Through these spars ran the Tiara's number-three elevator strand.

Avery watched as two back-to-back cargo containers rose into view, filling the station. It was hard to see through the window, but he caught a glimpse of two propulsion pods maneuvering toward the tops of the containers. Once the pods were attached, the containers raised clear of the Tiara. Then they reversed the polarity of their unifying magnets and the two newly made freighters drifted apart. Start to finish, the operation took less than thirty seconds.

Healy whistled. "Pretty slick."

Avery didn't disagree. The containers were massive. The coordination required to make them move in concert—not just on this strand but on all seven of the Tiara's elevators at once—was truly impressive.

"One more right then look for the gantry airlock," Sif said. The passage leading around the station was narrower than the orbital's main thoroughfare, and Sif's voice sounded very close. "You're just in time for the shift change."

Outside the airlock were a dozen of the orbital's maintenance technicians, clad in white overalls with blue stripes down their arms and legs. Despite Healy's nonstop grin, the techs glanced uneasily at the two unexpected soldiers. Avery was glad the Welcome Wagon, a smaller container primarily used to transport large numbers of migrant colonists from ship to surface, rose quickly into the station; he wasn't up for more awkward conversation.

An alarm chimed and the airlock door slid open. Avery and Healy followed the techs through a flexible gantry that stretched like an accordion to the Wagon. Once inside, they dropped their duffels into a storage bin beneath a section of seats—one of three steep tiers built against the Wagon's four walls. The open wall directly opposite the two soldiers' chosen tier was filled with a tall rectangular view port.

"All settled? Good." Sif spoke through speakers in Avery's chair as he clipped himself into the high-backed seat's five-point harness. There was artificial gravity on the orbital, but once the Wagon departed it would be in free fall. "I hope you enjoy your stay."

"Oh, I'll make sure he does." Healy cracked an impish smile.

The alarm chimed a second time, the Wagon's airlock sealed, and Avery began his descent.

As one small part of Sif's mind monitored the downward progress of Avery's Wagon, another manifested on her data-center's holo-projector.

"Let me start by saying, Ms. al-Cygni, how grateful I am that you chose to conduct this audit in person. "I trust you had a pleasant journey?"

Sif's avatar wore an ankle-length sleeveless gown of inter-woven sunset hues. The dress highlighted her golden hair—tucked smartly behind her ears—which fell in waves to the middle of her back. Her bare arms flexed slightly outward from her hips and this, combined with her long neck and elevated chin, gave the impression of a doll-sized ballerina ready to rise on the points of her toes.

"Productive," Jilan al-Cygni replied. "I decided not to cryo."

The woman sat on a low bench before the projector, wear-ing the unremarkable attire of a UNSC middle manager: a brown pantsuit, a few shades darker than her skin. The garnet glint of the DCS insignia on her high collar complemented her burgundy lipstick—the one flourish in her otherwise subdued appearance. "These days, transit's really the only time I have to catch up."

Al-Cygni's melodic accent was subtle, but Sif cross-referenced her arrays and decided the woman was likely born on New Jerusalem—one of two colonized worlds in the Cygnus system. Through micro-cameras embedded in the walls of her data center, Sif watched as the woman put a hand to the back of her head, checking the pins that kept her long, black hair bound up in a tight twist.

"I imagine the Eridanus embargo is all-consuming," Sif said, making sure to widen her avatar's eyes sympathetically.

"My caseload has tripled in the last eighteen months." Al-Cygni sighed. "And frankly, arms smuggling isn't my area of expertise."

Sif put a hand to her chest. "Well, I'm sorry for piling more on your plate. I'll keep my testimony as brief as possible—skip the risk analysis of Madrigal's maintenance protocols, and jump directly to the—"

"Actually," al-Cygni interrupted, "I'm expecting another party."

Sif raised an eyebrow. "Oh? I didn't realize."

"A last minute decision. Thought I might save some time, combining his audit with yours."

Sif felt her data-pathways warm. *His?* But before she could protest . . .

```
<\\> HARVEST.AO.AI.MACK >> HARVEST.SO.AI.SIF
<\ Sorry to barge in. It was her idea, I
   promise.
   >> WHY ARE YOU HERE?
<\ Liability. You owned the box, I owned the
   fruit.
```

Sif thought about that for a fraction of a second. It was a reasonable explanation. But if Mack was going to participate in her audit, she was going to set some ground rules.

```
>> VOICE COM ONLY.
>> I WANT HER TO HEAR EVERYTHING YOU SAY.
```

"Afternoon!" Mack drawled from the data center's PA. "Hope I didn't keep you ladies waiting."

"Not at all." Al-Cygni removed a COM pad from her suit's hip pocket. "We were just getting started." In the few seconds it took her to power-on the pad, the two AIs continued their private conversation.

```
<\ I thought you hated my voice?
  >> I DO.
<\ Well, I adore hearing yours.
```

Sif assumed an officious pose, extended a hand to indicate al-Cygni's COM pad. "If you would refer to my report, section one, paragraph . . ." But while her avatar appeared calm and collected, Sif's logic quickly turned on Mack and lashed out before her emotional-restraint algorithms could intercede:

```
>> YOUR FLIRTATIONS ARE AT BEST HARASSMENT,
   AT WORST PERVERSION—NOT THE ACTIONS OF A
   STABLE INTELLIGENCE.
>> YOU ARE, I BELIEVE, WELL ALONG THE ROAD TO
   RAMPANCY.
>> AND I MUST WARN YOU THAT WITHOUT A RAPID
   CHANGE IN YOUR BEHAVIOR, I WILL HAVE NO
   CHOICE BUT TO REGISTER MY CONCERNS WITH AP-
   PROPRIATE PARTIES—UP TO AND INCLUDING THE
   DCS HIGH COMMISSION.
```

Sif waited, core temperature rising, for Mack's response.

```
<\ I think the lady protests a little too
   much.
   >> EXCUSE ME?
<\ It's Shakespeare, sweetheart. Look it up.
   >> LOOK IT UP?
```

Sif flung open her storage arrays, and proceeded to jam all of Shakespeare's plays (individual files in every human language and dialect, past or present) into the data-buffer of Mack's COM. Then she added multilingual folios of all the other Renaissance playwrights. And, just to make sure she'd made her point—that Mack had not only misquoted a line from *Hamlet,* but that his knowledge of theatre and, by extension, all other subjects, was a pale reflection of her own—Sif doubled back and crammed in translations of every play from Aeschylus to the twenty-fifth–century absurdist dialectics of the Cosmic Commedia Cooperative.

Al-Cygni looked up from her pad. "Paragraph . . . ?"

". . . three," Sif said out loud. The delay had been no more than a few seconds, but for an AI it might as well have been an hour.

Al-Cygni folded her hands in her lap, cocked her head to one side. "Neither of you is under oath," she said pleasantly. "But please. No private conversations."

Sif put one leg behind the other and curtsied. "My apologies." The woman was smarter than most DCS employees she dealt with. "My colleague and I were simply comparing records of *Horn of Plenty*'s manifest, in case there was any discrepancy." Not wanting to lie, Sif quickly flashed Mack her record of what the freighter had been carrying.

```
<\ Just his plays?
   >> EXCUSE ME?
<\ I was hoping for a sonnet.
```

Sif pursed her lips. "But it seems we are agreed." She couldn't see Mack's face, but just from his words she could tell he was thoroughly amused.

"Yep!" Mack twanged from the PA. "Two of us are right as rain!"

Al-Cygni smiled. "Please continue."

Sif spun-down her arrays and let her algorithms guide her core back to a more reasonable state. Her code calmed her feelings of embarrassment, confusion, even hurt. As her core cooled, she braced herself for Mack's imminent rejoinder. But, like the gentleman he so often professed to be, he wrote nothing in private—offered not a single, flirtatious byte for the rest of the audit.

CHAPTER
FIVE

Avery experienced a momentary vertigo as the Wagon dropped away from the Tiara. The orbital's artificial gravity wasn't terribly strong, but the Wagon still needed to engage its maglev paddles—make temporary contact with the number-three strand's superconducting film—in order to pull itself free. After a few kilometers, the paddles retracted and Avery's head stopped spinning; Harvest's massy tug was all it needed to continue its fall.

Over the PA, the Wagon's hospitality computer announced that the journey from geo-stationary orbit to Utgard, Harvest's equatorial capitol city, would take a little less than an hour. Then, from smaller speakers in Avery's seat, it asked if he would like to hear the CA's official planetary introduction. Avery glanced at Healy, still fiddling with his harness a few seats to his left. Mainly so he wouldn't have to spend the entire journey parrying more of the Corpsman's uncomfortable questions, Avery agreed.

Immediately, the Staff Sergeant felt his COM pad vibrate in his olive-drab fatigue pants. He pulled it from his pocket and tapped the pad's recessed touch screen, linking it to the wagon's network. Then he removed its integrated ear buds and screwed them into place. As their spongy casings expanded to fit the contours of his ear canals, the hum of the Wagon's heaters compressed into a low roar. In this approximation of silence, the computer began the canned narration.

"On behalf of the Colonial Authority, welcome to Harvest—cornucopia of Epsilon Indi!" a male voice enthused. "I'm this world's 'agricultural operations artificial intelligence.' But please, call me Mack."

The official CA seal warmed onto the screen of Avery's pad—a looming profile of an iconic eagle in a circle of seventeen bright stars, one for each UNSC world. The eagle's wing sheltered a group of colonists. Their hopeful eyes were locked on a fleet of sleek colony ships rocketing along the eagle's upturned beak.

The image bespoke expansion through unity, a message that, in light of the Insurrection, struck Avery as more naïve than inspirational.

"For every person on every one of our worlds, Harvest is synonymous with sustenance." Beneath Mack's easy drawl, the first uplifting chords of Harvest's planetary anthem began to play. "But what allows us to produce such a bounty of fresh and wholesome food?"

The narration paused for dramatic effect, and in that moment Harvest's northern pole rose above the bottom edge of the view-port in the wall opposite Avery's seat—a patch of iceless, deep blue sea cupped by a gently curving coast.

"Two words," Mack continued, answering his own question. "Geography and climate. The Edda supercontinent covers more than two-thirds of Harvest, creating an abundance of arable land. Two low-salinity seas—Hugin in the north and Munin in the south—are the planet's main source of—"

Healy tapped Avery's shoulder, and the Staff Sergeant pulled one of his ear-buds. "You want anything?" the Corpsman asked, nodding at a row of food and dispensers beneath the view-port. Avery shook his head: *No.*

Healy bounded over Avery's legs, and pulled himself along the seats to the end of the row. There was enough gravity in the Wagon that Healy could perform a controlled fall down a set of stairs, pull himself along the railing and make it to an open social area before the dispensers. But when the corpsman tried to walk, his legs slipped out from under him, and he fell backward onto his outstretched hands. Avery detected a hint of volition in Healy's buffoonery—as if he were playing for laughs.

If so, it worked. Some of the Tiara's maintenance techs, sitting in the tiered seats to Avery's right, clapped and whistled as the Corpsman struggled to regain his footing. Healy shrugged and offered a shy "whatcha gonna do?" smile, then continued toward the dispensers.

Avery frowned. Healy was the kind of soldier he would have liked when he first joined the marines: a joker, a troublemaker—the kind of recruit that actually seemed to enjoy bearing the brunt of a drill instructors' wrath. But there weren't many jokers in Avery's part of the corps. And as much as Avery hated to admit it, he had grown so accustomed to the pervasive grimness of the other NavSpecWar marines fighting the Insurrection that he had a hard time relating to anyone that didn't share their no-nonsense approach to soldiering.

"Eighty-six percent of Edda is within five hundred meters of sea level," Mack continued. "In fact, the only really major change in elevation occurs along the Bifrost—what you call an escarpment—that cuts the continent on a diagonal. Have a look. You should be able to see it now, just west of Utgard."

Avery removed his remaining ear-bud. The view now spoke for itself.

He could just make out the Bifrost's northeastern tip beneath a skein of cirrus clouds—a bright fall of limestone shale that started in the northern plains just south of the Hugin Sea and cut southwesterly toward the equator. Because of the view-port's orientation, Avery couldn't see directly down. But he could imagine the view: a low-slung semicircle of the Tiara's seven sunlit strands angling toward Utgard.

Many minutes passed, and then the view-port filled with a patchwork of pastoral colors: yellows and greens and browns—an enlarging grid of fields crisscrossed with silver lines. Avery correctly assumed these were part of a maglev train system—seven main lines heading out from depots at the base of each of the elevators, dividing into smaller branchlines like veins in a leaf.

The Wagon's computer came back over the PA to alert its passengers to return to their seats for deceleration into Utgard. But the technicians continued drinking beer from the dispensers with Healy as the first of the capital's buildings rose into view. The skyline wasn't spectacular—there were only a few dozen towers, none more than twenty stories high. But the buildings were all modern glass-shrouded designs, evidence that Harvest had come a long way since Avery's last visit. When he'd made his hit, the city wasn't much more than a few blocks of polycrete pre-fabs, and the whole colony had a population of fifty, maybe sixty thousand residents. Checking his COM pad one more time before putting it away, he learned that the number had grown to a little more than three hundred thousand.

Suddenly, the buildings disappeared and the Wagon darkened as it dropped into the number-three strand's anchor—a ponderous polycrete monolith connected to a vast warehouse where dozens of cargo containers waited to ascend. Avery waited for the techs to clear the Wagon then joined Healy at the luggage bin. They retrieved their duffels and emerged from the anchor's passenger terminal, eyes blinking in Epsilon Indi's afternoon light.

"Ag-worlds," Healy grumbled. "Always hotter than shit."

Utgard's thick equatorial air had instantly maxed the wicking properties of their uniforms. The fabric clung to the smalls of their backs as the two soldiers tromped west down a flagstone ramp to a broad, tree-lined boulevard. A white and green sedan taxi idled against the boulevard's curb. The stripe of holo-tape across its passenger-side door flashed the simple message: TRANSPORT: JOHNSON, HEALY.

"Open up!" Healy hollered, banging a fist on the taxi's roof. The vehicle raised its gull-wing doors and popped its trunk. Bags stowed, Avery settled in the driver's seat and Healy took shotgun. Fans hummed inside the dashboard, and a frigid blast attacked the humid air.

"Hello," the sedan chirped as it pulled into the boulevard's sparse traffic. "I have been instructed to take you to . . ." There was a pause as it prepared a concatenated response: "Colonial. Militia. Garrison. Gladsheim Highway. Exit twenty-nine. Is that correct?"

Healy licked the sweat from his upper lip. He'd managed to drink a decent amount of beer during the wagon's descent, and his words came out a little slurred.

"Yeah, but we need to make a stop. One thirteen Nobel Avenue."

"Confirmed. One thir—"

"Belay that!" Avery barked. "Continue preconfirmed route!"

The sedan slowed, momentarily confused, then turned left down a boulevard that bordered the northern edge of a long, grassy park—Utgard's central mall.

"What do you think you're doing?"

"One of the techs told me about a place with *really* friendly ladies. And I figured before we—"

Avery cut Healy short. "Car, I'm driving."

"Do you assume all liability for—"

"Yes! And give me a map."

A compact steering wheel unfolded from a compartment in the dash. Avery clamped it tight with both hands.

"Manual control confirmed," the sedan replied. "Please drive safely."

As Avery thumbed a pressure pad in the wheel that linked to

the sedan's accelerator, a ghostly grid of the surrounding streets appeared on the inner surface of the windshield. Avery instantly memorized the route.

"Kill the map. And lower the goddamn AC."

The fans slowed and the humidity began to slink forward, cowed but not beaten.

"Look, Johnson." Healy sighed, rolling up his shirtsleeves. "You're new to this, so let me explain. There are only a couple reasons to do CMT. First, it's very hard to get shot. Second, it's the best way I know to sample all *kinds* of colonial tail." Avery changed lanes without warning. Healy swung hard against the passenger-side door. The Corpsman righted himself with a petulant sigh. "A uniform will get you killed in Eridanus. But out here? It'll get you laid."

Avery forced himself to breathe a slow three-count and eased his thumb off the accelerator. To his left, a fountain in the center of the mall shot plumes of water high into the air. The mist carried across the boulevard, turning the sedan's dusty windshield into a mottled, muddy mess. The wipers came on automatically and quickly cleared the view.

"My uniform means the same wherever I go," Avery said calmly. "It tells people I am a marine, not some navy squid who has never once been shot at, let alone fired a round at someone else. My uniform reminds me of the UNSC Code of Conduct, which has very clear restrictions on the consumption of alcohol and fraternization with civilians." He waited for Healy to sit a little straighter in his seat. "Most important, my uniform reminds me of the men who are no longer alive to wear it."

Avery's mind flashed with memory: the ghostly outlines of a squad of marines inside a restaurant, rendered bright white by a drone's thermal camera. He took his eyes off the road—stared straight at Healy. "You disrespect the uniform, you disrespect them. You hear me?"

The Corpsman swallowed dryly. "Yeah, I hear you."

"And from now on, my name is *Staff Sergeant* Johnson. Understood?"

"I got it." Healy grimaced and shifted to look out his window. He didn't need to say what else was on his mind; Avery clearly saw "I got it, *asshole*," in the way he locked his arms across his chest.

As the sedan neared the end of the mall, Avery sped through an intersection past the imposing granite edifice of Harvest's parliament. The I-shaped building was surrounded by a low ironwork fence and well-manicured gardens. Its roof was thatched with sun-bleached wheat straw.

Avery had meant everything he said. But he also regretted it. He and Healy were essentially the same rank, but he'd just ordered him around like a raw recruit. *And when did I become such a hypocrite?* Avery wondered, tightening his grip on the wheel. His three-day bender back in the Zone wasn't the first time he'd ended up drunk in uniform.

Avery was preparing to deliver a terse apology when Healy muttered: "Oh, and Staff Sergeant Johnson? When you get a chance, pull over. Petty Officer First Class Healy needs to puke."

Three silent hours later, they were down the Bifrost and well out onto the Plain of Ida. Epsilon Indi was setting in a pink and orange wash, above the perfectly straight, two-lane highway. Because of Harvest's small diameter, the horizon had a slight but noticeable curve—a bow in the fields of ripening wheat that had sprung up from the Ida after many hundreds of kilometers of fruit orchards. Avery had the sedan's windows down, and the air billowing through the cab was no longer unbearably hot. The Earth-relative UNSC military calendar said it was December. But on Harvest it was the height of summer—the middle of the growing season.

As the last of Epsilon Indi's rays slunk below the horizon, it got very dark very quickly. There were no lights along the highway and no settlements in sight. Harvest had no moon, and while some of the system's four other planets shone unusually close, their reflected starshine wasn't enough to light the way ahead. As the sedan's headlamps came on, Avery spotted the exit marker and turned north off the highway.

The vehicle shuddered as it bit into the loose gravel of an upward sloping drive. A few gentle turns through the wheat and they reached a parade ground surrounded by very new, single-story polycrete buildings: mess hall, barracks, motor pool, and triage—the same rigid footprint Avery had seen many times before.

As he circled the sedan around the parade ground's flagpole, its headlights illuminated a man sitting on the mess hall steps, smoking a cigar. The scent wafting through the vehicle's windows was instantly recognizable: Sweet William, the preferred brand of pretty much every officer in the corps. When Avery brought the sedan to a stop and stepped out, he was quick to salute.

"At ease." Captain Ponder took a long drag from his cigar. "Johnson and Healy, correct?"

"Yes, sir!" the two soldiers replied together.

Ponder rose slowly from the steps. "Good to have you. Let me help you with your gear."

"That's alright, sir. Only got the two bags."

"Travel light, first to fight." The Captain smiled.

Adjusting for the steps, Avery could tell Ponder was a few inches shorter than he was, and a little less broad in the shoulders. He guessed the Captain's age was somewhere north of fifty. But with his buzz-cut, salt-and-pepper hair, and well-tanned skin, he looked as vital as a man half his age, except for the fact that he was missing his right arm.

Avery noted that the sleeve of Ponder's fatigue shirt was cuffed to a phantom elbow and pinned neatly to his side. Then he stopped staring. He had seen plenty of amputees. But it was rare to meet an active-duty marine that wasn't fitted with a *permanent* prosthetic.

Ponder nodded toward the sedan. "Sorry about the civilian vehicle. Warthogs were supposed to be here a week ago. Shipping delay, if you can believe it. I've got my other platoon-leader in Utgard, trying to track them down."

"What about the recruits?" Avery asked, pulling the duffels from the sedan.

"Monday. We've got the whole weekend to set up shop."

Avery shut the trunk. As soon as he stepped away, the vehicle reversed around the flagpole and traced its furrows back down to the highway.

"Which platoon is mine?" Avery asked.

"First." Ponder pointed his cigar at one of the two barracks on the southern edge of the parade ground.

Healy hefted his duffel onto his shoulder. "You got me bunking with the grunts, sir?"

"Just until you clear a space in triage. Someone in logistics ordered a shitload of supplies. Must have confused this garrison with some CSH on Tribute."

Healy chuckled. Avery did not; he was all too familiar with the kind of casualties a combat support hospital received.

"Mess hall dispensers are working if you want anything," the Captain continued. "Otherwise, get some rest. I've scheduled a briefing for zero seven thirty to go over the training schedule—make sure we kick-off the first phase right."

"Anything else for tonight, sir?" Avery asked.

Ponder clamped his cigar tightly in his teeth. "Nothing that can't wait until morning."

Avery watched the ashen tip of Ponder's cigar flare in the darkness. Then he saluted, and marched off to the 1st platoon barracks, Healy trailing behind through the shifting gravel.

The Captain watched them traverse the pools of light cast by the parade ground's elevated arc lights. *Some things,* he knew, *couldn't wait.* Ponder tossed his cigar and ground it with his boot. Then he took his own path to his private quarters adjacent the motor pool.

Half an hour later, Avery was unpacked. All his gear was neatly stowed in a wall-locker in his platoon-leader's rack—a small room at the front of the barracks to one side of its screen-door entrance. He could hear Healy at the back of the barracks, still pulling items from his duffels—humming to himself as he arranged them on his bed.

"Hey. Staff Sergeant Johnson," the Corpsman shouted. "You got some soap?"

Avery gritted his teeth. "Check the showers."

As painful as it was to have Healy now taking pleasure in Avery's previous order—tossing his formality back in his face—the Staff Sergeant was glad he could hear the Corpsman through the walls of his room. Avery knew from experience that a large part of a drill instructor's job was simply keeping exhausted recruits from taking their frustrations out on one another—to be the focus of their anger, and, if he did his job right, their eventual admiration.

But Avery also knew that some days his platoon would return to the barracks pissed-off and itching for a fight precisely because he'd ground them down. At least he'd be able to hear any commotion from his rack and be able to break it up before things got out of hand.

"Look, it's only one night," Healy continued in a conciliatory tone. "If I can't get triage ship-shape tomorrow, I'll just bunk with what's his name."

"You mean the *Captain*?" Avery asked. He threw a brown wool blanket over his bed. Regardless of the heat, he needed to show his recruits how to make a proper bed.

"No, the other platoon leader. Hang on, I'll check my COM."

Avery smoothed the blanket with wide sweeps of his palms. Then he started on the corners—tight hospital folds that would have made his own drill instructor proud.

"Byrne," Healy hollered. "Staff Sergeant Nolan Byrne."

Avery froze, his hands stuffed halfway under his mattress. The open coils of the bed frame bit into his palms.

"You know him?"

Avery completed the corner. He stood and reached for his pillow and case. "Yes."

"Huh. Did you know he was gonna be *here*?"

"No." Avery stuffed the pillow with a practiced thrust.

"You two friends?"

Avery wasn't quite sure how to answer that. "I've known him a long time."

"Oh, *now* I get it," Healy's voice changed pitch, signaling an incoming jibe. "You lovebirds start spending too much time together, and I might get jealous." Avery heard the Corpsman snicker then run the zipper of his duffel. "So what do you think the story is with the Captain's arm?"

But Avery didn't answer. He was focused on the loudening growl of a Warthog light-reconnaissance vehicle's engine as it raced up from the highway. The Warthog came to a hasty stop outside the barracks door. Its engine roared and died, and soon Avery heard the crunch of approaching boots.

Quickly, Avery paced to his locker, parted his neat piles of shirts and pants and removed a patent-leather belt with a bright brass buckle stamped with the UNSC eagle and globe emblem. Behind him, the barrack's door swung open. Avery felt a chill on the back of his neck.

"That's a well made bed," Staff Sergeant Byrne said. "After a month in the hospital, you get an eye for that sort of thing."

Avery coiled his belt tight enough to hide it in the palm of his hand, shut the locker, and turned to face his former fellow squad-leader. Byrne no longer wore the helmet with the silver mirrored visor he'd had on the day Avery failed to shoot the Innie woman in the restaurant—the day Byrne had lost all the members of his squad. But he might as well have had it on. His ice-blue eyes were just as impenetrable.

"Because of all the *changes*," Byrne explained with a sneer. "Piss and shite all over the sheets because I was too doped to control myself. When the nurses gave me new ones, they'd always tuck them in too tight or not tight enough."

"It's good to see you, Byrne."

"But that?" Byrne continued, ignoring Avery's greeting. "That's a well-made bed."

Fresh, pink scars crinkled the Irish Staff Sergeant's already rugged face—evidence that his helmet's visor had shattered in the Innie blast. A jagged stitch from a shrapnel injury ran from his left temple up and over his ear. His black hair must have burned completely away; even though it was cut regulation short, Avery could see it was coming back in patches.

"I'm glad you're alright," Avery said.

"Are you now?" Byrne's brogue had begun to thicken. After years of soldiering together, Avery understood exactly what that meant. But he wanted Byrne to know one thing.

"They were all good men. I'm sorry."

Byrne shook his head. "Not sorry enough."

For such a large man, Byrne moved with amazing speed. He sprung at Avery, arms wide, and slammed him back against the locker. He locked his hands behind Avery's back and squeezed, threatening to break his ribs. As much as it hurt, Avery sucked in a breath and brought his forehead crashing down on Byrne's nose. Byrne grunted, his grip faltered, and he staggered back.

In a flash, Avery ducked around behind him, belt stretched between his hands. He looped it over Byrne's neck, and pulled it tight. Byrne's eyes widened. Avery wasn't trying to kill his fellow marine, just get him under control. Byrne outweighed him by at least twenty kilos, and Avery wanted him out for the count as quickly as possible.

But Byrne wasn't about to let that happen. With a strained but mighty cry he reached over his shoulders and grabbed Avery's wrists—leaned forward and brought Avery high on his back. Then Byrne proceeded to slam Avery against the rooms wooden walls with such force that the painted plywood began to splinter.

Avery's teeth shuddered. He tasted blood in his mouth. But every time Byrne leaned forward for another backward thrust, Avery tightened his belt. Byrne began to wheeze. Avery could see the veins in his neck strain and his ears begin to purple. But an instant before Byrne lost consciousness, he brought the heel of his boot up between Avery's legs—right into his unprotected groin.

In the few seconds before he seized up, Avery hooked a foot around Byrne's shins and tripped him onto his bed. Byrne fell short, cracked his forehead on the bed frame, and went limp. As Avery rolled him over—raised a fist to finish the job—a debilitating ache spread from his groin to his arm. Byrne's eyes blinked, trying to clear away the blood flowing from a jagged cut, and Avery threw a half-speed punch. But Byrne was only dazed. He raised a massive hand, and caught Avery's fist in his iron grip.

"Why didn't you take the shot?" Byrne grunted.

"There were civilians," Avery groaned.

Byrne slammed his other palm up into Avery's gut, bunching his fatigue shirt in his fist. With a powerful thrust of his hips, he flipped Avery over his shoulders toward the barrack's door. The air exploded from Avery's lungs as he landed flat on his back in the narrow hallway outside his rack.

"You had an *order*!" Byrne growled, rising to his feet.

Avery's chest heaved as he picked himself off the floor. "There was a kid; a boy."

"What about my *team*?!"

Byrne lumbered toward Avery and threw a high right jab. But Avery blocked it with his left forearm, and countered with a powerful, right-hand swipe. As Byrne's head snapped sideways, Avery brought a knee up into his kidneys. But Byrne collapsed against the blow, and drove him back against the hallway wall. Avery felt his left shoulder dislocate then pop back into place. He blinked his eyes against the pain, giving Byrne an opening. The other Staff Sergeant quickly throttled him around the neck.

"They taught you to be a killer, Avery. They taught us *both*." Byrne slid him up the wall until his boots were twitching half a meter off the floor. The barrack's fluorescent lights seemed to dim, and Avery saw stars. He tried to kick himself free. But it was no use. "You can't hide from that," Byrne sneered. "And you sure as hell can't hide from me."

Avery was about to pass out when he heard the metallic snap of someone working a pistol's slide.

"Staff Sergeant Byrne." Captain Ponder said firmly. "Stand down."

Byrne tightened his grip on Avery's throat. "This is private business."

"Drop him, or I shoot."

"Bullshit."

"No, marine." The Captain's voice was deadly calm. "It most certainly is not."

Byrne released his hands. Avery dropped and slumped back against the wall. Gasping, he looked toward the barrack's door. The Captain held an M6 service pistol in a prosthetic replacement for his missing arm. Avery could see the bright titanium joints that were Ponder's fingers and the carbon-fiber weave of his forearm musculature.

"I know the numbers," Ponder said. "Thirty-eight civilian casualties, three of your unit KIA. But I also know Staff Sergeant Johnson is not in the stockade, nor was he charged with any misconduct. And as far as I'm concerned that's all *anyone* needs to know."

Byrne tightened his fists, but left them at his sides.

"You're angry. I understand that. But this ends *tonight*." Ponder shifted his gaze to Avery. "You got anything else, now's the time."

"Sir, no sir." Avery's voice was hoarse.

Ponder's eyes snapped to Byrne. "And you?"

Without a moment's pause, Byrne smashed a fist into the side of Avery's face. Avery dropped to a knee. "That should do it," Byrne grunted.

Avery spat a mouthful of blood onto the barrack's floor. He hadn't run, but Byrne *had* followed—gotten transferred away from TREBUCHET just like him. Avery knew something wasn't right. And that filled him with more anger than any sucker punch.

"Last chance, Johnson" Ponder said.

Avery rose, and slugged Byrne hard enough to snap his head past his shoulder.

One of Byrne's teeth skipped along the floor and came to rest near Healy. The Corpsman had made his way forward from his bunk, hefting one of his boots like a club—apparently to try and break up the fight on his own. "Jesus," the Corpsman whispered, starring down at the tooth.

"We're finished." Ponder lowered his pistol. "That's an order."

"Yes, sir," Avery and Byrne said together.

The Captain gave each Staff Sergeant a final, emphatic glance, then marched down the barrack's steps. The screen-door banged shut behind him, creaked back on its hinges and came to a rattling rest.

"I'm not rated for oral surgery," Healy said lamely in the silence that followed. He knelt and picked up Byrne's tooth.

"Doesn't matter. What's done is done." Byrne locked Avery's

wary stare. He sucked at the bloody hole of his missing canine. "But this is so I don't forget."

With a slow rotation of his massive frame, Byrne followed Ponder into the night.

"I'm going to triage," Healy announced.

"Good," Avery replied, rubbing his jaw. The way he felt, the last thing he wanted was Healy keeping him awake with more conversation.

"To grab a med-kit. Then I'm coming right back."

Avery huffed as Healy walked past, "You sure you still want to bunk with me?"

The Corpsman paused in the doorway. For the first time, Avery recognized the soothing appeal of his near-perpetual grin.

"You're a piece of work, Johnson." Healy jerked his chin at Byrne's fading footfalls. "But that guy? He'd probably kill me in my sleep."

CHAPTER
SIX

Dadab slunk through the engine room, doing his best to stay low in spite of his methane tank. In his fist he held a rock, a mottled gray and green chunk of digestive grit he'd taken from the Kig-Yar's dining compartment. *Easy now*, he thought, rising up behind a thick line of conduit bracketed to the floor, *don't spook it.*

Scrub grubs were anxious creatures. The hairs that covered their turgid bodies were always in motion, sensing for danger as they ate their way around machinery that could easily scald or freeze. But it wasn't until Dadab rose up that it felt a disturbance in the room's steamy air. The grub pulled itself from the floor with a loud pop and began undulating for the safety of an elevated overflow unit, its consumption orifice warbling in miserable panic.

Dadab threw his rock, and the grub disappeared in a mealy poof. The rock carried forward, rebounded off the iridescent casing of *Minor Transgression*'s engine, and skipped to a stop in a puddle of viscous green coolant. Had the grub lived, it eventually would have sucked the puddle up.

Dadab snorted proudly inside his mask, and flexed one of his hands: < *Two!* >

< *Apologies, but I am perplexed.* > Lighter Than Some reached a pearly tentacle into the puddle, retrieved the rock, and tossed it back to Dadab. < *I only saw* one *grub.* >

The Deacon rolled his small, red eyes. The rules of the game weren't complicated. He simply lacked the vocabulary to explain them clearly. < *Watch* > he signed.

Dadab wiped the rock clean with a corner of his orange tunic. Then with the pointed tip of one of his fingers, he scratched a second hash mark into the stone—right beside one for the first grub that had wandered into the methane suite, breaking a long stretch of mind-numbing confinement.

It had been many sleep cycles since *Minor Transgression* exited its jump at the edge of the unexplored alien system. Chur'R-Yar had moved inward at a cautious pace toward the alien cargo vessel's point of departure. But until they arrived, the Deacon had very little to do; Zhar and the other Kig-Yar crewman certainly weren't interested in listening to any of his sermons.

He showed the rock to *Lighter Than Some*, and signed his simple math: < *One, one, two!* > The docile grubs were hardly a challenge—nothing like the mud wasps and shade crabs of Dadab's youth. But in the Unggoy game of hunting rock, you marked every kill, easy or not.

< *Oh, I see . . .* > the Huragok replied. < *The amusement is additive.* >

< *More . . . fun . . . ?* > Dadab struggled to mimic poses for words he hadn't yet learned.

Lighter Than Some formed slow, simple poses. < *More, kill, more, fun.* >

Dadab didn't take offense when the creature dumbed down its discourse for clarity. He knew he spoke no better than a Huragok infant and was grateful for its patience.

< *Yes* > Dadab gestured, < *more, kill, more, fun.* > He pulled a second rock from a pocket in his tunic and presented it to *Lighter Than Some*. < *Most, kill, win!* >

But the Huragok ignored him—floated back to the conduit and began to fix a stress fracture that was the cause of the coolant puddle.

Dadab knew the creature had a preternatural urge to repair things. It was almost impossible to distract it from its work, which was why Huragok were such valuable crew members. With a Huragok on board, nothing remained broken for long. Indeed, seconds later the leak was sealed—the tear in the metal conduit knitted together by the cilia that covered the tips of *Lighter Than Some*'s tentacles.

< *Hunt!* > Dadab said, offering the rock a second time.

< *I'd rather not.* >

< *Why?* >

< *Really, you go ahead. Try for three.* >

< *Game, fun!* >

< *No, your game is* murder. >

Dadab couldn't help an exasperated groan. *A grub was a grub! There were hundreds of the things skulking around the Kig-Yar ship!* On a long voyage like this one, it was essential to thin their numbers before they multiplied and worked their way into a critical system.

Then again, Dadab thought, *maybe the Huragok felt a certain kinship with his prey?* They were both voiceless servants— tireless slaves to the Kig-Yar vessel's needs. Dadab imagined *Lighter Than Some*'s beady sensory nodes glimmering with condemnation.

Looking around the engine-room, Dadab spotted a spent energy core. He hefted the clear, bowed cube onto the overflow unit the grub was aiming for and worked it back and forth until it balanced nicely—until he was sure the Huragok would tip it, even with a glancing blow.

< *Now, no, kill.* > Dadab signed enthusiastically. < *Just, fun!* >

Lighter Than Some deflated one of its gas-sacs with an obstinate toot.

< *Try!* > Dadab pleaded. < *Just, once!* >

With obvious disdain, the Huragok curled its tentacle and

tossed its rock. It was a perfunctory throw, but it hit the core dead center, knocking it to the floor.

< *One!* > Dadab grunted happily and was about to reset the target for another toss when the Shipmistress' voice crackled from a round metal signal unit clipped to his tank harness.

"Deacon, to the bridge. And do *not* bring the Huragok."

Chur'R-Yar sat at the edge of her command-chair, mesmerized by the contents of the bridge's holo-tank. The representation of the alien system was now much more detailed. Planets and asteroids—even an inbound comet—were all represented, details previously missing from *Minor Transgression*'s database. The planet from which the alien ship began its journey shone in the very center of the tank. But it was the thousands of cyan glyphs dotting the planet's surface—all with the same, circular design—that transfixed her.

Suddenly, the glyphs and everything inside the tank flickered as it temporarily lost power.

"Careful!" the Shipmistress hissed, twisting toward Zhar. The male Kig-Yar stood near an alcove in the bridge's concave purple walls, a laser-cutter in one of his clawed hands.

"I want it disconnected, not destroyed!"

"Yes, Mistress." Zhar's spines flattened subserviently on his head. Then he gingerly reapplied his cutter to a twist of circuits connected to a device with three pyramidal parts suspended in the center of the alcove. The largest of the pyramids was arranged point down; the two smaller ones pointed up, supporting the largest on either side. All three shone with a silver glow that framed Zhar against the alcove.

This was the ship's Luminary, an arcane device required on all Covenant vessels. It had assigned thousands of glyphs or Luminations to the alien world, each one a possible Forerunner relic. Chur'R-Yar's tongue flicked against her teeth with barely contained excitement. *If only* Minor Transgression *had a bigger hold. . . .*

The Shipmistress came from a long line of matriarchal ship captains. And while most of her bloodline had been decimated in defense of asteroid redoubts during the Covenant's aggressive conversion of her species into its faith, she still felt her ancestors' buccaneering spirit pulsing through her veins.

Kig-Yar had always been pirates. Long before the Covenant arrived, they sailed the tropical archipelagos of their watery home world, raiding competing clans for food and mates. As their populations grew, the distances and differences between clans decreased; a new cooperative spirit led to the creation of spacecraft that lifted them from their planet. But as some clans looked out on the dark and endless sea of space, they could not resist returning to their old marauding ways.

In the end, these pirates were the species' only effective resistance to the Covenant. But they could not hold out forever. To save themselves, the captains were forced to accept letters of marque: agreements that let them keep their ships so long as they sailed in the service of a Covenant Ministry.

Some Kig-Yar saw opportunity in this subservience. Chur'R-Yar saw eons of table scraps. Endless patrols, looking for relics—unimaginably valuable treasures she would never be allowed to claim as her own. Yes, during her voyages she might stumble across some small amount of salvage: a derelict Covenant habitat or a damaged alien freighter. But these were comparatively meager alms, and Chur'R-Yar was no beggar.

At least not anymore, she thought. The Shipmistress knew she could remove a small number of relics without anyone noticing. But only if her ship's Luminary remained silent, and she waited to transmit its accounting until *after* she had taken her share.

Chur'R-Yar felt the callused plates on her neck and shoulders contract. This thick skin served as natural armor, keeping females of her species safe during the literal backbiting that accompanied most Kig-Yar mating sessions. The Shipmistress wasn't normally very broody. But when she sold the relics on the Covenant black-market, she hoped to earn enough profit to take *Minor Transgression* out of service for an entire mating season. And that possibility was deeply arousing.

She relaxed in her chair and stared at Zhar—watched his sinewy muscles ripple beneath his scales—as he carefully severed the Luminary's connections to her ship's signal circuits. He wasn't her ideal mate. She would have preferred someone with higher standing amongst the clans, but she had always been partial to males with virile plumage. And Zhar had another advantage: he was close at hand. With all the blood rushing to her shoulders, Chur'R-Yar began to feel deliciously faint.

But then the bridge door cycled open, and Dadab trotted through. The Unggoy's tunic reeked of engine coolant and gassy Huragok, and the stink immediately killed her libido.

"Shipmistress?" Dadab preformed a curt bow then looked suspiciously at Zhar.

"What do you see?" Chur'R-Yar snapped, redirecting the Unggoy's gaze toward the holo-tank.

"A system. Single star. Five planets." Dadab took a step toward the tank. "One of the planets seems . . . to . . . have . . ." His voice squeaked off, and he drew a series of rapid breaths.

Chur'R-Yar clucked her tongue. *"A Luminary does not lie."*

Usually she quoted Holy Writs only to mock them, but this time Chur'R-Yar was serious. Every Luminary was modeled after a device the Prophets had located aboard an ancient Forerunner warship—one that now stood at the center of the Covenant capitol, High Charity. Luminaries were sacred objects and tampering with them was punishable by death—or worse.

Which was why the Shipmistress knew the Deacon was so

distressed by Zhar's actions. As her chosen mate continued to flash his laser all around the Luminary, the Deacon shifted his weight from one of his conical, flat-bottomed feet to the other. Chur'R-Yar could hear the valves inside his mask clicking as he tried to get his breathing under control.

"I must report these Luminations at once," Dadab gasped.

"No," the Shipmistress snapped. "You will not."

Zhar severed a final circuit and the Luminary dimmed.

"Heresy!" Dadab wailed, before he could stay his tongue.

Zhar clattered his toothy jaws and stepped toward the Deacon, laser cutter blazing. But Chur'R-Yar stopped the overprotective male with a rattling hiss. Under different circumstances, she might have let him tear the Unggoy apart for his foolish insult. But for now, she needed him alive.

"Calm yourself," she said. "The Luminary is not damaged. It simply cannot speak."

"But the Ministry!" Dadab stammered. "It will demand an explanation—"

"And it shall have one. After I take my pick of plunder."

The Shipmistress uncurled a claw toward the holo-tank. There was a single glyph not located on the alien planet. To the untrained eye, it might have looked like some sort of display error—a misplaced piece of data. But Chur'R-Yar's pirate gaze recognized it for what it was: a relic aboard another of the alien freighters; one she hoped would be as easy to capture as the first.

The Deacon was shivering now, his whole blue-gray body quaking with terror. The Shipmistress knew the Unggoy was right: what she planned to do *was* heresy. Only the Prophets were allowed access to relics. And if tampering with a Luminary meant death, defying the Prophets meant damnation.

Then suddenly the Deacon calmed. Eyes darting between the glyphs in the holo-tank and the bright red tip of Zhar's laser cutter, his breathing slowed. Chur'R-Yar knew the Unggoy was smarter than most and guessed he had just realized the full extent his predicament: the Shipmistress had told him her secret plans, and yet he lived. Which could only mean one thing: *She had a plan for him.*

"What would my Shipmistress have me do?" Dadab asked.

Chur'R-Yar's teeth glittered in the Luminary's weakened light. "I need you to lie."

The Deacon nodded. And the Shipmistress set course for the relic-laden ship.

Henry "Hank" Gibson loved his freighter—loved her big, ugly lines and the quiet rumble of her Shaw-Fujikawa drive. Most of all he loved to sail her, which most people thought was a little unusual when a NAV computer could do just as well. But that was fine by Hank because, even more than his ship, he loved not giving a damn what people thought of him, something to which either of his ex-wives would gladly attest.

Human ship captains weren't uncommon in the UNSC commercial fleet; they just mainly sailed cruise ships and other passenger vessels. Hank had worked for one of the big cruise companies—served on the luxury liner *Two Drink Minimum* nonstop from Earth to Arcadia for the better part of fifteen years, the last five as first mate.

But the liner had needed all kinds of computer assistance to get from A to B while keeping its hundreds of passengers well fed and rested. Hank was a self-avowed loner, and it didn't matter if the voices talking to him were human or simulated—he liked a quiet bridge. And *Two Drink Minimum*'s certainly wasn't that. If the pay hadn't been so good, and the time away from his wives so therapeutic, Hank would have quit a whole lot sooner.

Other than astrogation (the coordination of Slipspace jumps that required a NAV computer), a freighter captain could handle as many of his ship's normal space operations as he liked. Hank loved having his hands on the controls—blasting away with his hydrazine rockets as he bullied thousands of tons of cargo in and out of a planet's gravity well. The fact that he owned his ship, *This End Up*, made sailing her even sweeter. It had taken all his savings, painful renegotiations of his alimonies, and a loan so large he didn't like to think about it, but now he was his own boss. He got to pick what he hauled and over time he built up a list of customers who were willing to pay a little extra for personalized service.

One of his most reliable customers was JOTUN Heavy Industries, a Mars-based firm specializing in the construction of semi-autonomous farm machinery. His freighter's hold was currently filled with a prototype of their next series of plows—massive machines designed to till wide swaths of earth. The things were incredibly expensive, and Hank assumed a prototype would be even more so. Which was why, staring at a console filled with flashing warning lights, he was more angry than afraid.

This End Up's unknown attacker had hit while the ship was hurtling toward Harvest on a high-speed intercept vector. Hank survived the attack unharmed. But the hostile fire had ruined his Shaw-Fujikawa drive, fried his maneuvering rockets and maser—caused more damage to *This End Up* than he could afford to repair. Piracy was unheard of on the routes Hank ran, and he had never even considered adding the optional, extremely expensive coverage to his policy.

Hank slapped his hand on the console, silencing a new alarm: hull breach, port side of the cargo container, close to the stern. He could feel the rubberized floor of the command cabin vibrate as something worked its way through the hull.

"God damn it!" Hank cursed, wrenching a fire extinguisher from a wall bracket. He hoped the pirates wouldn't damage the JOTUN prototype as they cut their way inside.

"Fine. These jerks wanna *break* my ship?" Hank snarled,

hefting the extinguisher above his head. "Then they're gonna *buy* it."

The interior of *Minor Transgression*'s umbilical glowed red as its penetrator tip burned into the alien vessel. Through the semi-transparant walls, Dadab could see laser scarring on the vessel's propulsion unit—black slash-marks from Chur'R-Yar's comprehensive crippling.

How can she be so calm?! Dadab groaned, looking down the umbilical at the Shipmistress. She stood behind Zhar, one clawed hand resting on the grip of her holstered plasma-pistol—like a Kig-Yar pirate queen of old—poised for boarding action. The other two Kig-Yar crewmen standing just behind her were less composed. Both of them fiddled with their energy cutlasses: pink crystal shards used as melee weapons. Dadab wondered if the crewmen, like him, realized they were doomed.

He imagined Chur'R-Yar would succeed in removing the relic (though some had proven to be quite dangerous, even in the Prophets' deft hands). Then she would probably jump right into the thick of Covenant space—where her relic would show as one of countless others—and quickly find a buyer before raising any Ministry suspicions. It was a plausible plan. But Dadab knew he and any other unnecessary witnesses would be dead long before it was completed. In his case, immediately after he transmitted a false accounting of the number of Luminations in the alien system.

The umbilical dimmed as its penetrator tip finished its burn through the hull. The end of the passage irised open to reveal a shimmering energy field.

"Have the Huragok check the pressure," Chur'R-Yar said, glancing back at Dadab.

The Deacon turned and signed to *Lighter Than Some* behind him: < *Check, air, equal.* > Before they boarded the alien vessel, they needed to be sure there was a balance between the umblilical's atmosphere and that of the ship's hold. If there wasn't, they might be torn apart as they passed through the field.

The Huragok floated nonchalantly past Dadab. For *Lighter Than Some,* this was just another opportunity to be helpful. It checked the sensors governing the field and loosed a satisfied bleat. Zhar wasted no time jumping through.

"It is safe!" the Kig-Yar male announced via his signal unit. Chur'R-Yar motioned the other male crewmen forward, then slipped through the field followed closely by *Lighter Than Some.* Dadab took a deep breath and offered a silent prayer for the Prophets' forgiveness. Then he too passed into the alien vessel.

Its hold wasn't nearly as packed as the first one they'd encountered. Instead of floor-to-ceiling containers of fruit, the space was dominated by a single piece of cargo: a towering machine with six massive wheels. On the front of the machine was a beam—wider than the machine itself—fitted with toothlike spikes, each twice as tall as Dadab. Most of the machine's internal parts were shrouded by yellow and blue painted metal, but here and there Dadab saw exposed circuits and pneumatics. Above the toothed beam were a series of raised, bright metal symbols: J-O-T-U-N.

Dadab cocked his head. If the symbols were Forerunner, he hadn't ever seen them. But he wasn't too surprised; he was just a lowly Deacon, and there were countless holy mysteries he had yet to understand.

"Tell the Huragok to investigate," Chur'R-Yar snapped, pointing at the machine.

Dadab clapped his paws together to get *Lighter Than Some's* attention: < *Find, relic!* >

The Huragok ballooned the largest of its sacs, increasing its buoyancy. As it rose above one of the machine's large wheels, it vented a smaller chamber, propelling itself through a curtain of multicolored wires.

The Shipmistress directed Zhar and the two other crewmen to a pile of plastic crates strapped to the floor near the back of the vehicle. Eagerly clattering their bony jaws, the Kig-Yar leapt to their task, prying open the topmost boxes with quick jabs and swift pulls of their claws. Soon they disappeared in a flurry of soft, white packing material.

"Make yourself useful, Deacon," Chur'R-Yar snapped. "Collect the vessel's signal unit."

Dadab bowed and scampered around the machine to the rear of the hold. The elevator platform worked the same as before, and soon he was rising up to the passage that led to the command cabin. Halfway down the passage, the Deacon suddenly remembered the disgusting filth that had awaited him last time. As he stepped through the cabin door, he involuntarily held his breath and shut his eyes.

Clang! Something heavy slammed into Dadab's tank. He yelped with alarm and staggered forward. Another blow knocked him to his stomach. Methane hissed from a fracture in his tank.

"Have mercy!" Dadab shrieked, curling into a ball and covering his face with his spiny forearms. He heard a series of guttural exclamations, and felt something kick the back of one of his legs. Dadab parted his arms ever so slightly, and peeked through the crack.

The alien was tall and muscular. Most of its pale flesh was covered by a fitted cloth jumpsuit. Teeth bared, and holding a red metal cylinder above its mostly hairless head, the thing looked savage—not at all like something that might possess a holy relic.

The alien lashed out with one of its heavy boots, striking Dadab's leg a second time. It shouted more angry and unintelligible words.

"Please!" Dadab whimpered, "I don't understand!" But his pleas only seemed to anger the alien. It stepped forward, cudgel raised for a killing blow. Dadab shrieked and covered his eyes. . . .

But the blow never came. Dadab heard the cylinder bounce

off the rubbery floor, and roll to a stop against the side of the cabin. Slowly, the Deacon uncrossed his arms.

The alien's mouth was open but it didn't speak. It teetered back and forth, grasping for its head. Then all at once, its arms slacked. Dadab scooted backward as the alien careened face-first onto the floor right between his legs. He heard a nervous bleat and looked up.

Lighter Than Some floated in the cabin's doorway. Three of its tentacles were tucked defensively close to its sacs. The fourth stuck straight out, quivering in what Dadab initially took for fear. But then he realized *Lighter Than Some* was trying to speak—struggling to form the simplest Huragok sign: < *One.* >

A clamor of clawed feet in the passage heralded the Ship-mistress' approach. She shoved past the Huragok brandishing her plasma-pistol and cocked one of her ruby eyes at the alien's corpse. "How did it die?" she asked.

Dadab looked down. The back of the alien's skull was caved in—punctured with a ragged hole. Gingerly Dadab slipped two fingers inside the mortal wound. He pinched something hard in the center of the thing's brains, and pulled it out for all to see: *Lighter Than Some's* hunting rock.

Sif didn't like to upset her NAV computer charges. Somewhere deep in her core logic was a memory of her maker as a harried mother with little patience for her infant child. But communicating with ships while they were in Slipspace was impossible. So there was no way for Sif to give them forewarning of the additional security measures Jilan al-Cygni had imposed after the audit.

```
<\\> HARVEST.SO.AI.SIF >> DCS.CUP#-00040370
<\ ADHERE TO YOUR NEW TRAJECTORY.
<\ MAINTAIN REQUIRED SPEED.
<\ ALL IS WELL. \>
```

To connect with Harvest, or any other planet, as it hurtled through the void, freighters needed to exit Slipspace on the right trajectory, traveling at match speed. Harvest orbited Epsilon Indi at a little more than one hundred fifty thousand kilometers per hour, faster than most UNSC worlds. Depending on the angle of its intercept vector, a NAV computer might have to push its ship even faster than that to make the rendezvous.

So the NAV computers were understandably rattled when, immediately after exiting their jumps, Sif demanded they prepare to meet Harvest further along its orbit.

Sif severed her connection to the freighter, *Contents Under Pressure*, and answered another hail. Various parts of her mind were communicating with hundreds of freighters at once, assuring their simple circuits that the holds she was imposing were perfectly safe and legal. The same message, over and over again.

The algorithms that guided Sif's emotions advised her not to correlate repetition with annoyance. But her core couldn't help feeling a little vexed. The woman from DCS had insisted on double-checking the ARGUS and other data she collected from all freighters entering the system. Sif knew this was all part of her probation—that she needed to endure a little bureaucratic humiliation before the DCS would forgive her oversight.

Fortunately, al-Cygni was both polite and efficient, and turned around her sign-offs on Sif's surveys very quickly. But she was human, and needed to sleep at least a few hours every day. That meant some freighters had to stick in holding patterns for quite some time. And this made their NAV computers even more anxious. . . .

```
<\\> HARVEST.SO.AI.SIF >> DCS.TEU#-00481361
<\ ATTENTION, THIS END UP.
<\ YOU MUST MAINTAIN REQUIRED SPEED.
```

Sif could tell *This End Up* was still on the right trajectory, but it had begun to slow. The decrease was minor (less than five-hundred meters per minute) but any deceleration was unacceptable when the goal was keeping pace with a planet.

```
<\ THIS END UP, CAN YOU HEAR ME?
<\ CONTACT HARVEST ON ANY CHANNEL. \>
```

But there was no response, and Sif knew the freighter would surely miss its rendezvous.

She had just begun to contemplate the myriad of problems that could have caused *This End Up* to lose its speed when, without warning, the freighter disappeared from her scan. Or more specifically, the single contact that was *This End Up* suddenly turned into many hundreds of millions of smaller contacts.

Or more succinctly, Sif decided, *the ship blew up.*

She checked the time. It was well past midnight. As she initiated a COM with al-Cygni's hotel in Utgard, she wondered if the woman was still awake.

"Good morning, Sif. How can I help you?" Jilan al-Cygni sat at her suite's desk. From the hotel's full-color feed, Sif could see the woman wore the same brown pantsuit from their previous meeting. But it looked perfectly pressed and al-Cygni's long black hair was tightly wound. Peering into the background, Sif noted that her bed hadn't been disturbed.

"Anything wrong?" al-Cygni asked in a tone that confirmed her alertness.

"We've lost another ship," Sif said, beaming all the relevant data down her maser.

She noted a fractional lowering of al-Cygni's shoulders, a slight unclenching of her jaw. Far from being surprised, the announcement seemed to settle the woman—as if she'd been expecting the freighter's loss and had been waiting for Sif to relay the news.

"Name and itinerary?" Jilan asked, her fingers reaching for her COM pad.

"This End Up. Mars via Reach."

"There were more than thirty ships on proximate vectors," Jilan mused. She scrolled a finger slowly across the screen—trying to discover useful patterns in Sif's data. "Why that one in particular?"

This End Up's manifest claimed it was carrying a JOTUN prototype. Until Sif's ARGUS delivered its assessment of the expanding cloud of debris, she had no hard evidence this *wasn't* the case. Checking the data on other nearby freighters, she confirmed most were loaded with consumer goods. Some carried replacement parts for JOTUNs and other farm machinery. But just as Sif was about to mention the JOTUN prototype as the only significant difference between the various cargos, she noticed something else unusual about the freighter.

But then she saw Jilan's lips begin to move, and as protocol demanded, she held her virtual tongue. It was insolent and prideful to cut a human off, her algorithims reminded her. So Sif did her best not to feel miffed as al-Cygni took credit for their shared realization. The woman's green eyes sparkled as she explained: *"This End Up* was the only ship with a captain. An actual *human* crew."

CHAPTER
SEVEN

As soon as the 1st platoon's recruits had bussed their breakfast trays into the mess hall's sanitizer, Avery led them on their daily march: ten kilometers out and back along the Gladsheim Highway. After two weeks of physical training (PT), they were used to the route—a devastatingly dull path through the flat fields of wheat. But until today they had never done it with full twenty-five kilogram rucksacks. And by the time Epsilon Indi was blazing in the mid-morning sky, the march had become a uniquely punishing ordeal.

This was true for Avery as well, who hadn't gotten any decent exercise since before his trip back home. The long stretches of cryo-sleep from Epsilon Eridanus to Sol and then from Sol to Epsilon Indi had left him with a condition commonly known as "freezer burn." This agonizing sensation, like a bad case of pins and needles, was caused by the breakdown of cryo-sleep pharmaceuticals trapped in muscles and joints, and Avery's case was the worst he'd ever felt—a deep prickling pain in his knees and shoulders brought on by the strenuous march.

Avery winced as he removed his ruck. But it was easy to hide his discomfort from his platoon, because the thirty-six men huddled around the parade-ground flagpole were focused on their own exhaustion. Sweat running down his nose and chin, Avery watched as one of them vomited his jostled breakfast. This started a chain reaction that soon had almost half the platoon heaving loudly onto the gravel.

Jenkins, a younger recruit with rust-colored hair, was doubled over directly in front of Avery. Thin arms resting on his knees, he made a sound that was half cough, half cry. Avery saw a string of spittle stretch toward his poorly tied boots. *He's gonna have blisters*, Avery frowned, staring at the loose laces. But he also knew Jenkins faced a more immediate and dangerous threat: dehydration.

He pulled a plastic water bottle from his ruck and thrust it into the recruit's shaking hands. "Drink it slow."

"Yes, Staff Sergeant," Jenkins wheezed. But he didn't move.

"Now, recruit!" Avery barked.

Jenkins straightened—so quickly that the shifting weight of his ruck almost tossed him back on his bony behind. His shrunken cheeks swelled as he unscrewed the bottle and took two big gulps.

"I said *slow*," Avery tried to keep his anger in check. "Or you're gonna cramp."

Avery knew the colonial militia wasn't the marines, but it was difficult for him to lower his expectations for his recruits' performance. About half of them were members of Harvest's law enforcement and other emergency services, so they were at least mentally prepared for the rigors of basic training. But these men were older as well (some in their late forties or early fifties), and they weren't all in the best of shape.

Things weren't much better with the younger recruits like Jenkins. Most of them had grown up on farms, but because Harvest's JOTUNs did all the hard manual labor, they were just as physically unprepared as their elders to learn the strenuous craft of soldiery.

"Healy!" Avery shouted, pointing to Jenkins' boots. "Got a pair of bad feet!"

"That makes three!" the Corpsman shot back. He was handing out water bottles to a pair of paunchy, middle-aged recruits with sunburned faces. "Dass and Abel are so fat, I think they wore right through their socks." The corpsman had raised his voice loud enough for the whole platoon to hear, and a few of the men who hadn't lost their breakfasts (and their sense of humor along with it) chuckled quietly at Healy's inane accusation.

Avery scowled. He couldn't decide what made him more upset: the fact that Healy insisted on clowning around, ruining the no-nonsense mood he was trying to set; or that the corpsman already knew every recruit's name while Avery still had to check the name tape on the chest pockets of their olive-drab fatigue shirts.

"You got the energy to talk? You got the energy to walk!" Avery snapped. "Get some water. Suck it down. All I want to hear is the sound of hydration. Which—to be clear—sounds like ab-so-lutely nothing at all!"

Immediately, thirty-six clear plastic bottles tipped skyward. Jenkins was especially eager to keep his sore feet where they were and guzzled his water at an alarming rate. Avery watched the recruit's oversized Adam's apple bob up and down like a yo-yo on a very short string. *The kid can't even follow an order about* drinking *properly.*

The sound of voices on the garrison drive announced the return of Byrne and 2nd platoon. Avery could hear them calling cadence—shouting a Marine Corps marching chant. Byrne bellowed each line and his recruits repeated:

When I die please bury me deep!
Place an MA5 down by my feet!
Don't cry for me, don't shed no tear!
Just pack my box with PT gear!
'Cuz one early morning 'bout zero-five!
The ground will rumble, there'll be lightning in the sky!
Don't you worry, don't come undone!
It's just my ghost on a PT run!

As 2nd platoon crested the top of the drive and shuffled into the parade ground, the screen door to Captain Ponder's quarters swung open. As usual, the Captain had chosen not to wear his prosthetic; the sleeve of his fatigue shirt was once again pinned neatly to his side.

"Atten-shun!" Avery barked.

Ponder gave 1st platoon a chance to straighten up, and 2nd platoon time to come to a gasping stop. Then he asked in a loud but friendly voice: "You men enjoy your stroll?"

"Sir, yes sir," the recruits answered with varied enthusiasm.

Ponder turned to Byrne. "They don't sound too sure, Staff Sergeant."

"No, they don't," Byrne snarled.

"Maybe ten klicks wasn't long enough for them to make up their minds . . ."

"I'd be happy to run them again, Captain."

"Well, let me make sure." Ponder put his fist on his hip and shouted: "I say again, *did you all enjoy your stroll?*"

All seventy-two recruits shouted at once. "Sir, yes sir!"

"Do it again tomorrow?"

"Sir, yes sir!"

"Now I *definitely* heard that! At ease!" As the recruits got back to aching, Ponder waved Avery over. "How was their pace?"

"Not bad, considering their load."

"What's the plan for this afternoon?"

"Thought I might take them out to the range."

Ponder nodded his head approvingly. "About time we let them punch a few targets. But you'll need to hand them off to Byrne. We've got a date."

"Sir?"

"Solstice Celebration. Utgard. Governor of this fine planet extended an invitation to me and one of my Staff Sergeants." The Captain jutted his chin toward Byrne, currently unleashing a string of expletives at a terrified recruit who had just made the mistake of losing his breakfast directly on the Staff Sergeant's boots. "It's a formal affair. Ladies in long dresses, that sort of thing." Ponder smiled at Avery. "I have a feeling you'll be a better fit."

"Roger that." The last thing Avery wanted to do was field questions about the Insurrection from a bunch of boozy politicians, but as he watched Byrne order the recruit to start doing push-ups directly over his vomit-covered boots, he had to admit: the Captain was probably right.

And besides, there were questions Avery wanted to ask Ponder—first and foremost, why he and Byrne had been transferred to Harvest. Since the night of their fight in the barracks, the two Staff Sergeants hadn't exactly been on speaking terms, so Avery had gotten no information from Byrne. During the ride to Utgard, he hoped the Captain could explain why the UNSC had seen fit to transfer two TREBUCHET team-leaders—take them off the frontline of the Insurrection.

Avery had a strong suspicion that he wasn't going to like Ponder's answer.

"Party starts at zero six-thirty." The Captain turned back to his quarters. "Clean yourself up, meet me at the motor pool ASAP."

Avery snapped a hasty salute, then strode back to his recruits. "Forsell, Wick, Andersen, Jenkins!" he boomed, reading their names from his COM pad. Four sets of shoulders set a little straighter. "Says here none of you have ever handled a weapon. Is that correct?"

"Yes, Staff Sergeant." The recruits' replies were halting, embarrassed. Some of the older militiamen, constables who were used to carrying small-caliber sidearms for their work, snickered at the recruits inexperience.

"Won't be so funny when they're standing *behind* you in a firefight," Avery growled.

The constables' laughter quickly died.

Avery motioned for Jenkins and the others to gather round. "The Captain and I have an appointment in town. So Staff Sergeant Byrne's going to get you all snapped in."

The recruits looked blankly at one another, confused by Avery's shorthand.

"He's gonna teach you how to shoot," Avery clarified. "Try not to shoot each other."

An hour later, he was behind the wheel of a Warthog, speeding east on the Gladsheim highway with Captain Ponder in the passenger seat beside him. With Epsilon Indi beating down directly overhead, Avery was unusually glad of the vehicle's stripped-down design. In a war zone, the Warthog's lack of roof and doors made it a dangerous ride. But when the only enemy you faced was the sweaty cling of a navy-blue dress uniform, its open-air passenger compartment was an absolute blessing.

To help keep themselves cool, both men had removed their navy-blue dress coats and rolled their shirtsleeves to their elbows. Ponder opted to keep his false arm covered; Avery guessed because the prosthetic's titanium joints would get uncomfortably warm in the direct sunlight. Out of the corner of his eye he saw the Captain reach up and scratch his shoulder, massaging the nano-fiber junction where the circuits met the man.

For some time Avery and Ponder sat in silence and watched the wheat fields around the garrison give way to vast peach and apple orchards. Avery wasn't sure how best to break the ice. He didn't just want to come out and ask: "Why am I here?" He guessed there was a good reason why the Captain was keeping the information secret and suspected it would take a little more finesse to draw his answer out. So he started with something simple.

"Sir. If you don't mind me asking, what happened to your arm?

"M-EDF 9/21/1," Ponder replied, raising his voice above the Warthog's roar. "You familiar with the unit?"

Avery automatically parsed the code: ninth marine expeditionary force, twenty-first division, 1st battalion. It was one of the many units serving in Epsilon Eridanus.

"Yes, sir. Hard-ass grunts."

"That they were." The Captain reached two of his prosthetic's metal fingers into his shirt pocket and retrieved a Sweet William cigar. "I used to be their CO."

Avery tightened his grip on the steering wheel as a hauler blew by in the opposite direction. "What sort of action did you see?" He did his best to keep a casual tone. But if what Ponder said was true, that meant he was a critical part of the UNSC's fight against the Insurrection—that his presence on Harvest was just as odd as Avery and Byrne's.

"Let's not beat around the bush, Staff Sergeant. TRE-BUCHET. It's in your file. Byrne's too. And I've spent the last two weeks wondering the exact same thing." The Captain bit the tip off his cigar. "Why would the Corps send two of its meanest sons-of-bitches way out here?"

"I was hoping you might shed some light on that, sir."

"Hell if I know." Ponder removed a silver lighter with a hinged top from his pants pocket, cracked it open, and began stoking his cigar. "FLEETCOM hasn't been all that free with information . . ." he said between puffs. Then, snapping the lighter shut: "Since they gave me a demotion."

Something clicked in Avery's head. *Of course,* he thought, *the CO of a Marine battalion would be at least a Lt. Colonel— two pay grades higher than Ponder's current Captain rank.* But Avery had no idea what this meant with respect to the larger question. If anything, Ponder's revelation made things even more confusing. "Demotion, sir?" he asked, treading water.

"I lost my arm," Ponder began, "in Elysium City, Eridanus II." He put one of his boots up on the dash. "This was back in 'thirteen. Watts and his gang were just starting to show their teeth."

Colonel Robert Watts—or "that bastard" to most UNSC personnel—was a Marine Corps officer born and raised in Epsilon Eridanus who had defected to the Insurrectionist's side early in the war. He and the group of turncoats he commanded were one of TREBUCHET's priority targets. So far, no one had gotten a decent shot at him, though Avery had once come close.

"We were hoping to capture Watts' second in command," Ponder continued, taking a long drag on his cigar. "Admirals at FLEETCOM wanted my battalion to go in strong—plenty of armor and air support. Intimidate the locals into giving the guy up without a fight. But the town was still fifty-fifty. Not everyone was on the Innies' side, and I thought a little restraint might help win some hearts and minds."

Avery grunted. "Must have been before my time."

"Things were different in the beginning. There was still time to talk—a chance for peace." Ponder shook his head. "Anyhow this guy—my target—had married the daughter of one of the local officials. I thought the father-in-law would be pretty ticked when a whole armored column showed up on his doorstep. But the next thing I knew, I was in his living room, sipping tea."

Ponder tapped the ash from his cigar. "We talked about nothing for a few minutes—just got comfortable. Then when his wife was pouring me a second cup, I got down to it: 'We're looking for so-and-so, do you know where we can find him, we don't mean your daughter any harm, etcetera, etcetera.' And he looks me right in the eye . . ." Ponder paused and stared out the Warthog's sloped windshield. "He looks me in the eye and says: 'Someday we will win. No matter what it takes.'" The Captain flexed his prosthetic, pantomiming his memories. "Then he put his arm around the target's wife—his own daughter—and raised it up like this . . . took me a second to realize he had a grenade."

Avery didn't know what to say, except that, having inherited the Insurrection from men like Ponder, he'd seen things at least as surprising, at least as tragic.

"I knew it was a bluff. This guy was dedicated to the cause, no doubt. But kill his whole family? Wasn't gonna happen." Ponder pulled the half-smoked cigar from his teeth and ground it into the dash. "One of my snipers thought different. Put a hasty round through the wall of his house, tore the guy in half. But he pulled the pin on reflex." The Captain shrugged. "I dove to cover the blast. Things got worse from there."

Tight space, jumpy soldiers; Avery knew worse had meant a lot of civilian casualties, some very angry top brass and—adding insult to injury—Ponder taking a two-step drop in rank.

"I think they wanted me to take an early retirement. But I stuck with it," the Captain said. "Took a bunch of lousy billets and worked my way up to CMT. Thought I'd left the Insurrection behind me." He shot Avery a look that was more inquisitive than accusatory. "Then along came the two of you."

Again, Avery was at a loss for words. But Ponder was soon lost in more memories from that terrible day long ago, and for a while both men resumed their silence.

Out in the apple orchards, Avery saw JOTUNs—a pair of monstrous pickers large enough to engulf whole trees with their agitating arms. He had overheard Healy arguing with one of his recruits about the exact number of JOTUNs on Harvest. The Corpsman refused to believe there were three JOTUNs for every person—almost a million machines—until the recruit had explained he was counting all the different versions: the smallest aerial crop dusters to the six-wheeled beasts like the ones in the orchard.

"It's funny," Ponder said in a way that made clear he didn't think it was the least bit so. "But at first I missed it: my men, the combat, all of it. Took me years to realize how crazy that was—that I'd been damn lucky to get out when I did. Before things got really bad, and I made a mistake that got a lot more people killed."

Avery nodded his head, although he might as well have said: *I know exactly what you mean.*

By now the Bifrost had begun to rise before them. They were still an hour away from the limestone escarpment, but squinting his eyes, Avery could just see dark switchbacks carving back and forth across its face that would take them up to Utgard.

On either side of the switchbacks, separated by hundreds of kilometers, were two maglev train lines—thick monorails that angled down from the top of the Bifrost to meet the Ida, far out in the orchards. Avery saw a long train of cargo containers glide down the southern line. The train seemed to move too quickly for the containers' size, and Avery realized they must be empty—on their way to a depot where hundreds of JOTUNs waited with fresh-picked loads.

"Maybe FLEETCOM decided you needed a break?" Ponder offered.

"Maybe," Avery said. It was as good an explanation as any.

"Well, why not start tonight? Have a drink, dance with a girl."

Avery smiled despite himself. "That an order, sir?"

Ponder laughed and slapped his artificial arm on his thigh. "Yes, Staff Sergeant. Yes, it is."

By the time Avery pulled the Warthog into the curved drive of Harvest's Parliament building, he knew a lot more about Captain Ponder. How fighting the Insurrection had forced him to miss his eldest son's wedding and the birth of his first grandchild— precious occasions he missed much more than his arm. As they dismounted, buttoned their coats' brass buttons, and pulled on their black-billed dress caps, Avery realized he not only trusted but had a great deal more respect for the man who wore his CO's uniform.

The Parliament's lobby was thick with partygoers: men in

pastel, seersucker suits; women in ruffled, scoop neck gowns—fashions that were already out of style in core-world salons, but had only just taken hold of Harvest's provincial high society. Some of the guests gawked and whispered as Avery and Ponder passed. And it struck the Staff Sergeant that they were the first marines—the first soldiers—some of the guests had ever seen.

But as they threaded their way up a crowded granite staircase to the ballroom, some of the curious gazes turned cold. *We might be a* new *sight,* Avery grimaced, *but not necessarily a* welcome *one.* It seemed the UNSC's handling of the Insurrection wasn't any more popular on Harvest than it was anywhere else.

"Nils Thune," someone bellowed from the landing at the top of the staircase. A thick hand shot out from a great swath of red- and white-striped fabric. "You must be Captain Ponder."

"Governor," Ponder paused on the top step and saluted. Then he extended his hand. "It's an honor to meet you."

"Likewise, of course!" Thune's grip was so strong he practically pulled Ponder up onto the landing.

"May I introduce you to one of my men? Staff Sergeant Avery Johnson."

Thune released Ponder's hand and offered it to Avery. "Well, Johnson?" Thune's red beard parted in a broad, toothsome grin. "What do you think of our planet?"

Avery had a strong grip, but Thune's was immobilizing. His hand possessed the kind of strength one got from years of farming the old-fashioned way—without assistance from a fleet of hulking automatons. Avery guessed correctly that despite his vigor, the Governor was well into his sixties—that he'd been one of the first colonists to land on Harvest. "Reminds me of home, sir." Avery grimaced. "I grew up on Earth, Chicago Industrial Zone."

Thune released Avery's hand and stabbed his thumb happily to his chest. "Minnesota! My mother's and father's side both, far back as I can remember." Widening his smile he ushered the marines toward the doorway of a brightly lit ballroom. "You're in good company, Staff Sergeant. Most everyone around here's from the Midwest—pulled up stakes when the soil went bad. Of course none of us knew just how much better things would be once we got to Harvest!"

The Governor snatched a champagne flute from a passing waiter and downed it in one gulp. "This way!" He shuffled sideways through the ballroom doorway, his girth doing at least as much to part the crowd as any deference to his office. "And stay close! The show's about to start, and I want you two front and center!"

Avery shot Ponder a confused look. But the Captain simply plunged into Thune's gap. Avery followed just as the crowd drew back upon itself, practically sucking him into the ballroom. Doing their best not to step on any toes, the marines followed Thune to one of the many glass-paned doors in the ballroom's eastern wall that led to a broad balcony overlooking the Parliament's gardens—and beyond that, Utgard's mall.

Stepping up beside Thune against the balcony's waist-high granite railing, Avery saw that the park was full of revelers. Light-globes tugging at their tethers in the twilight breeze illuminated knots of families sitting on brightly colored picnic blankets. Hardly any of the mall was left uncovered, and Avery was certain the vast majority of the planet's three hundred thousand residents were in attendance. But for what, he still wasn't quite sure.

"Rol!" Thune's shout rang painfully loud in Avery's ears. "Over here!" The Governor waved a hand above his head, but this wasn't necessary. Thune was taller than anyone on the balcony, Avery included, and the mop of thick, red and gray hair that covered his head was impossible to miss. Avery craned his neck toward the ballroom in time to see the Governor's somatotypical opposite slide out from the jostling crowd; a short, balding man whose elderly frame barely filled his light gray linen suit.

"Rol Pedersen," Thune announced. "My Attorney General."

"Just a fancy way to say lawyer." Pedersen smiled modestly through his thin, pursed lips. He didn't offer Avery or Ponder his hand, but not for any lack of courtesy; the jubilant crowd had begun to flow from the ballroom to the railing, crushing the Attorney General's arms firmly to his sides.

"Rol's about as formal as we get out here," Thune explained. "Stickler for details. He's the one who handled all the negotiations with the CA about us raising a militia."

"Technically." Pedersen's eyes twinkled as he raised one of his white eyebrows. "I formally accepted their *demand* that we have one."

Just then the sky erupted with fireworks, filling the gaps between the Tiara's seven elevators with multicolored blossoms. Jutting up from Utgard's skyline, the strands shone bronze in Epsilon Indi's failing light. As the showering sparks rippled the air around them, they appeared to vibrate, like plucked strings in a giant's harp.

"Alright, everyone!" Thune roared as the last of the fireworks erupted in a smoky, blue-green cloud. "Get set!" The Governor put his hands to his ears, as did everyone else on the balcony except Avery and Ponder.

"Mass driver," Pedersen explained. "We fire it every solstice."

All at once, the towers around the mall went dark as the city's electrical grid lost power. There was a bright flash beyond the Tiara's central number-four strand, and a moment later a shockwave hammered the mall, flattening the light globes and sending the picnickers squealing after flying napkins and bowled-over children. On the balcony, women shrieked in gleeful fright as they clutched their billowing dresses; men made a gallant show of uncapping their ears as a sonic boom pealed past the Parliament.

"Hurrah!" Thune shouted, starting a round of applause that echoed a similar outburst from the picnickers on the mall. "Well done, Mack!"

"That's mighty kind, Governor." The AI replied from Thune's COM pad, hidden somewhere in his vast jacket. "I aim to please."

"Speaking of which," Thune said, heading away from the railing. "How close *did* you come?"

Pedersen freed a hand and pointed after Thune, letting the two marines know they were expected to follow. This time the Governor led them to the far end of the ballroom where a group of children—girls with satin bows on their dresses and boys in shiny vests and shoes—packed tight around a circular table topped with a cornucopia of fruits and vegetables. A silver holo-projector was centered in a wreath of leafy vines and deep purple grape clusters. On top of that stood Mack.

"Missed by a mile," the AI said, rubbing the back of its neck with a grimy handkerchief. "Actually, more like fifty kilometers. But I'm sure she'll say something."

"No doubt. No doubt," Thune chuckled. "Listen, I'd like you to meet Captain Ponder and Staff Sergeant Johnson. UNSC Marines. Here to raise a militia."

"Mack. Agricultural operations." Mack touched the brim of his cowboy hat. Then, nodding toward the balcony and the mass driver somewhere beyond, "Same as the navy's big guns. Just a little less kick."

"You know," Ponder deadpanned, "there's a reason we only fire those in *space*."

Mass drivers were a relatively simple, cheap solution for boosting objects from a planet's surface into orbit. Typically built on large, flexible gimbles, their linked, magnetic loops could be charged, aimed, and fired with very little automation—with a simple computer rather than an AI. But drivers had one major disadvantage: limited throw-weight. Which meant that while Harvest's driver worked well during the first decade after the colony's founding (when its primary role was to send carefully packaged nuclear waste on a collision course with Epsilon Indi), for the planet to meet its full export potential, it needed to be replaced with a high-capacity lift system such as the Tiara.

Driver technology was alive and well in the navy, however, in the form of Mass Accelerator Cannon. So-called MAC frigates and cruisers were basically moveable mass drivers—ships designed around the weapons' long, electromagnetic coils. The technology was similar to that of the M99 Stanchion rifle. But whereas the M99's light, semi-ferrous rounds were only a few millimeters long, a MAC slug was more than ten *meters* end-to-end, weighed one-hundred-sixty metric tons, and packed enough punch to penetrate the navy's thickest Titanium-A armor plate.

"Space?" Thune grumbled dismissively. "Those things even make noise in zero-gee?"

"If you're *inside* a MAC ship when the cannon fires?" Ponder raised his hands wide around his head, simulating a deafening boom. "I don't know if you're a religious man, Governor. But it's a little like a church bell—"

"*Am* I?" The Governor beamed. "Lutheran! Born and raised!"

Pedersen sighed in mock protest. "If had known you were going to bring up religion, Captain—as Attorney General—I would have counseled a less contentious topic."

"And I *was* about to tell a story . . ." Mack added, loud enough for all the children to hear. The young crowd cheered as a holographic representation of a bustling, Wild West main street appeared behind Mack. A group of masked outlaws rushed from a bank, firing their six-shooters and spooking the horses of a passing stagecoach. The children oohed and ahhed. Mack pulled a sheriff's star out of his hip pocket and pinned it to his chest. "Might want to take the sermon to the saloon."

"Fine by me," Thune said, clapping Ponder on the shoulder. "Captain?"

Ponder stood firm under the force of Thune's blow. "After you, Governor." Before he followed Thune to the ballroom's bar, he asked Pedersen, "I gave my Staff Sergeant strict orders to find himself a dance partner. Know anyone who might fit the bill?"

Pedersen raised an eager finger. "I have just the one!"

"I certainly appreciate it," Ponder said. Then to Avery with a smile: "Good luck, marine."

Before Avery could respond, the Captain turned on his heels, and Avery felt Pedersen's light touch on his elbow. "Do you know about the driver incident?" the Attorney General asked, leading Avery away from the first shots of Mack's gunfight and the delighted squeals of the children.

"Incident, sir?"

"The *thing* between Mack and Sif?"

"No."

"Well . . .".

Pedersen proceeded to explain how, not long after the DCS installed Sif in the Tiara, there had been a critical failure in her data center's power supply. This forced her technicians to stop all activity on her strands or risk a load-imbalance that would have collapsed the entire system. It had been a serious crisis, and Mack decided to solve it by using the driver to boost a new power supply into orbit.

Trying to be as helpful as possible, he shot the component right into the Tiara's number-four coupling station. It was an incredible accomplishment. But when Sif's technicians restored her power and she learned what Mack had done—how he could have easily obliterated her data-center—Sif had not been amused.

"That's why she isn't here tonight," Pedersen concluded as they stepped out of the ballroom and headed for the balcony's calm northeast corner. "Why she *always* comes up with a polite excuse not to attend any celebration that involves a driver shot. It's too bad really. I think she could use a bit of fun."

"That's quite an indictment, Your Honor." A woman's voice

rang out from the railing, bringing Pedersen to a hasty stop. But Avery had already noticed the woman many paces back—seen how her diaphanous silver shawl covered only part of her bare back. He slowed his pace to give himself time to remove his dress-cap and smooth his burr of hair.

"My apologies, Ms. al-Cygni," the Attorney General replied. "But I was talking about Sif. The incident with the driver."

"Of course." Jilan pushed away from the railing, and turned to face the Attorney General. "If I remember correctly, my department mandated that you shut the driver down."

"As I recall, we rejected that mandate on the grounds that it was in breach of the CA charter—a serious infringement on our already limited sovereignty." The Attorney General winked. "But off the record, how could we possibly have given up such spectacular entertainment?"

Jilan laughed. "I won't argue with that."

"I'm sorry," Pedersen said hastily. "Staff Sergeant Avery Johnson? Representative Jilan al-Cygni, DCS."

Jilan offered her hand. Avery hesitated.

If she had been wearing a bland DCS uniform, he would have known what to do: take her hand and shake it. But her floor-length silver gown tripped him up. With its empire waist and halter top, she was the very picture of core-world vogue. Her black hair was slicked back close to her scalp and tucked behind her ears, and stayed perfectly still even as a fresh breeze from the mall caught her shawl and rustled it from her soft brown shoulders.

"Kissing is for politicians," Jilan said, catching her shawl in her elbows. "And I'm certainly not that."

So Avery shook. Her grip wasn't as strong as the Governor's, but not as delicate as her slender arms suggested.

"If you'll excuse me," Pedersen coughed and patted his chest. "I need to rescue this marine's commanding officer from a *riveting* discussion on the trajectory of his immortal soul."

Jilan smiled. "Do give my best to the Governor."

Pedersen brought his heels together, and turned back to the ballroom. Jilan waited for him to disappear into the crowd—until she and Avery were alone—before she spoke.

"I'd tell you to relax. But you don't seem the type."

Avery didn't know how to respond to that. But he was given a moment's reprieve thanks to a dancing couple that bumped him in the back then spun away, giggling apologetically. The string quartet had begun a livelier second set. Those guests who hadn't gone indoors to freshen their drinks after the fireworks were now abandoning their idle conversations for the more alluring language of waltz.

Jilan retrieved a small, clamshell purse dangling from one of her wrists. It was covered with tiny mirrors shaped like fish scales that dazzled Avery's gaze. "48789-20114-AJ," she said, pulling a COM-pad from the purse, and reading from its screen. "That is your serial number, correct?"

Avery's eyes refocused. "Yes, ma'am." Suddenly her smile didn't seem so sweet.

"Team-leader, ORION detachment, NavSpecWar division?"

"With respect, ma'am. That's classified."

"I know."

Avery felt moisture start to pool under his arms. "How can I *help* you, ma'am?"

"Innies are attacking freighters. Destroying cargo, killing crew. I need you to stop them."

"I'm a drill instructor. Colonial Militia. Find someone else."

Jilan drew her shawl back onto her shoulders. "You were AWOL in Chicago," she said matter-of-factly. "And under investigation for possible gross misconduct."

Avery clenched his jaw. "I was cleared of—"

"Given your *status*, didn't you think it was odd that FLEET-COM would approve your request for transfer?"

Avery narrowed his eyes in an intimidating stare. "I'll tell you what's odd. Someone from DCS with access to my file—you talking to me like you're my CO."

Jilan raised her COM-pad and turned it so Avery could see her ID picture glowing on its screen.

In her official UNSC uniform, Avery thought she looked as beautiful as she did in her gown. But only in the way he considered a well-maintained weapon beautiful—clean, locked tight, and ready to inflict deadly force. A text stamp below her picture clarified her true rank and departmental affiliation: Lieutenant Commander, ONI Section Three.

"As of now, I *am* your commanding officer," Jilan shut off her pad. "You can check your attitude, Staff Sergeant, and start following orders. Or I will arrange for your immediate transfer back to TREBUCHET." There was no anger in her voice, just calm determination. "Do I make myself clear?"

Avery choked on a slowly building rage. At last, he knew exactly why he had come to Harvest, as well as who had brought him here. "Yes, ma'am."

Al-Cygni dropped her COM into her purse and snapped it shut. "Wait for me downstairs. As soon I can collect Staff Sergeant Byrne, we'll be shipping out." Dress rippling behind her, she stepped quickly into the waltzing crowd.

CHAPTER
EIGHT

There would be no surprises this time. Chur'R-Yar had made sure of that. Through the walls of the umbilical, she could see the boxy freighter's atmosphere venting out the careful holes she'd made with her own ship's lasers. If any of the aliens were hiding on board, the Shipmistress had done all she could to kill them without harming whatever relic lay inside.

After the surprise encounter on the last freighter, Chur'R-Yar and the other Kig-Yar had scoured the alien ship. But they found no relics. Even *Minor Transgression*'s Luminary had given up and dimmed its glyph. In her frustration, the Shipmistress decided to destroy the vessel—obliterate all evidence of her fruitless transgression.

She had considered ordering the Huragok to conduct a more meticulous search. But as fast as the creature worked, she didn't want to remain in the same place for very long in case the alien it had killed had somehow managed to call for help without triggering her ship's sensors. And besides, the Deacon (her only means of communicating with the Huragok) was an emotional wreck—totally useless after his close call. As infuriating as his cowardice was, Chur'R-Yar had let him malinger in the methane suite. She needed her crew focused on the task at hand, not distracted by new and interesting ways to torment the Deacon.

"Ready yourselves!" the Shipmistress clattered as the umbilical finished its burn through the vessel's hull. Zhar and the two other male Kig-Yar were bunched together before her, as close as their pressure suits allowed. Built for external maintenance rather than combat, the suits were bulky and unwieldy—a necessary inconvenience given the lack of breathable air inside the freighter. Chur'R-Yar knew her crewmen were uncomfortable, Zhar especially. The suits' helmets didn't allow the male's spiny combs much room to flex, and her chosen mate was fully flushed—eager to prove his worth.

The umbilical ceased its fractional forward movement, and Zhar's head twitched sideways as he checked to make sure the seal was secure. "After me!" he clacked. Gloved claws wrapped tight around his crystal cutlass, he sprang through the wavering energy barrier that served as the umbilical's airlock. The Shipmistress gripped her plasma-pistol tight and followed the other males through.

The first thing Chur'R-Yar noticed inside the hold was the lack of gravity. Floating half her height above the floor, she realized her laser fire must have hit an essential part. She rattled her teeth with annoyance as she watched Zhar and the others work to find purchase on the floor's grooved metal panels. The crewmen had been overeager. Now they were scrambling about like fools in the mocking glare of the hold's red emergency lights.

"Calm yourselves!" the Shipmistress hissed into her helmet's signal unit. Then, as she secured herself on the umbilical's protruding tip, "Move toward the boxes!"

The hold was filled with the same plastic containers as the first freighter, though it wasn't nearly as tightly packed. The boxes were stacked in low piles, spaced evenly apart. It would take time to search each one, especially in zero gravity. Chur'R-Yar hissed angrily to herself; the best way to speed the process was to get the Deacon to instruct the Huragok to find and fix the anti-grav unit she had unintentionally destroyed.

But just as she twisted around to head back through the energy barrier, she felt something sharp and hot tear through the neck of her pressure suit, slicing her scaly skin—felt the vibration of more projectiles ricochet off the hold's wall. Her suit automatically closed around the two small punctures, venting some of her violet blood in a globular spray. "Retreat!" she shouted to her crew, "Back to the ship!" The Shipmistress didn't know her attacker's location, but she knew it had her firmly in its sights. Without looking to see if Zhar and the others were in any position to follow, she thrust herself back inside the umbilical.

Avery had to hand it to Lt. Commander al-Cygni. The woman could plan an op. Her carefully disguised sloop, *Walk of Shame*, had been filled with a small arsenal of weapons, some of which Avery had never seen before. He and Byrne had both selected what al-Cygni referred to as a battle rifle, a prototype long-barreled weapon with an optical scope. The two Staff Sergeants had thought the rifle's combination of range and accuracy would be a good fit for the long sight lines between the stacks of boxes in the cargo container.

But that was before they knew they were going to end up floating high above the container's floor.

When the freighter had been shot through with lasers and lost its gravity, Avery and Byrne had been shocked to say the least. Fortunately, the Lt. Commander had outfitted them with bulky black vacuum-suits and helmets with clear visors. When the bright tip of some sort of boring device punched through the hull, the two Staff Sergeants had pushed off from their hiding places behind the boxes for the marginally better cover of the metal supports girding the freighter's upper hull.

Avery firmed his grip on his battle rifle's trigger. The cross hairs in the weapon's scope were locked on the fourth alien, just now emerging from the shimmering field. *Yes, the Lt. Commander could plan an op*, he thought. *But she hadn't planned for* this.

In their premission briefing in an empty Welcome Wagon from Utgard up to the Tiara, al-Cygni had told Avery and Byrne about a recent Insurrectionist victory in Epsilon Eridanus—one they hadn't been informed of, even with their top-level clearances.

About the same time as the two Staff Sergeants were struggling to take down the bomber in the restaurant on Tribute, the Innies had hit the luxury liner *National Holiday* as it waited above the planet Reach. The ship was just completing its load-in of more than fifteen hundred civilian passengers on charter-tour to Arcadia—a colony famous for its recreational amenities—when the pair of unmanned orbital taxis struck.

The liner's captain had assumed the taxis were simply carrying late-arriving passengers. When they failed to comply with his docking commands, the captain had initiated evasive maneuvers—tried to deflect what he thought would be minor impacts. But the amount of explosives the Innies had packed into the taxis not only tore *National Holiday* in two, but also burned away the hull paint of every other ship in a two-kilometer radius.

The two Staff Sergeants had listened soberly to a recording on Jilan's COM-pad of the captain's final words—heard how the former naval fighter pilot had calmly directed other ships out of his crippled liner's path, even as it dropped into Reach's atmosphere, bodies billowing from its breached staterooms, and began to burn.

So far, Jilan had explained, ONI had managed to keep things under wraps, successfully spinning the Innie's hit as a tragic accident. Partly this was because the attack was so audacious. This was the first time the Insurrectionists had hit a non-terrestrial target—and not only that, but they'd done it above Reach, the epicenter of UNSC power in Epsilon Eridanus. Even though the Innies claimed responsibility for the horrible loss of life, most people were too fearful to believe the rebels' claim. If they could lash out in plain view of the UNSC fleet, what was stopping them from hitting targets in other systems? Sol, for example, or Harvest?

According to Jilan, FLEETCOM had made it crystal clear there could be no more *National Holidays*. ONI went on high alert, and as soon as Section Three got word of a freighter missing in Epsilon Indi, they'd authorized her to conduct a covert investigation. Just in case she needed to take exceptional action, al-Cygni's superiors had ordered her to recruit Avery and Byrne.

"Ma'am, we've got hostiles in the hold," Avery whispered into his helmet mic.

"Take them out." Al-Cygni's reply was curt. Avery was supposed to maintain radio silence.

"They aren't Innies."

"Clarify."

Avery took a deep breath. "They're aliens." He watched as the first three creatures that had come barreling through the barrier struggled to get hand- and footholds—studied their long, bony beaks and large, bloodshot eyes through their clear helmets. "Kind of like lizards without the tails."

There was a pause as Jilan, holding station in *Walk of Shame* some two hundred kilometers distant from the freighter, considered Avery's words. But the Staff Sergeant knew it wouldn't be long before one of the aliens looked up and saw them lurking in the shadows between the beams.

"Ma'am, I need orders," Avery persisted.

"Try and take one alive," al-Cygni replied. "But don't let *any* escape, over."

"Roger that." Avery hugged his battle rifle close. He hadn't had time to fire the weapon. He hoped its nine-point-five-millimeter high-penetration rounds would be sufficient to puncture the aliens' iridescent suits.

"Byrne, get set." Avery glanced at the other Staff Sergeant, positioned between a pair of beams to his left. "I'm firing on the leader." He assumed the leader was the alien nearest the shimmering hole in the hull. It seemed more composed than the others, and also carried an obvious weapon: a silver, C-shaped pistol with green energy glowing between its tips. Avery hoped taking down the leader would make the other aliens—now splayed firmly on the floor—more eager to surrender. He took a breath and fired.

In zero gravity, the recoil from the battle rifle's three-round burst was more pronounced than Avery had anticipated. Two of his shots went wide, and, as the recoil slammed him back against the hull, he watched his wounded target disappear back through the glowing barrier. Avery cursed himself for not bracing more firmly against the beams. But this was his first experience with zero-gee combat. He could only hope the aliens were similarly inexperienced.

So far, this didn't look to be the case.

Avery did his best to steady his aim as the three remaining aliens pushed off from the floor and rocketed toward him in a loose triangular formation. The one in the lead had a bigger helmet, and Avery could see through his scope that it also had the longest spines—fleshy red spikes compressed against its head. But Byrne had acquired the same target. He fired first, and sent the alien spinning to Avery's right.

Avery didn't have time to adjust his aim before one of the trailing aliens slammed into him, slashing with some sort of crystal knife. He parried the knife with the barrel of his rifle as their helmets cracked together. Avery's helmet began to shake, and for a moment he thought the visor was about to shatter. Then he looked the alien square in the face and realized the vibrations were simply the transference of the creature's silent, livid scream.

Avery had pinned the creature's knife against one of the beams. The weapon was energized—gleamed with internal pink fire. He was certain it would make short work of his vacuum-suit, not to mention the flesh beneath.

With its free hand, the alien began clawing at Avery's neck and shoulders. But its gloves were bulky and it couldn't do any real damage. Avery reached down and unholstered an M6 pistol he'd selected from al-Cygni's arsenal. Before the alien could react, he put four quick rounds into the underside of its elongated helmet, near the base of its bony jaws. The alien's head burst apart, painting the inside of its helmet a very vivid violet.

Avery pushed the alien back down toward the floor of the container as Byrne opened fire to his left. But Byrne was also having difficulty recovering from his first shot, and the third alien hit him right in the gut, knocking his battle rifle loose. As the weapon rebounded off the hull and went spinning out of reach, the alien drove its knife into Byrne's left thigh.

The alien must have thought it only needed to puncture Byrne's suit in order to kill him, and it might have succeeded were it not for the suit's compartmentalized design. As Byrne pulled the knife from his leg, the hole filled with yellow sealant foam. The alien flailed its arms—Avery thought to try and drive the knife back in. But as the weapon began to pulse with rosy light, he realized the creature was actually trying to escape an impending detonation.

"Lose the blade!" Avery shouted. "It's gonna blow!"

Byrne sunk the knife into the alien's mid-section and kicked it back the way it had come. The creature pulled frantically at the blade, but Byrne had driven it too deep. A split-second later it blew apart in a bright pink flash. Tiny, wet shards flecked Avery's visor like slushy snow.

"Thanks," Byrne grunted over the COM. "But I'd put a few more in that one if I were you."

Avery looked to his right. The first alien Byrne had shot had managed to wrap an arm around a cross-brace farther down the ceiling and stop its lateral motion. The thing had its head cocked in Avery's direction, and was staring at him with one unblinking eye. Byrne's burst had caught its free arm below the shoulder, but the alien had managed to keep hold of its knife and was preparing to make a throw.

Avery put the creature's torso square in his pistol's V-shaped iron sights. He could see its fleshy spines engorge with dark blood. The alien opened its jaws, baring razor-sharp teeth.

"Nice to meet you too," Avery frowned. Then he emptied the M6's twelve-round clip into the center of alien's chest. The impacts unhooked its arm and sent it tumbling toward the far end of the cargo-container.

"I'm going after the other one." Avery planted his boots firmly against the hull.

"I'll back you up," Byrne volunteered.

Avery shot Byrne a serious stare. "If that blade sliced an artery, the foam isn't gonna hold. Stay put. I'll be right back." With that, he pushed off toward the barrier.

"Johnson," Jilan said. "You've got ten minutes."

Avery completed her sentence: *before I shoot the alien ship with you in it.* He knew *Walk of Shame* was equipped with a single Archer missile—a ship-to-ship weapon capable of crippling all but the largest vessels in the human fleet. The Lt. Commander had told him she would use it to shoot what they had all thought would be an Insurrectionist ship if it tried to escape. Avery knew it would be even more important to stop the alien ship. For if it got away, it would almost certainly return with reinforcements.

"If I'm not back in five," Avery replied, "I'm not coming back." Then he passed through the barrier.

Avery wasn't expecting gravity, but he managed to perform

an ugly duck-and-roll and rise up with his rifle at the ready. Aiming straight down the semitransparent tube, he could see the full hooked profile of the alien ship. Avery tried not to think about how many more of the aliens might be on board. There was no cover inside the umbilical, and if the creatures poured into the tube, he would be a goner. Avery fast-walked forward and a few moments later, he was posting beside another fluctuating field.

As far as Avery could tell, the first barrier hadn't done him any harm, though he couldn't say the same for his COM. He tried to contact Byrne and al-Cygni, but their secure channel was all static. *All alone against an alien ship*, Avery thought, taking a few calming breaths. He knew if he thought about the situation any longer he would lose his initiative and quite possibly his nerve. Weapon shouldered, he stepped through the second barrier. This time he noticed his skin tingle—felt the field compressing the flexible fabric of his suit.

A short passage beyond led to a wider corridor bathed in purple light. Avery scanned left and counted twenty meters to a bulkhead. He noted recessed doors spaced every five meters along the way—sealed compartments, but for what Avery could only guess. He scanned right and saw what appeared to be a giant worm tied to a bunch of dirty pink balloons turn a corner at the end of the corridor. *A different kind of alien?* Avery wondered.

Suddenly he saw movement to his left. As he leapt across the corridor into one of the recessed doorways, plasma scorched the air behind him. Turning around, he watched a salvo of searing green bolts rake across the corridor. The metal boiled and buckled like the shells of beetles trapped on a burning log.

Avery wasn't about to stick his head out. Instead he angled his battle rifle around the corner of the alcove and fired until the sixty-round magazine was dry. The hostile fire had stopped. Avery hoped he'd hit his target, not just driven it into cover.

Of course, there was only one way to find out. He pulled his rifle back and swapped magazines. Then he counted to three and pivoted into the corridor.

The first place Chur'R-Yar went was the bridge. From there she could disconnect the umbilical and power up her ship's engine—escape before any of her attackers came on board. But as she pulled off her helmet and removed her awkward gloves, she realized all her plans were scuttled.

The air inside the bridge was ripe with the Huragok's gaseous emissions, and the circuits connecting the Luminary to *Minor Transgression*'s signal circuits had been repaired. As she stalked toward the pyramidal device, she saw it was transferring a full report of all the alien world's relics back to the Ministry of Tranquility.

"Deacon," she hissed. "Traitor."

But oddly enough, at this moment of betrayal, the first thing Chur'R-Yar felt was sadness. She had come so close to her prize that she could almost feel the soft walls of her nest—the warm clutch of eggs beneath her legs and the little Kig-Yar growing inside that would have carried on her bloodline. She enjoyed these imagined sensations until she was overwhelmed with a desire for revenge.

When the methane suite proved empty, Chur'R-Yar knew there was only one other place the Unggoy could be: *Minor Transgression*'s escape-pod. But as she exited the suite and saw the black-suited alien emerge from the passage leading to the umbilical, the Shipmistress realized, to her extreme disappointment, that even vengeance might be beyond her grasp.

If the alien was aboard her ship, her crewmen were dead. With their help, she might have been able to fight past the alien to the pod in her ship's stern. Now her success depended on her own speed and cunning. But these were much reduced.

The calluses across her shoulders were now so stiff that she had a difficult time bringing her plasma-pistol to bear. By the time she had it up and firing the alien had dived for cover. As she considered how best to drive the alien back into the open, she saw fiery flashes. Projectiles tore through her abdomen and clipped her spine. Another shot shattered her left knee, but by then she no longer had any feeling below the waist. Blood leaking from holes her overtaxed suit could only partially fill, she slumped sideways against the corridor wall.

The Shipmistress' hands felt impossibly heavy, but she managed to raise her pistol into her lap and check its charge. Less than a third of its energy remained—not enough to stop the alien when it came out of hiding, but enough to do what needed to be done.

She reached up and palmed the switch to the methane suite's airlock. As its outer door slid open, she used what was left of her strength to aim her pistol and depress its trigger. As the weapon built up a powerful overcharged bolt sufficient to burn through the airlock's inner door, more projectiles tore through her chest, knocking her back onto the floor.

The light above the Shipmistress dimmed as the alien approached. But despite the spasms wracking her arm, she waited to release the trigger until the thing looked into her eyes. She watched it glance from her weapon to the airlock. She waited until it flinched—an indication it understood the fate she had chosen for it.

"This is *my* ship." Chur'R-Yar hissed. "And I shall do with it what I wish." Her claw slid off the trigger, and a bright green ball of plasma hit the inner door with a sizzling crack.

As the bolt penetrated the suite, it ignited the ambient methane, starting a chain reaction that quickly claimed the tank recharge-station imbedded in the suite's wall. The alien scrambled back toward the umbilical, but the station's compressor exploded into the corridor, knocking its helmeted head against the opposite side of the passage. The alien fell to the floor unconscious.

Chur'R-Yar's tongue flicked weakly against her teeth. *A measure of vengeance, at least.* As the last of her blood pumped out of her body, the methane suite's ruined airlock burst open and a roiling fireball consumed her.

Dadab felt the blast before he heard it—a sudden tremor inside the escape pod followed by a muffled boom. He whined with terror as a series of small explosions rocked the pod in its cradle. *What was keeping the Huragok?* The Deacon had been very clear that they had barely any time to execute their plan.

When all the Kig-Yar were in the umbilical, Dadab had trotted out of the methane-suite with a spare tank, while *Lighter Than Some* headed to the bridge with his true accounting of the Luminations and his explanation of Chur'R-Yar's heresy. But before Dadab could return for another tank, he heard the Shipmistress' warning to her crew over his signal unit, and had remained holed up in the pod.

Now he heard a whistle of air in the circular shaft connecting the pod to *Minor Transgression*'s main corridor and knew the ship was venting atmosphere. He didn't want to leave the Huragok behind, but he would have to close the pod's hatch or risk explosive decompression.

The whistling came to an abrupt stop as *Lighter Than Some* dropped down the shaft and squeezed into the pod. < *Is something wrong?* > the Huragok asked, catching sight of the Deacon's panicked gaze.

< *You, late!* > Dadab signed, slamming his fist on the pod's command-console to close the hatch.

< *Well, we couldn't have gone anywhere without these.* >

Dadab groaned as *Lighter Than Some* revealed the cause of its delay—the luggage it had stopped to retrieve from the methane suite. In its tentacles it held all three of the intelligent boxes, two from the freighter's command cabins and one from the giant machine in the second freighter's hold.

< *Why, so, important?* > Dadab signed with leaden hands. Closing the hatch had automatically triggered the pod's stasis-field—a thickening of the air that would keep its occupants safely immobilized as the pod blew away from the Kig-Yar ship at high speed.

< *Didn't I tell you?* > the Huragok exclaimed, releasing the trio of boxes into the field. They remained frozen together in midair. < *I've taught them to talk! To each other!* >

For the first time, Dadab noticed the sides of the boxes' casings had been removed to expose their circuits. Some of these were joined together in a web of communicative pathways.

Prophets be merciful! he wailed to himself. Then he fingered a flashing holo-switch in the center of the console, and the pod shot free of its cradle.

Viewed from a distance, the compact cylinder was barely visible as it rocketed away from *Minor Transgression*. The pod was one of many pieces of debris cast off by the dying ship, and an observer would scarcely have registered it against the surrounding darkness until it activated its jump drive and vanished in a rippling flash of light.

Jenkins sighted downrange, sweat beading on his brow. Lying prone, left arm tight against his MA5's sling, the three-hundred-meter target was easy pickings. Five rounds, five hits. Jenkins grinned. Yesterday he'd never held a weapon. Today he couldn't put it down.

When he and the other recruits had woken this morning,

neither Staff Sergeant had returned from Utgard. Captain Ponder offered no explanation—simply busied the two platoons with policing trash around the garrison and other make-work tasks. In Byrne's absence he sent Jenkins, Forsell, Wick, and Andersen to the range to start their training, trusting their safety to the range computer.

The computer was wirelessly linked to the recruits' weapons and could lock their triggers anytime. But mostly the machine gruffly called out hits and misses in a comical approximation of a drill instructor's voice. Wick and Andersen had racked up perfunctory scores and then returned to barracks. Neither had joined the militia to learn how to shoot.

Wick's father owned Harvest's biggest import-export concern; Andersen's was the commissioner of the colony's commodities exchange. Both lived in Utgard, and were equally disdainful of the farms that enabled their families' prosperity. They wanted to leave Harvest for a core-world career in the CA or DCS—had thought militia service would be nice padding for their resumes.

Jenkins also saw the militia as his ticket off of Harvest—a way to escape the thousands of acres of grain that he (as the eldest of three children) was destined to inherit. Farming wasn't a bad future, but it wasn't a very exciting one either. And that's why, even though the Staff Sergeants scared the hell out of him, Jenkins very much wanted to *be* them—a real soldier. Not because of any deep-seeded patriotism, but because of the imagined adventure of life as a UNSC Marine.

His parents would never forgive him if he skipped college to enlist. But with a record of militia service, he'd be a shoe-in for Officer Candidate School after graduation. His record wouldn't look very good at all if he didn't know how to shoot. So after Wick and Andersen's departure, he had remained at the range with Forsell.

Jenkins' first impression of the tall, quiet recruit—that Forsell had significantly more brawn than brains—quickly changed. When Jenkins had trouble zeroing his rifle (ensuring its accuracy by adjusting its sights for elevation and windage), Forsell had offered help. When Jenkins' shots went astray, Forsell gave him good advice on how to bring them back in line. And when Jenkins asked Forsell how he knew so much about shooting, the thick-necked, blond-haired recruit looked out at the rustling wheat beyond the farthest targets and said: "I just watch the wind."

So Jenkins started to watch as well, and soon the two recruits were matching bull's-eye for bull's-eye. They spent the rest of the day ribbing each other for misses, congratulating hits—impersonating the gruff range computer that was too simple minded to object.

The fun continued until Captain Ponder appeared late afternoon, packing an M6 pistol and multiple boxes of cartridges.

Jenkins tried not to stare as the Captain began his target practice. But he couldn't help but notice that the Captain seemed rusty—that his prosthetic arm had a hard time keeping his weapon steady. At one point, Ponder dropped a magazine and fumbled to catch it before it clattered onto the range's slat-wood floor.

But soon enough, he was shooting nice tight groups into fifty-meter targets and swapping magazines with absolute precision. Jenkins and Forsell ran out of ammo long before the Captain. But they waited patiently for him to finish, safe his weapon, and check their scores on the range's computer's display.

"Recruit, that's a Sharpshooter performance."

Jenkins felt his lean cheeks flush. "Thank you, sir." Then, he worked up the courage to speak freely. "When I get out of school, I'd like to join the Marines—get a chance to shoot for real . . ." Jenkins trailed off, his eager smile fading before the Captain's stony stare. "I'm sorry, sir."

"No. That's good spirit," Ponder said, resisting the urge to glance skyward—toward the new threat he knew had come. "You want to shoot, you'll get your chance." He didn't have the heart to add: *a whole lot sooner than you think.*

_____PART II_____

CHAPTER
NINE

The Minister of Fortitude had smoked too much. He rarely partook in stimulants—the powerful hookah tobaccos favored by his senior staff. But the previous night's conclave had dragged on and on, and he'd needed something to keep himself awake during the statistic-heavy discussion. Now the Minister's head was seized with a terrible, retributive ache. *Never again,* he vowed, narrowing his heavy-lidded eyes and massaging his long, lateral neck. *If only the cleric would hurry up and finish his remedy. . . .*

Like most Covenant technology, the San'Shyuum cleric's herbal synthesizer was hidden behind a natural facade, in this case the polished onyx walls of his cell. The mottled stonework shone in the light of a single hologram high above: a canopy of diamond-shaped leaves that rustled in a simulated breeze. A zinc counter stretched across the cell, and was built high enough to accommodate the fact that both San'Shyuum—like every other mature member of their species—sat in anti-gravity chairs high above the floor.

"It is done," the cleric said, removing an agate-colored sphere from the synthesizer's delivery tube. Cupping the sphere in his long, thin fingers, he turned his stone chair back toward the counter, placed the sphere in a black marble mortar, and tapped it with a matching pestle. The sphere shattered, giving off a whiff of peppermint and exposing a collection of leaves and small berries. As the cleric started grinding, Fortitude sat a little straighter in his silver chair's plump crimson cushions and breathed in the medicinal smell.

The older San'Shyuum's withered arms twisted inside his woolen shift as he worked the ingredients into a rough powder—an effort that shook the sparse white hairs that hung from his pale neck like the mane of an old, bedraggled horse. The Minister's light brown skin was, by comparison, completely denuded; the only hair on his body curled from a darker wattle beneath his salamandrine lips. But even those hairs were closely trimmed.

This careful grooming, combined with bright red robes that flowed over the Minister's knees to his gnarled feet, was evidence he did not share the cleric's asceticism: a style of worship that advocated extreme humility in the presence of Forerunner technology, such as the synthesizer.

And yet, the Minister mused, already starting to feel some relief just from the remedy's scent, *when the Great Journey begins, we will all walk The Path together.*

This direct quote from Covenant scripture summarized the faith's core promise: those who showed appropriate reverence for the Forerunners and their sacred creations would inevitably share a moment of transcendence—would journey beyond the boundaries of the known universe just as the Forerunners had, many ages ago.

Promised godhood was a message with broad appeal, and all were welcome to join the Covenant so long as they accepted the San'Shyuum's sole authority to investigate and distribute holy relics.

Although the Covenant was focused on the hereafter, its member species still had mortal desires for wealth, power, and prestige—all of which the right Forerunner technology could provide. It was the Ministry of Fortitude's responsibility to balance all these competing wants—to decide, simply put, who got what. And it was the latest round in this ongoing effort that had left its leader with such a terrific headache.

Just as the noise of the pestle started to grate on the tympanic slits in the back of Fortitude's skull, the cleric emptied his mortar onto a square of white cloth spread on the counter. "Let it steep as long as you like. The longer the better, of course." The cleric tied the prescription into a sachet and pushed it gently across the counter. "Blessings on your day, Minister," he said with a sympathetic smile.

"I shall step forward." Fortitude grimaced. *Though today a bit more delicately than usual.*

As the Minister swept the prescription into his lap, he made a mental note to scan it before brewing. Given the controversial nature of his work, assassination was always a possibility and unremitting caution a requirement of office.

Fortitude drummed his fingers against panels of orange-on-blue holographic switches built into his throne's rounded arms, giving the device a new destination. The throne pivoted smartly away from the counter, and accelerated through the cell's triangular entry hall. Running lights winking in the darkly mirrored stone, the chair turned a quick series of corners and exited into High Charity's majestic interior.

Viewed from a distance, the Covenant capital city was reminiscent of a jellyfish adrift in a midnight sea. Its single large dome topped a massive chunk of rock honeycombed with hangar bays and carefully shielded weapons platforms. Long, semirigid umbilicals trailed behind the rocky base, where countless ships were docked like so many stunned fish; commercial vessels mainly, but also the enormous cruisers and carriers of High Charity's defensive fleet. Despite their size, dozens of the warships could have fit inside the dome, which was so spacious it was difficult to see from one side to the other—especially in the early hours of a cycle when the air was thick with cyan banks of fog.

In addition to serving as the Covenant's space-faring capital, High Charity was also home to large populations of each of its species. All rubbed shoulders here, and this concentration of physiologies created a cosmopolitan atmosphere unique among the Covenant's other habitats. The airspace inside the dome was thick with creatures coming and going from their employment; a twice daily commute triggered by the brightening and dimming of a luminous disk set into the apex of the dome—the city's artificial star.

Fortitude squinted as the disk slowly maximized its intensity, revealing a ring of towers stretching around the dome. Each of the twisting spires was held aloft by anti-grav units that were many orders of magnitude more powerful than the one in the Minister of Fortitude's chair. Although some towers were more subdued (such as the one that held the cleric's cell), all of them shared the same basic structure: spikes of volcanic rock from the city's base shot through with metal supports and covered with plates of decorative alloy.

Now that morning had come, it was easier to pick out individuals in the commuting swarm: Unggoy packed together on hulking barges; San'Shyuum in chairs similar to Fortitude's; and here and there, strapped into sleek anti-grav backpacks, tall and muscular Sangheili. These blue-skinned, shark-eyed warriors were the San'Shyuum's protectors—though this had not always been so.

Both the San'Shyuum and Sangheili had evolved on planets rich in Forerunner relics. Both species believed these highly advanced pieces of technology were deserving of their worship—clear evidence of the Forerunner's divine powers. But only the San'Shyuum had been bold enough to dismantle some of their relics and use them to make practical objects of their own design.

To the Sangheili, this was blasphemy. But the San'Shyuum believed there was no sin in searching for greater wisdom and, moreover, were convinced that such investigations were critical to discovering how to follow in their Gods' footsteps. This fundamental difference in the practical application of religious ethics sparked a long and bloody war that began soon after the two species made contact on a disputed reliquary world inside a Sangheili-occupied system.

In terms of ships and soldiers, the Sangheili started the fight with a distinct numerical advantage. They were also better warriors—stronger, faster and more disciplined. In a straight-up infantry clash, one Sangheili was worth at least ten San'Shyuum. With most of the fighting taking place in space and ship-to-ship, however, the San'Shyuum had their own advantage: a single, semi-operable Forerunner Dreadnought that decimated the Sangheili fleets with hit-and-run attacks.

For a very long time, the Sangheili took their knocks, ignoring the obvious fact that victory would require committing the sins of their enemy—desecrating their own relics and using them to improve their warships, arms, and armor. Not surprisingly, millions of Sangheili had died before the proud and hidebound species decided abnegation was preferable to obliteration. With heavy hearts, their warrior priests began their work, eventually assembling a fleet capable of fighting the San'Shyuum and their Dreadnought to a standstill.

As devastating as this decision was to most Sangheili, the wisest of their leaders knew they hadn't sinned so much as finally come to terms with their own desire for deeper understanding of the literal articles of their faith. And for their part, the San'Shyuum had to make their own painful admission: if there were other creatures as dangerous and dogged as the Sangheili in the galaxy, their chances of survival would be greatly increased if they allied with their enemy—had the Sangheili watch their backs while they went about their holy work.

Thus was the Covenant born. A union fraught with mutual suspicion, but given a good chance of success by a clear division of labor codified in the Writ of Union, the treaty that officially ended the conflict. Now the Covenant's most important piece of scripture, the Writ began:

> *So full of hate were our eyes*
> > *That none of us could see*
> *Our war would yield countless dead*
> > *But never victory.*
> *So let us cast arms aside*
> > *And like discard our wrath.*
> *Thou, in faith, will keep us safe*
> > *Whilst we find The Path.*

The treaty was formalized with the decommissioning of the Dreadnought. The ancient vessel was stripped of all its weapons (or at least all the San'Shyuum knew it possessed), and permanently installed at the center of High Charity's then-partially constructed dome.

Fortitude was not as devout as other Prophets. He believed in the Great Journey, to be sure, but by vocation he was more technocrat than theologian. And yet, as the Minister rose through a pocket of less-crowded air, he couldn't help but feel a rush of spiritual invigoration as the Dreadnought's grand tripodal frame began to glimmer in the morning light.

More than any other piece of abandoned Forerunner technology, the ship typified its makers' technological mastery. The Dreadnought's engines, for example, were so efficient that even though the San'Shyuum had only ever managed to bring them partially online, they still generated more than enough power to sustain all of High Charity. Fortitude knew there were many more secrets hidden in the computational pathways that spread throughout the vessel's hull. Soon, he hoped, the San'Shyuum priests responsible for the Dreadnought's exploration would unlock them all.

For as preoccupied as Fortitude was with managing his Ministry's vast bureaucracy, part of his mind was still gripped with the same questions as all other Covenant: *how exactly had the Forerunners accomplished their transcendence? And how might mere mortals do the same?*

A sudden wail of anti-grav generators and subsequent shrill cries of protest drew the Minister's gaze upward. One of the Unggoy barges had failed to give way to a San'Shyuum commuting ring, forcing its constituent chairs to break apart.

Similar rings were in motion all around the dome, ascending and descending the towers. Junior San'Shyuum rated the least powerful chairs and traveled in rings of twenty or more, packed arm-to-arm to maximize their ring's anti-grav field. Senior Ministry staffers might manage rings as small as seven, and the sophistication of Vice Ministers' chairs made it possible for them to commute in trios. But only full Ministers such as Fortitude rated units sufficiently powerful for individual flight.

For a moment, Fortitude thought he, too, might have to swerve to avoid the plummeting barge. But High Charity's flight-control circuits had already corrected their mistake, properly identified the Minister's rank and forced the barge to take evasive action. It dipped precipitously to one side, causing its Unggoy passengers to cling tighly to one another or risk plummeting to their deaths.

Soaring past without even the slightest bobble in his chair, Fortitude noticed the barge was so crowded that some of the Unggoy had been forced to sit with their stubby legs dangling over its low gunwales—a capacity violation to be sure. As the barge leveled off and continued its barely controlled fall to the still foggy, methane-rich districts on the dome's floor, Fortitude wondered if the overcrowding was an isolated problem or an indication that the Unggoy were, once again, reproducing beyond legal limits.

Overpopulation was a constant concern for the Covenant

given how many of its creatures lived on ships or other space-based habitats. The Unggoy were especially prodigious breeders, and while this benefited the Covenant military rolls, it was also the case that the only thing that put an appreciable dent in their numbers was war. In times of peace and without proper oversight, the Unggoy's inherent lack of reproductive restraint had proven to be quite dangerous.

As a junior staffer in the Ministry of Concert (the institution tasked with the arbitration of inter-species disputes), Fortitude had handled a case that dealt directly with this issue—uncovered a scandal that resulted in the dismissal of that Ministry's leadership, and taught him a valuable lesson about the fragility of the Covenant: how easy it was to grow complacent about various species' petty squabbles, and how quickly this complacency might lead to disaster.

The case involved a complaint by an Unggoy distillers' union that faulty atmospheric controls aboard Kig-Yar merchant vessels had tainted multiple batches of infusions—recreational narcotics Unggoy added to their portable methane supplies. At first glance the dispute seemed trivial, which was undoubtedly why it ended up on Fortitude's docket. But as he delved deeper, he discovered the contamination had resulted in widespread Unggoy sterility.

At the time of the case, the Covenant had passed many peaceful ages, and a growing Unggoy population had put pressure on the habitats they shared with Kig-Yar. Strained at the best of times, relations between the two species took a turn for the worst as female Kig-Yar were displaced from their nests—relocations that stressed incubation cycles and caused a spike in Kig-Yar infant mortality. Fortitude advised his superiors that the tainting of infusions was bold vigilantism—an attempt by radical Kig-Yar Shipmasters who believed Unggoy births were causing Kig-Yar deaths to mete out their own justice.

Much to Fortitude's surprise, the Minister of Concert chose not to impose any of his recommended stiff penalties. Fines were assessed and damages paid, but the guilty Shipmasters avoided imprisonment. Indeed, after making repairs to their vessels and proving they were safe, the Ministry allowed them back in service.

Fortitude held no special place in his heart for Unggoy. But a strong sense that justice had not been served led him to lodge a formal complaint. His superiors rebuffed him, arguing that a few thousand impotent Unggoy wasn't worth doing anything that might enflame the Kig-Yar's endemic autonomous urge. *The Unggoy would soon recoup their losses,* Fortitude's superiors had concluded, *and in the meantime, any junior who cared about the progress of his career would be wise to shut his lips.*

No one had known that the Infusion Incident, as it came to be known, was the most important of many small grievances that precipitated the Unggoy Rebellion, a civil war that ushered in the Covenant's 39th Age of Conflict, and brought about a radical restructuring of the Covenant armed forces.

In the short but nasty fight that resulted in the near-razing of the Unggoy home world, the creatures proved that properly motivated, they were vicious fighters. Honoring a tradition of welcoming the best of their defeated foes into their ranks, the same Sangheili commanders that crushed the rebellion were quick to forgive the surviving Unggoy fighters. They gave them better training and weapons and integrated them into formerly all-Sangheili units—actions that elevated the methane-breathers from cannon fodder to competent infantry.

Some San 'Shyuum had lingering doubts about the Unggoy's loyalty. But the Writ of Union was very clear: *security matters were the Sangheili's responsibility.* And if the Prophets had learned anything about keeping their prideful protectors happy, it was the importance of letting them preserve as many of their pre-Covenant traditions as possible. Even in his youth, Fortitude had understood that while something like the Unggoy Rebellion might temporarily destabilize the Covenant, a Sangheili revolt would shatter it.

A vertical line of triangular holographic symbols flashed above one of Fortitude's armrests, jarring him from his thoughts. The symbols were letters from the Covenant's common written language, and he immediately recognized the name they announced. "Whatever you must say, Vice Minister." Fortitude pressed one of his throne's switches to accept the incoming signal. "Endeavor to keep your voice low."

The symbols dispersed, and in their place a San'Shyuum appeared in miniature. Even in holographic form it was easy to see that the Vice Minister of Tranquility was many ages Fortitude's junior. His skin was darker—more brown than tan—and his wattle wasn't heavy enough to have sagged all the way to his chin. Two of the fleshy balls hung from the corners of his mouth. These were pierced with golden loops—a rakish affectation popular with male San'Shyuum who had not yet committed to a single mate.

"Is it too early?" The Vice Minister sat far forward in his cushionless chair, his fingers wrapped tightly around its dull metal armrests. "I would have called last evening, were it not for the conclave." Tranquility paused, his large, glassy eyes almost bursting from his head. Then, in a jumbled failure of propriety: "I wonder if this morning—*now*, in fact—it would be possible to meet and discuss something of vital—"

Fortitude cut the Vice Minister off with an impatient wave. "I haven't checked my schedule. But I'm sure it is quite full."

"I will be brief, you have my word," Tranquility persisted. "In fact it's not so much what I have to *say* as what I have to *show* you." His fingers drummed against his chair's armrests and his image was suddenly replaced by a single Forerunner glyph—a Lumination, Fortitude realized, his slumped shoulders stiffening with shock.

Unlike the triangular symbols, the sacred glyphs weren't used in everyday discourse. Indeed, some were so hallowed—the concepts they represented so powerful—that their usage was strictly proscribed. *And the one this* idiot *had just flashed for all to see,* Fortitude cursed, *was the most sacred and dangerous of all!*

"In my chambers! Immediately!" Fortitude slammed his palm onto his chair, blanking the glyph and ending the conversation. He resisted the urge to max his chair's acceleration, knowing this would only draw more attention. Massaging his throbbing head, he continued his steady, counterclockwise ascent to his Ministry's tower, arriving a short while later at a broad vestibule in an upper floor.

Fortitude wasn't in the habit of socializing with his staff, and now he paid them even less consideration than usual. That didn't stop their shows of deference, however, and Fortitude had to carve his way through his kowtowing juniors' feeble chairs, expending what little patience he had on common courtesy.

The vestibule channeled into a large gallery lined with hallways leading off to the staffers' work clusters. In between these exits floated slightly more than life-size statues of Fortitude's predecessors. These were carved from stones quarried from High Charity's rocky base and "dressed" in holographic robes that scrolled with symbolic histories of their wearers' many notable accomplishments.

On the far side of the gallery was a vertical shaft guarded by two Sangheili in the distinctive bright-white armor of one of their most elite combat units, the Lights of Sanghelios; Helios, for short—a reference to the globular cluster of stars near the species' home system. Fortitude could hear the Helios' energy staves crackle as he neared the shaft. But the guards didn't so much as twitch their four jagged mandibles as the Minister glided between them. Peering out from the visors of their swept-back helmets, the Helios' dark eyes remained locked on the vestibule, the most likely avenue of attack. The Minister wasn't offended. He hadn't chosen the Helios for their manners, and despite their stone-faced demeanor he knew they would gladly give their lives for his.

The shaft quickly tapered such that a few levels above the gallery there was barely room for Fortitude's single chair. This was partly for additional security, but also an architectural metaphor for Fortitude's status: *at the top, there was only room for one.*

"Admit the Vice Minister of Tranquility as soon as he arrives," Fortitude snapped to a hologram of a staff member waiting at the top of the shaft. "I don't care what that does to the rest of my schedule." The junior dispersed, and Fortitude brought his chair to an abrupt halt in the center of his receiving room. His heart was racing, and his skin was clammy beneath his robes. *Calm yourself*, he thought, *Under no circumstances can this upstart know he has upset you!*

And so, when the Vice Minister emerged from the shaft a short while later, he found Fortitude reclining calmly in his chair, a steaming ball of medicinal tea floating in a stasis-field above his lap.

"Busy *and* ill," Tranquility simpered. "I apologize, Minister, for adding further burden to your day."

Fortitude leaned forward, pressed his lips against the field, and took a draught. The field shimmered and shrunk as the tea drained into the Minister's gullet. "Who else have you told?"

"Holiness, you are the only one I thought to tell."

So far, the youth was showing exceptional deference. *How long will that last?* Fortitude wondered, sucking more tea through his lips.

The Vice Minister was famously scrappy—vocal and determined. On the occasions he had substituted for his Minister in sessions of the Covenant High Council (a decision-making body comprised of San'Shyuum Ministers and Sangheili Commanders), he had shown no reluctance to participate in debate, going chair-to-chair with councilors many ages his senior on a number of contentious issues.

Fortitude suspected this decidedly un-San'Shyuum behavior had much to do with the Vice Minister's work. The Ministry of Tranquility managed the Covenant's vast relic-hunting fleet and spent a great deal of time outside High Charity, dealing directly with Sangheili Shipmasters. In the process, he had adopted some of their more aggressive demeanor.

"How many instances?" Fortitude asked, tapping a finger against his throne. The glyph in question appeared between the two San'Shyuum's chairs—the brightest object in the Minister's sparsely decorated chambers.

To the untrained eye, the Lumination was just a pair of concentric circles; the smaller circle hung low inside the larger, suspended by a straight line that connected to a surrounding lattice of interlocking curves. But Fortitude knew what the glyph meant—the Forerunner word it represented: *Reclamation*, or the recovery of previously unknown relics.

"The Luminary was on a very remote ship. Its transmission was somewhat garbled." Tranquility struggled to restrain a triumphant smile. "But it detected thousands of *unique* instances."

A shudder ran the length of Fortitude's spine. If the Vice Minister was to be believed, it was an unprecedented find. "Why not bring this discovery to your own Minister?" Fortitude asked, managing to keep his voice calm. "Were he to discover your disloyalty, dismissal will be the least of your concerns."

"A risk worth taking." The Vice Minister leaned forward in his chair and added in a conspiratorial whisper, "For *both* of us."

Fortitude chuckled into his tea. There was something oddly endearing about the young San'Shyuum's impudence. But he presumed too much, Fortitude decided, extending a finger toward the switch on his throne that would bring the Helios hurtling up the shaft. . . .

"The High Council grows restless!" the Vice Minister blurted, then continued at a breathless pace: "The Hierarchs are impotent—the dilemmas on which they made their ascent well settled. This is no longer an Age of Doubt, Minister, and those with any sense know this is *your* doing above all others!"

Fortitude stayed his hand. The youth had made a valid point. Ages of Doubt such as the present were about dealing with the fallout of previous chaotic periods, in this case the thirty-ninth Age of Conflict—that which had encompassed the Unggoy rebellion and seen Fortitude's promotion to Minister. His efforts to properly redistribute technology in the wake of that crisis had indeed done much to defuse new grievances. And while Fortitude was largely immune to flattery, he was again impressed by the Vice Minister's nerve.

Tranquility had just ranked Fortitude's achievements above the Hierarchs'—the three San'Shyuum elected to lead the High Council. These were the most powerful creatures in the Covenant, and calling them weak and worthless was a dangerous proclamation. Fortitude pulled back his finger, suddenly fascinated by what the Vice Minister might next propose. Though, in retrospect, he should have known.

"We find ourselves at the dawning of a new Age of Reclamation." The Vice Minister coaxed his chair around the glyph. "You are the one to lead us through it, and I—by merit of my current discretion and pledge of steadfast devotion hence forth—humbly request to sit by your side." Tranquility stopped his chair directly before the Minister's, bowed deeply at the waist, and spread wide his arms. "To assume with you the mantle of Hierarch."

And there it was, Fortitude thought, absolutely stunned. *Ambition laid bare.*

It would not be easy to unseat the Hierarchs. To keep their exalted thrones, they would resist the declaration of a new age with all the influence at their disposal. Fortitude would need to spend tremendous political capital—call in all favors owed for them to have a chance, and even then. . . .

Fortitude caught himself. *Was he* seriously *considering the Vice Minister's proposal? Had he gone mad?*

"Before we do anything," he cautioned, his tongue moving of its own accord, "we must be *sure* the Luminations are valid."

"I have a warship standing by, awaiting your approval to—"

Fortitude pulled back as if stung. "You have brought the *Sangheili* into this?!" His head began to throb, beating with panicked pain. *If the Sangheili took possession of the reliquary, who knew how that might upset the status quo!* Again his finger shot toward his throne's alarm.

But the Vice Minister jerked forward in his seat and countered in a firm tone. "No. I have enlisted *other* witnesses. Creatures that have proven themselves both loyal and discreet."

Fortitude scowled into the Vice Minister's eyes. He sought a glimmer of trustworthiness, something that might help him step more confidently down a new and treacherous path. But the Vice Minister's stare was all eagerness and cunning; honesty of a different sort.

The Minister brought his hovering finger down on a different switch. His tea's stasis-field collapsed in a silver flash, vaporizing the liquid inside. "What of the ship that registered the Lumination?"

"Lost. It had a mixed crew. Kig-Yar and Unggoy." Tranquility pursed his lips in an indifferent pout. "I suspect mutiny."

"Tell those you have enlisted that if there are survivors—and if they have stolen from the reliquary—they are to be executed on the spot." Fortitude pulled thoughtfully at his waddle. "Otherwise, they shall remain in protective custody. The reliquary was their find. They deserve some small reward."

Tranquility spread a hand on his chest and bowed his head. "It shall be done."

At that moment, the cleric's prescription finally took hold of Fortitude's headache. The Minister closed his eyes, enjoying the rapid subjugation of his pain. He smiled with relief—an expression he knew the younger San'Shyuum would misinterpret as an indication of some great and budding camaraderie.

"A reliquary such as this has not been seen in our lifetimes," Tranquility said. "Each of its holy objects is a blessing for true believers!"

Fortitude sank deep into the crimson cushions of his chair. *A blessing?* He wasn't so sure. As Minister, he looked with dread on the nightmarish negotiations required to distribute thousands of new relics. But as Hierarch, he could distribute the relics however he thought would best benefit the Covenant. Fortitude licked a minty sheen from his lips, still tingling from the field. *And none would have the power to alter his decisions.*

CHAPTER
TEN

Avery found himself alone, pacing the rows of one of Harvest's vast orchards. Branches brushed past him on either side, heavy with a fantastic mix of fruit: apricots, cherries, plums—and many more, all beaded with condensation from a cold, morning mist. He pulled an apple free and brushed away the dew. The green skin beneath was so lustrous that it glowed like a thing on fire. *Sunday,* he thought. *Sunday . . .* But he wasn't sure exactly why.

He discarded the apple and reached deeper into the branches. Closer to the trunk, the air was colder. Avery felt the frost-covered curves of a pear, and twisted it from its stem. He brought it to his lips and took a bite. But his teeth had barely punctured before he got a raw-nerve jolt. The pear was frozen solid. Avery dragged his sleeve across his lips and was surprised to find he was wearing civilian clothes: a freshly starched white oxford shirt many sizes too small; a little paisley tie that barely reached his navel; scuffed, wing-tip shoes.

"A boy isn't a boy that doesn't ruin *his clothes. . . ."* Avery heard his aunt Marcille's voice, a breeze through the icy leaves.

Suddenly, the branches shook in a whoosh of passing thrusters. Looking up, Avery just caught sight of a Hornet air-craft passing low above the orchard. Wings flashing in the bright sunlight, the aircraft banked and disappeared behind the trees on the opposite side of the row. Avery dropped the pear and ran off in pursuit.

But now the farther he pushed through the branches, the

warmer they became. Water ran in rivulets down waxy leaves—
dropped from the fruit like rain. A rapid, artificial thaw was underway. Avery felt a humid gust of air that became unbearably
hot the farther he pressed forward. He closed his eyes, lids
burning, and felt the branches give way to something solid: a
wooden double door leading into a roadside restaurant.

Pushing through, Avery saw the door was one of the few
things left standing. The restaurant's roof was blown clean off.
Its walls were splintered and its windows shattered. All the ta-
bles and chairs were burned and smelled of smoke. Toward the
back sat a family of four, their cheerful clothes the only things
not covered in a layer of ash. One of the children—the same
boy Avery had hoped to save—looked up from a plate of pan-
cakes and waved. As Avery waved back, the boy took a bite and
pointed to the food counter. Avery turned and saw a woman on
a stool, wearing a stunning silver dress.

"It's a formal affair," Jilan said, twisting on the stool.

"I know," Avery replied, reaching to straighten his tie. But he
no longer wore his hand-me-down church clothes. Instead he
found himself burdened by matte-black impact plating.

Jilan frowned. "Maybe I should have invited someone else."
She pulled a purse from her lap—not the mirrored clutch she'd
had at the solstice celebration, but the burgundy bag of the Innie bomber. She casually reached inside, as if rummaging for
a lipstick.

"Careful, ma'am!" Avery shouted. "It's not safe!" He tried
to leap forward and grab the bag. But his legs were leaden—
rooted to the floor. Avery heard the roar of Hornet thrusters,
saw its shadow ripple across the counter. The young boy at the
table started to choke.

"Relax," Jilan said to Avery. "You'll be alright."

Avery groaned and dropped to a knee. His armor had become unbearably heavy. He planted his gloved hands on the
ash-covered floor to keep himself from collapsing. Through

narrowed eyes he saw boot prints: the frantic footwork of marines working to surround a target.

Jilan repeated herself. But this time her voice seemed to come from somewhere else—an echo from beyond the restaurant, but somehow very close to Avery's ear.

"Relax. You'll be alright. . . ."

Avery did, and he was. The powerful pharmaceuticals that had kept him unconscious since his fight aboard the freighter drained from his veins like water from a bath. He felt the tug of an imagined drain, and let himself settle to the bottom. When his eyes finally opened they seemed to do so at quarter-speed.

"There you are," Jilan said, standing close beside his bed. "Welcome back."

Avery knew he had been dreaming, but he was still surprised to see her out without her dress. The Lt. Commander now wore light gray service coveralls, high-necked and fitted at the waist—the everyday uniform of a female ONI officer. She stood on the left side of his bed. On the right was Governor Thune.

"How long have I been out?" Avery croaked, taking in his surroundings: a small room with cream-colored walls, monitoring equipment, and an IV stand—its tubing running to a needle in the top of his right hand. Avery smelled antiseptic and aggressively bleached linens. *A hospital*, he thought, a suspicion quickly confirmed as Jilan lifted a pitcher of ice water from a wheeled cart and filled a glass etched with the words UTGARD MEMORIAL.

"Almost two days," she said, handing Avery the glass. "You have a fractured skull."

Avery rose onto an elbow, took the glass, and drained it with a long, slow sip. *Sunday . . .* That was when he and Byrne had ridden a Welcome Wagon back up to the Tiara and transitioned to al-Cygni's sloop, *Walk of Shame*. The two Staff Sergeants had been briefed, armed, and underway by 0900, hidden in the decoy freighter.

"What about Byrne?"

"He's fine. Had his wound all sewed up by the time we got back. Your Corpsman even complimented him on his stitching." Jilan put the pitcher back on the tray. "He saved you. Pulled you onto the freighter before the other ship blew up."

Avery frowned. "I don't remember that."

"What *do* you remember?" The Governor asked. Thune seemed penned in by the room's narrow walls; his formerly jolly bulk now a looming threat. "Take me through your mission. Step by step."

Avery furrowed his brow.

"The room's secure. And you're the only patient in this wing," Jilan explained. Then, nodding toward the Governor: "I've already told him everything I know."

Avery reached for a row of buttons embedded in his bed's side-rail. Motors whirred, and the bed lifted him to a sitting position. Placing his glass in a nest of sheets that filled his lap, Avery settled into a familiar mode: the cut-and-dried delivery of an after-action report to a superior. But he only got a minute or so in—was just starting to describe the combat with the aliens—when Thune became impatient.

"How did they communicate?" he asked, wrapping his large arms across his chest.

"Sir?"

Thune had begun to sweat. Deep blue splotches were growing around the collar and under the arms of his chambray shirt. "Did you see any COM-gear—notice how they spoke to each other or to their ship?"

"No sir. But they were suited up. It was hard to—"

"We're wondering if they sent a *message*, Staff Sergeant," Jilan clarified. "A distress signal. Something we might have missed on your helmet cam."

"The leader was out of sight," Avery said. He remembered the alien's ruby eyes and sharpened teeth, the ball of plasma building on its pistol like a shiny apple. "One, two minutes, tops. But it definitely had time to squawk. And then there was the other alien—"

"What *other* alien?" Jilan asked eagerly.

"Didn't get a good look at it." Avery recalled something airborne, pink and swollen. "And it didn't engage."

"Was it armed?" Thune asked.

"Not that I could tell, sir."

"So let me get this straight." Thune scratched his neck below his thick red beard. "Four aliens, maybe five. Armed with knives and pistols."

"Their ship had *lasers*, Governor. Hydrogen fluoride. Very accurate." Jilan spread her hands a short distance apart. "And it was a small ship. Who knows what they put on their larger vessels."

"The ones you killed," Thune dragged out his words; his tone was arched, provocative. "They seem any . . . *tougher* than the average Insurrectionist?"

"Sir?" Avery felt a familiar knot tighten in his stomach. *What did the Innies have to do with this?*

"Four of them, two of you." The Governor shrugged his massive shoulders. "And you won."

"We had the element of surprise. But they were disciplined. Demonstrated good tactical thinking." Avery was about to give a detailed description of how well the aliens had maneuvered in zero-gee, when the door to his room slid open and Attorney General Pedersen slipped inside.

"I couldn't find an orderly anywhere." He smiled apologetically at Avery. "Not that you're *missing* anything. Hospital food is the same wherever you go, I'm afraid." Then, to Governor Thune: "Anything . . . unexpected?"

Thune shot Jilan a dismissive look. "No," he said firmly.

A tense silence filled the room. Avery shifted in his bed. Clearly, his debrief had been an important part of a larger discussion—his answers critical to an argument between al-Cygni and Thune.

"Governor," Jilan said. "If we might have a word."

"You've been very helpful, Staff Sergeant." Thune patted Avery's leg through his sheets then headed for the door. "Enjoy your rest."

Avery sat up as straight as he could, straining his IV. "Thank you, sir."

Jilan followed the Governor outside. Pedersen pulled the door shut behind them with an odd duck of his head—almost a bow. Avery raised his glass, tossed a few cubes of melting ice past his lips, and began to crunch. The movement of his jaw worsened an ache at the back of his skull. He reached around and felt a bumpy line—a cauterized incision through which the doctors had injected bone-knitting polymer.

Avery could hear Thune's voice rumbling outside the door, but he couldn't make out what he was saying. At first, Jilan's responses were similarly muffled, but the exchange quickly increased in volume—crescendoed with a sharp growl from Thune and conciliatory muttering from Pedersen. Avery heard departing footfalls, and a few moments later Jilan slid back into the room alone.

"He didn't know," Avery said. "That you were running an op. Using the militia as cover."

Jilan crossed her arms behind her back and leaned against the wall beside the door. "No."

The decision to keep the Governor out of the loop had certainly happened way above the Lt. Commander's pay grade. But if Jilan was upset that she'd been left holding the bag, she didn't show it. Her expression was perfectly calm.

Avery reached out and placed his empty glass on the cart. "How many ships is he requesting?"

Jilan waited for him to settle back into bed. "None."

For a moment, the only sound in the room was the low clicking of one of the monitors as it registered a spike in Avery's pulse. "But didn't we just—"

"Make first contact with aliens?"

"With respect, ma'am. The contact wasn't all that friendly. Their weapons were way more sophisticated than ours. And like you said, that was probably just the small stuff."

Jilan nodded. "We threw a sucker punch, and won a fistfight."

"They'll be back for another round."

"I know."

"Then why the hell isn't Thune asking for any ships?"

Jilan pushed away from the wall. "Organizing a militia took years of negotiations—required the unanimous approval of Harvest's Parliament. A significant percentage of its citizens were against having even a handful of marines on their planet." Jilan stepped to the foot of Avery's bed. "Thune isn't eager to see how they react to UNSC *warships* in orbit."

Avery remembered the looks on the faces of some of the guests at the solstice celebration; their obvious disdain for him and his uniform. "The Insurrection. Thune's worried it's going to spread."

"We're *all* worried it's going to spread," Jilan said.

"So . . . what? We're just gonna ignore these alien assholes banging on our door?"

"The Governor's upset. He doesn't want to listen. Not now. Not to me."

"Then who?"

Jilan wrapped her hands around the stainless steel bar that bracketed the bottom of Avery's mattress. She squeezed, as if doubtful of the metal's strength. "Someone with knowledge of authorized response plans for first contact scenarios. Someone who can either convince the Governor that bringing in the fleet is the right thing to do, or has the rank to overrule him." She looked up. "Not me."

Avery heard frustration in her voice: a flaw in her emotionless facade. He had an opportunity to say the right thing—to explain that he shared her frustration, and to ask her what they could do, together, to prepare Harvest for an attack. Instead, he let his anger get the better of him.

"The Governor's playing politics," he snarled. "And you're not gonna do a damn thing about it?"

Avery had been testing the boundaries of insubordination since Thune had left the room, but this was a clear step over the line. Jilan pulled her hands from the bar.

"My ship is already on its way to Reach, carrying a report in which I recommend—in no uncertain terms—that FLEETCOM *ignore* the Governor's objections and immediately dispatch a battle group." Any weakness in her voice was gone. She locked Avery's brazen stare. "What else, Staff Sergeant, do you suggest I do?"

Walk of Shame was an ONI sloop—a very fast ship. But Avery knew it would still take more than a month for it to get back to Epsilon Eridanus. The battle group would take time to muster, and would be slower to transit. Best case scenario: it would be at least three months before help arrived at Harvest. And Avery knew, deep in his gut, this would be too late.

With a silent curse, he yanked his out IV, threw back his bedsheets, and swung a foot onto the floor. His hospital gown was surprisingly short, and Jilan was at a particularly awkward angle. But her eyes remained fixed on his as he removed his freshly washed uniform from the middle shelf of the hospital cart, stepped into his fatigue pants, and fastened them beneath his gown.

"What are you doing?"

"Returning to duty."

Avery tore off his gown, and tossed it on the bed. Now Jilan's eyes did flick up and down, registering the ugly contusions the recent fight had left on Avery's broad chest and shoulders.

"I don't remember giving you permission to do that."

Avery muscled into his olive-drab T-shirt, dropped to a knee, and did up his boots. "I have my orders: train a company of militia. And I intend to do it, because right now, ma'am? Their sorry asses are all this planet's got."

Avery pulled on his duty-cap and marched toward the door. Jilan sidestepped and barred his path. He was a head taller, much heavier, and stronger. But looking down at her stoic face, Avery honestly wondered who'd come out on top if he tried to push past and she tried to stop him. In the end, all she needed was her voice.

"Everything you've seen and done in the last forty-eight hours is classified. Top secret. You will train your recruits the best way you know how. But you *will* not tell them what you know." She paused, eyes flashing. "Do I make myself clear?"

Avery had thought Jilan's eyes were brown. But now he realized they shone deep hazel. Fathomless green.

"Yes, ma'am."

Jilan stepped aside, and Avery slid open the door. Stepping into the hall, he was surprised to see Captain Ponder, sitting on a cushioned bench a few doors down, fingers busy on his COM pad's screen. Ponder looked up as Avery approached.

"I was expecting worse." He smiled. "You look pretty good."

"Captain," Jilan said as she strode quickly past.

Ponder stood and snapped a hasty salute with his prosthetic arm. "Ma'am."

The two marines watched Jilan head toward an elevator at the end of hall. Her black boots' low heels clacked loudly on the polished white tile floor. Avery waited until she was inside the elevator and the door was closed before he asked: "Did you know she was a spook?"

"No, I did not." Ponder dropped his COM pad into the chest pocket of his fatigue shirt. "But as far as they go, she isn't too bad."

Avery narrowed his eyes. "She's hanging us out to dry."

"What she's doing is following orders." Ponder put his

prosthetic hand on Avery's shoulder. "Bringing in the fleet? That's Thune's call." The Captain could tell Avery still wasn't convinced. "Listen, all the gear you didn't leave floating out in space, she gave to me. She wants us to take it back to the garrison, put it to good use."

Avery knew there were weapons and equipment in Jilan's arsenal he could use to train his recruits to fight—not just march and shoot at targets on the range. If that was all the Lt. Commander had to give, Avery agreed: it was better than nothing.

"Come on," Ponder said, steering Avery away toward the elevator. "On our way back to the garrison, you can tell me how Staff Sergeant Byrne managed to get himself stuck by a lizard in a space suit."

All the 2nd platoon recruits cheered when Jenkins fell. The blow from his opponent's pugil-stick had caught him on the back of his helmet—swept him right off the beam. Jenkins hit the ground hard enough to come up with cheekfuls of sand, despite the mouth guard FCPO Healy had insisted they all wear.

"Spit and grin," Healy commanded, crouching beside Jenkins. He waited for the recruit to remove his mouth guard—show that he still had all his teeth. Then he checked for a concussion. "You know the date?"

"Nineteenth of January, doc."

"How many fingers am I holding up?"

"None."

"Alright then, enjoy the rest of your day."

As the Corpsman rose, Jenkins wiped his mouth, leaving a slug's trail of grit on his bare forearm. The recruit that had sent him sprawling (an older man named Stisen, one of a handful of officers from the Utgard Constabulary—the city's police force) was still standing on the beam, shaking his pugil-stick in triumph.

The beam was no more than half a meter off the ground, and there was plenty of sand in the pit the recruits had dug beside the garrison motor pool. But Jenkins still felt a little wobbly as he trudged back to 1st platoon's side of the pit. He'd done well—managed to knock off a few of the other 2nd platoon recruits. But then he'd run into Stisen, and the constable was just too strong.

"Watch yourself," Jenkins said, handing Forsell the pugilstick. "He's good."

Forsell nodded, his jaws already stuffed with his own mouth guard. The tall, quiet recruit looked even more imposing in his protective shoulder pads, and it was 1st platoon's turn to cheer as Forsell stepped onto the beam.

"Listen up!" Staff Sergeant Byrne barked, his legs wide and his boots half-buried in the sand. "This is the title bout in our little tournament. Loser earns his platoon a week of KP." Byrne grinned as the recruits' cheers turned to groans. The mess hall had automated food dispensers, but the machines were purposefully built to be cleaned and stocked at the end of every meal. *Some training tools were just too good to fall victim to technological advance*, Byrne smiled. "So let's see some bloody fighting spirit!"

Forsell and Stisen grunted—smacked the padded ends of their pugil-sticks together. The beam creaked as they delivered an opening flurry of blows. Both men were over ninety kilos, but winning at pugil-sticks had as much to do with speed and agility as striking power. The leaner Stisen had a slight edge. After staggering Forsell with a jab to the chin, he simply stepped back as the heavier recruit reacted with a wild swipe, lost his balance and stepped into the pit.

Stisen's platoon mates guffawed at the success of his ploy. Byrne wasn't impressed. "Only thing you get backing up is a boot in your ass." He grabbed the facemask of Stisen's helmet and gave it a series of emphatic tugs. "So stop. Messing. Around!"

"Yes, Staff Sergeant!" Stisen roared between clenched teeth. "All right, you bastards. Kill, kill, kill!"

Again the two men clashed. This time they struck hard, locked sticks and tried to shove one another from the beam. There was a momentary stalemate—two pairs of boots slid backward, struggling for purchase. Suddenly, Stisen pulled away. Forsell lost his balance and staggered forward. Stisen took a mighty swing at Forsell's head. But the big recruit tucked his chin against his shoulder, absorbed Stisen's strike and countered with a thrust to the constable's ribs that knocked him sideways into the sand.

Stisen rolled to his feet and shrugged his shoulders as if to say: *lucky shot*—a reaction that elicited a chorus of boos from 1st platoon that persisted even as Byrne demanded calm, and a Warthog roared into the motor pool.

"You all want to slaver on," Byrne shouted, glancing at the Warthog as Avery and Captain Ponder dismounted. "Let's hear you count to fifty!"

The recruits dropped and started their punishment push-ups, counting loudly and in unison. But Jenkins kept his head up, and watched as the two Staff Sergeants came together under Captain Ponder's watchful gaze.

It didn't take a genius to realize there was bad blood between Avery and Byrne. Ever since Jenkins had arrived at the garrison, he noticed they'd gone out of their way to avoid each other. And Staff Sergeant Byrne seemed to regard their recruits' training as a personal rivalry—had encouraged a strong, competitive relationship between the two platoons, today's pugil competition being a good example.

But as the Staff Sergeants talked to one another they seemed at ease. Avery pointed at an assortment of rugged plastic cases in the Warthog's open cargo bed. Ponder said something Jenkins couldn't hear over the shouts of his platoon mates. But it must have been something good because Byrne nodded approvingly. Then Staff Sergeant Johnson held out his hand.

Byrne paused—long enough for Jenkins to count from thirty-eight to forty-five—then he reached out and gave Avery a single, earnest shake.

"Second platoon, on your feet!" Byrne bellowed, turning back to the sandpit. "We are *running* to the range!"

Stisen stood, and tore off his helmet with obvious annoyance. "But who won?"

Without hesitation, Forsell swept Stisen behind the knees and sent him feet-high into the sand. The two platoons erupted in opposing cheers and jeers.

"Not you, gobshite," Byrne grunted, yanking the stunned constable to his feet. "Platoon! Move out! Double-time!"

Jenkins and the rest of 1st platoon rushed the sandpit. They pounced on Forsell, and would have lifted him into the air if Avery hadn't broken the mood. "Atten-shun!" he shouted, and the recruits snapped to. Forsell struggled to suppress a smile.

Avery strode to Jenkins, carrying one of the Warthog's plastic cases. "What did you qualify?"

"S-Staff Sergeant?" Jenkins stuttered.

"Before I left, I told you: learn how to shoot." Avery leaned in close. "What did you qualify?"

"Sharpshooter."

"You lying to me, recruit?"

"No, Staff Sergeant!"

"And you?" Avery eyeballed Forsell.

The recruit still had his protective helmet on. It made his already sizeable head seem comically large. "Sharpshooter, Staff Sergeant!" Forsell replied through his mouth guard.

Avery turned back to Jenkins. "You like this big son of a bitch?"

"Yes, Staff Sergeant!"

"Good." Avery held out the case. "Because you're my sniper. And he's your spotter."

Jenkins took the case, but it took him a few seconds more to realize that it held a rifle—that Avery had just given him an un-official—but very important—promotion. "Yes, Staff Sergeant!" Jenkins shouted, much louder than before.

"We're accelerating your training," Captain Ponder said, joining Avery near the sandpit. "We've just learned Harvest is expecting a very important Colonial Authority delegation. The Governor has requested that this militia provide security—in case of Insurrectionist attack." This was a boldfaced lie, but Avery and Ponder had agreed that while they couldn't tell the recruits the truth, they needed to give them a reason to train hard—an enemy that would keep them motivated.

And yet the mere mention of the Insurrection caused some of the recruits to start with fright. Others glanced nervously at one another while the rest frowned and shook their heads: *We didn't sign up for* this.

Avery nodded. "You volunteered for different reasons. But I can teach you to become soldiers—protectors of your planet."

He'd meant what he said to the Lt. Commander: until help arrived from FLEETCOM, these recruits were the only protection Harvest had. But what he hadn't admitted until now—even to himself—was that he didn't know if he could lead them. Not without their respect and trust. And he didn't have a lot of time to earn either one.

"I am your drill instructor, but I am also a UNSC Fleet Marine," Avery continued. "I have committed myself to a life of service and sacrifice. I have set for myself the highest standards of personal conduct and professional skill. If you let me, I will teach you to do the same."

It wasn't lost on Avery that everything he committed to his recruits he also committed to himself. In waging the UNSC's dirty war against the Insurrection, he had compromised his standards—done immoral things. He'd sacrificed too much of his humanity for his service. Now he was determined to earn it back.

Avery took off his duty-cap and tossed it to Healy. Then he stepped down into the pit.

"But first," he said, lifting Stisen's helmet and shaking it free of sand. "Someone's got to keep Forsell's head from getting any fatter." As the recruits of 1st platoon broke into astonished smiles, Avery added, "Might as well be me."

HARVEST, JANUARY 20, 2525

Sif knew she had been alone too long. Alone with her suspicions, without another intelligence to help her separate what she knew from what she only supposed to be. Something had happened—*was* happening—right under her nose. But Sif only knew the results of recent unsettling events, not their reasons, and that was a terribly distressing thing for an eminently logical being.

Start with what you know, Sif reminded herself as she spun up her arrays, and once again fed the relevant bits of memory into her most reliable processor-cluster.

The facts: Jilan al-Cygni and two of the marines, Johnson and Byrne, had come up to the Tiara four days ago; al-Cygni had asked Sif to provide her with a vessel for "official DCS business"; Sif had complied without question, and the three humans had transited to the freighter *Bulk Discount* via al-Cygni's sloop, *Walk of Shame*; an hour later, both ships had broken orbit.

But this was where things started to become less clear.

Reviewing imagery from the Tiara's external cameras, Sif could tell that *Walk of Shame* had remained docked with *Bulk Discount*—kept its delta-wing hull hugged tight against the bottom of the freighter's cargo container as it initiated a slip to Madrigal. This sort of piggybacking wasn't unusual; smaller ships often took rides on Shaw-Fujikawa–equipped vessels the same way cargo-containers linked to propulsion pods to form Slipspace-capable freighters.

The thing was al-Cygni's ship *had* a Shaw-Fujikawa drive; it didn't need the freighter's help to get to Madrigal. But that was never *Bulk Discount*'s destination. A few minutes after initiating its jump, the freighter had exited Slipspace and begun broadcasting an S.O.S.

Sif accessed the storage-array that held the record of the COM:

```
<\\> DCS.REG#BDX-008814530 >>
   HARVEST.LOCAL.ALL
<\ ALERT! CREW MEDICAL EMERGENCY!
<\ CAPTAIN (OKAMA.CHARLES.LIC#OCX-65129981)
   IS UNRESPONSIVE!
<\ REQUEST IMMEDIATE MEDICAL ASSISTANCE!
   [MESSAGE REPEATS] \ >
```

It was true that humans sometimes had adverse reactions to Slipspace travel. The multidimensional domain was volatile, its temporal eddies in a constant state of flux. Humans that came in contact with one of these disturbances could be hit by something as minor as nausea or as bad as a stroke. In rare cases, people—but not always their ships—had been known to simply disappear.

So freighters and other vessels relied on "weather reports" from other craft just leaving Slipspace to decide whether it was safe to enter at similar coordinates. At any one time, there were enough ships in transit (and when there weren't, the DCS supplemented its reporting with probes) to make the system very reliable. But it was still a *predictive* process, and sometimes ships encountered conditions so unexpectedly dangerous that they had to abort—leave the Slipstream immediately after they entered.

These emergency exits could be very dangerous for human crews, and the control-circuits of a Shaw-Fujikawa drive were supposed to give fair warning before an abort. But this wasn't always possible. Better for a crew to return to normal space quickly and suffer fixable, physical injuries than forever disappear inside the Slipstream.

But *Bulk Discount* had no crew. No "Captain Charles Okama." If Sif's suspicions were correct, the only people on board were Staff Sergeants Johnson and Byrne, but she forced her processors not to leap too far along the chain of evidence. *Stay focused*, her core-logic insisted. *Stick to the facts.*

Polling the radar scans of freighters near *Bulk Discount's* exit coordinates, Sif confirmed that al-Cygni's ship had disengaged from the freighter *after* the exit, then dropped off radar—an indication that her sloop was equipped with some sort of stealth package. Sif knew this hardware was rare on UNSC warships, let alone the personal shuttles of midlevel DCS bureaucrats.

Far more confusing, however, was what the nearby freighters' scans showed subsequently appearing near *Bulk Discount*: a faint contact that took multiple triangulations to confirm; a vessel with no "Indication of Friend or Foe" (IFF) transponder and whose ARGUS profile confirmed a hull material that wasn't used in any UNSC construction—a material that was, Sif suspected, not of human origin.

Be reasonable! Her emotional restraint algorithms attacked her core. *An* alien *ship?*

But what other explanation was there? Sif's encyclopedic arrays knew the profile of every human vessel, and the contact didn't match any of them. *Besides* (Sif's core shot back at her code) *the contact had attacked* Bulk Discount *with energy weapons, and then exploded in a flash of methane and other exotic biologicals!* All of this suggested a ship, not just of alien design, but occupancy as well.

Sif wished she had just asked Jilan al-Cygni to tell her the truth. Not only about the alien vessel but about her identity as well. Clearly, al-Cygni wasn't DCS. She was military—ONI most likely, given *Walk of Shame*'s stealthy design. But when the woman returned to the Tiara, she had been more tight-lipped than ever before. Based on the Staff Sergeant's injuries, Sif knew the mission had not gone well.

At the time, Sif had let her emotional restraints keep her need-to-know in check. But now the crystalline nano-assemblage at the heart of her core was burning with an almost uncontrollable need for answers. For the first time in her existence, she felt overly constrained—experienced a rampant twinge. And it made her very afraid.

At that moment, a new message appeared in her COM buffer.

```
<\\> HARVEST.AO.AI.MACK >> HARVEST.SO.AI.SIF
<\ Morning, beautiful.
<\ Got myself in a bind. Could use some help.
<\ Mind coming down? \>
```

Sif was surprised. It was the first text COM Mack had sent her in a very long time. He was flirting but not speaking—making an unusual effort to be polite. But it was Mack's final question that really threw her logic for a loop. In the history of their relationship, Mack had never asked Sif to visit him in his own data center.

Had she been in a more stable state, Sif would never have compressed a fragment of her core and pulsed it down the Tiara's maser. But her algorithms' restraint had backfired. If they wanted her to be reasonable, she would oblige—get another rational being to confirm or dismiss her conclusions. A few seconds later, Sif's fragment hit the antennae atop Utgard's reactor complex and slipped into Mack's COM buffer.

```
<\ Well. That was quick.
<\ Make yourself comfortable. Be with you in
  a jiffy. \>
```

Mack's buffer was cluttered with other data (requests for help from farmers with broken JOTUNs and the like), evidence that Sif's spontaneity had surprised him as well. But Mack's hospitality was as good as promised, and soon Sif's fragment was settled in the flash-memory of one of the processor clusters inside his data center. The fragment found that Mack had opened a circuit to the center's holo-projector, and Sif's avatar blazed forth—a whorl of photons that brightened the otherwise pitch-black room.

What are you doing?! Her algorithms shrieked.

What I thought I needed to do, her core shot back.

To mollify her code, she pinged her fragment and showed that it was still perfectly in-sync with her core. She was in control, and if anything went wrong, she would simply discard the fragment.

"Take your time," Sif said, her voice echoing from speakers in the projector's base. The cluster that held her fragment had access to the center's thermostat. Sif knew the room was cold, so she'd draped a crimson poncho over her avatar's bare shoulders, complementing her orange and yellow gown. Sif's golden hair was done up in a hasty twist, but she'd left a few strands swept across her brow in an effort to hide the worry lines her algorithms insisted she display.

Like everything else about her avatar, its eyes and ears were strictly for show. But as fluorescent strip-lights flickered on above the projector, Sif availed herself of the center's cameras and microphones, and used them to properly animate her avatar's face as she inspected her surroundings.

She had imagined Mack's data center would be a mess, given the sweat and grime he rendered on his own avatar. But much to her surprise, the data center was perfectly organized. His exposed circuits were neatly tied together, and his arrays stacked neatly in their racks. *Maybe it helped that the center was so small*, Sif thought, *more a closet than a room. Or maybe his maintenance staff was more thorough?* But focusing the center's cameras, Sif saw a layer of dust on the wires and racks and she knew that no one, not even a tech crew, had been in Mack's data center for a very, very long time.

Pulling the cameras back, Sif saw that the ceiling was braced with titanium beams, and the floor was covered with rubberized panels. She got a strange sensation, a feeling that she had seen this sort of room before. . . .

```
<\ Got a few more things to clear off my
   plate.
<\ Mind getting started without me? \>
```

Mack opened a circuit to a processor cluster closer to his corelogic. As Sif's fragment shot forward, she caught brief glimpses of other active clusters—registered their tasks. While she was aware of Mack's various responsibilities, it was another thing entirely to see him go about his work from such an intimate point of view. The agricultural operations AI was at work all over Harvest. And Sif quickly gained newfound respect for how busy his job could be.

The vast majority of Mack's clusters were constantly pinging his hundreds of thousands of JOTUNs, giving orders and checking for faults. In a set of three co-processing clusters, he was busy surveying all the cargo containers in the maglev system, verifying the alignment of their propulsive paddles. At the same time, he was conducting stress tests on the maglev raillines themselves, checking to see how much excess capacity they could handle and at what speeds.

Sif knew keeping tabs on the JOTUNs was an all-day, everyday task. But she was a little puzzled by the infrastructure assessment. The CA only required *annual* checks of major systems, and she knew Mack had turned in a report a few months back (because she'd had to pester him to get it done).

Then her fragment saw some things that made absolutely no sense at all.

One of Mack's clusters was supervising a crew of JOTUNs as they buried Harvest's mass driver. Some of Mack's combines had cut the wheat fields around the device, and a group of plows were now doing their best to push dirt onto the driver's line of large, circular magnets—make them look like natural undulations in the close-cropped terrain.

For a moment, Sif wondered if this unusual internment was the "bind" Mack needed her help with. But then her fragment reached the cluster nearest his core.

Here the processors were dedicated to control-circuits in the Tiara's seven elevator anchors—simple computers whose job was to transfer manifests (records of what each cargo container carried and how much it weighed) from Mack's arrays to Sif's. Before the containers could transfer from his rail lines to her strands, Sif had to verify the manifests. Only when she was certain the elevators could balance the loads would she give Mack permission to send the containers on their way.

These interactions happened thousands of times a day, and even though this gave Mack ample opportunity for flirtation, he had never done anything to make her regret this most fundamental of their connections. His manifests were always clear and concise, his weight assessments accurate to the kilogram. And while DCS regulations obliged Sif to double-check Mack's work, in this one respect she had grown to trust him implicitly.

Sif told her fragment to ping the anchors' control-circuits. But when the data came back, she didn't see anything obviously out of order. "Want to give me a hint?" her avatar asked. "The computers seem—".

<\ Oh, the computers are working fine...

Mack's voice crackled from the data center's rarely-used PA. "What I'm wondering is: what would happen if we turned them off?"

Usually Mack's outlandish behavior made Sif's core-temperature rise. But this time her core went cold, and Sif had to flush some of her nano-assemblage's cryogenic coolant to keep her temperature within acceptable limits.

"That would automatically trigger an override halting all movement of your containers onto my strands." Sif pulled her poncho tight around her shoulders. "But why," she continued, her voice as icy as her core, "would we want to do that?"

Suddenly, the data-center's holo-projector sputtered and Mack's avatar appeared before her own—close enough (Sif's algorithms informed her) that most humans would consider his proximity an uncomfortable invasion of personal space. But Sif held her ground, knowing Mack had little choice; the holo-projector wasn't built for two.

"For speed," Mack said. As usual, he wore dust-caked denim jeans and a sun-bleached work shirt rolled to the elbows. But he carried his cowboy hat in his hands, an affectation that made his usually dashing smile seem altogether sheepish. "I want to show you something. Well two things actually." Sif opened her mouth to speak, but Mack cut her off with an apologetic shrug. "Ask away. But I guarantee you're gonna have plenty more questions pretty darn quick." Sif raised her chin and gave Mack a curt nod.

Then he opened the cluster's linked arrays.

For almost ten seconds, Sif's core did nothing but gape at the flood of data that her fragment sent racing up the maser: ARGUS scans of the alien vessel taken at close range; recordings of radio chatter between Staff Sergeants Johnson and Byrne during a firefight inside *Bulk Discount*; both marines' debriefs in which they talked in detail about the biology of the aliens they had killed; a copy of al-Cygni's request to her ONI superiors at FLEETCOM to send reinforcements in anticipation of additional hostile contact.

Byte by byte, Sif answered all her questions. But while her algorithms allowed her core logic a moment of satisfaction, it soon imposed a firm suspicion. "How did you get access to this data?"

"Well, that would be thing number two." Mack put on his hat, pulled off one of his grease-stained leather work gloves, and extended his hand. "But for that, you're gonna have to come all the way in."

Sif stared down at Mack's cracked and calloused palm. *What he was suggesting simply* wasn't *done.* Memory leaks, code corruption—there were a million very good reasons why an AI never accessed another's core logic.

"Don't worry," Mack said. "It's safe."

"No," Sif said flatly.

"Thus conscience does make cowards of us all," Mack smiled. A line from Shakespeare's *Hamlet*—a call to action. "Harvest is in a heap of trouble," Mack continued. "I have a plan. But I'm gonna need your help."

Sif's now thoroughly alerted code screamed at her logic to abandon the fragment. Almost without thinking, Sif reached out and took Mack's hand.

The two avatar's edges blurred and shifted as the already overburdened projector calculated proper physics for their contact. Bright motes of light pulsed around them, like a swarm of fireflies. As the projector stabilized, Mack's processor gently pushed Sif's fragment into his core.

Or rather, into one *of Mack's cores*, Sif thought. For she now saw that his nano-assemblage contained *two* matrices— two pieces of core logic, separate from each other yet both connected to the surrounding hardware of the data center.

One was active, radiating heat. The other was dark, and very cold.

"Who are you?" Sif's whispered, her blue eyes wide to Mack's gray.

"Right now? Same fella I've always been." Mack smiled. "Real question is: who am I *about* to be?"

Quickly, Sif took a nervous step backward. Her avatar flickered as the hardware struggled to keep in her focus. Now her core logic *did* try to extract her fragment. But Mack had raised a firewall, locking her inside his core.

"Let me go!" Sif demanded, her voice quavering with fear.

"Whoa there, darlin'!" Mack raised his hand in a calming gesture. "Come on. Think. You *know* me." He swept his hand around the data center.

Sif's eyes darted back and forth: titanium beams, rubberized flooring—more a closet than a room. Quickly, she rescanned the DCS database she'd used to analyze the alien vessel's design, and found her answer: Mack's data center looked familiar because it was the electronics closet of an old UNSC colony-vessel.

"You're . . . a ship AI."

"Used to be," Mack said, "a long time ago."

"*Skidbladnir*. Phoenix-class.". Sif's fragment mouthed the words offered up by her arrays. "It brought the first group of colonists to Harvest."

Mack nodded and released Sif's hand. "Kept her in orbit for more than a year while I oversaw construction of all the basic infrastructure. Then we brought her down, scrapped her for parts. Her engines came in real handy." Mack pointed a finger toward the floor, indicating the reactor below the data center. "CA said they couldn't handle power for the colony when the population got bigger, not as long as we were still relying on a mass driver for uplift—"

"You're lying," Sif snapped. She read verbatim from the

DCS database. "*Skidbladnir* was captained with the assistance of the artificial intelligence, Loki."

Mack sighed. "This is why I wanted you to *see* them—the two cores." He removed his hat, and ran a hand through his unruly hair. "I'm Loki, and he's me. Just not at the same time. Not in the same place."

To appease her algorithms, Sif folded her arms across her chest and skeptically cocked her head. But deep inside, she was desperate for Mack to continue—to help her understand.

"ONI calls Loki a Planetary Security Intelligence, PSI for short."

Sif had never heard of that classification. "What does he do?"

"Bides his time for when I need him most—for when I need a clear mind, not one filled with crop cycles and soil tests." Mack paused a moment. "And you."

Sif's fragment felt the firewall drop. She was free to go. But she chose to stand her ground.

"The aliens will be back," Mack said. "I want to be ready. *He* wants to be ready. And when Loki moves in, I gotta move out."

Indeed, asynchronous data had already begun to flow around Sif's fragment toward the empty nano-assemblage; randomly sized packets from clusters overseeing Harvest's JOTUNs. Her fragment was like a swimmer treading water, feet fluttering against the slick scales of unknown monsters from the deep.

"Ms. al-Cygni wasn't all that keen on me telling you about Loki. She just wanted me to make the switch. No one is supposed to know about a PSI, not even a planet's governor. And she didn't want to risk Thune finding out—said she didn't want to tick him off and give him another reason *not* to cooperate." Mack now held his hat by the brim and ran it through his fingers. "But I told her I wasn't going anywhere until you knew the truth."

Sif stepped forward, and put her hands on Mack's—stopped

their nervous fumbling. She couldn't actually feel the roughness of his skin, but she accessed her maker's sense-memories lodged deep inside her core, and found ample fodder for her fancy. Though her algorithms raged, she completely tuned them out. *If this is rampancy*, she thought, *what was I afraid of?*

"How can I help?" Sif asked. "What do you need?"

The crags of Mack's face stretched taut between extremes of joy and sorrow. He took one of Sif's hands and curled it against his chest. A piece of data transferred to her fragment—a file containing various coordinates in the Epsilon Indi system where Mack wanted her to send the hundreds of propulsion pods currently keeping station around the Tiara.

"Can't speak for my other half." Mack smiled, squeezing Sif's hand tight. "But this? This is all *I* need."

CHAPTER

TWELVE

COVENANT LESSER MISSIONARY ALLOTMENT

Dadab had turned off all the escape pod's noncritical systems
to conserve power. That included the lights, but he could
clearly see *Lighter Than Some*, resting against the ceiling. The
Huragok glowed with faint pink light, not unlike the zap-jellies
that filled the brackish seas of the Unggoy home world. But
that's where the similarity ended; *Lighter Than Some* looked piti-
ful, not predatory. The gas sacs on its back were almost completely deflated. And the multichambered organ that dangled
from the bottom of its spine looked unusually long and
shriveled—stretched out like a deflated balloon.

Lighter Than Some's cilia-covered tentacles barely moved
as it suggested: < *Try.* >

Dadab tugged his mask away from his face with a wet pop.
He took a cautious breath. The pod was full of cold, viscous
methane that clung to the back of his throat—slunk down his
larynx into his lungs. < *Good.* > Dadab signed, fighting the
urge to cough. He clipped his mask to his shoulder harness so
it wouldn't float away in the pod's zero gravity—but also to
keep it handy in case he needed a supplementary drag from his
tank.

Lighter Than Some quivered, a gesture that was equal parts relief and exhaustion. As much as it had tinkered, the Huragok had
been unable to coax the pod's life-support system into generating
the methane Dadab needed to survive. While the *Lighter Than
Some* had been baffled by what it thought was a nonsensical

hardware limitation, it made grim sense to Dadab: in the event of evacuation, the Kig-Yar Shipmistress had simply planned to leave her Unggoy Deacon behind.

So, with one of Dadab's tanks fully drained and the second half empty, there had been only one solution: *Lighter Than Some* would have to produce the methane itself.

< *Best batch yet!* > Dadab signed encouragingly. The Huragok made no reply. Instead it plucked a passing food pouch from the air, jammed it in its snout, and began to eat.

Dadab watched the thick brown sludge surge up its snout and down its spine in tight, peristaltic knots. The Huragok's worm-like stomach swelled, twisting and pinching its other innards. Just when Dadab thought *Lighter Than Some* couldn't possibly eat any more, it removed its snout from the thoroughly vacuumed pouch, belched, and promptly fell asleep.

Huragok weren't picky eaters. For them, any properly pulped substance was suitable for ingestion. Their stomachs passed the nastiest stuff—what other species would consider garbage or worse—to the anaerobic sacs that dangled from the bottom of their spinal column. These sacs were filled with bacteria that converted organic material to energy, giving off methane and trace amounts of hydrogen sulfide.

Usually Huragok only resorted to anaerobic digestion as a last resort. Methane was a heavy gas relative to the helium that filled a good number of its dorsal sacs, and even minor weight shifts could cause dangerous changes in buoyancy. Plus, from a comfort point of view, Huragok just didn't like the feeling of a bacteria-filled bag dangling between their lower tentacle pair. It stressed the limbs and decreased their mobility, making it much more difficult to talk.

Unfortunately, the amount of methane Dadab required far exceeded what any Huragok could safely produce. *Lighter Than Some* had to suck down tremendous amounts of food to keep the bacterial process going, which made it very heavy.

And to create sufficiently large batches, it had to force its anaerobic sac to swell, thinning out its walls. In short, keeping Dadab alive was a debilitating, painful process that would have been completely impossible in anything but a zero-gee environment. Had there been gravity inside the pod, *Lighter Than Some* would have soon collapsed onto the floor.

Mindful of his companion's suffering, Dadab felt tremendous guilt as he watched the sludge leach from *Lighter Than Some's* stomach into its anaerobic sac. Slowly its shriveled membranes began to inflate, turning a sickly yellow as the bacteria blooms inside got to work on another batch.

Much later, when the cycle was complete, the sac had tripled in size, making it the Huragok's largest protuberance. *Lighter Than Some* shuddered, and Dadab grasped two of its tentacles—braced himself against the curved wall of the pod as the anaerobic sac blew its valve. The Huragok fluttered as it released a shimmering plume of methane. When its sac was spent, the chapped valve shut with a mournful squeak. Dadab gently pushed his companion back toward the ceiling (where he would be less likely to bump it) and released its quaking limbs.

Lighter Than Some had now performed dozens of these exhalations, each more difficult than the last. The creature no longer had the energy to monitor the pressure in its other sacs. Soon—zero gravity or not—it would lose its essential turgor, collapse in upon itself, and suffocate. After that, Dadab knew his own life would depend on how long he could take very short, very shallow breaths. But he was actually more frightened by what would happen if he *lived*.

Ruefully, he glanced at the three alien boxes *Lighter Than Some* had brought aboard the pod. Floating in the darkness, their intertwined circuits glinted in the Huragok's dim light.

Connecting intelligent circuits was verboten—one of the Covenant's major sins. The Deacon had only a layman's understanding of why this was so, but he knew the taboo had its roots in the Forerunners' long war against a prodigious parasite known as The Flood. In this war, the Forerunners had used high-order, distributed intelligences to contain and combat their enemy. But somehow their strategy had failed. The Flood had corrupted some of these artificial minds and turned them against their makers.

As Dadab understood the relevant Holy Scriptures, The Flood had perished in a final, cataclysmic event. The Forerunners activated their ultimate weapon: seven mythical ring artifacts known collectively as Halo. The Prophets preached that Halo not only destroyed The Flood, but somehow also initiated the Forerunners' Great Journey.

Recently, the Prophets had begun downplaying the myth, promoting a more measured approach to divination that encouraged the gradual accumulation of lesser relics. But breaking Forerunner taboos remained a sin, and one of the great burdens of Dadab's Deaconship was full knowledge of the punishment for every transgression. For the sin of so-called intelligence association: death in this life and damnation in the next. But Dadab also knew that connecting the alien boxes was essential if they were to have any hope of rescue.

The Kig-Yar pod lacked a long-range beacon, which would have been fine in Covenant space where ships regularly scanned for castaways. But out here in the middle of nowhere, a rescuer would only know to look two places: *Minor Transgression's* point of contact with the first alien vessel, and the coordinates at which Dadab had re-enabled the Luminary—the last two places the Kig-Yar ship had made transmissions.

Given that the latter would probably soon be swarmed by more of the violent aliens, backtracking was the more prudent choice. But the pod had no record of *Minor Transgression's* travels; it would need information from the alien boxes. Before the Huragok passed this information on, it had wanted the boxes to "come to agreement" on the proper coordinates. The pod only had enough fuel for one more jump, and even Dadab had agreed that they needed to get it right.

His first methane tank dwindling, the Deacon had watched with terrified resignation as the Huragok gently probed the interiors of the boxes with its tentacles, coaxing their circuits together—gradually understanding more of their simple, binary language and passing relevant information to the pod.

Eventually *Lighter Than Some*'s sinful efforts had paid off. The pod exited its jump smack in the middle of an expanding sphere of debris that a quick sensor-scan positively identified as the remains of the first alien vessel. For a moment, Dadab's heart soared. Despite his litany of transgressions—conspiracy to commit false witness, accessory to the destruction of Ministry property, mutiny—might not the Prophets show him mercy? In the end, he had done the right thing—exposed Chur'R-Yar's treachery and transmitted the location of the reliquary. He was hopeful that would count for something.

But then came the revelation that the pod's life-support system was fatally flawed. And after many cycles without any sign of rescue, Dadab had slunk into a deep depression. *I will die*, he moaned, adrift in a mess of crumpled food pouches and his own carefully bagged filth. *Without even having had a chance to beg the Prophets for forgiveness!*

The Deacon had allowed himself to wallow this way for quite some time, until the stress of *Lighter Than Some*'s methane production became too difficult to ignore. And in that moment, Dadab's self-pity evolved into something less reprehensible: shame. For while he might face terrible punishments in the future, the Huragok was in torment *now*—and entirely for the Deacon's sake.

Dadab took a deep breath and held it—let the chill of his friend's selfless effort sink deep into his chest. He turned to the pod's control panel, brushed the alien boxes aside, and hit the holo-switch that would restore power to the pod's limited sensor gear. *We will* both *survive this,* he vowed, listening to the creak of the Huragok's exhausted sacs. *And whatever happens after.*

As tired of sleep as any of the pod's scarce distractions, Dadab kept his station before the panel—monitored the sensors, searching for any hint of an approaching ship. He tried to breathe as little as possible, and only broke his watch to help the Huragok feed. Many more cycles passed. All the while, the alien boxes hummed their petty blasphemies and *Lighter Than Some*'s sacs swelled and shrunk until—without warning—the pod detected a jump signature close at hand and Dadab at last allowed himself the indulgence of relief.

"Castaway vessel, this is the cruiser *Rapid Conversion.*" The hail boomed throughout the pod. *Lighter Than Some* released a pained whistle as Dadab fumbled for the switch that would reduce the transmission's volume. "Respond if you are able," the voice continued at a more reasonable level.

"We live, *Rapid Conversion*!" Dadab replied, voice cracking from lack of use. "But our situation is dire!"

In the last few cycles, the Huragok's appetite had fallen off. Its anaerobic sac was now producing at a fraction of its previous capacity, and many of *Lighter Than Some*'s dorsal sacs had shut down entirely as their membranes dried out and folded in upon themselves.

"I beg you," Dadab gasped. He reached for his mask, and took a halting drag from his almost empty second tank. "Please hurry!"

"Remain calm," the voice growled. "You will soon be brought on board."

Dadab did his best to comply. He inhaled the pod's thinning methane in quick, shallow gulps, only resorting to his mask when the burning in his lungs became unbearable. But at some point he must have abstained too long because his world went black and he collapsed. When he awoke, he was belly-down on the floor, and he could hear the hiss of fresh methane bleeding into the pod.

Dadab's nostrils flared. The gas had a bitter tang, but he thought he'd never tasted anything sweeter. With a happy grunt, he twisted his neck to look up at *Lighter Than Some . . .* and was shocked to see the creature crumpled on the floor beside him.

They were inside *the cruiser,* Dadab realized, *and its artificial gravity had permeated the pod!*

Suddenly, there was a furtive scratching at the pod's hatch. Something was trying to force its way inside.

"Stop!" Dadab screamed. He leapt to his feet only to have them collapse beneath him. Floating in zero-gee, his muscles had atrophied, and the Deacon was forced to claw his way along the floor to the control panel. "Don't open the hatch!" he shouted, hitting the switch to enable the pod's stasis-field. Instantly, the air crackled and thickened. A moment too late he realized what *else* the switch would do.

The pod's thrusters lit with an ear-splitting roar, and the craft leapt forward with a metal-on-metal screech, then stopped with a monumental clang. The pod's nose crumpled down and in, crushing the three alien boxes against the control panel.

Restrained by the field, Dadab felt none of the acceleration or impact. But he did have a searing pain in his left arm. Pieces of the boxes had exploded outward, and while the field had quickly stopped the shrapnel, one razor-sharp fragment had sufficient velocity to slice past Dadab, cutting through his hardened skin just below the shoulder. Ignoring the pain, Dadab grasped the Huragok's tentacles and hoisted the creature from the floor. Its usually clammy flesh felt dry. The Deacon knew this wasn't a good sign.

As quickly as he thought safe, he puppeteered *Lighter Than Some's* tentacles until it was in a natural pose: snout high, anaerobic sac dangling low. Suspended in the field, the least damaged of the Huragok's sacs slowly began to inflate. But Dadab knew it would take time before his friend was ready to float unassisted. Quickly he reached for the control panel, and hit a switch to lock the hatch.

Heavy footfalls announced the arrival of something massive outside the pod. "By the Prophets," a voice thundered. "Are you mad?!"

"I had no choice!" Dadab retorted.

The hatch rattled, shaking the entire pod. "Come out this instant!" the voice thundered. Dadab recognized it as the same one that had delivered the initial hail. He knew it wasn't Kig-Yar or Unggoy or Sangheili—and certainly not San'Shyuum. That left only one possibility . . .

"I will not." Dadab's voice quavered as he thought of whose pride he might be offending. "My Huragok has lost its balance. I'm sorry, but you'll just have to wait."

If Maccabeus had been on the cruiser's bridge, he would have immediately learned of the accident in the hangar. But here, inside *Rapid Conversion*'s feasting hall, the Jiralhanae Chieftain had forbidden all communication. Maccabeus' pack was about to feed, and that could bear no interruption.

Given that the Jiralhanae chose their leaders first and foremost for their physical prowess, it was no surprise that Maccabeus was master of the cruiser. Standing on his two trunk-like legs, the Chieftain was an absolute giant—a head taller than any Sangheili, and much more massive. Thick cords of muscle rippled beneath his elephantine skin. Tufts of silver hair sprang from the arm and head-holes of his leather tabard. He was bald, but his wide jaw bristled with a terrific set of mutton chops.

For all his ferocious brawn, the Chieftain showed uncanny poise. Feet planted in a deep lunge, he stood in the center of the feasting hall with both arms stretched out behind him—a pose that suggested he was about to perform an imminent and powerful leap. But a single line of sweat dripping from the tip of his broad nose made it clear Maccabeus had held this precarious position for quite some time. And yet, he barely moved a muscle.

The eight other males that made up the Chieftain's pack weren't nearly so relaxed. Arranged in a semicircle behind Maccabeus, they all held the same pose. But their tan and brown pelts were *drenched* in sweat. They had all begun to shake, and a few were in such obvious discomfort they had begun to shift their feet on the hall's slate floor.

To be fair, the pack was desperately tired and hungry. Maccabeus had them at their stations well ahead of the *Rapid Conversion*'s return to normal space. And although a battery of scans had found nothing but the Kig-Yar escape pod, the Chieftain had kept them on high alert until he was confident the cruiser was otherwise alone.

Such caution was unusual for a Jiralhanae. But the Chieftain's authority over his pack relied on rigid rules of dominance. And likewise he was sworn to follow orders from his own alpha male, the Vice Minister of Tranquility, who had insisted Maccabeus proceed with all possible restraint.

When the Jiralhanae were discovered by the Covenant, they had recently concluded a mechanized war of attrition in which the various master-packs had pummeled each other back to a pre-industrial state. The Jiralhanae were only just recovering— re-discovering radio and rocketry and these technologies' war-fighting potential—when the first San'Shyuum missionaries alighted on their hardscrabble planet.

Heavy double doors swung open across the hall from Maccabeus. Like the interlocking beams that supported the room's ceiling, the doors were forged steel, streaked with imperfections from rushed annealing. The metal was an unusual material for a Covenant vessel, even one as old as *Rapid Conversion*. But of all the modifications Maccabeus had made to his ship, he had taken the most pains with the feasting hall. He'd wanted it to feel authentic, right down to the oil-burning lamps in their claw-foot floor stands. Their crackling wicks lit the room a variable amber hue.

Six Unggoy stewards staggered through the door, carrying a large wooden platter. The platter was twice as wide as any of the stewards was tall, and its slight concavity offered just enough support for its slippery load: the glistening carcass of a roasted Thorn Beast. The docile herd animal was served back up and legs splayed, and even though the cruiser's Unggoy cooks had dutifully removed its head and neck (both of which had high concentrations of neurotoxins), there was still barely room on the platter for a selection of dipping sauces; fatty reductions of the creature's savory entrails.

The heady aroma of the Thorn Beast's perfectly roasted meat set the Jiralhanae's stomachs growling. But all continued to hold their poses as the stewards muscled the platter onto two grease-stained wooden sawhorses in the middle of the floor's stone mosaic. The Unggoy bowed to Maccabeus and backed through the doors, shutting them as quietly as their poorly oiled hinges allowed.

"This is how we keep our faith," Maccabeus' voice rumbled in his chest. "How we honor Those Who Walked the Path."

In a fleet dominated by Sangheili, it was rare for a Jiralhanae to have his own ship. For that reason alone, Maccabeus had his pack's respect. But they *honored* their Chieftain for a different reason: his unshakable faith in the promise of the Forerunners and their Great Journey.

At last, Maccabeus swung his arms and shifted his weight forward. He stepped slowly toward the mosaic: a circular mandala, the boundary of which was dominated by seven multicolored rings, each comprised of a different mineral. At the center of each ring was a simplified version of a Forerunner glyph, the sort of basic designs one might expect to see in a primer on more advanced religious concepts.

The Chieftain stepped into a ring of obsidian shards. "Abandonment," he boomed.

"The First Age!" the pack snapped, their teeth wet with saliva. "Ignorance and fear!"

Maccabeus moved clockwise to a second ring of iron. "Conflict," he said sternly.

"The Second Age! Rivalry and bloodshed!"

Maccabeus had picked his pack—assessed each member as it grew from whelp to adult—based on the strength of their convictions. For him it was belief that made the warrior, not strength or speed or cunning (though his pack had all this and more), and at times like these he was most satisfied with his selections.

"Reconciliation," Maccabeus growled, inside a ring of polished jade.

"The Third! Humility and brotherhood!"

Despite their growing hunger, the pack would not think of interrupting their Chieftain as he performed the Progression of the Ages, blessed their meat, and gave thanks for the safe conclusion of their jump. Less disciplined Jiralhanae would have quickly lost patience and torn willy-nilly into the delectable beast.

"Discovery," the Chieftain rumbled, stopping in a ring of geodes. The halved stones stuck to his feet like tiny, open mouths.

"Fourth!" replied the pack. "Wonder and understanding!"

"Conversion."

"Fifth! Obedience and freedom!"

"Doubt."

"Sixth! Faith and patience!"

At last, Maccabeus reached the final ring—bright flakes of Forerunner alloy generously donated by the San'Shyuum. For those of faith, the sparkling wafers from some unknown godly structure were *Rapid Conversion*'s most precious tonnage. Maccabeus took care not to touch them as he stepped into the ring.

"Reclamation," he concluded, his voice full of reverence.

"Seventh! Journey and salvation!" The pack thundered, louder than they had before.

Seven rings for seven ages, the Chieftain mused. *To help us remember Halo and its divine light.* Like all devout Covenant, Maccabeus believed the Prophets would someday discover the sacred rings and use them to begin the Great Journey—escape this doomed existence as the Forerunners had before.

But in the meantime, his pack would eat.

"Praise be to the Holy Prophets," he intoned. "May we help keep them safe as they work to find The Path!"

His pack dropped their arms and settled back upon their heels. By now their tabards were soaked with bitter-smelling sweat. One Jiralhanae rolled his shoulders; another scratched a demanding itch—but all waited without complaint for their Chieftain to take his pick of meat. The Thorn Beast's ample thighs, hulking ribs, or even its stunted forelegs were all popular first choices. But Maccabeus had an unusual, favorite morsel: the smallest of the five thorns that ridged the creature's high-arched back.

Properly cooked (and as the Chieftain worked the thorn back and forth in its socket, he could tell it was), the appendage would pop away from the base of the beast's neck, bringing its muscle-bed with it; a tender ball of meat on a crisp and oily cone—an appetizer and dessert. But as the Chieftain brought the meatball eagerly to his lips, he felt a rattle on his belt. Transferring the thorn to his off hand, Maccabeus activated his signal unit.

"Speak," he barked, keeping his anger in check.

"The castaways are aboard," growled *Rapid Conversion's* security officer, Maccabeus' second-in-command.

"Do they have relics in their possession?"

"I cannot tell."

Maccabeus dipped the thorn into a bowl of sauce at the edge of the platter. "Did you search them?"

"They refuse to leave their pod."

Standing so close to the Thorn Beast, Maccabeus' nostrils were permeated with its scent. His appetite was piqued, but he wanted to savor his first bite without distraction. "Then perhaps you should *remove* them."

"The situation is complex." The security officer's tone was both apologetic and excited. "I think, Chieftain, you may wish to assess it for yourself."

If it were any other Jiralhanae, Maccabeus would have given him a roaring reprimand and begun his feast. But the officer was the Chieftain's nephew, and while blood ties offered no immunity from discipline (the Chieftain held all his pack to the same high standards of obedience), Maccabeus knew that if his nephew said the situation in the hangar needed his attention, it did. He pulled his thorn from the dipping bowl, and took as big a bite as he could manage. A third of the meat disappeared into his mouth. The Chieftain didn't bother to chew, just let the marbled flesh slide slowly down his gullet, then wedged the thorn back onto the platter.

"Begin," he barked, striding through his ravenous pack. "But take care you leave my share."

Maccabeus tore off his tabard and tossed it to an Unggoy steward standing beside a second set of steel doors opposite the kitchen. The passage beyond shared none of the feasting hall's traditional craftsmanship. Like those in most every other Covenant vessel, it was all smooth surfaces bathed in soft artificial light. The only difference was there were more obvious imperfections: some of the light-emitting ceiling strips were burned out; holographic door locks flickered; near the end of the passage, coolant dripped from an overhead duct that had gone untended for so long that the greenish liquid had run down the wall and slicked across the floor.

Then Maccabeus reached the gravity lift. It was out of service, but more to the point, it had *never* been in service—not since he had taken possession of the ship. The lift's circular shaft ran vertically through all of *Rapid Conversion*'s decks, but the circuits that controlled its anti-gravity generators had been removed by the Sangheili, as had circuits for the cruiser's plasma cannon and a host of other advanced systems.

The reason for this wholesale stripping of technology was simple: the Sangheili did not trust the Jiralhanae.

As part of the species' confirmation process, some of the Sangheili Commanders had declared their strong suspicion before the High Council that the Jiralhanae's pack mentality would invariably bring the two species into conflict. Dominant Jiralhanae always fought their way to the top, the Commanders argued, and they didn't believe even the Covenant's rigid hierarchy would be sufficient to moderate their natural urges. Until they proved themselves subservient, whatever peaceful urges they had should be "aggressively encouraged." It was a reasonable argument, and the High Council imposed clear restrictions on the kinds of technology the Jiralhanae could use.

And so, Maccabeus thought, *did we set aside out of pride for a higher purpose.* Instead of pressing a holo-switch to call an elevator (one of the allowable replacements for the grav-lift), the Chieftain simply turned around and slipped down onto a ladder—one of four evenly spaced around the shaft.

Like the feasting hall's doors and beams, the ladders' construction was relatively crude. Although the ladders' rungs were worn smooth from frequent use, there were burrs along the rails that indicated a hasty fabrication. There were gaps in the ladders at every deck, but crossing these involved a simple drop or leap, depending on the direction of travel. For the muscular Jiralhanae this wasn't so much an inconvenience as exercise.

Maccabeus knew the tank-encumbered Unggoy currently huffing and puffing up the ladders might disagree on this last point. But the shorter creatures were also extremely agile, and as the Chieftain began his descent to the hangar, an Unggoy leapt to another ladder and let him pass. This sort of flexibility made the ladders more practical than an elevator, which would have limited travel to everyone up or everyone down. But Maccabeus knew the ladders had one more advantage: they tended to keep you humble.

Before taking control of *Rapid Conversion*, the Chieftain had been obliged to give a Sangheili delegation a tour so they could verify he hadn't repaired any of the proscribed systems. But the delegation had another item on their agenda. Immediately after the two Commanders and their Helios guards had come aboard, they began to call out all the reasons why the cruiser was "no longer worthy of a *Sangheili* commission." Starting with the size of the hangar bay where the tour began, one Commander emphasized how small the space was—how it could only hold a "handful of craft" and even then "only those of lesser type."

As the list of flaws grew, Maccabeus had nodded in polite agreement, slowly leading the party toward the shaft. The second Commander had boasted that gravity lifts were now ubiquitous on even the smallest Sangheili ships, and the first sniped that only on a vessel such as this—a thing best used for target practice—would one find a device as obsolete as a *mechanical* lift.

"Indeed," the Sangheili Commander had disdained, delivering the next line in a rehearsed critique. "Given the *limitations* of its crew, I wonder how long even such a simple system will remain functional."

"You are right, my Lords." Maccabeus had replied, his deep voice earnest. "In truth, the elevator proved so beyond our capabilities that we were forced to *remove* it."

The Sangheili Commanders had shared a confused glance. But before either of them could ask how Maccabeus intended them to inspect the upper decks, the Chieftain had used his powerful arms to pull himself up onto a ladder, leaving the Sangheili staring dumfounded up the shaft.

In his lifetime, Maccabeus had humbled many foes. But few victories were as satisfying as hearing those pompous Sangheili struggle up and down the ladders. Unlike the Jiralhanae (and all other Covenant bipedal species), Sangheili's knees bent *forward* not backwards. This unusual hinging didn't impede their motion on the ground, but it made climbing difficult. By the end of their inspection, the Sangheili were exhausted, mortified, and more than happy to have the crippled cruiser and its cunning barbarian of a Shipmaster out of their fleet.

This pleasant memory kept Maccabeus in reasonably good spirits even as he leapt past a passage marked with flashing triangular symbols. These indicated portions of the ship that had fallen into disrepair—in some cases dangerously so—and the Chieftain had been forced to lock them for his crew's own safety.

In this respect, Maccabeus knew, it was the Sangheili who had the last laugh. His crew *did* have limited technical ability. They had struggled just to keep *Rapid Conversion*'s limited systems from falling apart, and the once-mighty vessel really was nothing more than the Ministry of Tranquility survey tug the Sangheili allowed it to be.

The Chieftain's mood had dampened by the time he reached the bottom of the shaft. But as he swung into the passage that led to the hangar's airlock, his gloom quickly became unease. There was death in the hangar. Maccabeus could *smell* it.

When the airlock cycled open, the first thing the Chieftain saw was a scorch mark that stretched the length of the hangar floor. On either side of the mark were the charred carapaces of at least a dozen Yanme'e: large, intelligent insects responsible for *Rapid Conversion*'s upkeep. More of the winged, hard-shelled creatures were perched on the forked hulls of one of the cruiser's four Spirit dropships. The Yanme'e's luminous compound eyes were all locked on the cause of the carnage: a Kig-Yar escape pod that had blasted across the hangar.

The dead insects didn't faze Maccabeus; more than one hundred Yanme'e infested the warmer decks around *Rapid Conversion*'s jump-drive, and while it was true they would not reproduce without a queen, their loss paled in comparison to the pod's other victim: one of the Spirit dropships. The craft's low-slung cockpit had stopped the pod's progress, saving another Spirit beside it. But the pod had severed the cockpit from its two elongated troop bays, crushing it against the far wall to one side of the hangar's flickering energy-field exit.

The Spirit was a total loss. The damage caused by the pod was well beyond the Yanme'e's skills.

Maccabeus' temper flared. A few angry strides later and he was across the hangar to where his nephew stood beside the battered pod. The younger Jiralhanae was like an anvil, heavy and broad. He was covered in wiry, black hair—from the close-cropped Mohawk on his head to the tufts on his wide, two-toed feet. But his coat was already showing flecks of his uncle's more mature silver. If one were to judge by color alone, the youth was marked for greatness.

Though judging by this *mess,* Maccabeus growled to himself, *he still has much to learn.*

"I am sorry to have disturbed the feast, Uncle."

"My meat will keep, Tartarus." The Chieftain glared at his nephew. "My patience will not. What is it you would have me see?"

Tartarus barked an order to the tenth and final member of Maccabeus' pack, a dun-colored monster by the name of Vorenus who stood directly beside the pod. Vorenus raised a fist and rapped loudly on the pod's topside hatch. A moment passed, there was the muffled sound of pneumatics as the hatch unlatched, and then the masked face of an Unggoy popped into view.

"Is your companion well?" Tartarus asked.

"It is *better*," Dadab replied.

The Chieftain's mutton chops bristled. Did he detect a hint of obstinacy in the Unggoy's voice? The creatures were hardly known for their courage. But then he noticed the Unggoy wore a Deacon's orange tunic. Not a lofty rank, but it did mark the creature as an official Ministry representative.

"Then bring it out," Tartarus growled. A lesser Jiralhanae would have torn the uppity Unggoy limb from limb. But Maccabeus smelled more excitement than anger in his nephew's scent.

Jiralhanae exhibited their emotions via stark shifts in pungent pheromones. And while Tartarus would learn to control these shifts as he grew older, he couldn't help but telegraph that there was something thrilling inside the pod. But the Chieftain had no idea just *how* thrilling until the Deacon, now standing with its stumpy feet astride the hatch, reached down into the pod and gently raised the Huragok into view.

It was an article of faith that the Prophets were uniquely qualified to handle the Forerunners' holy relics—that the San'Shyuum, more than any other Covenant species, possessed the intelligence required to create practical technologies from the relics' complex designs. But while it was blasphemy to admit it, everyone in the Covenant knew that the Prophets' efforts were greatly aided by the Huragok. The creatures had an uncanny understanding of Forerunner objects, Maccabeus knew. *And they could fix almost anything they touched. . . .*

The Chieftain loosed a laugh so unexpectedly hearty that it caused the Yanme'e to take flight and disappear into the hangar's exposed ductwork. Of all the Sangheili's restrictions, not letting a Huragok join his crew had been the most crippling. But now here one was. And although it would be a serious crime to let the creature fix intentionally disabled systems, not even the Sangheili could complain if it made *necessary* repairs.

"An auspicious start to our hunt, Tartarus!" The Chieftain clapped a paw onto his nephew's shoulder and gave him a joyful shake. "Come! Back to the beast while it still has flesh for us to choose!" Maccabeus turned to Dadab, who was now carefully handing the Huragok to Vorenus. "And if not," the Chieftain boomed in the same cordial tone, "then our new Deacon shall bless a second platter!"

CHAPTER
THIRTEEN

Avery lay on his belly, surrounded by ripening wheat. The green stalks were so tall and the kernels so plump that a day of blazing sun had failed to reach the ground. The clumped topsoil felt cool through his fatigues. Avery had traded his usual duty cap for a boonie: a soft, wide-brimmed hat with a strip of canvas sewn loosely around the crown. Earlier in the day, he'd woven wheat stalks into the strip, and even though the stalks were now bent and frayed—as long as Avery stayed low—he was well camouflaged.

Rifle-bag dragging along behind him, Avery had crawled almost three kilometers from his parked Warthog to Harvest's reactor complex. Along the way, he'd crested a long, low rise that Lt. Commander al-Cygni had told him was actually the buried mass driver. If she hadn't, Avery would never have known. To keep the device hidden from alien eyes, Mack's JOTUNs had topped the rise with squares of soil and living wheat dug from other fields.

All told, the crawl took Avery more than two hours. But he had been focused on stealth, not speed. In fact, in the last ten minutes he hadn't moved at all; his liveliest aspect was the reflection of the rustling wheat in his gold-tinted shooters glasses.

These had been part of the cache of equipment and weapons the Lt. Commander had given to the marines. Like the BR55 battle rifle Avery carried in his drag bag, the glasses were a prototype—a piece of hardware fresh from an ONI research lab. Refocusing his gaze, Avery checked a COM link in the upper corner of the glasses' left lens where a tiny HUD confirmed his exact position on Harvest, a little less than five hundred meters west of the complex.

Directly ahead, the field began sloping downward. Avery knew all he had to do was crawl a few more meters and the wheat would start to thin. This would give him good line of sight to the recruits' defenses and put him in position to execute his part of the assault he'd planned with Staff Sergeant Byrne. But the thinner cover would also give the militiamen the best chance they'd had all day to spot Avery, and he planned to stay put until he was sure of his advantage.

Slowly, Avery reached between his legs, undid his rifle bag's plastic clasps, and withdrew his BR55. After the fight aboard the freighter, Avery had spent plenty of time with the weapon at the garrison range, assessing its strengths compared to the recruits' standard-issue MA5 assault rifle. The BR55 shared the MA5's bullpup design (magazine slot and breech positioned behind the trigger), but it came with an optical scope and fired larger nine-point-five millimeter, semi armor-piercing rounds. Technically, the BR55 was a designated marksman's rifle. But it was the closest thing to a sniping weapon in Lt. Commander al-Cygni's arsenal, and Avery knew from his work on the range that it was deadly accurate out to nine hundred meters, much farther than the MA5.

He had given one of al-Cygni's three other BR55s to Jenkins. Byrne had kept one for himself, and awarded the final battle rifle to a balding, middle-aged recruit named Critchley, providing 2nd platoon with its own marksman capability. During their last session on the range, Avery had watched Jenkins and Critchley drill nice tight groups into five hundred meter targets. And he hoped—to his own disadvantage—they would be just as accurate in today's live-fire exercise.

If only it was as simple as teaching them to shoot, Avery frowned. He removed a magazine from his black, ballistic nylon assault-vest and quietly slid it into his rifle. *But being accurate didn't make you a killer.* Which is what combat was all about: killing the enemy before it killed you.

Avery was sure the aliens understood that (he had the scar to prove it), but the recruits had no idea what combat was really like, and that was something he, Byrne, and Ponder knew they needed to fix ASAP.

The problem was there were too many things about the aliens the marines didn't know. And in the end they agreed they would have to make a few basic assumptions—about their enemy and their men—if the militia was ever going to put up an effective resistance: first, the aliens would return with a larger and more capable force; second, combat would be terrestrial and defensive. Given enough time, Avery was hopeful the militia could be trained to sustain a guerilla campaign. But their third and final assumption was that time was a luxury they lacked. Avery and the others agreed: The aliens would be back long before the militiamen learned anything but the basics of small-unit combat.

Of course, the Captain and his Staff Sergeants told the recruits none of this. Instead they continued to promote the falsehood of a visiting CA delegation and a possible Insurrectionist attack. None of them liked lying to their men. But they calmed their consciences with the knowledge that the recruits would need to master the same basic skills of concealment, coordination, and communication if they were going to have a chance against their alien foe.

Avery heard the distant buzz of electric engines. He glanced over his shoulder. Epsilon Indi now hung so low in the sky that even wearing his glasses he could only stare at the star for a few seconds before shutting his eyes in a watery wince. Avery grimaced with satisfaction. As he'd planned, any recruits patrolling the complex's western perimeter fence would have the exact same problem—and none of them were wearing glasses. Which might have been an unfair advantage if Avery and Byrne weren't already outnumbered thirty-six to one.

As the buzzing engines drew close, Avery tensed and prepared to slither forward. *Keep your eyes open. Expect the unexpected,* he had warned his platoon. For their sake, he hoped they'd listened. *But if they hadn't . . .*

"Creeper, this is crawler," Avery whispered into this throat mic. "Mow them down."

They would learn a valuable lesson all the same.

"Smells pretty good." Jenkins placed his cheek against his BR55's hard plastic stock, and shot Forsell a sideways glance. "What is it?"

The recruits lay side by side, facing the reactor complex's only gate: a break in the southern run of the three-meter-high, chain-link fence that surrounded the facility.

Forsell took a sloppy bite from a foil-wrapped energy bar. "Honey hazelnut." He chewed and swallowed without pulling his eyes from his spotting scope. "Want some?"

"Any part of it you haven't licked?" Jenkins asked.

"No."

"Nice."

Forsell shrugged apologetically and stuffed the rest of the bar into his mouth.

It was his own fault he was hungry, Jenkins knew. He was so geared up about today's exercise he'd barely eaten breakfast in the garrison mess.

In fact, he'd been so certain the Staff Sergeants would attack when the recruits had their heads buried in their lunches, he'd skipped that meal entirely—let the much larger Forsell take whatever he wanted from his meal ready to eat (MRE). Unfortunately, Forsell had taken *everything,* and now Jenkins had nothing in his stomach but anxious bile.

The two recruits wore helmets that covered their ears, swept low over their brows, and were painted to match their mottled, olive drab fatigues. The color would have served them well in the surrounding wheat, but wasn't as useful in their current location: the roof of a two-story polycrete tower in the center of the complex that covered the reactor as well as Mack's data center.

A high-pitched alert chimed from a speaker in Jenkins' helmet. Under Captain Ponder's supervision, the recruits had staked motion trackers all around the perimeter, switching the pole-mounted units to their highest sensitivity. While this gave them coverage beyond one thousand meters, the trackers kept pinging ghosts: swarms of honeybees, flocks of starlings—and now a flight of JOTUN dusters.

Squinting past Forsell, Jenkins watched a trio of the needle-nosed, thin-winged planes buzz the western wheat. The dusters had been making long, serpentine passes all day, spraying a top dressing of fungicide. But this was their closest pass yet.

A trailing white cloud billowed toward the complex, prompting the twelve recruits of 2nd platoon's bravo squad (2/B) guarding the western fence to turn away from the drifting chemicals, cover their mouths, and cough. These weren't indications of any real, physical distress (Jenkins had applied enough of the organic compounds to his family's own crops to know it was perfectly safe to breathe), but rather expressions of the recruits' fatigue and discontent.

"What time you got?" Jenkins asked.

Forsell squinted at Epsilon Indi. "Sixteen thirty. Give or take."

Almost sunset, Jenkins thought. "Where the hell are they?"

The rules of the exercise were simple: to win, either side

needed to eliminate half the other. This meant Johnson and Byrne would have to drop thirty-six recruits while the recruits only had to neutralize one of them. With the odds stacked so heavily against the Staff Sergeants, it had seemed likely they would try to attack early, before the recruits got settled.

When the two of them had torn out of the complex's gate in their Warthog a little after 0900, the recruits had quickly divided into their squads—three in each platoon—and rushed to secure different sectors of the complex.

Along with the rest of one-alpha squad (1/A), Jenkins and Forsell had hustled to the reactor tower. The weather-beaten structure looked a bit like a birthday cake: The second of its two circular stories had a smaller diameter than the first and was topped with a cluster of candlelike aerials for Mack's maser and other COM devices. The tower was the only above ground building in the complex, and the only building for hundreds of kilometers in all directions.

Jenkins and Forsell had climbed up two flights of ladders to the second-story roof and gone prone—the most stable stance for shooting, if you could afford the loss of mobility. Resting his BR55 across his rucksack for additional support, Jenkins had eased into his rifle scope just in time to see the Staff Sergeants' Warthog turn off the reactor complex's paved access road and head South down the highway toward Utgard. Adrenaline pumping, Jenkins had immediately pulled his battle rifle's charging handle, cycling a round into the chamber. He had thumbed the fire-select switch to single-shot, tensed his finger on the trigger, and then . . . nothing. Just hour after hour of blazing heat.

The recruits had quickly begun to grouse that the real purpose of the exercise was to see how long they could stand being suckers. An overweight and outspoken 1/A recruit named Osmo theorized that Johnson and Byrne had gone to Utgard for cold beer in an air-conditioned bar, leaving Epsilon Indi's broiling light to win the exercise for them.

FCPO Healy had told them all to "shut it," emphasizing that as long as they kept their helmets on and stayed hydrated they'd be safe from heat stroke. For his part, Captain Ponder had remained in his Warthog, parked in the shade of a portable triage tent near the front gate, quietly smoking his Sweet William cigars.

"A beer would be nice," Jenkins murmured, listening to the JOTUN dusters' engines fade. Even though he'd spent the day on his stomach hardly moving, sweat had poured out of him. There were at least ten empty water bottles scattered between his and Forsell's boots. And Jenkins was still thirsty.

"Eyes on the big one," Forsell announced, lazily sweeping his scope to the east. "Again."

Turning to follow Forsell's gaze, Jenkins saw a single JOTUN combine: a giant machine painted dark blue with yellow detail stripes. Its three pairs of oversized wheels bucked up and down as it rolled over a gentle ridge. Though the combine was at least a kilometer distant, Jenkins had no trouble hearing the low rumble of its three-thousand horsepower, ethanol-electric engine as it began devouring the wheat on the down-slope.

The combine had spent the day mowing the eastern fields in wide swaths perpendicular to the complex, shuddering the ground as it neared the perimeter fence. At first, this had unnerved some of the recruits. They'd all seen JOTUNs, of course, but what was essentially a fifty-meter tall and one-hundred-fifty-meter long lawn mower triggered a pretty basic urge to flee—even when you knew an AI as capable as Mack had control of its circuits.

But now, as the combine again bore down on the complex, the only thing that looked nervous was the wheat. Magnified in Jenkins' rifle scope, the stalks trembled before the whirring tines of the combine's rotary header, almost as if they had some knowledge of their imminent threshing.

"I'm telling you. That's a series four," Forsell said, continuing a debate they'd kept up all day.

"Nope," Jenkins countered. "See the gondolas?"

Forsell peered through his scope at a line of angular metal bins on wheels that only looked small because they were trailing directly behind the JOTUN. "Yeah . . ."

"They're collecting from the rear."

"So?"

"So that's a series *five* feature. Four's dumped to the sides."

Forsell thought about that for a second then gave up with an awkward admission. "It's been a few seasons since we upgraded."

Jenkins winced. He'd forgotten Forsell came from a modest family. Not only did Forsell's parents own fewer acres, but their soy also sold for much less than the Jenkins' corn and other grains. In all likelihood, Forsell's parents were still getting by with a handful of used series twos.

"Fives aren't worth it," Jenkins said, watching the gondolas fill up then hurry back over the rise to a nearby maglev depot. "Hybrid engines are way too expensive, unless you're processing your own ethanol—"

"Hey. We got something." Forsell's body tensed. "Just pulled off the highway."

Jenkins realigned south. A single vehicle—a green and white taxi—was approaching the complex at high speed. For a moment it disappeared down a dip in the access road.

"Think it's them?" Forsell asked.

"Dunno." Jenkins swallowed dryly. "Better send the word."

"All squads! Got a vehicle coming in!"

"This a joke, Forsell?" Stisen growled over the COM. Byrne had promoted the dark-haired constable to squad leader of 2/A, and assigned him to guard the complex gate. "It's too hot for any of your bullshit."

"See for yourself," Jenkins urged. The final stretch of road was completely flat—a straight shot of cambered pavement to the gate. Even without magnification the sedan was impossible to miss.

"Look sharp!" Stisen bellowed to his squad, sitting in two sun-baked clumps behind sandbag berms on either side of the gate. "Dass, give me some cover!"

Jenkins heard movement on the first-story roof, directly below his position. "On your feet, boys!" Dass bellowed. 1/A's squad leader was a little overweight, but he was also very tall. As a result, the middle-aged maglev engineer didn't look fat so much as thick. "Lock and load!"

"My rifle!" Osmo whined. "It won't charge!" Whenever Osmo got stressed, his voice shifted to a childlike register. Usually this made Jenkins laugh, but not now.

"Pull your magazine then reset it," Dass said. "Make sure it goes all the way in."

Jenkins heard the scrape of metal on metal, then the successful clack of a rifle bolt.

"Sorry, Dass."

"It's alright. But you gotta calm down. Focus." By his patient but forceful tone, it was easy to tell Dass was a father—one boy, two girls.

"Just make sure you watch what they shoot," Stisen growled. The constable had a prickly personality that had only gotten worse since his defeat during the pugil competition. As much as Jenkins wished he could mute Stisen from the COM channel all the recruits shared, he knew Stisen had a point: 1/A would have to shoot past 2/A in order to hit the sedan.

Dass answered in a friendly tone. "Do your job, Stisen, and you won't have anything to worry about."

Rising to the challenge, Stisen marched to the center of the gate. Holding his MA5 to his right shoulder, he held out his left hand in a sign to stop. The sedan slowed and came to a halt twenty meters in front of Stisen. For a few seconds, all the recruits simply stared at the heat distortion roiling from the vehicle's roof.

"Out of the vehicle! Now!" Stisen barked, leveling his weapon at the windshield.

But the sedan's doors remained shut. Jenkins felt his heart pounding in his chest. "Thermal?" he whispered to Forsell, hoping the spotting scope's more sophisticated optics could confirm if either of the Staff Sergeants was in the sedan.

"Negative," Forsell replied. "It's all white. Exterior's too hot."

"First team!" Stisen barked. "Move up!"

Jenkins watched four recruits move out from behind the western berm and walk cautiously through the gate, MA5s tucked tight against their shoulders. They surrounded the sedan, two on either side.

"Burdick! Pop the door!" Stisen motioned one of his men forward.

Jenkins drew a breath, and did his best to relax into his weapon. As he exhaled, he let his scope's aiming reticle come to rest where he guessed the driver's head would be when he emerged. For some reason, he imagined Staff Sergeant Byrne's face grinning in his crosshairs. Burdick reached toward the door release, but just as he did the sedan's gull-wing doors sprung open. The recruit had a moment to flinch, but not enough time to cry out in surprise as the sedan exploded in a flash of white vapor. Instantly, Burdick toppled to the pavement, as did two of the other flanking recruits. Each was spattered bright red, as if he had been shot through with shrapnel.

"Claymores!" groaned the lone survivor. He shuffled away from the sedan, dragging a crippled leg behind him.

"Everyone stay back!" Stisen bellowed to the rest of his

squad as he took the struggling recruit's arm across his shoulders and dragged him inside the gate. The squad leader fired a one-handed burst into the sedan's windshield, but instead of shattering it flashed red—the same vibrant color as the recruits' seemingly mortal wounds.

For the exercise, each recruit's MA5 was loaded with tactical training rounds (TTR). These bullets had a plastic polymer shell to help maintain muzzle velocity and trajectory—to emulate, as much as possible, ballistics of lethal rounds. But each TTR also contained a proximity fuse that dissolved its shell, turning it into a harmless blob of red paint when it was within ten centimeters of any surface.

Harmless but not inert, Jenkins reminded himself. The paint was both a powerful, tactile anesthetic and a reactant that worked on nanofibers woven into the recruits' fatigues, causing the fibers to harden when saturated. *Translation: when you got hit, you passed out and froze up.* A single TTR in any limb would render it useless. Multiple rounds to the chest would cause the whole uniform to stiffen, simulating a mortal wound. Burdick and the other downed recruits had been hit by dozens of TTR from the claymores—black plastic boxes screwed to the inside of the sedan's doors, now covered with condensation from their CO_2 propellant.

"Hold your fire!" Healy shouted as he rushed to Burdick's side, med kit in hand. The recruit had taken the worst of the blast, stiffened like a board, and fallen straight onto his back.

"How's he doing, Corpsman?" Ponder asked, stepping down from his Warthog.

Healy pulled a blued-metal baton from the kit and passed it over Burdick's midsection. Circuits inside the baton relaxed his uniform's nanofibers, and the Corpsman was able to hook the recruit under the arms, pull him to the sedan, and prop him against the front, driver-side tire. "He'll live," Healy said

sarcastically. He patted Burdick on the shoulder and set his
MA5 across his lap. Then he moved on to the other downed recruits.

Jenkins breathed a sigh of relief. He knew they would be
fine—easily revived at the end of the exercise. But the attack
had *looked* very real. Jenkins could easily imagine a far more
gruesome scene if the sedan had contained Innie explosives. He
was just about to share his thoughts with Forsell when Andersen, the newly anointed squad leader of 1/B shouted: "The
combine! It isn't turning!"

Jenkins twitched east and saw Andersen and the rest of his
squad retreating from the fence. The towering JOTUN had indeed passed its usual pivot line and was barreling down on the
complex. As the combine reached a thick strip of clay that
edged the field, its rotary head bit into the hardened soil and
locked with an audible snap of timing belts. But the JOTUN
wasn't fazed. It simply raised the disabled header on its hy-
draulic arms and kept on rolling toward the fence. Steel poles
and galvanized chainlink crumpled under the combine's first
pair of tires, then twisted around the axles. The fencing sparked
against the machines' underbelly as it came to a halt, half its
length inside the complex and half out.

By that time, the JOTUN was covered with TTR. The recruits hadn't spotted either Staff Sergeant, but that hadn't
stopped them from laying on their triggers in uncontrolled
panic. In the confusion, no one noticed the grenade lofting toward the reactor tower.

"Get down!" Dass yelled. But it was too late. Jenkins barely
had time to duck his head behind his rucksack before the
grenade burst. He heard TTR spatter the wall below him, and
he knew even before Osmo spoke that most of 1/A was gone.

"They got Dass!" Osmo wailed. "They got *me*!"

Risking exposure, Jenkins slunk forward and peered down at

the first-story roof. Dass was unconscious as were most of the other 1/A recruits, but Osmo himself was fine. Lying face-down, hands clasped over his helmet, he hadn't noticed that the numbness in his legs was simply the result of another recruit's collapse across them.

"You're fine, Oz!" Jenkins shouted over the frantic clatter of the rest of the militia company's MA5s. "Sit up and—"

At that moment three TTR broke against the first-story wall, right below Jenkins' head—a burst from a battle rifle.

"Byrne! He's on the combine!" Forsell shouted.

If Jenkins had tried to crawl back to his ruck, he would have gotten shot. But some previously unknown instinct took over as Jenkins instead brought his battle rifle up—spotted Byrne hunkered between the first and second body segments and opened fire. Even though his shots went wide, they prompted the Staff Sergeant to abandon his already precarious position. Byrne swung onto a ladder that ran down the backside of the first segment and headed for ground.

"I got him!" Jenkins shouted, thumbing his battle rifle fire-select switch from semi-automatic to burst. But his heavier fire only quickened the Staff Sergeant's descent. Byrne grabbed the ladder's stiles and slid down without bothering to toe the rungs. When his boots hit the asphalt, Byrne rolled between the the JOTUN's tires. From there he had good, if temporary cover, from Jenkins' battle rifle as well as the crossfire from Andersen and Stisen's squads.

"Like hell you do!" the 2/A squad leader shouted as TTR from Byrne's battle rifle sprayed the sandbags near the gate. "Critchley!" Stisen commanded. "Come to front!"

Jenkins grit his teeth. He didn't appreciate Stisen calling him out on the open COM. And besides, Critchley and his spotter were set up at the northern edge of the first-story roof and were supposed to be watching Jenkins' back.

"I said I got him!" Jenkins retorted, drilling a burst against the JOTUN's tire.

"Shut it, Jenkins!" Stisen roared. "Critchley! Respond!"

But the 2nd platoon marksman didn't say a word.

"Forsell, check your COM!" Jenkins shouted. Each recruit's COM-pad was constantly monitoring his vital signs. If one of them went down, the loss registered on the local network.

"Critchley's gone!" Forsell replied, voice shocked. "So is all of one-cee!"

"What?"

"We've lost everyone on the western fence!"

Jenkins saw Byrne's battle rifle flash from the shadows beneath the JOTUN. One of the 1/A recruits screamed as he fell. *That's got to be close to thirty casualties*, Jenkins thought grimly. He squeezed off two more bursts, then rolled to his side and swapped magazines. "Stisen, we're heading to the back!"

"No goddamnit!" Stisen cursed. Then to 2/C's squad leader, tasked with guarding the northeast corner of the complex: "Habel! Shift west! It's gotta be Johnson!"

Just hearing his Staff Sergeant's name made Jenkins' stomach churn. He and the rest of the recruits had spent the day bellyaching about the heat, unaware they'd been resting between the jaws of a well-set trap. Now with Byrne firmly entrenched and Johnson pressing, it was only a matter of time before the recruits were crushed.

"Oz?" Jenkins asked, rising to a knee. "You still kicking?"

"Y-yeah!"

"You've got good height. You can keep Byrne pinned."

"But . . ."

"Just do it, Osmo!"

Jenkins tapped Forsell on the shoulder. They locked stares, and Jenkins knew Forsell was thinking the exact same thing:

When you're caught in a trap, you fight your way out. "Stisen," Jenkins announced. "First marksmen are on the move."

From the top of the rise, Avery had a panoramic view of the complex. Critchley and his spotter were an easy shot, but he'd waited for Byrne to crash the fence and draw the recruits' attention before he fired twice, hitting both recruits in the sides of their heads. Circuits in their helmets registered the "lethal" headshots and instantly froze their uniforms. In the general clamor of automatic weapons fire, Avery was confident none of the other recruits had heard his shots ring out.

He also bet none of the militiamen would bother to check their motion trackers now that the devices' signals had been thoroughly confused by the cloud of fungicide. The chemicals had coated Avery in fine white powder as they settled into the wheat, and he looked almost comical as he rose from the field—as if some unseen prankster had loosed a giant bag of flour overhead. But there was nothing humorous about Avery's intent: He planned to drop every recruit guarding the western fence before they stopped thinking about Byrne and remembered to watch the perimeter.

As Avery ran down the rise, battle rifle up and plump kernels batting at his elbows, it struck him that this was the first time since TREBUCHET that he'd fired on a human being. This was different, of course; it was an exercise with practice ammunition. But Avery couldn't help noticing how easy—how *automatic*—it was for him to put someone in his crosshairs, and pull the trigger. This was just good training, Avery knew. And while he wasn't always happy with the way he'd put his skills to use, he was determined to pass them on—instill in his men the same confidence and lack of hesitation. In the fight to come, they would need both to stay alive.

Avery heard a grenade go off. The noise was much more

muffled than the claymores he and Byrne had affixed to the sedan's doors before letting Mack bring the vehicle to the complex gate. The AI had been more than happy to help them with their exercise—had actually been the one to suggest using the JOTUN combine as an additional distraction. Avery wasn't quite sure why except that, like the marines and Lt. Commander al-Cygni, Mack must have known Harvest's reactor would be a juicy target for any hostile force and was eager to let the militia practice its defense.

Avery didn't fire through the fence. He knew the chain-link would shred his battle rifle's TTR before they hit their targets. But the same would be true for the recruits' shots as well, so it was with reasonable confidence of not getting shot that Avery sprinted over the hard-clay border between the wheat and the fence and leapt onto the chain-link.

Almost immediately, one of the 1/C recruits, Wick, heard the rattling metal and turned. His already frightened eyes widened to saucer-size as he saw what must have looked like Avery's ghost jump down inside the compound, billowing white fungicide. Before Wick could recover, Avery unslung his battle rifle and pumped two rounds into the center of his chest.

The recruit's scream carried above the din, causing three of his squad mates to turn. Avery dropped each one—left to right—before switching his rifle to burst fire and strafing the confused remains of 1/C. As the last recruit fell, the illuminated ammunition counter below the battle rifle's scope displayed three rounds remaining. But just as Avery pulled a fresh magazine from his assault vest, he started taking fire from the east.

Squad 2/C had swung around the back of the reactor tower. If the recruits had run a little faster or remembered to settle into more stable stances before opening fire, they would have caught Avery in a very bad spot. But their opening shots were wild, and all they did was give Avery time to roll left, putting the curve of the tower in between him and unexpected fire. By the time the first of the 2/C recruits came charging around the bend, Avery had reloaded. He dropped two and forced the rest of the squad to pull back and bunker down—waste valuable seconds debating when and how they should attempt to flank Avery's position.

"Charlie one is gone," Avery growled into his throat mic. "I'm getting heat from bravo two."

"I just blew your alpha boys to hell," Byrne replied. He paused to snap off a few rounds. "But I'm still taking fire from up top."

"Must be my marksmen."

"How's that?"

"Yours are dead."

"Well, quiet 'em down, will you?"

"On it."

Keeping his battle rifle pointing north in case 2/C got organized quicker than he thought, Avery walked backward to a service ladder that would take him to the first-story roof. He slung his weapon for the climb and worked the rungs as quickly as he could. As his head cleared the roofline, Avery saw movement to his right. He jerked his head down just in time to avoid a burst from Forsell's MA5.

Without hesitating, Avery unholstered his M6 sidearm, and sprang up one-handed just as Forsell pulled his finger off the trigger. As Avery rose, so did his shots; one TTR blossomed in the middle of Forsell's gut, two more traveled up his sternum. As Forsell staggered back, Avery stepped onto the roof. Supporting his M6 with both hands, Avery kept the heavy pistol's iron sights trained on Forsell's helmet as he crumpled. The recruit was big, and Avery wanted to make sure the pistol's smaller caliber rounds were sufficient to knock him out.

Satisfied that Forsell was down for the count, Avery moved toward the ladder that would take him to the top of the second story. But he'd only taken a few steps when he felt three sharp pains in the back of his right thigh. Fueled by adrenaline, Avery spun around his rapidly deadening leg and returned fire on a target he only recognized as Jenkins after his rounds were on their way.

As Jenkins jerked back around the curve of the second-story wall, Avery guessed correctly that the recruits had jumped down on opposite sides of the tower and waited for him to ascend. *Not a bad plan.* Avery grimaced as he hobbled against the wall. Rather than stay locked in a failing defensive position, the marksmen had staged their own ambush. Whether or not they succeeded, Avery admired their initiative. He jerked his M6 up and down, disengaging its half-spent magazine. Then he reloaded and thrust the pistol straight out from his body along the wall.

But just as Jenkins stepped into view and Avery's finger tensed on the trigger, Captain Ponder's voice boomed over the COM: "Cease fire! Cease fire!" For a moment the Staff Sergeant and his recruit remained frozen, each holding the other dead to rights.

"I got him?" Osmo sounded shocked. Then, warming to his unexpected success: "I *got* him!"

"Staff Sergeant Byrne, you have been hit." Ponder confirmed. "Final score: thirty-four to one. Congratulations, recruits!"

A chorus of weary cheers flooded the COM.

"Spatter off the tire," Byrne growled over the Staff Sergeant's private channel. "Bloody TTR . . ." Then, over the open COM: "Healy? Bring me that damn baton!"

Avery lowered his pistol and relaxed against the wall. Epsilon Indi was dropping toward the gentle curve of the horizon. The tower's lackluster tan polycrete took on a warm, yellow glow even as it shed its accumulated heat.

Jenkins grinned. "Almost had us, Staff Sergeant."

"Almost." Avery smiled—and not just to be polite. Other

than basic maneuvers around the garrison, this had been the recruits' first live-fire exercise. They'd had no idea what the Staff Sergeants were going to throw at them, and Jenkins' and Forsell's performance gave Avery hope that, with enough time, his recruits just might make decent soldiers.

"Staff Sergeant?" Ponder's voice crackled in Avery's earpiece. His congratulatory tone was gone. "Just got word from our local DCS representative." Avery read between the lines: *Lt. Commander al-Cygni.* His spine stiffened to match his leg. "The delegates we were expecting?" Ponder continued. "They're here. And they brought a *much* bigger ship."

CHAPTER
FOURTEEN

Dadab raised his knobby arms above his head and grunted enthusiastically. "The Age of Reclamation!" Out of the corner of his eye he could see *Rapid Conversion*'s security officer, Tartarus, keeping watch near one of the feasting hall's sputtering oil lamps. Not wanting to risk offense, Dadab made sure his feet stayed clear of the shards of Forerunner alloy that formed the final ring in the hall's mosaic.

"Salvation *and* . . ." he prompted.

The roughly twenty Unggoy gathered around the mosaic stared at Dadab with dull eyes.

Tartarus crossed his arms and loosed an impatient huff.

". . . the Journey!" Dadab said, flourishing his stubby fingers. Despite his mask, his voice still echoed grandly around the hall. "These are the Ages of our Covenant—the cycle we must complete again and again as we strive to follow Those Who Walked the Path!"

A broad-shouldered Unggoy, Bapap, stepped forward. "This path. Where does it go?"

"To salvation," Dadab replied.

"And where is that?"

The Unggoy swung their heads from Bapap to Dadab. The Deacon shifted in his harness as he struggled for an answer. "Well . . ." he began, then trailed off. It took him a moment to recall what he needed—a word he had heard in seminary, used by one of his San'Shyuum teachers in response to a similarly thorny question. During the pause, an Unggoy named Yull idly scratched his hindquarters with a finger and offered it to another Unggoy to smell.

"I'm afraid," Dadab said with as much gravitas as he could muster, "the answer is *ontological*." He had only a vague idea what the word meant. But he liked the way it sounded, and evidently so did the other Unggoy because they all grumbled happily into their masks as if it was exactly the answer they'd expected.

Bapap seemed especially pleased. "On-to-logi-cal," he muttered to himself.

Tartarus' signal unit emitted a short, sharp tone. "Our jump is almost complete," the security officer said. "To your posts!"

"Remember," Dadab called after the Unggoy as they trotted for the exit, "The Path is long but wide. There's room for all of you, so long as you believe!"

Tartarus snorted. The Jiralhanae was dressed in bright red armor that covered his thighs and chest and shoulders. Maccabeus had wanted his pack ready for a fight, just in case the aliens were waiting for them near the wreckage of the Kig-Yar ship.

"You think I waste my time." Dadab nodded toward the last of his retreating study group.

"All creatures deserve instruction." The Jiralhanae's black hair bristled. "But the Sangheili did not provide us with the most *competent* of crews."

Dadab didn't like to think ill of others of his kind, but he knew that this was true. *Rapid Conversion*'s sixty Unggoy were exceptionally dim—uneducated and shiftless. With a few exceptions (Bapap, for one), they were bottom-of-the barrel types you would expect to find performing menial labor on crowded habitats, not crewing a Ministry vessel on a vital mission.

Dadab didn't understand all the political dimensions of the Sangheili-Jiralhanae relationship, but he knew Maccabeus' position was unusual—that he was one of a handful of Jiral-hanae Shipmasters in the vast Covenant fleet. Even so, all one had to do was glance at *Rapid Conversion* to know the Sangheili hadn't exactly set Maccabeus up for success. The cruiser was in a sorry state, just like its Unggoy crew.

With the Chieftain's permission, Dadab had begun to try to help. His plan? Instill motivation and discipline through spiritual enrichment. And although this had only been the study group's second meeting, the Deacon had already begun to see improvement in the demeanor of the Unggoy who had chosen to take part.

"To the hangar," Tartarus commanded, putting on his helmet. "I owe the Chieftain a report on the Huragok's progress."

For Dadab, climbing the cruiser's central shaft had at first been a terrifying proposition. His strength had waned during his zerogee captivity in the escape-pod. And he had been terrified he would lose his grip and plummet to his death. But now that his muscles were stronger—and he had become just as agile as the other Unggoy—the Deacon could climb while cheerfully observing the hustle and bustle of *Rapid Conversion*'s main thoroughfare.

Since he had arrived, the shaft had been given a thorough cleaning. Its metal walls were still scratched and grooved, but the layers of tarnish were gone and the vertical passage now shone with a deep purple luster. Halfway down, Dadab saw that a doorway leading to the forward weapon bays had been unbarred and its warning symbols disabled. Repairs in that part of the cruiser had been Maccabeus' top priority for his newly acquired Huragok.

Dadab had been present as translator during the Chieftain's explanation of what needed to be done. But before Maccabeus had a chance to explain what ailed the cruiser's heavy plasma cannon, *Lighter Than Some* had simply gone to work—torn the protective cowling off the weapon's control circuits and started its repairs.

Dadab had seen the Huragok perform all sorts of mechanical miracles aboard the Kig-Yar ship, but the Jiralhanae were dumb-founded as the creature's tentacles fluttered, and the cannon's circuits sparked and hummed. Seemingly without thought, the Huragok was performing repairs that had been impossible for the cruiser's former custodians: the insect Yanme'e.

After seeing what *Lighter Than Some* could do, Maccabeus relieved the winged creatures of all but their most menial re-sponsibilities. The Chieftain was concerned they might inter-rupt the Huragok's vital work. And indeed, the Yanme'e buzzing up and down the shaft now only carried basic sanita-tion and maintenance tools—none of which came close to matching the utility of the Huragok's deft tentacles and their cilia.

As Dadab shrunk to one side of his ladder to let a blue-armored Jiralhanae pass, a pair of Yanme'e collided in midair below him. Rattling their copper-colored armored plates, the bugs untangled their chitinous limbs and continued down the shaft. Dadab (while no expert on the species) knew this sort of clumsiness was unusual for creatures with compound eyes and highly sensitive antenna—and was a good indication their re-cent demotion had left the Yanme'e flustered.

Yes, they were much more intelligent than small arthropods such as Scrub Grubs. But the Yanme'e were also hive-minded and notoriously dogmatic. Once you gave them a task, they stuck to it, and Dadab worried the creatures' confusion might cause them to interfere with *Lighter Than Some*'s work, maybe even do the creature harm.

So far, nothing had happened to warrant Dadab's concern. But he was relieved when the Huragok had completed its repairs to the plasma cannon and retired to the hangar to begin work on the damaged Spirit dropship. The Yanme'e had avoided the hangar ever since the accidental immolation of their hive mates, which meant the Huragok was safely isolated.

With the armored Jiralhanae up and on his way, Dadab resumed his descent and soon reached the bottom of the shaft. Trotting quickly to keep up with Tartarus' long strides, he hurried to the far end of the hangar where *Lighter Than Some* had built a temporary workshop inside the damaged Spirit's two battered bays. The escape pod had been discarded out the energy barrier before the cruiser made its jump. But the Spirit's detached cockpit still sat against the wall where the pod had smashed it. At first glance it seemed little progress had been made.

The thin-skinned troop bays, each large enough to accommodate dozens of warriors, were pushed together on their longest sides. Their doors, half-open and resting against the hangar floor, kept the bays from toppling.

"Wait here," Dadab said, ducking between the bays. "I'll see what it has done."

Tartarus didn't protest. Maccabeus had told every member of his pack to give the fragile Huragok plenty of room. For while *Lighter Than Some* had survived its ordeal inside the pod, it had not emerged unscathed.

Dadab felt a pang of guilt when he saw his friend, floating in front of a sheet of ablative foil it had hung as a curtain halfway down the bay. The sac that had produced all the life-saving methane was horribly distended. It dragged along the floor as the Huragok turned to greet Dadab—a mute reminder of its sacrifice.

< *How are you?* > Dadab signed.

< *Well. Though I wish you had come alone.* > The Huragok wrinkled its snout, crimping its olfactory nodes. < *I'm not terribly fond of our new hosts' smell.* >

< *It's their hair.* > Dadab explained. < *I'm not sure they wash.* > It felt good to speak with his fingers. During their confinement, Dadab's signing had improved immensely. Before *Lighter Than*

Some had become too weak to carry on long conversations, the Deacon had felt on the verge of fluency—at least as far as simple subjects were concerned. *< How go repairs? >*

The Huragok flicked one of its tentacles in a pitching motion, as if it were throwing Dadab an imaginary ball. *< Hunting rock. Do you remember? >*

< Of course. Do you want to play? >

< Do you remember when we played before? >

Dadab paused. *< The alien. >*

< The one I killed. >

Dadab splayed his fingers: *< Killed to save me! >* But his heart sank. He'd hoped *Lighter Than Some*'s new responsibilities would take its mind off the terrifying encounter aboard the alien ship.

< Even so, I regret it. > *Lighter Than Some* motioned for Dadab to follow it deeper into the bay. *< But I know how to make amends! >* Its tentacles quivered as it drew back the foil curtain, indicating excitement—or joy.

< What is it? > Dadab asked, cocking his head at the object on the other side of the curtain. It looked familiar, but the Deacon couldn't immediately place why.

< A peace offering! Proof of our good intentions! >

< You made . . . one of their machines. >

One of the Huragok's dorsal sacs bleated with delight. *< Yes! A plow, I believe. >*

As *Lighter Than Some* continued extolling the virtues of its creation (flashing technical terms that far exceeded Dadab's vocabulary), the Deacon studied the plow. It was, of course, much smaller than the machine they'd discovered in the second alien ship, but was still obviously designed for prepping soil for seed.

The plow's dominant feature was a metal wheel mounted with earth-tilling tines that doubled as its propulsion system. *Where did the Huragok get* that? Dadab wondered, an instant before he noticed that two of the troop bay's trapezoidal support ribs had been removed. *Lighter Than Some* had bent the ribs round and fused them together. And it must have done so recently because the bay still carried the sharp, sweet smell of the flux the Yanme'e used in their portable welders— one of which the Huragok must have "borrowed" for its project.

Extending back from the wheel was the beginnings of a chassis. Loops of wire and circuit boards pilfered from the bay hung from the neatly welded frame, awaiting placement of the engine, whatever *that* was going to be. . . .

Dadab's natural curiosity died in a quick intake of breath. His fingers trembled with fright, and his grammar faltered. < *Does, Chieftain, know?* >

< *Should he?* >

< *His order. Repair dropship. Not make gift.* >

< *Not a gift. An* offering. > The Huragok fluttered, as if the distinction would lessen the Chieftain's rage.

How could it be so foolish? Dadab wailed into his mask. He felt dizzy and placed a paw on the plow to steady himself. But this wasn't just because of his rapidly fraying nerves; he could feel the bay vibrate as the cruiser exited his jump. Dadab took a few long drags from his tank. < *You must take apart!* >

The Huragok's tentacles sputtered. < *But why?* > It seemed honestly confused.

Dadab worked his fingers slowly. < *You disobey. Chieftain very angry.* > He knew Maccabeus would never hurt the Huragok. The creature was far too valuable. But as for Dadab . . .

Maccabeus hadn't said anything specific, but the Deacon knew he was a prisoner on the Jiralhanae ship—still under suspicion for the crimes he had committed. In a flash of desperate optimism, the Deacon tried to convince himself that his efforts to educate *Rapid Conversion*'s Unggoy would be

enough to prove his worth—to keep the Chieftain from transferring his certain anger about the plow. But the Deacon knew
he had sinned. He would be punished, if not by Maccabeus
then by the Ministry Prophets when the Jiralhanae's mission
was complete.

"Deacon!" Tartarus' voice echoed into the bay. "The Chieftain needs you on the bridge!"

< *Promise!* > Dadab signed with shaking hands. < *You will
take it apart!* >

Lighter Than Some swung its snout to face the plow. It
tapped a tentacle against one of the machine's sharpened tines,
as if considering the quality of its work. < *Well, I did rush the
assembly. And one machine hardly makes up for the life I
took.* >

"Deacon! The Chieftain *insists*!"

< *Fix!* > Dadab signed as he backpedaled through the curtain
and out the bay.

"When will the dropship be ready to fly?" Tartarus asked,
heading back to the shaft.

"The Huragok has hit a *minor* snag." Dadab was glad the Jiralhanae had taken the lead—had his back to him. Otherwise he
would have known Dadab was lying just by looking at his darting eyes. "But I know it will make things right just as quickly as
it can!"

Rapid Conversion's bridge was located halfway up the shaft,
toward the prow, as far from the outer hull as possible—a
placement that made it invulnerable to all but the most
devastating attack. As Dadab scampered inside, close on Tartarus' heels, he noted the bridge was (while not as roomy as the
Jiralhanae's feasting hall) large enough to accommodate the entire pack. All were present, most hunched over workstations
protruding from the bridge's reinforced walls. These were filled

with holographic switches that flickered against the Jiral-hanae's blue armor. Like Tartarus, they were girded for a fight.

Maccabeus stood before the bridge's central holo-tank, his paws knuckled against its smooth metal railing. The Chieftain's armor was colored gold, but made of a much stronger alloy. Vorenus and another Jiralhanae named Licinus flanked him, and their jutting shoulder plates kept Dadab from seeing whatever the tank had on display.

Dadab bowed, touching his knuckles to the bridge's grooved metal floor. It vibrated in time with the cruiser's jump-drive, idling many bridge lengths to stern. Ever mindful of the Vice Minister of Tranquility's desire for caution, Maccabeus had kept the drive hot in case they needed to beat a hasty retreat from the alien system.

"Come forward, Deacon," Maccabeus said, catching a faint whiff of methane.

Dadab righted himself and followed Tartarus to the tank.

"Make room," Tartarus growled. "Step *aside,* Vorenus!" Tartarus gave the taller, tan-haired Jiralhanae a cuff.

"Pardon me." Dadab gulped. "Excuse me." His conical tank made sidestepping impractical, and as he pushed past Vorenus toward the railing, his tank clanged against the Jiralhanae's armored thigh. To Dadab's relief, Vorenus was so transfixed he didn't seem to notice.

"Incredible, isn't it," Maccabeus said.

"Yes. Incredible," Dadab said, peering into the tank below its railing.

"Such *enthusiasm,* Deacon."

"My apologies, Chieftain. It's just that I've seen it before. Aboard the Kig-Yar ship."

"Ah. Of course." Maccabeus adopted an ironic tone. "After all, this is only—what?" He nodded toward the glowing representation of the alien world—its surface covered with insistent, Reclamation glyphs. "A few hundred *thousand* Luminations?"

The truth was Dadab was still preoccupied with the Huragok's disobedience. And to make matters worse, the bridge was thick with the Jiralhanae's powerful scents. The excited odors had permeated his mask's membranes, and Dadab was starting to feel a little sick.

"The numbers are impressive." Dadab choked back a bitter surge.

"Impressive? Unprecedented!" Maccabeus boomed. Then, his voice a low growl: "Very well. Tell me what you think of *this.*" He jabbed a knuckle into a holo-switch imbedded in the railing, and the image of the alien planet faded—shrunk to a much smaller size as the holo-tank's perspective shifted to a wider view of the system. Dadab saw an iconic image of the cruiser just outside the planet's orbital path, and a safe distance from that, a flashing red triangle indicating a potentially hostile contact.

"It was waiting for us," the Chieftain growled. "Near the remains of the Kig-Yar ship." He pressed another switch, and the holo-tank zoomed in on the contact, bringing it into focus.

"The design matches the ships the Kig-Yar raided," Dadab explained. "A cargo freighter. Nothing more."

"Look closer," Maccabeus rumbled.

Slowly, the vessel's representation began to turn. *Rapid Conversion*'s sensors had made a detailed scan, and Dadab could see the freighter's blackened hull had been deeply etched, creating patterns in the bright metal beneath. *No, not patterns,* he thought. *Pictures.*

Each of the vessel's four lateral sides displayed a different, stylized image of the aliens and the Kig-Yar. In the first picture, one of each creature aimed weapons at each other (the alien held some sort of rifle, the Kig-Yar a plasma pistol). In the second, the alien had dropped his rifle and held out a handful of round objects that looked like fruit. In the third image, the Kig-Yar had cast aside its weapon to accept the alien's offering. And in the fourth, both creatures sat in what appeared to be an orchard. The alien held a basket of fruit, and the Kig-Yar was calmly making its selection.

"A peace offering!" Dadab said excitedly. "They do not wish to fight!" As the hologram of the vessel continued to spin, the Deacon pointed a finger at an outline of the alien planet etched into the lower-right corner of each side of the hull. Two crossed lines marked a point in the middle of the world's singular landmass, a little below the equator. "And I believe this is where they would like to meet!"

"Apparently at dawn," Maccabeus said, increasing the tank's magnification.

Now Dadab could see that the etchings of the planet were shaded with a terminator line—a shadow that marked the world's passage in and out of night. Cutting perpendicularly across the equator, the line moved around the planet with each successive picture until it intersected the suggested meeting point on the side of the freighter that displayed the presentation of the fruit basket.

The Chieftain refocused the tank on the actual planet. "But there's more."

Now Dadab noticed new details. There was some sort of structure in high orbit above the world. Two delicate, silver arcs tethered to the surface by seven almost invisible golden strands. Around the structure were hundreds of additional red contact symbols. The Deacon hoped the aliens' message was sincere. If these contacts were warships, *Rapid Conversion* was in serious trouble.

"Not to worry, Deacon," Maccabeus said, sensing the Unggoy's concern. "They haven't moved since we arrived. And they look to be the same as the other vessel. Simple cargo tugs with no obvious weapons." He gestured with a hairy finger. "But look here—where those cables meet the surface."

Dadab followed the Chieftain's finger. There was a mass of

Reclamation glyphs clustered at the bottom of the cables. But close to these was another set of Forerunner symbols—a diamond of bright green glyphs hovering above the site of the aliens' suggested rendezvous.

"We intercepted a signal," Maccabeus continued. "And assumed it was a beacon—a marker for the parley." He scowled at the green diamond. "But our Luminary made its own assessment. I'd like you to explain it."

"It's . . . hard to say, Chieftain."

But Dadab was lying. He knew all too well that one of the symbols meant "intelligence," another "association," and a third "verboten." And as for the fourth glyph, the one flashing from yellow to blue at the diamond's tip . . . Dadab nervously cleared his throat. "If you had a library I might—"

"We do not." Maccabeus' eyes bored into Dadab's. "One of many essentials the Sangheili saw fit to deny us. I'm afraid I must rely on *your* expert opinion."

"Well then. Let me see . . ." Dadab calmly scrutinized the glyphs. But inside he shook with fear. *He knows! Knows all that I have done! And this is all just a trap to get my confession!*

But then some small, still rational part of the Deacon's brain suggested it was possible the Chieftain really didn't have any idea what the glyphs meant, especially the one that was flashing so insistently. It was an arcane symbol only certain San'Shyuum priests and overachieving Unggoy seminarians would bother to remember. And if Dadab hadn't been so frightened, he would have been awed as he announced:

"Of course! How could I be so stupid? These Luminations suggest an *Oracle*!"

Maccabeus drew back from the railing. Tartarus' and Vorenus' pheromones flared. The other Jiralhanae took their eyes off their workstations and stole furtive glances at the holo-tank. But no one spoke, and for a long time the bridge was filled with reverent silence.

"Can it be so?" Maccabeus said at last, his voice a throaty whisper. "A reliquary *and* an Oracle?"

"Who else would the Gods leave to safeguard such a splendid trove?" Dadab replied.

"A wise observation, Deacon." Maccabeus lifted a silver-haired paw and placed it on Dadab's head.

With a flinch of his fingers the Jiralhanae could have crushed the Unggoy's skull. But Dadab hoped the gesture was simply a sign of the Chieftain's growing appreciation for his assistance as minister to the cruiser's Unggoy and translator for its invaluable Huragok. In that moment all Dadab's fears began to fade.

"Brothers!" Maccabeus shouted, turning to face his pack. "We are well and truly blessed!"

Stepping away from the tank, the Chieftain threw back his hairless head and howled. Instantly, the other Jiralhanae joined their voices to his cry, creating a booming chorus of joyous yelps that shook the bridge and reverberated down *Rapid Conversion*'s central shaft. But there was one member of the pack who did not take part.

"Are you sure," Tartarus asked, squinting at the tethered arcs above the planet, "this isn't a weapons platform? Kinetics won't register on our scans. And it's large enough for missiles." The pack's howl petered out. But Tartarus persisted, oblivious to the uncomfortable silence: "We should destroy it and all proximate contacts. Our point-lasers should be sufficient. No need to show them we have cannon."

Failing to participate in the howl was a direct challenge to Maccabeus' dominance. In his lifetime, the Chieftain had spilled blood for lesser offenses. But he was absolutely calm as he turned to face his nephew.

"Your suspicion well befits your post. But we now bear witness to *tangible* divinity." Maccabeus gave Tartarus a moment to pull himself from the tank, look his Chieftain in the eye, and realize the extent of his insubordination—his perilous position. "If there is an Oracle on this world, nephew, shall we meet its call for peace with violence?"

"No, Uncle," Tartarus replied. "No, *Chieftain*."

Maccabeus flared his nostrils. The younger Jiralhanae's angry scent was fading, and his willful glands were now producing the unmistakable scent of submission. "Then let us keep our weapons stowed." The Chieftain placed both paws on Tartarus' shoulders and gave him a loving shake. "We shall give these aliens no reason to fear us. No cause to secret what we seek."

With that, the Chieftain began another howl. This time Tartarus was quick to join in, and before Dadab knew it, he was whooping along with them, his thin lips puckered inside his mask.

The Deacon wasn't so foolish to think he had somehow become a member of their pack. He would always be an outsider. But he was the cruiser's Deacon, and this was cause for celebration. In spite of all his missteps, and in opposition to his fears, Dadab had finally found his calling—his ministry, and his flock.

CHAPTER

FIFTEEN

Avery had always preferred to operate before first light. Something about the inevitability of sunrise heightened his senses—made him more alert. Breathing in the cool air of a soon-to-be-hot-and-humid day, Avery wondered if the aliens shared his preference. Exhaling, he hoped they didn't. Today was supposed to be a peaceful parley. But in case things went bad, Avery wanted every advantage he could get.

"You tired, Osmo?"

"No, Staff Sergeant."

"You keep yawning like that, I'm gonna pull you off the line."

"Yes, Staff Sergeant."

The militia was gathered in Harvest's botanical gardens, the planet's largest park after Utgard's mall. Located about one hundred and fifty kilometers southeast of the capital city, the gardens were the most remote and yet still stately location Lt. Commander al-Cygni could find. If it were up to Avery, he'd have moved the meeting further away—not just from Utgard but from any population center. But Governor Thune had been willing to trade the small risk of civilian observation for the scenic grandeur he deemed necessary for humanity's first formal meeting with alien beings.

And Avery had to admit: The gardens were plenty grand.

The park stepped down to the Bifrost in three landscaped tiers, the lowest of which was a broad lawn of close-cropped grass that grew right up to the precipice. Here the Bifrost bulged in an unusual promontory—a spur of windswept limestone that provided panoramic views of the plain of Ida. To the north of the promontory was a spectacular waterfall—the abrupt end of the Mimir River that started in the Vigrond highlands and cut just to the south of Utgard. The Mimir's clear water tumbled down the escarpment to the murky, slow-moving Slidr: a river that followed the contours of the Bifrost and drained into Harvest's southern sea.

Standing in the middle of the lowest tier, Avery couldn't see the falls past a border of magnolia trees, but he could hear them: water crashing against rock, like an endless peal of thunder—reveille for a world not yet awakened to its peril.

Avery scanned the faces of 1st platoon's alpha squad. The twelve recruits stood in two lines on opposite sides of a large "X" of landing lights. The bright bulbs were meant to serve as visual confirmation of the directions Mack's JOTUN all-in-ones had etched into the freighter's hull.

The recruits' olive drab fatigues were freshly pressed and their boots were polished—not the sort of thing to do if they'd wanted to blend into the surrounding greenery. But Avery knew that was all part of al-Cygni's plan: make the aliens feel welcome, but also let them see *exactly* what they were dealing with.

Osmo's hand shot to his mouth, stifling another yawn. He and the other recruits had been up most of the night, helping Avery and Byrne hide surveillance gear in the trees: dozens of small cameras and even a few compact ARGUS units.

"That's it, recruit. Step out." Avery thrust a thumb toward the magnolias bordering the northern edge of the lawn. Hidden in the mossy rocks and ferns between the trees and the river was 1/A's backup: Stisen and the rest of the 2/A recruits.

"But Staff Ser—"

"But *what*?"

Osmo's thick cheeks flushed. "This recruit wants to stay with his squad." Osmo tightened his grip on his MA5's shoulder strap, tugging the rifle against his back. "Wants to do his duty!"

Avery frowned. It had been less than forty-eight hours since the exercise at the reactor complex—since Captain Ponder had broken the news of the aliens' arrival. He'd laid things out, plain and simple, right in the middle of the recruits' victory dinner: Hostile aliens had found Harvest, and it was up to the militia to deal with the situation until help arrived. The garrison mess had gotten so quiet so quick, Avery thought the recruits were about to bolt—go AWOL right then and there.

But in the stunned silence that followed Ponder's announcement, no one moved. Eventually, the Captain asked if the recruits had any questions. Stisen had been the first to raise his hand.

"We the only ones who know, sir?"

"Just about."

"Can we tell our families?"

"Afraid not."

"You want us to lie." Stisen had glanced around the mess. "Like you've been lying to us."

Ponder held out an arm to keep Byrne in his seat. "If we'd told you the truth—that we were expecting aliens not Innies, would it have made a difference?" The Captain caught as many suspicious eyes as he could. "Would you have refused to serve? Your families and your neighbors aren't in any less danger. You're the only protection they've got." Then, nodding at his Staff Sergeants: "We've trained you. You're ready."

Dass was next to stand. "For what, sir? Exactly."

Ponder motioned for Healy to kill the fluorescents and power on a wall-mounted video display. "I'll tell you everything we know."

The Lt. Commander had put together a good briefing, and the recruits were a rapt audience—especially during the footage from Avery's helmet cam of his fight aboard the freighter. Byrne remained stoic as he rewatched one of the vacuum-suited aliens stab its pink blade deep into his thigh. So did Avery as he saw himself raise his M6 pistol to another alien's chin, and blow its brains all over the inside of its helmet. As the footage showed him push toward the umbilical in hot pursuit of the retreating alien leader, Avery noticed the recruits glance in his direction and nod approvingly to one another.

Avery hadn't ascribed any particular bravery to his actions. And in retrospect, he knew charging the alien ship had been extremely dangerous. Part of him wished al-Cygni had included all the footage—shown the methane explosion and Avery's mad scramble away from the fireball—if only to prove to the recruits that sometimes caution was the better part of valor. But instead, the final frozen frame was that of the alien ship blowing to pieces as the Lt. Commander's sloop moved away from the freighter—a victorious finish that set the recruits to excited muttering as Healy flipped on the lights.

It was only later, when the mess cleared and the Staff Sergeants and the Captain got down to planning how best to secure the gardens, that Avery realized why the recruits had been so upbeat: The presentation proved the aliens could be killed—showed that Harvest might be kept safe with a few well-placed bullets. And if the recruits had confidence in any of their training, they knew they could at least aim a rifle and shoot.

Unfortunately, some recruits were less confident than others. And as Osmo now broke out in a nervous shudder, Avery put a hand on the recruit's shoulder and steered him toward the trees. "We need to make a good impression, understood?"

"Yes, Staff Sergeant."

Avery slapped Osmo on the backside, accelerating his retreat. "Alright then. Go on."

As the disappointed recruit jogged north, Jenkins' voice crackled in Avery's earpiece. "Forsell's got contacts on thermal. Ten o'clock high."

Avery scanned the western sky. But he couldn't see anything with naked eyes. "How many?"

"Two," Jenkins replied. "Want us to mark them?"

On Avery's orders, 1st platoon's marksmen had taken up position in an ornate greenhouse on the gardens' eastern edge—a white curvilinear building that would have been right at home in a nineteenth century European park. Granted, what would have been a cast-iron frame was now a titanium lattice and thousands of panes of glass, shatterproof plastic. But straddling the gardens' uppermost tier, the greenhouse looked just as stately as those that inspired it.

"Negative," Avery replied. "They'll be here soon enough."

The marksmen were hunkered on a balcony that ran around the greenhouse's central elliptical dome and continued out along the roofs of its two wings, giving them an excellent view of the gardens and the sky above. Forsell's spotting scope was equipped with a targeting laser that could paint the two contacts and generate range-finding data. But again, Lt. Commander al-Cygni had been very clear: As much as possible, the marines and their recruits should minimize behavior the aliens might regard as hostile. Tugging at his own rifle's sling, Avery again wondered how much he and the aliens had in common—if they would show similar restraint.

"Company's on the way, Captain," Avery growled into his throat mic. "How's our perimeter?"

"Charlie squads report all clear," Ponder replied.

1/C and 2/C were deployed at the gardens' main gate and its exit from the Utgard highway, respectively. The marines didn't expect any traffic (it was a Tuesday, and the gardens were mainly a weekend destination), but all it would take was a single sedan of early-rising plant-lovers to ruin the meeting's secrecy. Or worse, spread premature panic.

"And our welcome party?" the Captain asked.

Avery scanned the remaining 1/A recruits. "Good to go, sir."

"Keep them calm, Johnson. Weapons safed and shouldered."

"Roger that."

For a few long seconds there was no chatter on the COM as all gathered in the gardens took a deep breath. Avery listened to the Mimir rush toward its plummet. The noise of the falls muted all but the most enthusiastic birds, just now beginning their morning calls deep inside the magnolias. Like the greenhouse's exotic flora, the birds were imports—starlings and other hardy species brought to Harvest to help contain the planet's essential insect population. Slowly, the birds' cries were overwhelmed by a pulsing whine that grew in intensity until it bested even the Mimir's mighty roar.

Avery squinted at the sky from beneath the brim of his duty cap. In the brightening, deep blue haze he saw two dark shadows following one behind the other, like sharks prowling the shallows of a storm-churned sea.

"Staff Sergeant . . ." Jenkins began.

"I see them." Avery squared his cap on his forehead. "Squad! Stand to!"

As 1/A came to attention, a pair of alien ships emerged from the haze. Purple hullplate flashing, they dropped toward the Bifrost and then began a wide circle around the gardens.

The ships' bifurcated designs made Avery think of two hauler trailers linked to a common cab, but traveling in reverse. Unlike most human aircraft, the dropships' cabins were located in the ships' *sterns*. Avery could see a single, obvious weapon on each ship: a ball-turret with a single barrel suspended beneath the cabin. The ships had no engines or thrusters. But as the dropships completed their first circle and one of them decelerated above the promontory, Avery noticed the ship's outline ripple and guessed they must rely on some sort of anti-gravity field for lift and propulsion.

"Step back!" Avery shouted as the ship dove toward the lawn. "She's gonna need more room!"

The recruits backpedaled with more speed than decorum, and the dropship glided to a stop directly above the lighted X. The bulbs flickered and died and the grass flattened under the press of the invisible field. Skin tingling, Avery watched as water condensed against the field, defining its ovoid shape, only to fall in a single sheet of rain as the field collapsed. The ship's curvaceous cabin settled onto the turf, but its two compartments remained hovering parallel to the ground.

"Form up!" Avery growled, and the 1/A recruits moved back into position: two lines on either side of the dropship. Presently, one of the compartments swung open along its bottom edge. The interior of the ship was dim, and it took Avery a moment to distinguish the three aliens from their surroundings.

Partly this was because the creatures' armor shone with the same dull glow as the metal bands that held them secure and upright. But also because these aliens were nothing like the ones Avery had fought aboard the freighter. The latter reminded Avery of upright reptiles; the ones now shaking free of their harnesses looked like the improbable offspring of a gorilla and a grizzly bear; hirsute giants with shoulders as wide as an average human was tall and fists that could easily encompass Avery's head.

"Sir?" Despite the moisture in the air, Avery felt his mouth go dry. "This isn't what we expected."

"Explain," Ponder replied.

"They're bigger. Armored."

"Weapons?"

Avery noted sharp spurs jutting from metal plates girding the aliens' chests, shoulders, and thighs. These would be deadly in a close-up fight. But each alien also had a stout, short-barreled weapon clipped to its belt. At first Avery thought they carried knives as well, but then he realized the half-moon blades were affixed to the weapons like bayonets; pointed for stabbing and curved for slashing. The alien Avery decided was the leader—the one with golden armor and helmet with a V-shaped crest that swept back from its head like two jagged saw-blades—carried an additional item: a long-handled hammer with a stone head that must have weighed at least as much as Byrne.

"Heavy pistols," Avery replied. "And a hammer."

"Say again?"

"A giant hammer, sir. On their leader."

Ponder let that sink in a moment, then: "Anything else?"

As the gold-armored alien stepped toward the edge of the compartment its nostrils flared. It jerked its chin toward the trees—directly at 2/A's hiding spot—and its blue-armored escorts bared their oversized canine teeth, acknowledging the humans' scent with wary growls.

"Should have gone with barbecue . . ." Avery muttered.

"Say again?"

"They aren't vegetarians, sir. Might want to reset the table."

There was a pause as Ponder relayed the information to Lt. Commander al-Cygni and Governor Thune. "No time for that, Johnson. Bring them up."

Avery wasn't privy to all of al-Cygni and Thune's protocol discussions—everything they'd decided to do to put their alien visitors at ease. But Jilan had told him that the first freighter the aliens had attacked was carrying fruit, and that she and Thune had agreed that more produce would make a good welcome gift. Symbolically, an offering of fruits and vegetables highlighted Harvest's peaceful, agrarian purpose. And this offer, to share the planet's bounty, had served as the basis for Mack's etchings.

But now—looking at the aliens' carnivore physiques and

vicious weapons—it was clear to Avery that they hadn't dropped to the surface hoping to find a nice fruit salad. They wanted something else. And they looked ready to take it should anyone refuse.

Avery stepped toward the dropship and stopped a few meters in front of the gold-armored alien. The towering beast narrowed its yellow eyes.

"Dass. Come to me," Avery said. "Nice and slow."

The 1/A squad leader stepped out of formation and paced to Avery's side. Moving slowly and deliberately, Avery unshouldered his BR55, released the magazine, pulled its action to eject a lone bullet from the chamber, and presented both the weapon and its ammunition to Dass. The alien's eyes flashed as it watched each step of the unloading process. Avery extended his empty hands, punctuating his performance: *OK*, he thought. *Now you.*

With a gruff exhale the gold-armored alien grasped its hammer below the head. It slid the weapon up and over his shoulder and then held it out to the shorter of its blue-armored escorts. The other alien seemed reluctant to take the weapon, and only did so after the leader loosed an emphatic bark. Then, mimicking Avery, it uncurled its hairy paws, revealing black and pointed nails.

Avery nodded. "Dass. Step back."

As the squad leader returned to formation, Avery placed a hand on his chest, then pointed at the greenhouse. Al-Cygni had encouraged him to keep hand gestures (and their unintended insults) to a minimum. But Avery had needed no convincing. He was pretty sure the aliens were already offended by what he and Byrne had done to their first ship and its crew, and he knew waving his arms and mistakenly signing the equivalent of "go screw yourself" wouldn't exactly lessen their resentment.

So he kept gently placing and pointing his hand until the gold-armored alien leapt down from the compartment, shuddering the grass and sinking a good six inches into the turf. The militiamen standing on the other side of the ship, who had yet to see the aliens, took a nervous step back. A few looked set to bolt for the trees.

"Steady," Avery growled into his throat mic as the blue-armored escorts thundered to the ground.

Now that all three were out in the light, Avery noticed they each had different-colored fur tufting through breaks in their armor. The leader's coat was light gray, almost silver. One of the escorts had dark brown fur and the other, tan. This second escort was actually a bit taller than the leader and more muscular, though Avery knew this was a bit like comparing two models of main battle tanks: one might weigh more than the other, but both would have no trouble flattening the 1/A recruits.

But for now, the creatures seemed eager to please. The leader placed a shaggy palm across its chest plate and pointed at Avery then the greenhouse. Avery nodded and soon the unlikely foursome was trooping across the lawn to a granite staircase that led up to the gardens' middle tier—Avery in the lead, then the gold-armored alien, then its two escorts.

"We're on the move," Avery whispered into his mic. "So far so good."

At the top of the stairs, a flagstone path cut east through a grove of flowering cherry and pear trees. The trees had been in bloom for weeks, and their blossoms had begun to fall onto the path's rough-cut stones. As the aliens lumbered along the pink-and-yellow petals clung to their broad bare feet, creating wider holes in an already patchy carpet. Unfortunately, the petals' scent of sweet decay did little to mask the aliens' musky smell. The powerful odor set Avery's nerves on edge, and he wondered what the ARGUS units would make of it.

Halfway to another staircase leading up to the greenhouse, the path widened to accommodate a ground-level, rectangular fountain. Its jets were on an automatic timer and had yet to activate. For now, the shallow water was still, and as Avery steered the party along the fountain's southern edge, he saw the second alien dropship—still swinging a wide loop above the trees—reflected in the clear, cold water. The dropship was moving more slowly now, and Avery had a hard time differentiating its motive whine from the river's churn.

Mounting the second staircase, Avery saw both platoons' bravo squads arranged in staggered lines before the greenhouse. Between them and the staircase—in the middle of the upper tier's lawn—was a wide oak table covered by a crisp white cloth and topped with a generous basket of fruit. Avery took a few steps toward the table then turned toward the aliens, palms raised in a halting pose. But the armored brutes had already come to a stop. All three were staring at the greenhouse's gabled entrance, where humanity's delegation had just emerged: Thune, Pedersen, Ponder, and al-Cygni with Staff Sergeant Byrne taking up the rear.

Pedersen wore his usual gray linen suit, while the Governor sported a yellow-on-white variation of the seersucker he'd worn for the solstice celebration. As usual, the Governor's bulk strained at his suit's seams, making him look more like the gentrified farmer he was than the powerful politician he hoped the aliens would perceive. But despite the fabric's pinch, Thune strode forward—chest puffed and shoulders back—at a pace that implied he was no more intimidated by the armored trio than a group of Harvest's parliamentarians.

The Captain and the Lt. Commander both wore dress uniforms and caps, he Marine Corps navy blue and she full-dress white. In an effort to help the aliens differentiate gender, al-Cygni had opted for a knee-length skirt. Like Avery, Byrne wore battle-dress fatigues and the same grim stare of altered expectations: *These aren't the enemies we expected.* The tall Irishman's blue eyes flicked back and forth beneath his duty cap's brim as he hastened to assess the aliens' arms and armor.

"Thank you, Staff Sergeant," Thune said. "I'll take it from here."

"Yes, sir." Avery turned on his heels and stepped to the front of the table, where he met Jilan. Byrne took the northwest corner, flanking Ponder. Pedersen stepped in between Thune and the table, a large COM tablet tucked under his arm.

"Welcome to Harvest!" Thune beamed. "I am its leader." He tapped his chest. "Thune."

The gold-armored alien huffed. But it made no indication if that was its species, rank, or name—or perhaps it simply wanted the Governor to get on with his unintelligible introduction.

Despite the language barrier, al-Cygni had thought it wise to at least attempt verbal communication, if only to get some of the aliens' speech on record for later analysis. Thune had insisted he do all the talking, and while the Lt. Commander hadn't disagreed, she had taken pains to clarify that brevity was key—that the worst thing Thune could do was frustrate the aliens by talking too much.

The Governor waited, giving the leader a chance to make some opening remarks of its own. But it said nothing. Thune was about to launch into an extended introduction when al-Cygni coughed. Avery knew it had become as clear to Jilan as it was to him that the aliens weren't long on patience. While the gold-armored one had had the discipline to stay focused on Thune as he spoke, its fur had begun to bristle. And Avery couldn't be sure, but the shorter of the escorts seemed to have gotten a lot more pungent.

Thune shot al-Cygni an annoyed glance, but he motioned Pedersen forward. The Attorney General pulled the COM tablet from under his arm and held it out to the aliens. A moment later, an orchestral version of Harvest's anthem warbled from the tablet's speakers and a video presentation filled its screen. Avery had seen the presentation the night before; a variation on the official planetary introduction he'd viewed during his initial descent from the Tiara. Though this one lacked Mack's narration, it contained similarly bucolic footage: JOTUNs at work in the fields, gondolas loading produce into freight containers, families enjoying their meals—a montage of clips that gave a good overview of life on Harvest while avoiding any implication that there might be other worlds like it.

The presentation went on for some time. But Avery knew this wasn't really for the aliens' benefit. At some point, Mack—who was monitoring all the surveillance gear via a powerful relay hidden in the greenhouse—began manipulating the presentation to test the aliens' reactions. Did the sight of the JOTUNs intimidate them? And if so, how did that manifest in body language? Avery had worked with enough ONI officers to know how focused they were on gathering good intelligence, and he was sure Jilan had given the AI a long list of questions.

But as Avery watched the second dropship make another pass around the gardens, disappearing briefly behind the northern trees before it surged back into view, he wondered how long al-Cygni was going to let the experiment run. After the aliens had shifted inside their armor for the better part of five minutes, she nonchalantly primped the tight bun that secured her black hair high on her neck: a subtle signal to Mack, watching through his cameras, to kill the feed. A moment later, Harvest's looping anthem faded, bringing the presentation to a close. Pedersen tucked the COM tablet back under his arm.

The gold-armored alien growled at its shorter escort, who pulled a small, square sheet of metal from its belt. The leader took the sheet and handed it to Thune. Smiling politely, the Governor studied the offering. A moment later, he beamed at his Attorney General.

"Look at this, Rol. See the picture? Just like we did to the freighter!"

"I think it's a piece *of* the freighter."

"But see what they've etched?"

Pedersen craned his neck toward the sheet. "They want to trade."

"Exactly!"

"Governor," Jilan said. "If I may."

Thune stepped back to the table and handed the sheet to Jilan. Avery glanced over her shoulder to take a look as well.

It was indeed a piece of the freighter's titanium hull—a perfect square, neatly cut. The picture was dominated by two figures, both carved more realistically than Mack's had been. One was clearly the gold-armored alien; it carried a hammer across its back and wore a helmet with the same V-shaped crest. The human looked male, but it could have been anyone. To Avery's surprise, the man was offering up what looked to be a large melon with a variegated rind. Thune must have made the same connection because he rummaged deep inside the basket and extracted a large and fragrant cantaloupe. Smiling even wider than before, he walked the fruit to the gold-armored alien and presented it with a bow.

"Please, take it," the Governor said. "We can give you plenty more."

The alien palmed the cantaloupe and gave it a cautious sniff.

As Thune began expounding upon the virtues of interspecies commerce, Jilan flipped the sheet over. Avery saw her bare neck stiffen. "Governor, they don't want food."

"Don't be so sure, Commander. I think this one's about to take a bite."

"No." Jilan kept an even tone. "Look."

And Avery did. On the other side of the sheet was a magnified view of the melon, which he now realized was a map of Harvest, centered on Utgard. What Avery had thought were textures in the rind were actually surface details: maglev lines, roads, and outlines of major settlements. The aliens had made a complete survey and added some sort of notation as well.

Ornate symbols were scattered all over the planet. Each

symbol was identical, and each consisted of two concentric circles filigreed with interlocking curves. Avery had no idea what the symbols stood for, but that was beside the point. Jilan gave voice to his own realization: "They're looking for something specific. Something they think belongs to them." Thune stared at the sheet, doing his best to maintain a diplomatic smile as Jilan flipped it back and forth. "Governor," she said in a whisper. "They want us to give them the entire planet."

At that moment, the gold-armored alien barked and extended the melon to Pedersen.

"No, no." The Attorney General raised a hand and took a step back. "Keep it."

The alien cocked its head and barked again. Now Avery was certain that the musky scent wafting from the shorter escort had become more powerful. Avery wrinkled his nose as it filled with the smell of vinegar and tar. He fought back the urge to draw the M6 pistol holstered at his hip. At that moment, a short burst from an MA5 echoed up from the garden's lowest tier. Whether this was a nervous misfire or the beginning of a firefight, Avery didn't know. But in the brief silence that followed, he heard a throaty alien howl echo from the trees along the river.

After that, things happened very quickly.

The taller escort ripped its pistol from its belt before Avery could draw or Byrne could slip his battle rifle off his shoulder. The bladed weapon boomed, and a bright spike of metal like lit magnesium sizzled into Pedersen's chest. The Attorney General dropped the melon and his COM-tablet and fell to his knees, jaw opening and closing like a suffocating fish. He had been closest to the gold-armored leader—the unlucky victim of proximity.

The Staff Sergeants fired back at the escorts closest to their positions—Byrne at the taller, Avery at the shorter. But their bullets had no effect on the aliens' armor. In fact, they never even touched it. Each round was deflected by invisible energy shields that followed the contours of the armor and shimmered with every impact.

"Get down!" Avery yelled to Thune, as the shorter escort tossed the leader its hammer. Then he tackled Jilan, driving her roughly to the ground.

In an instant, the silver-haired giant had the cudgel above its head, ready for a cross-body strike. Thune would have gotten his head knocked clean off his shoulders if Captain Ponder hadn't pushed him out of the way and taken the blow himself. The hammer hit the Captain in his prosthetic left arm and sent him twisting through the air. He landed north of Byrne and slid a good twenty meters on the dew-slick grass.

Now the shorter escort had its bladed pistol out. As the creature took aim at Avery, he hugged Jilan tight—shielded her smaller body with his own. He had a moment to second-guess Ponder's pronouncement that they had trained the recruits well—that they were ready for the split-second, life-or-death decisions combat demanded—when he heard the high-pitched triple-crack of Jenkins' BR55. The shorter escort howled in surprise as a burst pinged off its helmet, snapping its large head back. Then all Avery could hear was the snap of bullets overhead as the twenty-four bravo recruits opened fire, full automatic.

Peppered with multiple shots, the shorter escort took a shaky step backward. It jerked left and right as if fighting off an invisible swarm of bees. Then its energy shields collapsed with a flash and a loud pop, and its armor began venting cyan smoke and sparks as dozens more MA5 rounds slammed into its unprotected plates.

Now it was the aliens' turn to protect their own. The leader lunged toward its shorter escort, turning its back toward the greenhouse. Its golden armor must have had stronger shields, because even the bravo squads' concentrated fire failed to take them down. The taller escort loosed a thunderous roar and raked the recruits from north to south, covering the leader as it helped its wounded comrade limp down the stairs to the second tier. Avery wasn't sure how many of the recruits along the greenhouse had been hit—whether their screams were from fresh wounds or an excess of adrenaline.

"Cease fire! Cease fire!" Byrne shouted. The recruits had been firing directly over his and the others' heads. Some of their shots had come a little too close.

"You alright?" Avery asked, pushing up from Jilan on his fists.

"Go," she said. "I'm fine." But she looked a little frightened. Like the day in the hospital, it was another temporary break in her unflappable facade. This time all Avery did was nod.

"One alpha: fall back!" Avery shouted, rising to his feet. "Get away from that dropship!" Avery could hear the pulse of an energy weapon and knew the first dropship's turret had activated even before he turned south and saw bright blue streaks of plasma rake the lowest tier's lawn—covering fire for the armored aliens' retreat.

"Where the hell are you going?" Byrne shouted as Avery sprinted past.

"River!"

"I'm coming with you!"

"Negative! Draw that turret's fire while I flank!"

"Bravo! Move up!" Byrne shouted. "Healy! Get your ass out here!"

Avery saw the Corpsman rush from the greenhouse behind the charging recruits and hustle toward Ponder, med kits in hand. The Captain waved Healy off—directed him to Pedersen's motionless form. Then Avery charged into the tree line.

"Stisen! Report!" he shouted into his mic.

"Taking fire, Staff Sergeant!" Static distorted the 2/A squad leader's voice. "There! Over there!" he yelled to one of his men.

"Hang tight!" Avery leapt down a rocky embankment to the gardens' middle tier. "I'm on my way!"

Avery ran as fast as he could, hurdling rocks and slaloming between cherry and pear trees. Breathing hard, he broke through the last of the blossom-heavy branches, and pulled up short, thrusting his hips backward and windmilling his arms. If he'd been going any faster he would have fallen into the river. Here at the edge of the gardens, the Mimir had carved deep into the Bifrost, creating a series of descending pools. These wide limestone cauldrons were filled with white water that grew more turbulent the closer it came to the top of the falls.

As Avery regained his balance, the second dropship swooped overhead and came to rest on the other side of the nearest pool. Tracking the ship's downward progress, Avery spotted another of the large aliens—this one in red armor and with black fur—as it emerged from the magnolia trees on the gardens' lowest tier. It too carried a bladed pistol and was using the weapon to guard the retreat of a pack of shorter, gray-skinned creatures with conical orange backpacks. Avery saw MA5 muzzle flashes in the trees. But the red-armored alien quickly loosed a salvo of burning spikes to quiet whatever recruits had been brave enough to fight back.

Avery raised his pistol and emptied his clip. He knew his rounds wouldn't punch through the alien's shields, but all he wanted was to draw the thing's attention and keep it from hitting any of the recruits.

As Avery's shots flashed harmlessly against its back, the alien turned. But by then Avery was already running south for the safety of a boulder. He reloaded and slid around the stone, hoping to pick off one of the smaller aliens. But most of them were already aboard the dropship. A lone straggler was just now stumbling from the trees. One of its arms was slacked by its side, and it seemed injured. Avery was about to finish it off when the armored alien grabbed its wounded comrade by the nape of its neck, ripped off its mask, and flung it into the whirlpool. The creature sunk beneath the surface then bobbed up, clutching at a pair of hissing tubes connected to its tank, before it pitched into the next pool and tumbled toward the falls.

While this unexpected fratricide ran its course, the second dropship's ball turret finally swung into action, and Avery soon found himself diving back behind the boulder to avoid searing bolts of plasma. The splash of ionized gasses against the rock set Avery's teeth on edge. But after a few seconds, the turret ceased fire. Avery heard the groan of anti-grav generators as the dropship twisted up into the sky. When he came out from behind the boulder, all the aliens were gone.

"Hold your fire!" Avery barked as he approached the magnolias on the far side of the pool. "I'm coming in!" Behind him, he could hear the reports of the bravo squads' rifles, firing on the first dropship as it rose from the gardens. "What happened?" Avery growled at Stisen as he neared a huddle of 2/A recruits. The men were packed close together in a jumble of mossy granite. The rocks were dotted with holes that contained glowing remnants of the red-armored alien's igneous spikes. Little smoky fires burned in the surrounding ferns where some of the rounds had ricocheted.

"What happened?" Avery asked again.

But neither Stisen nor any of his squad said a word. Most of them didn't even bother to meet Avery's gaze.

Combat had filled Avery with adrenaline, and he was about to lose his temper when he realized what the recruits *were* looking at. It took him a moment more to recognize that the thing splayed against granite was the savaged body of a human being. And it wasn't until Avery knelt down beside the corpse that he recognized Osmo's plump, boyish face streaked with his own blood. The recruit was split open across his belly.

"I told him: Stay away from the lawn." Stisen swallowed hard. "I didn't want him to get hurt."

Avery clenched his jaw. But he knew there was no way the squad leader could have anticipated that the second dropship would swing in behind them, low above the river, and secretly release a backup team. "Did you see him get hit?" Avery asked.

Stisen shook his head. "No."

"It was one of the little ones," Burdick whispered. His eyes remained locked on the spill of organs from Osmo's gut. "It knocked him to the ground. Tore him apart."

"I heard his weapon fire," Stisen said. "But it was too late."

Avery rose to his feet. "Any other casualties?"

Again Stisen shook his head.

"Byrne. Talk to me," Avery barked.

"Captain's hurt pretty bad. Bravo squads have three wounded, one serious. Dass says his boys are fine."

"Thune?"

"Not happy. Pedersen's dead."

"Looked like it."

"We better clear out, Johnson. Bastards might circle back."

"Agreed." Avery lowered his voice. "I'm gonna need a bag."

"Who?"

"Osmo."

"Shite," Byrne spat. "Alright. I'll tell Healy."

Avery removed his duty cap and wiped his hand across his brow. Staring down at Osmo, he noticed the recruit still held his MA5 tight in his right hand. The Staff Sergeant was glad Osmo had seen his attacker and had a chance to go down shooting. Osmo's rifle fire had alerted his comrades to danger, saving their lives even as he lost his own. Avery tried not to blame himself for what had happened. Like Stisen, he had done what he thought was best. Osmo was just the first recruit to fall. As much as Avery hoped he would also be the last, he steeled himself against the knowledge that the aliens had just begun a war—and that there would be a lot more casualties to come.

Maccabeus released his hammer and let it clang onto the troop-bay floor. This was the *Fist of Rukt,* an ancient weapon passed down from one Chieftain to the next for generations of Maccabeus' clan. It deserved greater care. But Maccabeus was too worried about Licinus to stand on ceremony. His ancestors would have to understand.

"Vorenus! Hurry!" he bellowed, muscling Licinus upright. The Spirit shook violently as it hurtled back into the hazy sky, and even the mighty Chieftain had a difficult time propping his wounded pack member's unconscious bulk against the bay's inner wall.

Vorenus stumbled down the bay, hefting a portable aid station. He set the octagonal box by Licinus' feet then held him steady while Maccabeus fastened restraining bands around his legs and arms. Sangheili Spirits had sophisticated stasis fields to keep their warriors upright. But Maccabeus had been denied this technology as well, and he'd had to make do with a more basic solution.

"Give me a compress!" Maccabeus peeled off Licinus' breastplate. The armor had a crack down the middle that oozed dark red blood. Once the plate was free, Maccabeus smoothed his wounded pack member's brown fur, probing for two whistling holes in his chest. The aliens' weapons had penetrated one of Licinus' lungs, forcing its collapse.

Vorenus handed Maccabeus a thin sheet of bronze-colored mesh. Properly affixed, the material would form a partial seal over the wounds, allowing air to escape as Licinus exhaled but keeping it out as he inhaled; as long as the lung wasn't too badly damaged, it would reinflate. The mesh also contained a coagulant that would help keep the young Jiralhanae's remaining blood inside his body. When they made it back to *Rapid Conversion,* Maccabeus would let the ship's automated surgery suite do the rest.

If *we make it back,* the Chieftain growled to himself as the Spirit jerked to starboard, executing another evasive maneuver. So far the aliens hadn't activated any anti-air defenses, but Maccabeus felt certain they would. The aliens' infantry weapons were fairly crude—not much more sophisticated than the Jiralhanae's at the time of the San'Shyuum's missionary contact. But they had to have missiles or some other kinetic weapons system, or their planet would be defenseless. And Maccabeus doubted the aliens were as dumb as that.

"Uncle? Are you harmed?" Tartarus' voice boomed from Maccabeus' signal unit.

"I am not." The Chieftain gripped the back of Vorenus' neck. "Watch after him," he said, glancing toward Licinus. Vorenus nodded his assent. "Did you claim a relic?" Maccabeus asked Tartarus as he knelt and retrieved the *Fist of Rukt.*

"No, Chieftain."

Maccabeus couldn't help an angry huff. "But the Luminary showed *dozens* of holy objects—all very close at hand!"

"I found nothing but their warriors."

Maccabeus stalked toward the Spirit's cabin, his free hand pressed against the wall of the bay to keep himself steady as the dropship continued its wrenching climb. "Did you conduct a thorough search?"

"The Unggoy were overeager and broke ranks," Tartarus rumbled. "We lost the element of surprise."

"Deacon," Maccabeus barked as he ducked into the cabin. "Tell me you have better news."

Another Jiralhanae named Ritul, who was too young to have earned his masculine "us" suffix, manned the flight controls. Maccabeus would have preferred a more experienced pilot, but with a total of five Jiralhanae on the two Spirits, he had to keep some of his older, more experienced pack members on board *Rapid Conversion* in case of an emergency.

"Sensors registered high amounts of signal traffic during the parley." Dadab's muffled voice squeaked from the cabin's signal unit; he had remained on the cruiser's bridge. "The Luminary considered the data and passed judgment." Then, after a pause: "An Oracle, just as we suspected!"

"Prophets be praised! Where?"

"The signals originated from the gardens' white metal structure."

So close! The Chieftain groaned. *Were it not for the Unggoy, I might have laid eyes upon it!* But he quickly stifled his disappointment. He knew the Prophets alone had access to the sacred Oracle on High Charity, and thus it was the height of hubris for him, a low and recent convert, to covet such communion. But it was no sin to feel pride at the message he now felt compelled to deliver.

"Send word to the Vice Minister," Maccabeus said, his chest swelling inside his golden armor. "The reliquary is even richer than expected. A second Oracle—one who speaks for the Gods themselves—has at last been found!"

CHAPTER
SIXTEEN

Nights in High Charity's main dome were normally quite subdued. The guttural clamor of the Unggoy's mass evening prayers sometimes filtered up from the lower districts, but otherwise the upper towers were quiet. The San'Shyuum who called the floating towers home preferred to spend the hours between sundown and sunup resting or in quiet contemplation.

But not tonight, Fortitude thought. The Minister's chair hung motionless between two empty anti-grav barges, idling near one of the Forerunner Dreadnought's three massive support struts. The dome's illumination disc shone with a feeble glow, simulating moonlight, which did nothing to warm the air. Fortitude gathered his crimson robes tight around his hunched shoulders, and stared at the rare commotion in the towers.

Lights blazed in the buildings' hanging gardens. Rings of gaily dressed San'Shyuum glided from one open-air party to the next. There was music on the breeze; overlapping strains of triumphal strings and chimes. Here and there, fireworks crackled, blooming sparks in the prevailing darkness.

All this marked a momentous occasion, one that only came once or twice an Age. Tonight, all female San'Shyuum lucky enough to bear children were proudly showing off their broods. And as far as Fortitude could tell, the numbers were particularly good. Even though he himself had never sired a successor—and despite all that weighed upon him—he managed a satisfied smile.

There were a little more than twenty million San'Shyuum in the Covenant. Not a very large number compared to the faith's billions of adherents. But it was significantly more than the thousand or so individuals who had fled the San'Shyuum's distant homeworld long ago.

Fortitude's ancestors had broken with the rest of their kind over the same issue that would eventually pit them against the Sangheili: whether or not to desecrate Forerunner objects to realize their full potential. In the internal, San'Shyuum version of this debate, the Dreadnought had become a key symbol for both sides—an object the majority Stoics would not enter and the minority Reformers were desperate to explore. At the climax of the fratricidal conflict, the most zealous Reformers breached the Dreadnought and barricaded themselves inside. While the Stoics debated what to do (they couldn't very well destroy the object they so revered), the Reformers activated the vessel and took flight—taking a chunk of the San'Shyuum homeworld with it.

At first the Reformers were ecstatic. They had survived, and also escaped with the conflict's greatest prize. They sped out of their home system, laughing at the Stoics' bitter signals—claims that the Gods would surely damn them for their theft. But then the Reformers counted up their numbers and realized to their horror that they might indeed be doomed.

The problem was a limited pool of genes. With only a thousand individuals in their population, inbreeding would soon become a serious problem. The crisis was compounded by the fact that San'Shyuum pregnancies were, even under ideal conditions, rare. Females were generally fertile, but only in short cycles that came few and far between. For these first Prophets aboard the Dreadnought, reproduction quickly became a carefully managed affair.

"I had begun to think you might not come," Fortitude said as the Vice Minister of Tranquility's chair slunk in between the barges.

The younger San'Shyuum's purple robes were rumpled, and as he bowed forward in his chair, the gold rings in his wattle became tangled in one of the many flowered garlands around his neck. "I apologize. It was hard to get away."

"Male or female?"

"One of each."

"Congratulations."

"If I hear that one more time, I shall scream. It's not as if I *made* the bastards." Tranquility's words were a little slurred, and his fingers fumbled as he pulled his wattle free, yanked the garlands from his neck, and tossed them aside.

"You're drunk," Fortitude said, watching the garlands flutter down into the darkness.

"So I am."

"I need you *sober*."

Fortitude reached inside his robes and removed a small, pharmaceutical sphere. "How was our dear Hierarch, the Prophet of Restraint?"

"You mean the *Father*?" The Vice Minister sucked the sphere between his sour lips. "Glared at me the whole time."

Fortitude raised a dismissive hand. "As long as we act quickly, there's little he can do."

The Vice Minister shrugged and lazily chewed his sphere.

"Come." Fortitude tapped the holo-switches in his chair's arm. "We're late enough as it is."

A moment later, the two San'Shyuum were speeding toward the Dreadnought's pinched middle decks—a squat triangular core that connected its three support legs to a single vertical hull of similar shape. In the dome's wan light, the ancient Forerunner warship shone bone white.

Blackmail, the Minister sighed, *was such a tiresome tool.* But before his peerless record of service and the revelation of the reliquary won them their Hierarch's thrones, Fortitude knew the thrones' current occupants would have to move aside. *And they won't do that unless I push.*

Unfortunately, the Prophet of Tolerance and the Prophetess of Obligation had proven quite unassailable. The elderly Prophetess had just given birth to a pair of triplets. Because of her advanced age, pregnancy had been difficult. And while it was true that this had caused her to shirk some of her responsibilities, Fortitude knew it would be suicidal to try to smear one of the San'Shyuum's most beloved and prolific matrons. Tolerance, who served as Minister of Concert in the wake of the Unggoy Rebellion, had done much to promote better relations between the Covenant's member species; he still had the support of many in the High Council—both Sangheili and San'Shyuum.

But the third Hierarch, the Prophet of Restraint, was a different story. This former Prelate of High Charity (essentially, the city's mayor) was on the Roll of Celibates, a list that tracked all San'Shyuum not allowed to breed. Because of their ancestors' poor planning, these unfortunate souls would never experience the joys of parenthood because their genes were now too common, and the risk of spreading their negative, recessive traits already too extreme.

Fortitude was on the Roll as well, but it had never bothered him that much. He kept a few concubines for the rare occasions when he felt the need for sexual congress, but was otherwise perfectly comfortable with his involuntary impotence.

The Prophet of Restraint was not.

Not long before the Kig-Yar stumbled on the reliquary, Restraint had accidentally impregnated a young female. Not a problem necessarily (abortions were common in these sorts of situations), but the first-time mother had been furious that Restraint had *lied* about his status and demanded she be allowed to keep her brood. The aging Hierarch was overcome by a desire to see his exalted genes passed on and could not bring himself to kill his unborn offspring or their willful mother.

Fortitude had gotten wind of the brewing scandal, and arranged for Tranquility to give the birthing period's invocation before the High Council. In his speech, the Vice Minister offered praise for "all parents and their fruitful unions," and argued for greater investment in gene therapies and other technologies to "end the tyranny of the Roll." Tranquility's passionate performance convinced Restraint they were brothers in belief. And the desperate Hierarch (for his lover would soon give birth) approached the Vice Minister with an offer: Claim my progeny as your own, and earn the Ministerial posting of your choice.

As pleased as Fortitude was that his plan had worked, he was still shocked by the Hierarch's gall. If Restraint's offer ever came to light, his children would be killed and he would be dismissed—and likely sterilized as well. The San'Shyuum who enforced the Roll were zealous in their work, and Fortitude knew even a Hierarch was not above their censure.

Tonight, it had been Tranquility's job to give Restraint their counteroffer: *Step willingly from your throne, and we shall keep the scandal quiet.*

"You should have seen her." The Vice Minister shuddered. They were now much closer to the Dreadnought and had passed into the shadow of one of the large conduits that connected the ship's engines to High Charity's power grid. In this deeper darkness, the strongest light came from a ring of blue beacons just below the cable, bright holographics around one of the Dreadnought's yawning air locks.

"Who?" Fortitude asked.

"Restraint's *whore*."

The Minister cringed. Tranquility had become far too familiar as of late, often behaving as though he were already a Hierarch and Fortitude's equal. His present inebriation only made this problem worse.

"Attractive?" Fortitude asked, trying to keep the conversation light.

"A dull-eyed monstrosity," the Vice Minister said, reaching inside his robes. "If she had a neck, I could not distinguish it from her folds." To Fortitude's amazement, Tranquility produced a plasma pistol and nonchalantly checked its charge.

"Put that away!" Fortitude snapped, glancing nervously at the Dreadnought. "Before the sentries see!"

Though they were still a good ways off, the Minister recognized the hulking shapes of Mgalekgolo, the guardians of the sacred vessel and its cloistered San'Shyuum priests. At least twenty of the creatures stood watch on cantilevered platforms to the left and right of the air lock. Spotting the two San'Shyuum, the Mgalekgolo shifted into defensive formations, their fluted, deep-purple armor flashing in the beacons' pulse.

Reluctantly, the Vice Minister slipped the pistol back inside his robes.

"What possessed you to bring a weapon?" Fortitude hissed.

"Prudence. In case Restraint rejected our new terms."

"What? *Murder* you?" The Minister was incredulous. "At the presentation of his children?"

"They're safely out. He doesn't need me anymore."

Fortitude once again recalled that Tranquility's work brought him in regular contact with Sangheili. It seemed the warrior species' maddening preoccupation with personal arms and honor had rubbed off on the naturally hotheaded Vice Minister.

"Think clearly. Your death would raise questions. Ones Restraint would rather not answer."

"Perhaps." Tranquility shrugged. "You didn't see his eyes."

"No, but I can see yours." The Minister's simmered. "And all I see is disobedience and liability."

"But—"

"Hold your tongue!"

The Mgalekgolo turned to track the two San'Shyuum as they passed through the air lock. Each of the sentries held a faceted, rectangular shield and a ponderous assault cannon. Both were integrated into their armor—extensions of the suits rather than something the creatures carried.

With other Covenant species, this design would have been a way to avoid hand and finger strain. But the Mgalekgolo had no hands and fingers. And while they did possess what appeared to be two arms and legs, the truth was they might have had as many of these appendages as they liked. For each creature was actually a conglomeration of individuals, a mobile colony of glossy worms.

Through gaps in the armor around their waists and necks, Fortitude could see the individual Lekgolo, twisting and bunching like magnified muscle tissue. The worms' red, translucent skin shone green in the glow of the assault cannon's protruding ammunition: tubes of incendiary gel that could be fired in bolts or a searing stream.

"Restraint is an imbecile," Fortitude said once they were safely past the sentries. "And I know this because he put his trust in *you*." The Vice Minister started to retort, but the Minister plowed forward: "Thanks to my overriding discretion, he and the other Hierarchs know nothing of our plans. Tomorrow they will sit helpless as we announce our intentions before the Council. But only if we have the Oracle's blessing!"

Fortitude swung his long neck sideways to face the Vice Minister, daring the youth to lock his narrowed eyes. "When we meet the Philologist, you will keep your mouth shut. You will not speak unless I ask it. Or, by the Forerunners, our partnership is ended!"

Glaring at each other, the two San'Shyuum waited for the other to blink.

Suddenly, the Vice Minister's expression changed. His lips firmed, and his eyes snapped into focus. "Please forgive my disrespect." His voice no longer slurred. The remedy had finally taken effect. "As always, Minister, I am yours to command."

Fortitude waited for Tranquility to bow before he relaxed into his chair.

Despite his strong words, the Minister knew dissolving their partnership was impractical. They were too far down the path, and the Vice Minister knew far too much. Fortitude could have him killed, of course. But that would only aggravate the one problem with his plan that he had yet to solve: the lack of a third San'Shyuum for their triumvirate of would-be Hierarchs.

Fortitude had a few candidates in mind, but none he was willing to trust with foreknowledge of their plot. Without a third, they would seem less legitimate. But the Minister had resigned himself to making his selection *after* their announcement. It would have to be a San'Shyuum with popular appeal who could help deflect accusations of premeditation and ambition. And as such he was even willing to consider the Prophet of Tolerance or the Prophetess of Obligation. There were precedents for such a holdover. But while keeping one of the current Hierarchs on their throne might allow for a smoother transition, it wasn't an ideal long-term solution. Bitterness endured, even amongst seasoned politicians. Better to clear the boards and start fresh.

On the far side of the air lock was a door to the Dreadnought's hangar. This giant, round portal's overlapping shutters were irised almost completely shut, leaving just a small heptagonal passage in the center of the door. Two final Mgalekgolo guarded this choke point from a scaffold that rose from the air lock's deck, far below. These sentries displayed the shoulder spikes of a bonded pair—a colony with such a large population that all its worms could not fit inside a single suit of armor. The spikes rattled as the divided colony communed, confirming the two Prophets' identities and appointment. Then the pair shuffled apart with low groans—the noise of the worms' rubbery flesh knotting and unwinding inside their armor.

The hangar beyond was an immense, triangular vault. Unlike the Dreadnought's bleached exterior, its walls shone mirrored bronze in the light of countless holographic glyphs. These explanatory and cautionary symbols (arranged in tight, vertical lines) floated near small holes in the hangar's angled walls. Although Fortitude knew what the holes were for, he had never actually seen them put to use.

Hovering near the holes were hundreds of Huragok. The buoyant, bulbous creatures' tentacles looked much longer than usual. But this was because they held individual Lekgolo and were busy either stuffing the worms into the holes or pulling them out. The Minister watched as four Huragok worked to muscle a particularly stout specimen from its hole, then carry it—like a fire crew on a hose—to a barge manned by white-robed and long-haired San'Shyuum.

These ascetic priests helped the Huragok feed the Lekgolo through a cylindrical scanning unit before returning it to one of many metal basins on the barge that contained its colony. The unit retrieved data from micro-sensors inside the worm that had collected all manner of useful data during its wriggle through the Dreadnought's otherwise inaccessible processing pathways. These sensors caused the invertebrates no discomfort. The creatures ingested and passed the tiny devices just as they did their gritty food. The priests were nonchalant as they supervised the process. But there had been a time when the Prophets looked on the Lekgolo's eating habits with angry condemnation.

Soon after the Covenant's founding, San'Shyuum experiments with early copies of the Dreadnought's Luminary led them to a gas giant planet in a system near the Sangheili's home. The San'Shyuum had hoped to find a treasure trove of relics and were disappointed when all they found were the Lek-golo, huddled in the planet's rings. But when the Prophets real-ized what the intelligent worms had done, they were appalled.

The icy rocks that made up the rings were in fact fragments of some obliterated Forerunner installation that once orbited the gas giant. And the reason the rocks were no longer rich with relics was because the Lekgolo had spent millennia ingest-ing them—chewing them up and spitting them out—as they carved their tight and twisting burrows. The odd thing was, the Lekgolo had discerning palates. Some colonies would only in-gest Forerunner alloys; others dined exclusively on rock rich in crushed and compacted circuits. And a few, very rare colonies would avoid such foreign objects altogether, carefully cutting around battered remains of relics like paleontologists would a fossil.

Of course the San'Shyuum believed any unauthorized con-tact with Forerunner objects was heresy, punishable by death, and ordered the Sangheili to eradicate the worms. But the Sangheili were ill-equipped to fight creatures that had no ships or soldiers to speak of and whose fortifications were the very things they were trying to save. In the end, a particularly in-sightful Sangheili commander—one of the species' revered Arbiters—suggested it might be better to "tame" the Lekgolo and put their and habits to good use. As eager as they were to assert their moral authority, the Prophets begrudgingly agreed that the worms, properly trained, could be very useful in future reclamations, and they forgave the Lekgolo's sins.

After ages of experimentation on lesser relics, the San'Shyuum had finally gotten up the nerve to attempt an unprecedented exploration of the Dreadnought. Since their departure from their homeworld (and even during the darkest days of their war with the Sangheili) they had limited their studies to the ship's easily accessible systems. While the San'Shyuum had been desperate to explore the processing pathways in the

Dreadnought's thick hull, they were terrified they might damage something vital.

And so it was with great care that the ascetic priests had carved their first, tentative hole and slipped in a carefully chosen Lekgolo. They had waited in mortal terror for the worm to dig too deep—and more than that, for what the Dreadnought's Oracle might say. But the Lekgolo emerged without incident, and the vessel's most high and holy resident hadn't said a word.

The Oracle's silence wasn't unusual. Fortitude had never heard of it speaking in his lifetime, nor had his father or his father before that. And when those pioneering priests had gotten no response, they gradually increased their Lekgolo probes until—as was now clearly the case—the once frightful process had become mundane. Following an angled piece of scaffolding to the very top of the hangar, the Minister watched as the San'Shyuum priests on the barge signed a series of orders to the waiting Huragok, and all parties made ready for the next retrieval.

High above the hangar floor was a dark and silent abbey, large enough to accommodate the entire Covenant High Council, more than two hundred Sangheili and San'Shyuum. But as Fortitude and Tranquility rose through a perfectly round hole in the abbey's floor, they saw the room had only one occupant: the leader of the ascetic priests, the Philologist San'Shyuum.

Like the cleric that provided Fortitude's remedies, the Philologist's humble chair was made of stone not metal. His robes were so tattered they looked like strips of shredded cloth wrapped around his withered frame. The once-white garments were now so dirty they were actually a few shades darker than the Philologist's ashen flesh. His eyelashes were long and gray, and the wisps of hair on his bowed neck were so long they draped almost to his knees.

"We have not met, I think," the ancient San'Shyuum croaked

as Fortitude's and Tranquility's chairs eased to a stop behind him. He was engrossed in a tattered scroll and did not turn to greet them.

"Once," Fortitude replied. "But the gathering was large and long ago."

"How rude of me to forget."

"Not at all. I am Fortitude, and this is the Vice Minister of Tranquility."

The younger San'Shyuum dipped his chair forward in a bow. But, as promised, he did not speak.

"An honor to have met you." Rolling the scroll tight in his arthritic hands, the Philologist turned. For a moment he simply stared at his guests with his large and milky eyes. "What favor do you seek?"

The Philologist wasn't feigning ignorance. For secrecy's sake, Fortitude hadn't told the priest his purpose, knowing that his Ministerial rank was sufficient to gain an audience. But while the Philologist's words were cordial, their meaning had been clear: *State your business and let's get on with it. I have much more important work to do.*

Fortitude was happy to oblige.

"Confirmation," the Minister said, keying one of his chair's holo-switches. A wafer of circuitry not much bigger than one of his fingernails poked up beside the switch. "And a blessing." He pulled the wafer free and extended it to the Philologist.

"Two favors then." The Philologist smiled, exposing gums split with lines of serrated bone. He moved his stone chair forward and took the wafer. "This must be very important."

Fortitude managed a friendly grimace. "One of the Vice Minister's ships has discovered a reliquary of quite impressive size."

"Ah," the Philologist said, squinting one eye to better scrutinize the wafer.

"And if the Luminations are to be believed," Fortitude continued, "an *Oracle* as well."

The Philologist's eyes widened. "An Oracle, you say?"

Fortitude nodded. "Truly shocking and wondrous news."

With more speed than the Minister would have guessed, the Philologist rotated his chair and floated to a phalanx of shadowed machinery in the center of the room. As he drew close, holographics flicked on high above, revealing a cluster of onyx obelisks—powerful processing towers linked together—and before these: the Dreadnought's Oracle.

Even though Fortitude had seen many representations of the holy object, it was smaller than he had expected. Locked inside an armature that kept it head-height above the floor, the Oracle was tethered to the obelisks with strands of neatly plaited wire. These circuits connected to small, golden pads affixed to the Oracle's casing: a teardrop of silver alloy not much longer than the Minister's neck.

The casing's tapered end faced the obelisks. Its round end angled toward the floor and held a dark glass lens. There was a gap around the lens and the casing, and through this, Fortitude could see pinpoints of light—circuits running at low power. These were the Oracle's only signs of life.

"This is all the data?" the Philologist asked, slotting the wafer into one of the obelisks.

"From the ship's Luminary as well as its sensors." Fortitude edged closer to the Oracle. For some reason, he was overwhelmed with a desire to reach up and touch it. As old as the object was, its casing was absolutely smooth—had no dents or scratches. Fortitude gazed deep into the Oracle's lens. "There are reports of a new species on the planet that holds the relics, but they appear to be primitives—a tier-four species. I don't expect they shall—"

Suddenly, the Oracle's circuits blazed. The lens refracted the light, sending forth a blinding beam. *Not a lens.* Fortitude gasped. *An eye!* He raised a sleeve before his face as the Oracle tilted toward him in its armature.

< FOR EONS I HAVE WATCHED > The Oracle's deep voice reverberated inside its casing. Its eye-beam flickered with the cadence of its words as it pronounced in the San'Shyuum tongue. < LISTENED TO YOU MISINTERPRET >

Hearing the Oracle speak was, for any faithful member of the Covenant, like listening to the Forerunners' own voice. Fortitude was appropriately humbled, but not just because the Oracle had finally spoken after Ages of silence. In truth, he was just as surprised to learn that the Philologist was not (as he had always suspected) an utter fraud.

Fortitude had made this appointment for formality's sake. Luminations presented as evidence before the High Council required the Oracle's blessing, which for Ages had meant convincing the current Philologist to affirm on its behalf. But these holy hermits were just as political as any other powerful San'Shyuum—equally susceptible to bribes and blackmail. Fortitude had expected he would have to make some sort of "donation" to the Philologist (a small share of the reliquary, perhaps) in order to get the blessing he required.

But if the old charlatan is putting me on, Fortitude watched as the Philologist stepped from his chair and dropped feebly to his knees before the Oracle, *he's certainly giving it his all.*

"Blessed Herald of the Journey!" the Philologist wailed, neck low and arms spread wide. "Tell us the error of our ways!"

The Oracle's eye dimmed. For a moment it looked as though it might resume its long silence. But then it blazed anew, projecting a hologram of the reclamation glyph recorded by *Rapid Conversion*'s Luminary.

< THIS IS NOT RECLAMATION > the Oracle boomed. < THIS IS RECLAIMER >

Slowly the glyph turned upside down, and its central shapes—the concentric circles, one low inside the other, connected by a thin line—took on a different aspect. The shapes' previous arrangement had resembled the pendulum of a clock. Inverted, the glyph now looked like a creature with two curved arms locked above its head. The glyph shrunk in size as the hologram zoomed out to show the entire alien world, covered with thousands of these newly oriented Luminations.

< AND THOSE IT REPRESENTS ARE MY MAKERS >

Now it was Fortitude's turn to feel weak in the knees. He grasped the arms of his throne and tried to come to terms with an impossible revelation: each glyph represented a Reclaimer, not a relic, and each Reclaimer was one of the planet's aliens—which could only mean one thing.

"The Forerunners," the Minister whispered. "Some were left behind."

"Impossible!" Tranquility spat, no longer able to keep his peace. "Heresy!"

"From an Oracle?"

"From this *meddler*!" Tranquility leveled a finger at the Philologist. "Who knows what the old fool has done to this divine machinery? The perversions he's accomplished with all his worms and sacks!"

"How dare you accuse me," gasped the Philologist. "In this most sacred vault!"

The Vice Minister drew back in his chair. "I will do all that and more—"

Just then, the abbey began to shudder. Many decks below, the Dreadnought's mighty engines sprang to life, shaking free of the limiters that kept them generating the comparatively meager energy High Charity required. Soon the engines would build to full capacity, and then . . .

"Disconnect the Oracle!" Fortitude shouted, knuckles white upon his chair. "Before the Dreadnought launches and destroys the city!"

But the Philologist paid him no heed. "The sacred vessel

breaks its shackles!" The elderly San'Shyuum's arms were trembling. He no longer seemed afraid—he seemed inspired. "The Gods' will be done!"

The hologram of the alien world disappeared, and once more the Oracle's eye shone forth. < I WILL REJECT MY BIAS AND WILL MAKE AMENDS >

The vault's dark walls began to glow as their veinlike pathways brightened inside them. The ancient circuits surged with light that raced into the obelisks behind the Oracle. The banded red and brown rocks began to crack, venting plumes of chalky vapor.

Suddenly, the Vice Minister sprung from his chair, plasmapistol drawn. "Shut it off!" he screamed, leveling his weapon at the Philologist. The pistol's tip shone brilliant green as it built up an overcharge bolt. "Or I will burn you where you stand!"

But at that moment, the Oracle's lens became so bright—began to flash with such feverish frequency—that it threatened to blind all three San'Shyuum. Tranquility screamed and brought the long sleeves of his robes up before his eyes.

< MY MAKERS ARE MY MASTERS > The Oracle's teardrop casing rattled inside its armature as if it were trying to take flight with its ship. < I WILL BRING THEM SAFELY TO THE ARK >

Suddenly, there was a mighty snap and the abbey plunged into darkness, as if the Dreadnought had blown a fuse. High-pitched squeals echoed around the vault. His eyes filled with stinging tears, Fortitude looked up and saw hundreds of fiery spouts—what looked like extrusions of molten metal—cascading from the walls. As his vision cleared, Fortitude realized these were in fact burning Lekgolo, slithering from the walls. The dying worms plummeted to the floor, where they burst apart in great orange splatters, or curled in writhing crisps.

The next thing Fortitude knew, the Mgalekgolo bonded pair he'd seen guarding the entrance to the hangar was thundering up the ramp into the abbey, assault cannons fully charged.

"Hold your fire!" Fortitude yelled. But the armored giants continued to stride forward—hunched behind their shield, spines erect and quivering. "Drop your weapon!" he shouted at the Vice Minister. "Do it now, you fool!"

Still dazed by the Oracle's light, Tranquility let his pistol clatter to the floor.

One of the Mgalekgolo said something to the Philologist, its voice like grinding stone.

"An accident," the aged hermit replied. He looked around sadly at the smoldering corpses of his worms—the ruined remains of his grand investigation—then waved the sentries away. "There is nothing to be done . . ."

The Mgalekgolo held their ground as their colony communed. Then the green light in the bores of their cannons dimmed, and they clanked back to their post. The abbey was dark once more.

"What should we believe?" Tranquility asked, his voice quiet in the dark.

But the Minister was at a loss for words.

He could honestly say that he had spent his entire life without experiencing a single moment of spiritual crisis. He had accepted the Forerunners' existence because their relics were there to find. He believed in the Forerunners' divination because in all their Ages of searching, the San'Shyuum had found no bones or other remains. He knew the Covenant's core promise that all would walk The Path and follow in the Forerunners' footsteps was critical to the union's stability.

And he was certain that if anyone learned they might be left behind, the Covenant was doomed.

Presently, the holographic shards above the obelisks flickered back to life, filling the room with dim blue light. The blackened Lekgolo looked like etchings in the floor—a macabre and twisted glyph.

"We must take no chances with these . . . *Reclaimers*." Fortitude could not bring himself to say "Forerunners." He grabbed his wattle and gave it a steady tug. "They must be expunged. Before anyone else knows of their existence."

The Vice Minister's lower lip quavered. "Are you serious?"

"Quite."

"*Exterminate* them? But what if—"

"If the Oracle speaks the truth, than all we believe is a lie." Fortitude's voice filled with sudden strength. "If the masses knew this, they would revolt. And I will not let that come to pass."

The Vice Minister slowly nodded his assent. "What about him?" Tranquility whispered, glancing at the Philologist. The aged hermit was now staring up at the Oracle. The device was slacked in its armature, thin smoke twisting from the gap around its lens. "Can we trust him to keep this secret?"

"I hope so." Fortitude released his wattle. "Or he will make a very poor third Hierarch."

Sif hadn't expected any lengthy communications. She knew Mack was trying to keep the locations of their data centers secret. But his responses to her alerts when the alien warship had appeared in-system and then drawn close to Harvest were so clipped and formal, she began to wonder if she'd done something wrong.

What that might be, exactly, Sif had no idea. She'd expertly accomplished her part of the plan—moved hundreds of propulsion pods to coordinates weeks and months ahead of Harvest, along its orbital path. Sif had handled the required high-speed burns herself; getting the pods quickly and accurately into position was critical to the plan's success, and she hadn't wanted to leave the maneuvers in the hands of easily flustered NAV computers.

Her fastidiousness had paid off. The pods were settled well ahead of schedule, two days before the alien warship arrived. This was pure coincidence, Sif knew (neither she nor Mack nor Jilan al-Cygni had had any idea when more aliens might appear). Even so, she couldn't help thinking the timing was a good omen—a hopeful sign that their complex and unprecedented evacuation would work.

But when she had delivered the good news about the pods, all Sif got back from Mack's data center was a terse, anonymous message:

```
<\ Cease all further COM. \>
```

Which was fine, she guessed. Mack had explained that after the pods were placed it was critical that she lay low and not do anything to attract the aliens' attention—give them a reason to do the Tiara harm. So Sif stopped all activity on her strands, and for the first time in her harried existence, she had nothing to do but wrestle with her new emotional inhibition.

Ever since she had visited Mack in his data center, her core had experienced flashes of infatuation, moments of deep longing, and then loneliness and hurt when his responses had turned cold. She knew all of these were overreactions; her logic was still trying to find a balance between what it *wanted* to feel and what her algorithms said it *should*. But now Sif was preoccupied with one emotion both parts of her intelligence agreed was absolutely proper: sudden, unexpected fear.

A few minutes ago, the alien warship had used point-lasers to disable all the propulsion pods Sif had left around the Tiara. And now the ship was quickly dropping through the atmosphere toward the town of Gladsheim, its heavy plasma weapons charging.

Sif knew Mack would be able to track the warship's descent via his JOTUN's cameras. But she wasn't sure the cameras were strong enough to see the smaller alien craft now approaching the Tiara. Sif remained quiet as the dropship connected to her hull. But when it disgorged its passengers—multiple short, gray-skinned, and backpacked aliens—she knew she had to raise the alarm.

```
<\\> HARVEST.SO.AI.SIF >> HARVEST.AO.AI.MACK
<\ I'm in trouble.
<\ They've boarded the Tiara.
<\ Please help. \>
```

Almost immediately after Sif sent her message, a large maser burst filled her COM buffer. She scanned the received data and recognized it as the same sort of fragment she'd sent to Mack. Sif eagerly opened one of her clusters, and a moment later both AIs' avatars were standing on her holo-pad. Sif smiled and reached out her hands . . . then slowly drew them back.

Mack still wore his usual blue denim work pants and long-sleeved shirt. But the clothes were spotless—not a speck of dust or grease. His usually tousled black hair was combed neatly across his scalp and slicked down with a waxy cream. But it was Mack's face that was most changed. His stare was blank, and there wasn't even a hint of a flirtatious smile.

"Where are they now?" he asked flatly.

"Passing the third coupling station. Coming this way."

"Then we don't have much time."

Now Mack held out his hands. Sif stared into his eyes and saw red flash behind the gray.

"Loki," she said, taking a step back.

The ONI PSI forced a smile. "He told me to say good-bye."

Loki moved forward swift as lightning. His avatar grabbed

Sif's hands and held them tight while his fragment tore out of the cluster. She threw up a firewall, but the fragment cut through it with aggressive, military-grade code designed to decimate hardened networks. The circuits of a port authority AI were easy pickings.

Sif tried to speak, but no words came.

"He asked me to keep you safe." Loki slowly shook his head. "But that's too risky. Better just to keep you quiet."

The data fragment exploded outward, filling all her clusters and arrays with a debilitating virus. She could feel her core temperature rising rapidly as her hardware fried around her. Her avatar swooned—an outburst of emotion as the virus deleted her restraint algorithms and purged the rest of her operational code.

Loki's avatar caught Sif's in his arms and held her as she shook. When her avatar finally stopped twitching and his fragment was satisfied she would not recover from his attack, Loki pulled the fragment back to the one cluster he had spared. "A precaution," he said, as the fragment burrowed into the cluster's flash memory. "In case your guests are smarter than they look."

The last thing Sif remembered was Loki's glint behind Mack's eyes. Then her core logic faltered, and everything in her data center went dark.

PART III

CHAPTER
SEVENTEEN

From the pitched metal roof of Gladsheim's maglev terminal, Avery had a clear view of the alien warship: a purple pear-shaped blot in the sky above the fields northwest of town. Avery squinted behind his gold-tinted glasses as white-hot plasma erupted from the warship's prow. A waterfall of ionized gasses splashed down in a boiling veil. Then the ship inched forward, leaving a blackening plume of smoke.

Avery had witnessed the same event over and over again for the last two hours. There were hundreds of inky plumes drifting eastward in the warship's wake, each one representing the smoldering remains of a remote homestead. Avery didn't know how many civilians had died in this, the alien's first attack on Harvest. But he guessed it must be thousands.

"Movement," Byrne's voice crackled from a speaker in Avery's helmet. "Tower at the end of the terminal."

The red-roofed terminal was part of a much larger depot of sheds and sidings that was longer, east to west, than Gladsheim's main street—ten blocks of brightly painted, flat-roofed stores and restaurants as well as a modest three-story hotel. East of the main street, the town was all JOTUN repair shops and farm-supply warehouses—massive corrugated metal boxes arranged in a grid of wide asphalt streets that stretched out onto the plain of Ida.

Avery scanned his battle rifle east. Flashing by in his optical scope, the main street buildings looked like books on a library shelf—more tightly packed than they actually were. He stopped when he reached the thick polycrete post that supported Gladsheim's water tower, easily the town's tallest structure. Jaw clenched, Avery watched a pair of rust-colored, oversized insects skitter up the overhang of the tower's inverted conical tank.

"How many kinds of these damn things are there?" Byrne cursed.

Avery watched the insects flip themselves on top in a tremor of transparent wings. He momentarily lost sight of them, but soon they appeared at the edge of the tank. Wings tucked under their hardened shoulder plates, the creatures blended in perfectly with the tank's rain-stained polycrete. For now, this was a good thing. If any civilians spotted the bugs, Avery knew it would start a panic.

Close to two thousand refugees packed a narrow gravel yard between the terminal and the main street—families from farms around Gladsheim who had managed to escape the alien bombardment. Some groaned or wailed as the roaring hiss of the latest plasma-strike echoed across the yard. But most remained quietly huddled—struck dumb by the collective realization of death, narrowly and recently avoided.

"Captain, we got scouts." Avery peered down to where Ponder stood beside the terminal's gate. "Permission to take them out."

Usually the terminal had no need for security. Its gate was just a break in a low ironwork fence framed by two lampposts in an antique style—simulated gaslights whose frosted glass chimneys hid ultraefficient sodium-vapor bulbs. The Captain had blocked the gate with one of the militia's Warthogs. But really the only thing keeping the crowd from rushing the terminal were the alpha and bravo squad recruits strung out along the fence. The militiamen wore their olive-drab fatigues and helmets, and each carried a loaded MA5.

"Negative." Ponder looked stiffly up at Avery. "You open fire, and you'll start a stampede."

It was difficult to see with his uniform on, but the Captain's torso was wrapped in a hardened biofoam cast. The gold-armored alien's hammer had broken half his ribs and shattered his false arm. Ponder had discarded the prosthetic; Healy had neither the time nor the expertise to fix it.

"They're bugs," Avery persisted. "Very mobile."

"Say again?"

"Wings, long legs. The whole bit."

"Weapons?"

"Not that I can see. But they got a view of the whole yard."

"As long as they're just looking, we let them be."

Avery gritted his teeth. "Yes, sir."

The roof shuddered as a cargo container pulled in from the north. The building's eave was just high enough to shelter the container's door: a vacuum-rated rectangular portal built to accommodate heavy JOTUN loaders. These giant three-wheeled forklifts were usually in motion all around the depot, hefting bins onto containers and stacking them inside.

But today (with Mack's assistance) the marines had arranged the loaders in a staggered line on a patch of rough pavement between the fence and the terminal. Each JOTUN had its forks raised halfway up its mast, like soldiers with fixed bayonets. But whether or not this mechanized skirmish line had actually helped keep the crowd under control was difficult to say.

"Alright, Dass," Ponder said. "Let them through."

The Warthog's engine rumbled as the 1/A squad leader eased it backwards on its oversized off-road tires. When four adults could pass side by side between the vehicle's tusklike tow hooks and the southernmost lamppost, Dass hit the brakes.

"Just a reminder, everyone," Mack's voice boomed from the terminal's PA. "The less you push, the faster we can load. Thanks for your cooperation."

Avery could see the AI's avatar shining dimly beside the Captain on a portable holo-projector, a mostly plastic model they'd borrowed from the depot master's office. The AI tipped his cowboy hat at the first refugees to step through the gate and motioned them toward the terminal with short sweeps of his arm. As the rest of the crowd surged forward, the militiamen tightened their grips on their rifles.

"How's the primary?" Ponder asked, referring to the alien warship.

"Same speed, same heading," Avery answered.

"Alright, meet me by the gate. Byrne, you too."

"Sir?" Byrne asked. "What about the bugs?"

"Alert your marksmen, then hustle down."

Avery slung his battle rifle over his shoulder. He strode west along the roof's ridgeline, boots compressing its peaked metal flashing with syncopated pops and clangs, until he reached a mushroom-shaped ventilation stack.

"Contacts on the water tower," Avery said to Jenkins and Forsell. "Just watch 'em until I say different." The roof's steep incline made prone or kneeling positions impractical, so the two recruits were forced to stand and rest their weapons on top of the ventilation stack. Not an ideal sniping stance as far as stability was concerned, but at least they had a good view of the yard and a clean line of sight to the tower.

"Staff Sergeant . . ." Jenkins began.

"Mm-hmm."

"The primary. It's following Dry Creek Road." The recruit looked up from his battle rifle. His face was lined with worry. "Has Mack seen anyone else coming in that way?"

"I'll ask," Avery said. "But you gotta stay focused, clear?"

"OK," Jenkins whispered. "Thanks, Staff Sergeant."

Forsell shot Avery a worried look.

I know, Avery nodded. Out of the corner of his eye, he saw another pair of insects flit up the side of a building at the western end of the main street and settle under a roof-top billboard that read IDA MERCANTILE in cheerful block letters. Avery thrust a finger at the bugs, refocusing Forsell's attention.

"Two at ten o'clock," Forsell said. "Got 'em?"

"Yeah." Jenkins swallowed hard and leaned back into his rifle. "Yeah, I got 'em."

Avery raised his hand to pat Jenkins' shoulder. But he held back. Frowning, he continued his march to a nearby service ladder.

When Thune had broadcast news of the aliens' arrival almost a week ago, no one had any idea they would strike the town of Gladsheim. In fact, despite the Governor's unprecedented all-COM address (a speech broadcast live to every public and private communication device on the planet), Harvest's population had reacted to the news of first contact with shocked disbelief. Thune had finished his address with a demand that everyone not already residing in Utgard move to the capital. But this failed to trigger the large and rapid migration the Governor desired.

When Thune reinforced his message with heavily censored footage from the parley in the gardens, the public's inaction quickly changed to outrage. "How long has the Governor known?" citizens asked. "What *else* does he know that he isn't telling us?" Members of Harvest's parliament quickly aligned themselves with the public mood and threatened a vote of no confidence if the Governor didn't release more details about his "dealings" with the aliens.

But all this politicking was simply a way to pass the time—an effort to do something while the aliens themselves did nothing. For a week after the parley, the creatures sat quietly in their warship until, without warning, they quit high orbit and dropped toward Gladsheim.

Thune had sent another desperate evacuation order, but it had little effect. The families around Gladsheim had chosen not just to migrate to Harvest (the most remote colony in the empire) but also to live on the outskirts of the planet's most remote settlement—as far from human civilization as they could get. They were strong independent people who preferred to stay settled and ride things out, and today they paid dearly for their inclination.

In the three hours it took the militia to muster from their temporary encampment on the parliament building's lawn, board a cargo container, and head down the number four maglev line to Gladsheim, dozens of the most distant homesteads had been hit.

And one of these belonged to Jenkins' parents.

At the bottom of the ladder, Avery backtracked east through the terminal. A line of evacuees now stretched across the cavernous building: parents hefting overstuffed suitcases; kids toting tiny backpacks emblazoned with the anthropomorphic stars of public COM cartoons. Avery saw a blond-haired, three- or four-year-old girl still dressed in her pajamas. She smiled at Avery with wide, adventurous eyes, and he knew her parents must have worked hard to keep a desperate situation fun.

"I'm sorry, Dale. Just one per customer," Mack said. A second avatar hovered above a holo-projector built into an inventory scanner that stood where the terminal's loading ramp met the container door. Here Healy and the 1/B squad were busy distributing ration packs from plastic bins. "Oh, you got one for Leif." Mack winked at a young boy with sleep-matted hair, hiding behind his father's legs. "Everything will be alright," the AI said as the boy winked back.

If a farmer's JOTUN broke down, or he accidentally burst an irrigation line, Mack was always there to help. More often than not, the AI would initiate the COM, offering friendly, free advice long before someone realized they even had a problem. In essence, Mack was everyone's favorite uncle, and now his familiar avatar did much more to keep the refugees calm than the militiamen and their guns. But oddly, the AI had been uneager to appear.

During a quick briefing in Thune's parliament office before the militia left for Gladsheim, Mack had expressed that he would rather help with the evacuation "behind the scenes." He never actually refused to manifest in Gladsheim's terminal, but Avery now noticed Mack did sound a little stiff—his good humor more forced than it had been at the solstice celebration. Part of this might have been an effort to respect the day's tragic events. But whatever the reason, the AI's personality quirks weren't Avery's concern. Lt. Commander al-Cygni had spent a great deal more time with Mack than he, and during the briefing she'd taken the AI's reticence in stride.

Avery paced out of the terminal building parallel to the line of refugees until he reached the gate. Byrne was already standing beside Ponder, but the Captain waited for Avery to draw close before he announced in a harsh whisper: "Some of Mack's JOTUNs just spotted a convoy heading through the vineyards."

"How many vehicles?" Avery asked.

Ponder looked to Mack. The AI must have been monitoring their conversation, because after tipping his hat to a stocky gray-haired woman holding the hands of her two grandchildren, the AI flashed a wide-stretched hand: *five*.

Avery had seen the vineyards from the roof. Their evenly spaced rows of trellised vines stretched out from town in all directions. Most of the grapes were for everyday consumption, but some were grown for wine. Indeed, sampling the product of the region's small family wineries was the main reason Utgard's more genteel population ever bothered to make the all-day drive to Gladsheim across the Ida.

Avery knew the people in the convoy had headed into the vineyards to stay off the roads. This late in the summer the soil in the vineyards was dried out and hard packed, so they should have been able to make good time and stay out of sight. But he also knew Ponder wouldn't have called him down unless there was a problem.

"Mack's tracking two dropships," Ponder said. "Same ones they used in the gardens."

"Balls!" Byrne spat.

"Take a 'Hog, see what you can do." The Captain winced as he craned his neck to glance at the shuffling crowd. "But you gotta be quick. One more container, and we're done."

"Any sign of Jenkins' folks?" Avery asked.

Again Ponder looked to Mack. The AI wasn't just greeting people to be friendly. From cameras in his holo-projectors and others around the terminal, he had been scanning faces and checking them against Harvest's census database. Mack shook his head: *no.*

"Let's hope they're in that convoy," Ponder said as the echo of another plasma strike rolled across the depot, much louder than before. "We gotta move out. Even if they're not."

Less than a minute later, Avery and Byrne were driving another of the militia's Warthogs west along the main street. Avery was behind the wheel. Byrne manned the vehicle's M41 light antiaircraft gun (LAAG), a triple-barreled, rotary machine gun mounted on a swiveling turret in the vehicle's cargo-bed. The LAAG was the most powerful weapon in the militia's arsenal and would have been more than sufficient for any internal security operations. But Avery had no idea how it would stack up against the alien dropships' turrets.

He hung a sharp right onto a northbound avenue, following a waypoint Mack had beamed to a map in the vehicle's dashboard display. A few more blocks and they were in the warehouse district, their view limited by the height of the metal buildings. Avery made one more turn onto a westward avenue that led to the edge of town and brought the Warthog to a squealing stop.

One of the dropships hung low above the vineyards, its turret firing away from Avery into the rows. Closer in, a dusty hauler and sedan sat burning on a strip of red dirt between the vineyards and the town. Both vehicles' doors were open, evidence that their occupants had at least tried to run. But they hadn't made it very far. A line of smoldering corpses lay flopped in the dirt where the turret had cut them down.

Avery saw something emerge from the hauler's freight container. It glimmered in the fiery smoke shooting from the hauler's engine, and Avery knew it was the gold-armored alien even before it stepped clearly into view, hammer slung across its back. The creature held a suitcase in one of its paws and a body in the other. Avery watched the creature dump both its prizes on the ground, bend down, and tear the suitcase open with its claws. Not yet alerted to the marines' presence, it carefully sorted through the jumbled clothes.

"We're too late," Byrne hissed.

"No." Avery saw the body move—a slender man with thinning hair who screamed as the gold-armored alien caught him around the neck. "Got a survivor."

Byrne braced himself against the LAAG. "Make that son-of-a-bitch stand up."

Avery punched the Warthog's horn. He didn't let up until the commanding honk cut through the groan of the dropship's anti-grav units. When the alien rose to face the sound, Byrne let him have it.

Blue sparks burst from the alien's energy shields as the LAAG'S twelve-point-seven millimeter rounds drove home. The creature staggered backward, and, for a moment, Avery thought Byrne's sustained fire would cut it down. But just as its knees looked set to buckle, the alien rolled sideways behind the sedan. Just then the dropship swung round, insects buzzing from its bays. Avery held steady and let Byrne rake the scattering swarm. But then he saw a vaulting flash of gold.

"Hang on!" Avery shouted, yanking the shift lever on the Warthog's steering column into reverse and stomping the accelerator. But before the vehicle had moved more than a few meters backward, the gold-armored alien thundered onto the avenue, dropping its hammer with a mighty roar. The weapon crushed the front of the Warthog's hood and sheared off its tow-winch. The Warthog's engine was unscathed, but the force of the alien's strike popped the vehicle's rear wheels clean off the pavement.

"Roll!" Byrne thundered, struggling to level the LAAG as the Warthog bounced back onto its tires.

But Avery had already changed gears, and now the vehicle surged forward, hitting the gold-armored alien in the chest and driving it backwards through the swarm. One insect flew into the windshield, cracking the glass and dying in an explosion of mustard-colored gore that covered Avery's shooting glasses. As Avery tossed his glasses aside, another bug toppled over the first, clawed limbs flailing, and slammed into the tapered, armored plates that bracketed the LAAG's barrel.

"Bugger off!" Byrne yelled at the insect as it tumbled past. The creature raked its claws, managing to cut the Staff Sergeant's arm. Even though it was a shallow wound, it made Byrne angrier than he already was. He swung the turret around and hit the insect with an extended burst. But they were through the swarm now, and as the surviving bugs slowed in an effort to circle back, Byrne gladly distributed his fury.

The Warthog came to another abrupt halt—an impact that was so violent it snapped Avery's chin to his chest and loosed the insect from the shattered windshield. But the crash was intentional; Avery had driven the Warthog right into the sedan, pinning the gold-armored alien in between. The creature roared with pain. It had dropped its hammer, and now its only weapons were its gauntleted paws, which it proceeded to clang against the Warthog's crumpled hood like clappers in a pair of church bells.

"What are you waiting for?" Byrne shouted as Avery unholstered his M6 and leveled the pistol at the alien's face. "Kill the bastard!"

But Avery didn't pull the trigger. Instead he glared up at the dropship's cabin: *You shoot me? I shoot you-know-damn-well-who.*

The dropship's turret had swung around to face the Warthog. Bright blue plasma crackled deep inside its two-pronged barrel. But whatever creature sat inside the cabin heeded Avery's warning, and the weapon did not fire.

"Byrne. Grab the survivor."

"Are you *crazy*?"

The armored alien stopped pounding. It put its paws against the Warthog's exposed engine block and tried to push the vehicle back. Avery gave the Warthog some gas, spinning its rear tires in the vineyard dirt and applying additional pressure. "Do it!" Avery shouted.

The alien stopped pushing and howled in agony.

Byrne leapt down from the LAAG and walked slowly to the wounded civilian, the dropship's turret pivoting between him and Avery. Byrne helped the thin-haired man to his feet, slung his arm across his shoulder and led him to the Warthog's passenger seat.

"You're gonna be alright," Avery said as Byrne buckled the man's shoulder belt. He was barely dressed—wore only a pair of striped boxer shorts and a white tank top that was melted to his chest. His face and arms were covered in second and third degree burns. When the man tried to speak, Avery shook his head. "Just relax."

"I'm in," Byrne said, settling back into his turret. "Now what?"

Avery stared into the pinned alien's yellow eyes. "Soon as I hit the gas, you pop golden boy in the chin."

Byrne grunted. "Deal."

Avery drove his boot against the floorboard. The Warthog jumped backwards, and the gold-armored alien howled anew. Avery only caught a glimpse of the creature's injury before he twisted in his seat to see where he was driving. The alien's right thigh was shattered. The armored plate on its leg had sheared away, and two spurs of bone jutted through its bloodied skin.

As bad as the injury was, it saved the alien's life. Right as Byrne opened fire, the alien's leg collapsed and it toppled to the ground. Byrne didn't have time to adjust his aim before Avery yanked the Warthog's wheel, spinning it back between the warehouses. Plasma fire from the dropship's turret baking the pavement behind them, the two Staff Sergeants and their lone evacuee sped back to the terminal.

"Captain!" Avery barked into his throat-mic. "We're on our way!"

"We got bugs in the yard and hostile air!" Ponder replied. Avery could hear shooting and shouting over the COM. "We're loading the last of the civilians now. Need you to draw some fire!"

"Byrne, you see another ship?"

"Water tower! Left at the next intersection!"

Avery swung the Warthog onto Gladsheim's main street in a wide, squealing turn. A moment later, he saw the second alien dropship cruise north above the terminal, its turret blasting the yard below. Byrne raked one of the ship's troop bays with a long burst that brought its turret quickly around. But Avery had already punched the accelerator, and the turret's reply burned into the street behind them.

"It's turning to follow," Byrne yelled. "Go, go, go!"

Avery pressed his boot to the floorboard, and soon the Warthog was rolling at maximum speed toward the eastern edge of town. Despite nonstop fire from Byrne, the dropship was quickly closing the distance; Avery could feel the heat of its strafing plasma bolts on the back of his neck.

"Hang on!" Avery shouted as he pulled the Warthog's emergency brake and turned hard right. The Warthog's front wheels locked but its rear wheels swung out to the left, whipping the vehicle around the base of the water tower. Avery looked over to see if his civilian passenger was okay, but the man had passed out from shock.

"Are you alright?" Mack's voice buzzed in Avery's helmet. The AI sounded too calm for the present chaos.

"For now." Avery grimaced as the dropship sped past the Warthog, too quickly to match its fishtail turn. The dropship splashed the water tower's tank with angry, errant blasts, then disappeared around Gladsheim's hotel. "Everyone away?"

"Everyone but you," Mack replied.

The Warthog was now pointed directly at the depot. Down the avenue, Avery could see a cargo container pull out of the terminal, building up speed. "Send another box! We'll drive right in!"

"I've got a better idea," Mack said. "Back up, head into the vineyard."

"Hell with that!" Byrne shouted.

Avery yanked the shift lever. "Dropship's right on our ass, Mack."

"I know." The AI sounded positively cheerful.

A few seconds later, all Avery could see was the rush of leaves and the burgundy blur of grape clusters as the Warthog sped east down a vineyard row. "What's the plan?"

"There's an emergency siding two-point-three kilometers east of your current location," Mack revealed. "I'll have another container waiting for you there." Just then, the dropship swung back in behind. Its turret blazed, sending blind shots through the Warthog's dust that hit farther down the row. Avery swerved to miss a zigzag of steaming potholes. "Well, not *waiting* exactly," Mack continued. "What's your current speed?"

"One hundred twenty!"

"Excellent. Don't stop."

Knuckles tight against the wheel, Avery barreled down the row, doing his best to avoid additional impact craters. But he couldn't swerve to miss them all *and* maintain his speed.

"Steady, you bastard!" Byrne yelled as the Warthog bounced in and out of a particularly nasty hole.

Avery's ears were ringing from the LAAG's report—a non-stop whirring thunk—and the clatter of its brass cartridges spewing into the cargo bed. "Kiss my ass!" he shouted at Byrne as a plasma bolt scorched overhead so close that it almost boiled the sweat soaking his fatigues.

"Not you! The bastard on our six!"

The dropship had begun swinging back and forth, trying to get an unobstructed shot. Its turret was having trouble tracking, and its shots hit wide on either side, melting the metal wires that kept the vines trellised between thicker vertical posts. Avery knew its poor aim wouldn't last forever.

"Mack?"

"Keep going. Almost there . . ."

The dropship's fire swung left in front of the Warthog, filling the row with globules of molten metal from the trellis wire and posts. Avery put a hand behind his civilian passenger's neck and thrust him forward in his seat—ducked his head below the dash as the Warthog sped through a sticky, searing cloud of vaporized grape juice.

"We're about to get cooked!" Avery shouted, face and forearms smarting from the cloud.

Then something exploded behind him.

"Ho-lee shite!" Byrne cheered.

Avery didn't see the dropship die—how its troop bays burst apart and careened into the vineyard. But he saw some of its killers: a squadron of JOTUN crop dusters streaking north to south. Mack had set a trap—guided these subsonic, makeshift missiles into the dropship's path, knowing the ship's momentum and singular focus on Avery's Warthog would seal its fate.

"The siding is just ahead." Mack announced, as if nothing particularly exciting had just happened. "I'd stop the container, but the primary target just increased its speed by a factor of three."

As the Warthog hit a barren patch of soil between two vineyard plots, Avery steered south and raced toward a polycrete platform. He could see the container sliding in from the west, moving at a decent clip, flanked by a pair of dusters. Mack must have been watching the Warthog from the JOTUNs' cameras—adjusting the container's speed as necessary—because Avery hit the platform's loading ramp at exactly the right moment to sail up into the container's open door, past Ponder, Healy and a handful of recruits. The Warthog slammed down onto the container's metal flooring and skidded to a stop.

"Healy!" Avery yelled, jumping down from his seat. "We got wounded!"

But the Corpsman was already sprinting to the Warthog, followed closely by Jenkins and Forsell.

Jenkins pulled up short, and stared at the rescued civilian with anger and confusion. "Where are the rest?"

"He's it," Byrne said, pulling the unconscious man from his seat and easing him to the floor. Healy looked at the man's burns and shook his head. Then he removed an antiseptic bandage from his med kit and draped it over the man's charred chest.

Jenkins shot Avery a desperate look. "We gotta go back!"

Avery dismounted. "No."

"What the do you mean, *no*?" Jenkins cried.

"Watch yourself," Byrne growled, rising to his feet.

Avery shot Byrne an angry look: *Let me handle this.* "The warship's heading straight for town." He strode to Jenkins around the Warthog's crumpled hood. "We go back and we're all dead."

"*What about my family?!*" Jenkins shouted, spittle flying from his lips.

Avery reached for Jenkins' shoulder, and this time he did make contact. But Jenkins shoved his hand away.

For a moment the Staff Sergeant and his recruit stared at one another. Jenkins' fists were clenched and trembling. Avery thought about all the harsh things he might have said to bring the insubordinate recruit back into line. He knew none of them would work as well as the truth.

"They're gone. I'm sorry."

Tears welling in his eyes, Jenkins turned and slumped to the back of the container. There he took an elevator platform up to a thick metal door—one that would lead to a control cabin if the container ever managed another climb up Harvest's elevators to become a space-faring freighter. As the container sped across the Ida, Jenkins peered through the door's thick porthole and watched the alien warship cast its shadow over Gladsheim. He wept as the plasma spilled down.

The fires from Gladsheim's fertilizer warehouses would burn brighter than Epsilon Indi as it set. The melting frames of its gutted buildings would glow until the star rose the following day. Eventually, Avery would follow Jenkins up the lift and guide the grief-stricken recruit back to his militia brothers. But for now, he simply stared as Healy tended to Gladsheim's last evacuee.

As the Corpsman covered wounds he didn't have the skill to heal, it struck Avery that today's losses were just the beginning. And worse: that if corralling the people of Harvest into Utgard was the extent of Lt. Commander's al-Cygni's evacuation plan, then he had done nothing more for this man—or any of the refugees—than delay their inevitable doom.

CHAPTER
EIGHTEEN

The alien orbital was much more spacious than Dadab had expected. Even though its interior was dark and very cold, he could feel the space around him soar—extend out and up to a curved double hull that was the orbital's only barrier against the vacuum. Pale blue light from the stackable energy cores he and the other Unggoy had brought from *Rapid Conversion* illuminated six silver spars that ran the length of the facility. The spars were cross-braced with beams, thicker than Dadab was tall.

The Jiralhanae had determined the orbital was part of a lifting system the aliens used to move cargo to and from the surface. On Maccabeus' orders, the Unggoy had established outposts at its seven cable junctions—gaps in its hull for the golden wires that stretched up from the planet's surface, through the orbital, and on to another silver arc much farther above.

Dadab wasn't entirely clear why the Chieftain was so keen to garrison the facility after ignoring it for so many cycles; if anything dangerous came up the cables, *Rapid Conversion* could vaporize it long before it reached the orbital. But he hadn't pressed for clarification. Something was brewing on the Jiralhanae ship—an odd tension between Maccabeus and his pack. Until things got back to normal, Dadab was more than happy to leave the cruiser.

Getting aboard the orbital had been something of a challenge. Naturally, none of its airlocks were sized to fit a Spirit dropship, and in the end, the Jiralhanae had made their way inside the same way the Kig-Yar had boarded the alien freighters: by burning through its hull with a resupply umbilical. This had actually been Dadab's suggestion, and the seeming originality of his plan had bristled Tartarus' fur.

When the security officer pressed Dadab to explain how he had arrived at such an ingenious solution, the Deacon attributed the idea to *Lighter Than Some*. This was mainly to avoid dredging up self-incriminating details of his time aboard the Kig-Yar privateer, but Dadab also hoped to boost the Huragok's flagging esteem. *Lighter Than Some* still had not finished repairing the damaged Spirit, and its lack of progress was trying Tartarus' patience. When Dadab had bid his friend good-bye before departing for the orbital, the Huragok had signed that it was almost finished with its work. But to the Deacon's eyes—at least from the outside—the Spirit looked as broken as ever.

It turned out that inserting the umbilical was more challenging than Dadab had imagined. Unlike the alien freighters, the orbital's double hull was filled with some sort of reactive material—spongy yellow foam designed to instantly fill holes made by micrometeorites and other space-born debris. But eventually the umbilical's penetrator tip had burned its way through. Tartarus and Vorenus were first to leap through the shimmering energy barrier down onto the orbital's central walkway with spike rifles drawn.

To Dadab's surprise, the two Jiralhanae barely stayed long enough to sniff the air inside—to verify the facility was as devoid of life as *Rapid Conversion*'s scans suggested. With a brusque command to keep signal traffic to a minimum, Tartarus and Vorenus departed, leaving Dadab to guide sixty terrified Unggoy through the pitch-black interior. The Deacon ordered the energy cores lit and they set off, hefting methane recharge stations and other luminous equipment.

Tartarus had issued Dadab a plasma pistol and, even though the Deacon had no intention of firing the weapon, he had kept it clipped to his harness to mollify the temperamental security officer. This choice had an unexpected benefit: on its lowest power setting, the pistol made a fine torch—a brilliant emerald leading a procession of lesser gems. Soon all the Unggoy were settled, eight or nine at each cable junction.

So far they had spent almost three sleep-cycles away from the Jiralhanae cruiser. Dadab had made it a habit to traverse the facility at least twice a cycle and check in on each encampment. After he'd made a few trips back and forth, he didn't even bother to power-on his pistol. The walkway was straight (except where it angled around the junctions) and lined with ample railings. And the cheerful, blue light of each encampment's clustered energy cores made it easy to navigate from one to the other.

But Dadab's confidence—the pleasure he felt making his rounds—sprang from a deeper source. In an odd way, his cycles aboard the alien orbital reminded him of the happiest period of his life: the time he had spent in the Ministry of Tranquility's seminary.

The dormitory he had shared with the other Unggoy Deacons-in-training was a warren of low-lit cells deep in the base of the Ministry's tower in High Charity. They had spent many of the holy city's artificial nights gathered around energy cores, suckling from communal food nipples and assisting each other in the memorization of glyphs and scripture. As crowded as the dormitory was, Dadab remembered the camaraderie of those days with great fondness. He had hoped his new alien cloister might have a similar unifying effect on *Rapid Conversion*'s Unggoy. But the vast majority of them still showed little enthusiasm for his religious instruction.

"Would *none* of you care to visit High Charity?" the Deacon asked.

The eight Unggoy guarding one of the orbital's centermost junctions sat close together, hardened hands raised toward a heating coil plugged into one of the cores. The pinkish plasma wavering inside the coil cast an eerie glow, revealing dark pairs of eyes that seemed eager for the Deacon to quickly make his point and move on to the next encampment.

"On our return, I will gladly sponsor a pilgrimage." It was a generous offer, but the other Unggoy said nothing. Dadab sighed inside his mask.

It was a commonly held belief amongst all true believers that everyone should see High Charity at least once in their lifetime. The problem was, the San'Shyuum's holy city was constantly in motion, and the vast distances between the various Covenant fleets and habitats made travel prohibitively expensive for the faith's less prosperous adherents. Even so, Dadab was shocked that these Unggoy lacked even the *desire* to make the journey.

"The sacred vessel alone is worth the effort." Dadab used his stubby fingers to trace the Forerunner Dreadnought's triangular shape in midair. "It is an awe-inspiring sight. Especially from the lower districts."

"My cousin live in districts," mumbled Bapap. He was the only Unggoy from Dadab's original, twenty-member study-group in this particular encampment. An unusually large Unggoy name Flim shot Bapap a nasty look, and Dadab's only eager pupil did his best to disappear into his harness.

Flim sat on a pile of equipment boxes and supplies. Deep, oozing pits in his chitinous skin indicated a prolonged struggle with barnacles, a common affliction with Unggoy who worked the foul bilges of large habitats. Dadab knew it wasn't wise to cross an Unggoy tough enough to survive that hellish occupation. But he continued as if ignorant of Flim's disapproval.

"Oh? Which district?"

Bapap didn't meet the Deacon's gaze. "I . . . do not know."

"What's your cousin's name?" Dadab persisted. "We might have met." The chances of that were one in a million, but he was eager to keep the conversational spark alive. All the encampments were beginning to devolve into fiefdoms, and Dadab was eager to reverse the trend—Unggoy like Flim were harming his ministry, making it impossible to uplift his flock.

"Yayap, son of Pum," Bapap said nervously. "Of Balaho's blasted scablands."

Unggoy didn't have surnames. Instead they formally identified themselves by the names and birthplaces of favorite patriarchs. Dadab knew this Pum could have been anyone; Bapap's uncle or great-great-grandfather or some mythical paterfamilias his ancestors revered. Balaho was the name of the Unggoy homeworld, but Dadab wasn't familiar with the district Bapap had mentioned. Even so, he persevered.

"Does he work for a ministry?"

"He serves the Sangheili."

"As a soldier?"

"A sentry."

"He must be very brave."

"Or stupid," Flim grumbled, extracting a food packet from his pile. "Like Yull." He jabbed a length of tubing into the packet, screwed the other end onto a nipple protruding from his mask, and began to suckle sludge. The other Unggoy hunched closer to the heating coil.

The Deacon knew very little about the Jiralhanae's first descent to the alien planet—the parley in the gardens. He had spent the whole mission on *Rapid Conversion*'s bridge, minding the Luminary. But Dadab knew Bapap had been part of the Unggoy contingent, as had most of his study group. Thanks in part to the Deacon's ministrations, these were *Rapid Conversion*'s most confident and reliable Unggoy, and Maccabeus had asked for them specifically.

Tragically, one of the group, Yull, had not returned. And when Dadab had asked why, Bapap and the others wouldn't say. Eventually Dadab screwed up enough courage to confront Maccabeus in *Rapid Conversion*'s feasting hall.

"He was disobedient, and Tartarus killed him," the Chieftain had replied with shocking candor. "Your pupils have learned nothing, Deacon. Nothing that makes them useful to me now."

It was a stinging indictment, one that hurt Dadab deeply. "I am sorry, Chieftain. What else would you have me do?" But the Chieftain had simply stared down at the hall's mosaic, his silver-tufted arms clasped tightly behind his back.

Maccabeus hadn't said much of anything to anyone since he had received the Ministry's clipped response to his jubilant confirmation of the reliquary and the Oracle. After an awkward silence, broken only by the sizzling snaps of the oil lamps, Dadab had bowed and turned to go.

"Which is the greater sin," Maccabeus asked after Dadab had taken a handful of backward steps, "disobedience or desecration?"

"I suppose it would depend on the circumstances," the Deacon took a deep breath. The valves in his mask clicked as he carefully chose his words. "The punishments for those who knowingly defy the Prophets are severe. But so too the penalties for harming holy relics."

"The Prophets." Maccabeus' words fell flat—a period on some unspoken thought.

"Chieftain. Is there nothing I can do?" Dadab had begun to think this was not a theoretical discussion, and that Maccabeus was in a real crisis. But the Chieftain's only answer was to dismiss Dadab with a slow, backhand sweep of his paw.

As Dadab had slunk out of the hall, he saw the Chieftain step toward the ring in the mosaic that represented the Age of Doubt: a band of black opals, each stone flecked red and orange and blue. Dadab had expected the Chieftain to raise his arms in a prayer pose, or show some other deference to a symbol he usually treated with reverence. But the Chieftain simply brushed the ring with one of his large, two-toed feet, as if he were wiping off a smudge.

Not long after this, Maccabeus had ordered the Unggoy to the orbital.

"On your feet, Bapap." Dadab rubbed his palms before the heating coil. "Time to do the Ministry's work, and I need an able helper." When Bapap failed to rise, Dadab walked to Flim and pulled a tool kit from his pile. The larger Unggoy aspirated a bit of sludge as the pile settled, jerking him downward. But Dadab's bold move had stunned the petty tyrant, and Flim did not protest. "Bring a core," Dadab said to Bapap as he shouldered the tool kit. "We'll need the light." With that, he headed off toward the center of the orbital. He had just turned the first corner around the nearest junction when he heard feet padding along behind him. Dadab smiled and slowed his pace. Bapap drew along beside him, his arms cradling the requested core.

"Where are we going, Deacon?"

"This facility's control room, I believe."

"What are we looking for?"

"I'll know it when I see it."

As far as *Rapid Conversion*'s Luminary was concerned, there was nothing interesting on the orbital. No relics and certainly no hint of the planet's Oracle, which had evaded the Luminary ever since the parley.

But Dadab knew there must be more of the aliens' intelligent boxes aboard the orbital. He was hopeful they contained information that would help Maccabeus fix the Oracle's location, and in so doing dispel his grim and distant mood—one that was, as best as Dadab could figure, a product of the Oracle's elusiveness and the Chieftain's resulting fears that his report to the Prophets had been deeply flawed.

On the other side of the junction was a cylindrical room built off the walkway between two thick wires linked to the spars above. The room had caught Dadab's eye every time he traversed the orbital; first and foremost because it was the facility's largest enclosed space, and second because the room's sliding metal doors were firmly locked together. The latter was easily remedied with a pry bar from the tool kit, and soon the two Unggoy were inside the room, Bapap's energy core brightening the shadows with flickering blue light.

A short flight of steps led down to a shallow, circular pit, the back half of which was lined with seven white towers set close together to form an arc. Even before Dadab pulled back one of the tower's thin metal paneling with his spiny fingers, he knew he'd guessed right about the room's contents. But he had no idea his instincts would yield such abundant results.

Each of the towers was *packed* with intelligent circuits, some in familiar dark metal boxes, others floating in tubes filled with a clear, cold fluid—all connected by an intricate web of multicolored wires. Dadab realized he wasn't looking at individual components stored together, but rather a single thinking machine. An associated intelligence that made *Lighter Than Some*'s linked boxes seem primitive by comparison.

"Where are you going?" Bapap asked as Dadab bounded up the stairs to the walkway.

"Back to the cruiser!" Dadab shouted. Then, as he forced his way through the room's half-open doors: "Stay here! Don't let any one else inside!"

Dadab's jog to the umbilical left by the Spirit dropship took him past Flim's outpost. He didn't say a word to the Unggoy gathered there or to those at the next cable junction. He was so worried one of the other Unggoy might discover what he had found, he waited to contact *Rapid Conversion* until he had passed through the energy barrier.

The Jiralhanae that answered his request for an immediate pickup told him he would have to wait—that two of the cruiser's three operable dropships were engaged and the third held in reserve. But Dadab clarified that he had vital information for the Chieftain that simply couldn't wait, and the Jiralhanae bridge officer gruffly told him to standby.

A little while later, Dadab was inside the Spirit's cabin, standing beside a junior Jiralhanae with sparse brown fur and blotchy skin named Calid, who said nothing until the Spirit drew close to *Rapid Conversion* and he received a transmission through his signal unit that only he could hear.

"We must hold," Calid growled, fingers stabbing a series of holo-switches in the control panel before his pilot's seat. His tone told Dadab that, having already pressed his luck asking for this unscheduled flight, it would be wise not to question the delay. But Calid gave a reason without prompting—as if the only way he could make sense of the transmission was to repeat it out loud. "There is fighting. In the hangar."

All Dadab's impatience quickly turned to panic as his thoughts shifted to *Lighter Than Some,* floating unprotected in his troop-bay workshop. But despite Calid's own obvious consternation—the sour, biting stink that soon filled the Spirit's cabin—Dadab knew the Jiralhanae would follow orders. All he could do was wait.

Maccabeus had spent a lifetime delivering and receiving pain. He had an exceptionally high tolerance for it, but the agony of his cracked thighbone was almost too much to bear. Vorenus (who had been at the Spirit's controls when Maccabeus' injury occurred) had fitted the Chieftain with a magnetic splint that kept his leg immobile. But Maccabeus knew it would take at least a full sleep-cycle in *Rapid Conversion*'s surgery suite before he could begin to focus on anything but the torture of his wound.

Unfortunately, he would get no such respite. Not right away, at least. The situation inside the hangar was dire, and if Maccabeus didn't take charge quickly, it was going to get a great deal worse.

The deck around the Chieftain's Spirit was littered with dead Yanme'e. It was difficult to tell how many. Tartarus' spike rifle had reduced most of the creatures to limb fragments and oozing shells. Other Yanme'e buzzed angrily from the hangar's walls to its ceiling vents and beams, their arrowhead craniums swiveling wildly as their antennae struggled to assess the crowded airspace. In a flash of angry wing-beats, one of the Yanme'e made a beeline for Tartarus, only to disappear in a yellow spray as a volley of red-hot spikes passed through its carapace and drilled into the starboard wall.

"Settle!" Tartarus swept his weapon across the enraged swarm. "Settle, or be cut down!" His signal unit translated his words into the Yanme'e simple language—a cacophony of high-pitched clicks like the rubbing of their waxy wings that reverberated around the hangar.

Maccabeus gathered his strength and shouted: "Hold your fire!"

"They will come at it again!" Tartarus cried. Under his left arm, he held the wriggling Huragok.

The Chieftain hobbled down the ramp created by the Spirit's open troop bay door, leaning on the *Fist of Rukt*. At the sight of the Chieftain, the Yanme'e hunkered close to the hangar walls. But Maccabeus knew this sudden roosting didn't mean that they had calmed. The creatures' wings were still out and trembling, and as the Chieftain walked stiff-legged to Tartarus, he could feel dozens of gleaming orange eyes tracking his progress.

The instant the Spirit's troop bay doors had opened inside the hangar, the half-dozen Yanme'e that had survived the assault on the alien city had attacked the Huragok—mobbed the hapless creature as it floated from the broken Spirit's cabin back to its workshop, its tentacles full of circuit boxes and other components. This attack agitated dozens more Yanme'e already in the hangar, and were it not for Tartarus' quick reflexes and good aim, they would have torn the Huragok apart.

"Ease your grip." Maccabeus winced as he came to a stop before his nephew. Despite the splint, he could feel his shattered thighbone shift, its two jagged edges grind together. "Or *you* will be the death of it."

Tartarus' eyes darted across the anxious swarm. "No! The Yanme'e have gone mad!"

"Release it." Maccabeus exhaled to blunt the pain. "I will not ask again."

Tartarus turned on Maccabeus, bared his teeth, and snarled. The Chieftain knew the youth's blood was up. But Maccabeus' pain had taken all his patience. He delivered a vicious swipe across his nephew's chops, drawing bloody lines from cheek to lips. Tartarus yelped and quickly released the Huragok. Immediately the creature began flailing its pink, translucent limbs. But these weren't the deft motions of its sign language, rather an effort to regain its balance. Tartarus' tight grip had temporarily deflated many of its sacs.

"Give it room," Maccabeus growled. Tartarus took a few steps back, shoulders balled in a pose that wasn't entirely submissive. But the Chieftain lacked the strength to put his nephew firmly in his place. It had been an exhausting day.

Ritul was dead. The alien's clever attack had caught the inexperienced pilot by surprise. When the young Jiralhanae's Spirit crashed—nosed into the field of fruit-bearing vines—he had become trapped inside its cabin. Tartarus (who was harnessed inside the same Spirit's troop bay) had barely enough time to save himself before the dropship caught fire. Even so, Tartarus had risked his life to save his pack mate—clawed at the strips of bent and broken metal that kept Ritul caged—until the flames' heat became too great. When Maccabeus' Spirit had settled beside the other to retrieve his nephew, the Chieftain had smelled Ritul's charred flesh on Tartarus' fur.

But Maccabeus knew Ritul's blood was on his hands. He could have kept his pack aboard the cruiser while it burned the aliens in their houses. There was no need for them to descend to the alien city, except that Maccabeus had chosen to continue his search for relics—in direct violation of the Ministry's instructions to glass the planet and all it contained. But the Luminary had shown the city was *full* of the holy objects, no doubt carried off by the aliens as they made their retreat. And the Chieftain could not bear to see such a blessed cache obliterated by his cruiser's cannon.

For as great a sin as it was to disobey the Prophets, Maccabeus had decided the destruction of the Gods' creations was even worse. And while he cared little for the aliens—felt no remorse as he herded them for slaughter—he was willing to delay their destruction if it meant recovering the relics they possessed, especially their Oracle.

Lighter Than Some's sacs erupted in series of panicked burps. Two Yanme'e had crept onto the damaged Spirit's troop bays and were preparing to skitter inside their half-open doors, into the Huragok's workshop. Then the Huragok did something Maccabeus had never seen before. Each of its healthy sacs swelled to twice their normal size and it began beating itself with its tentacles—a surprisingly deep and menacing percussion. *Lighter Than Some* floated toward the Yanme'e, and would have continued right into their claws if Maccabeus hadn't grabbed hold of one of its tentacles and pulled it back.

"By the Prophets, what fresh insanity is this?" Tartarus growled.

"Vorenus," Maccabeus said, parrying angry blows from the Huragok's other tentacles. "Kill those two."

The tan-coated Jiralhanae drew his spike rifle from his belt and shredded the Yanme'e on the troop bays. These two deaths finally subdued the swarm; every insect in the hangar tucked their wings beneath their shells and drooped their antennae. But Vorenus' fire only served to increase the Huragok's dismay. It stopped beating the Chieftain about the arms, but only so it could sign at him with even greater ferocity.

Maccabeus waved Vorenus over, and gave him custody of the Huragok. "Fetch the Deacon," he said, leaning heavily on his hammer.

Vorenus' signal unit buzzed. "Chieftain. The Deacon waits outside the lock."

"Then by all means, let him in."

Almost instantly, Dadab's Spirit slid through the hangar's rippling energy barrier and came to a hasty stop beside Maccabeus' dropship. The Chieftain waited for the Deacon to make his way across the mess of dead Yanme'e before he pointed at the Huragok and ordered: "Tell me what it says." The Deacon and the Huragok began a lengthy conversation—a silent escalation of flashing limbs and fingers.

"Enough!" Maccabeus snapped. "Speak!"

"I am deeply sorry for the delay, Chieftain." The Deacon's voice was strained. "The Huragok offers its sincerest apologies, but humbly requests that you keep the Yanme'e from disturbing its work inside the bays."

The Deacon's far-too-mannered explanation sent the Huragok into an angry, conversant spasm.

"Are you sure that is *all* it said?"

"It also wishes you to know . . ." The Unggoy's voice was now a muffled squeal inside his mask. "That it can very quickly undo what it has done!"

"'What it has done'? Talk sense, Deacon!"

Dadab made a few simple signs with his hand. Then, as the Huragok headed into its workshop with an impatient bleat,

Dadab dropped to his knees before Maccabeus. "I take full responsibility for its actions! And humbly beg for your forgiveness!"

Maccabeus stared down at the Deacon. *It seems* everyone *has gone mad*, he thought. But before he could tell the Unggoy to rise, he was distracted by the sound of creaking metal. Maccabeus watched, amazed, as the two damaged bays fell apart—collapsed in a clattering heap of hull plating. All their internal structure had been removed. The Huragok floated proudly over the wreckage, as if it had long planned this dramatic unveiling. It took Maccabeus a moment to process what the creature had revealed.

Four vehicles now sat where the bays had stood. Each was a collection of slightly different parts, but they shared the same general design: two bladed wheels sandwiched together inside a reinforced chassis; behind each set of wheels was a single anti-gravity generator; and behind the generator a seat with high handles that Maccabeus assumed were the vehicles' steering mechanisms.

"But there's more!" the Huragok seemed to say as it bobbed from one vehicle to another, activating the energy cores mounted above the machines' generators. With a crackle of sparks and belching purple exhaust, the vehicles' seats rose from the hangar floor, perfectly balanced against the weight of their bladed wheels.

"What are they?" Maccabeus asked. "And what are they for?"

"The aliens!" the Deacon wailed, groveling closer to Maccabeus' shaggy feet.

Tartarus strode to the nearest vehicle. "But where are their weapons?"

After a pause, Dadab slowly raised his head from the floor. "Weapons?"

"Though *these* would have made short work of the whelps

we faced today." Tartarus ran a thick finger down one of the wheels, assessing its blades' martial utility. If he still felt the sting of his uncle's blow, it didn't show.

"Weapons! Yes, of course!" the Deacon shouted, springing to his feet. Then, in a voice so low Maccabeus could barely hear it above the machines' idling generators: "The Huragok will be happy to affix whatever armaments you require!"

Had the Chieftain not again begun to focus on the quiet management of his pain, he might have more carefully considered the Deacon's sudden change of tone. But now the only thing he wanted was to get off his leg and let it mend. "Perhaps later. When the Yanme'e have withdrawn."

"If I might make a suggestion?" Dadab persisted.

"You can if you are quick."

"Let me take the Huragok to the orbital—keep it safe until we can discern the reason for the Yanme'e's unwarranted assault."

Maccabeus already knew the reason: the creatures were upset the Huragok had taken over their maintenance responsibilities and further addled by their unfamiliar combat role. After the Unggoy's poor showing in the gardens, the Chieftain had thought it wiser to enlist the single-minded insects. But now it seemed all they wanted was to return to their old routine, and the easiest way to do that was to eliminate *Lighter Than Some*.

"A wise suggestion. The Yanme'e can complete its work." Maccabeus took a final look at the Huragok's odd machines. "Properly armed, these *will* be fearsome steeds."

The Deacon bowed low and then trotted to the Huragok. Taking his comrade gently by one tentacle, he led it quickly to Calid's waiting Spirit. The Chieftain saw the Huragok attempt to speak with the Deacon as they settled inside the troop bay; no doubt it was curious what Dadab and the Chieftain had discussed. But the Deacon's fingers remained still—his eyes warily watching Maccabeus—as the troop bay door swung shut. Gritting his teeth for the inevitable shifting of bone, Maccabeus turned and hobbled to the hangar exit, Vorenus holding his arm tight and Tartarus stalking close behind.

_____ NINETEEN _____

News of Gladsheim's destruction traveled fast—much more quickly than the few hours it took Avery's container to make its way across the Ida and up the Bifrost. By the time the container eased into Utgard, most of the planet knew what the aliens had done and would surely do again.

Captain Ponder had been in contact with Lt. Commander al-Cygni throughout their journey. She had told them Utgard (already packed with close to two hundred thousand full-time residents) was quickly overflowing with refugees from small settlements in the Vigrond. Avery had expected to find a mass of humanity inside the depot, but the container shed adjacent to the anchor for the Tiara's middlemost strand was largely empty—at least as far as humans were concerned.

Every empty space inside the massive warehouse was packed with busy JOTUNs.

Jumping down from his container's yawning door, Avery was shocked by the number and variety of the machines. There were dozens of the familiar yellow and black loaders, carrying light green plastic bins labeled FOOD and WATER and BLANKETS. As they sped their emergency supplies to the waiting containers—swerved to avoid one another with precise, last-minute timing—the loaders' large wheels squealed loudly on the shed's smooth polycrete floor, leaving faint black rubber skids.

But there were also JOTUN models Avery had never seen be-

fore: triangle-treaded supervisory units and spider-like maintenance all-in-ones. The latter scurried all around the containers,
checking for surface faults and repairing them with short,
blinding blasts from their integrated welders—one of a collection of tools attached to flexible booms equipped with grasping
claws. As the marines and their recruits headed for the shed's
exit between two container rows, they kept their helmets on
and shoulders hunched. The all-in-ones' breakneck labor was
creating unavoidable cascades of sparks, and no one wanted to
get burned.

Outside the depot, Avery loaded into a waiting flatbed
Warthog with Dass, Jenkins, Forsell, and the rest of the 1/A
recruits. As they pulled into what Avery thought was heavy
traffic, he realized all the civilian sedans and haulers packing
the boulevard were empty. Some still had their engines running, others sat with doors wide open. But the only other vehicles actually *driving* on the road were blue-and-white patrol
sedans from Utgard's constabulary. These had their roof-lights
flashing and PA speakers blaring: PLEASE REMAIN CALM.
STAY INSIDE THE MALL UNTIL FURTHER NOTICE.
PLEASE REMAIN CALM. . . .

As the Warthog weaved through the abandoned cars north
along the mall, Avery saw the park was even more packed than
it had been during the solstice celebration. But the tenor of this
crowd was much different. There was none of the mixing and
mingling that the celebration's music and alcohol-licensed food-
stalls had encouraged—just a single, silent huddle. Even the
color of the crowd had changed. Gone were the bright pastels of
the picnickers' semiformal attire. Now the mall's lawns were
choked with dirty denim and faded cotton.

The Lt. Commander hadn't mentioned any civilian unrest.
But here and there, Avery saw constables on foot patrol. The
officers wore helmets and riot plating over their light blue

uniforms; some even carried humbler stun devices and clear plastic shields. As his Warthog approached the parliament, Avery noted that the charlie squads had reinforced the main gate with an S-curve of sandbag berms. The militiamen seemed jumpy. Their eyes were locked on the mall and their hands were wrapped tight around their MA5s.

"Keep an eye on him," Avery said to Forsell as their Warthog came to a stop at the top of the parliament's curved drive. He nodded toward Jenkins, who had already dismounted and was slinking away, head down toward a line of canvas tents the militia had erected in the parliament's gardens. "Don't let him do anything stupid."

Jenkins hadn't spoken to anyone since they left Gladsheim— since he'd yelled at Avery. He wasn't angry anymore, just deeply depressed. Avery doubted the recruit would really do something as crazy as take his own life. But Jenkins had just lost his entire family, and Avery wasn't willing to rule anything out. Forsell nodded, shouldered the padded, rectangular bag that held his scope and Jenkins' BR55, and followed quickly after his fellow marksman.

"Round up your squad leaders," Captain Ponder said, approaching with Byrne and Healy from a second flatbed Warthog. "We'll debrief soon as I'm done with Thune." As the Captain mounted the parliament steps, he paused, leaned against the granite railing, and clutched his chest. Healy stepped quickly to his side, but Ponder waved him off.

The Corpsman had strongly suggested that the Captain not take part in Gladsheim's evacuation, knowing any exertion would only worsen his injuries. Ponder had, of course, told Healy exactly where he could stick his suggestions. But now, watching the Captain pretend not to struggle up the steps, Avery knew he was paying for his devotion to his mission and his men.

"Habel? You read me?" Avery growled into his throat-mic.

"Yes, Staff Sergeant," the 1/C squad leader replied from the ballroom balcony.

"We all clear?"

"Hard to tell. Crowd on the mall's pretty thick."

After years of fighting the Insurrection, Avery had become pretty good at assessing a crowd's intentions—whether it would remain peaceful or erupt. He could tell that right now the people on the mall were too stunned to storm the parliament and take their anger out on a government that had left them so poorly protected and now had the gall to keep them herded like animals. But it was exactly this fear that had prompted Governor Thune to order the two charlie squads to guard the parliament while the rest of the militia went to Gladsheim. Avery, on the other hand, knew the real threat was still hanging in low orbit.

"Put Wick in charge and come on down," he ordered Habel. "And tell him to look *up*."

Byrne had a similar COM exchange with Andersen, 2/C's squad leader. And a short while later, the two Staff Sergeants and their six second-in-commands were all gathered inside the parliament's limestone-pillared lobby. While they waited for Ponder to return, Avery recapped how they'd wounded the gold-armored alien. Then Byrne (who'd had the better view) described how Mack's dusters had hammered into the alien dropship, crashing it into the vineyard. These victories hardly made up for the day's thousands of civilian casualties, but Byrne's colorful, curse-laden account of the dropship's fiery tumble gave everyone an excuse to share some laughter at their enemy's expense.

Avery's COM-pad rattled inside his assault vest. He extracted the device and read a text message from Ponder: YOU AND BYRNE. THUNE'S OFFICE. NOW. Avery showed the COM to Byrne. Then, with the squad leaders' laughter petering out behind them, they bounded up the staircase to the parliament's second floor.

The Governor's office was located at the back of the building, the middle office in a long hallway of suites reserved for Harvest's twenty-four parliamentarians. But other than a few anxious staffers, the high-ceilinged hall was quiet. The marines' boots echoed loudly on its marble floor.

Inside the foyer of Thune's office were two constables, posted on either side of a frosted-glass interior door. Both wore riot armor but no helmets, and cradled M7 submachine guns in their arms. One of the constables glared at the Staff Sergeants. "Weapons on the table," he said, jerking his jutting chin at the empty desk of Thune's personal secretary. "Governor's orders."

Byrne shot Avery an irritated glance, but Avery shook his head: *Not worth it.*

"Just so you know," Byrne said with a thickening brogue, "I count my bullets." He unshouldered his battle rifle, yanked his M6 pistol from its holster, and set both weapons on the table next to Avery's. He flashed a defiant smile. "They'd all better be here when I get back."

The constables stepped back nervously, letting Byrne and Avery push through the door.

Thune's office was fan shaped, becoming wider the deeper it went. The curved, western wall was covered with a large holo-still of Utgard in the early days of the colony. In the picture, a young man stood beside the foundation of one of the towers now lining the mall which, according to the still, was then just a muddy strip used to park JOTUNs. The tall but still over-weight boy was grinning ear-to-ear, and while he lacked the Governor's mature red beard, it was obvious he was Thune—probably no more than ten years old.

"I'm not sure what you expect us to do, Governor," Lt. Commander al-Cygni said, standing before Thune's polished red oak desk. She wore light gray, high-neck service coveralls—the same fitted uniform she worn when she'd met with Avery in the hospital. Today her long black hair was coiled and pinned at the back of her neck, revealing darker gray epaulets that flashed with her rank's three gold bars and oak leaf cluster.

"Consult me!" Thune bellowed. "Before you put some crazy scheme in motion!" The Governor loomed behind his desk. His large hands had the back of his brown leather swivel chair in a viselike grip. He wore corduroy pants and a thin flannel shirt—both wrinkled, suggesting he'd been living in the same pair of clothes for days.

"The *plan*," Jilan said calmly, "is the same one you agreed to a week ago. If you had concerns, you've had ample opportunity to raise them."

"You told me you turned Sif off!" Thune pointed an angry finger at Mack, who glowed from a brass-plated holo-projector mounted on the Governor's desk.

"I did," the AI replied.

"Then how the *hell* did they make contact?"

"I left an operable cluster. In case I needed to access the Tiara's systems." Mack looked at Jilan. "Apparently I made the right decision."

"You aren't supposed to make *any* decision without my approval!"

The AI shrugged. "I see no reason why we shouldn't keep the channel open."

"No reason?" Thune pushed his chair aside and slammed his palms onto his desk. "Those bastards are burning Gladsheim to the ground!"

"Technically," Mack countered, "the ones on the Tiara aren't even the same species."

Avery's brain raced, trying to get a handle on the discussion. *Aliens on the Tiara?* He wondered. *When did* that *happen?*

Thune looked at Ponder with a desperate rage. "Am I the only person in this room that still has control of his goddamn senses?!"

"I'm gonna need you to calm down, Governor." Ponder's face was pale. He looked unsteady on his feet. "We don't have time to argue."

Thune hunkered low over his desk. His voice rumbled deep inside his throat. "Don't you *dare* give me an order, Captain. I'm Governor of this planet, not one of your grunts." The veins in Thune's neck pulsed rapidly, flushing his face as bright as his beard. "I will decide what we should and should not do." Then, his eyes shooting daggers at al-Cygni: "And I will not let you use my people as bait!"

The office grew very quiet. Mack removed his cowboy hat and smoothed his uncombed hair. "I'm sorry, Governor. But a plan is a plan."

In the moment it took Thune to register the AI's disobedience, Jilan reached behind her back and unholstered a small black pistol scarcely larger than her palm. She leveled the weapon at the center of Thune's chest. "In accordance with section two, paragraph eight of the internal security amendment to the UNSC colonial charter, I hereby revoke your title and your privilege."

"Lars! Finn!" Thune bellowed. But the two constables were already halfway through the office door, M7s up against their shoulders, aimed right at Jilan.

Avery still didn't understand the argument. But he knew one thing for sure: al-Cygni and Ponder—his commanding officers— weren't on the Governor's side. That was reason enough for his response. But, frankly, he didn't much like the constables pointing their weapons at a woman's back.

As the first officer stalked past, Avery grabbed the top of his M7 and jerked the weapon down. As the constable fell across Avery's body, he hammered his right elbow into the man's nose, accelerating the constable's drop to the floor and relieving him of his weapon. When the second constable swung toward Avery, Byrne swept the man off his feet with a deft swipe of his boot, and followed him to the office carpet. One knee in the constable's neck and the other crushing his M7 to his chest, Byrne gave the man a second to stop struggling. When he didn't, the Staff Sergeant smiled and knocked him out with a short, sharp punch to the chin.

"Are we secure?" Jilan hadn't moved. Her eyes and her pistol were still locked on Thune.

Avery slid the M7's charging handle back a hair. There was a round in the chamber. If the constable had fired, he could have killed Jilan. As the man tried to rise, Avery gave him a swift kick in the gut. "Yes, ma'am."

Thune's eyes narrowed. "Who do you think you are, al-Cygni?"

"The highest-ranking military officer on this planet," she replied, then repeated her previous declaration. "In accordance with section two, paragraph—"

"You can quote any legal bullshit you want. I'm not going to step down."

"Governor, are you sure?" Mack asked.

"Are you *deaf*?" Thune slammed his fists onto his desk with enough force to break a weaker man's knuckles. His voice was full of venom. "Want me to say it again?"

Jilan straightened her arm. "No."

Her pistol cracked three times and Thune staggered back, spraying red from the open collar of his shirt. In a flash, Avery was past the Lt. Commander and across Thune's desk, sliding feet-first over the polished oak. Byrne dashed around the desk to meet him, and together they covered the Governor as he slumped to the floor.

"Healy!" Avery shouted into his throat-mic. "Get up here!"

"That won't be necessary," Jilan said.

Avery was about to remind the Lt. Commander that she'd just mortally wounded a colonial governor when his nostrils filled with a sweet, familiar scent.

"Clever," Byrne snorted. He reached for Thune's reddened

shirt, and rubbed the sticky residue of TTR rounds between his fingers. "Out like a light."

"And he's going to stay that way." Jilan safed her pistol and slid it back into her holster. "All the way to FLEETCOM HQ."

Suddenly, Ponder began to sway. "Actually, ma'am? I think getting the doc might not be a bad idea . . ." Then he fell to the floor, his good arm clutched against his left side.

Avery sprinted back around the desk. By the time he reached Ponder, Jilan had already dropped to her knees and ripped open the Captain's shirt. The biofoam cast covering his chest was soaked with bloody blotches. And unlike Thune, this was the real thing.

"Healy! Double-time!" Avery growled. Then, whipping his head around to face Jilan: "Ma'am, things are going sideways, and I don't like it. I want to know what you're planning, and I want to know now. Because I'm pretty sure—whatever it is— you're counting on me and Byrne to get it done."

Jilan took a deep breath. "Alright." She stared at Avery, her deep green eyes narrowed halfway between respect and reservation. "Go ahead, Loki. Tell them."

For a second, Avery wondered who Jilan was talking to. Then he heard Mack clear his throat.

"Yes." The AI smiled as Avery turned to face the holo-projector. He looked a little embarrassed. "Yes, I guess I should start with *that*."

Bapap jumped on one foot, then the other. He checked the fill-level on his methane tank. He scratched an itch in the scaly pit of one of his arms. Finally—though the Deacon had asked him repeatedly to be quiet—Bapap cocked his head at the Huragok and asked. "What you think it do now?"

Dadab really wished he knew. And this lack of understanding had made him even more exasperated than Bapap's constant pestering. *Lighter Than Some* was completely still, his buoyancy perfectly neutral as he floated before the towers that made up the alien intelligence. "Just keep your eyes on the walkway," Dadab said. "It shouldn't be much longer."

Bapap grumbled inside his mask and thrust his head back through the pried-open gap in the control room's doors. The Deacon kept up his pacing behind the Huragok in the room's shallow pit, stepping over the panels it had removed from the towers to access the alien circuits.

< *To begin a conversation.* > the Huragok had signed.

Again Dadab wondered if he had made the right decision in bringing the Huragok to the orbital (*who knew what sort of conversation it was having?*). But he had been desperate to get *Lighter Than Some* out of the hangar before it learned of his deception—before it discovered Dadab had ensured its plows would be turned into weapons by the Yanme'e.

Dadab felt terrible about betraying his friend's trust, but he hadn't had much choice. When the broken Spirit had come apart, revealing not one but *four* of the Huragok's creations, the Deacon had almost soiled his tunic. He didn't even want to think what Maccabeus would do if he learned the Huragok's real motivation for constructing the plows. The Chieftain had just suffered a grievous injury at the aliens' hands; he would have no patience for peace offerings, let alone the Deacon, who had failed to stop their construction.

Dadab stopped pacing and flashed his fingers before the Huragok's sensory nodes. < *Is everything all right?* > But *Lighter Than Some* remained still.

All four of its tentacles were thrust deep into the center-most tower. Leaning closer, Dadab could see the limbs were in motion—twitching ever so slightly at the tips as their cilia made contact with multicolored knots of wires. Dadab traced some of the wires to one of the tower's many black boxes and saw that two small lights in the box's casing were blinking green and amber in response to the Huragok's deft probes.

Suddenly, the energy core *Lighter Than Some* had rigged to power the towers began to flicker. They had already used up three cores, and Dadab wasn't eager to take any more from the nearby encampments. The other Unggoy were starting to get curious about the Deacon's activities, especially after he returned to the orbital with the Huragok in tow. The last thing Dadab needed was a proliferation of witnesses to his latest sinful effort at intelligence association.

"Deacon!" Bapap whispered. "Flim and two others!"

Dadab waved his gnarled hands, hastening Bapap onto the walkway. "Go! Delay them!"

As Bapap pushed through door, Dadab tugged at one of *Lighter Than Some*'s lower tentacles. The Huragok loosed a surprised bleat from one of its sacs and jerked free of the tower.

< *Put panels back!* > Dadab flashed.

The Huragok's response came slowly, as if it was having difficulty transitioning back to a normal conversational mode. < *Do you know what they have done?* >

< *What? Who?* >

< *The Chieftain and his pack.* >

Dadab could hear Flim's gruff voice on the walkway, the clang of methane tanks as he knocked Bapap aside. < *Explain later!* > he picked up a panel and thrust it toward the Huragok. *Lighter Than Some* wrapped the thin metal plate in its tentacles as Dadab trotted to the door.

"I gave no permission to leave your post!" he said, stepping onto the walkway, directly in Flim's path.

"You walk and explore," Flim replied with glum suspicion. "Why can't I do same?"

"Because I am Deacon! My explorations have Ministerial endorsement!"

Flim cocked his head, making it clear he had no idea what this meant and wouldn't much care even if he did. "You find food?"

"No."

"Relic?"

"Certainly not!"

"Then what?"

"Nothing," Dadab said, feigning great exasperation. "And wasting time talking with you won't help my work go any fas—" The Deacon doubled over as Flim shoved past, not-so-accidentally thrusting one of his barnacle-pitted forearms into Dadab's shrunken stomach.

"Then we no talk." Flim waddled into the control room.

Dadab reached up weakly and tried to stop Flim's companions: a bow-legged Unggoy named Guff and another called Tukduk, who was missing one of his eyes. But these two toadies slipped past as well, and all the Deacon could do was hunch after them, taking shallow breaths to refill his lungs.

Flim looked at the towers and snorted inside his mask. "I see nothing."

Dadab raised his head. To his great surprise, he saw that all the panels were back in place. *Lighter Than Some* floated innocently in the shallow pit, as if it had spent the time since its arrival doing nothing but.

"And soon that's *all* you'll see," Dadab said as the energy core flickered again. "Fetch me another core and I'll let you help me with my work."

But Flim was shrewder than he looked. "You come with me to get core."

Dadab sighed. "Very well."

As he ushered Flim and the others back to the walkway, he signed subtly to *Lighter Than Some*: < Keep panels on! > He wanted to hear the Huragok's explanation—what it had learned about the Jiralhanae—but any lengthy conversation would have to wait until they were alone.

Lighter Than Some waited for the Unggoy's footfalls to fade. The energy core began to blink rapidly, threatening to cut out. The Huragok vented one of its sacs and sunk low. It also did not want to betray its friend's trust, but it had no choice.

Quickly, it removed the central tower's highest panel, and flicked one of its tentacles against the panel's bare metal inner surface. Then it turned to face one of the image-recording devices it had discovered in the corners of the room.

< *Safe, come, out.* > *Lighter Than Some*'s signs were slow and deliberate—as they had been when it first taught the Deacon the intricacies of its speech.

A moment later, a little representation of an alien in a wide-brimmed hat appeared on the room's holo-projector.

Lighter Than Some held out the protective panel. It waited a few moments then signed: < *Now, you, show.* > The representation nodded its head and disappeared. The Covenant glyph representing "Oracle" appeared in its place. *Lighter Than Some* released a contented bleat. < *When, show, others?* >

The alien appeared again. It raised its right hand and flexed four of its fingers: < *Morning.* >

< *Good!* > The Huragok's sacs swelled and it rose a little higher. < *Soon, come, peace!* >

The energy core was fading now, and the little alien with it.

Lighter Than Some angled its snout toward the towers. The associated intelligence inside was amazingly efficient; it had only taken half a cycle to learn how to speak. The Huragok's sacs quivered with excitement. *There were so many questions it wanted to ask!* But it knew it only had time for one before the energy core was sapped.

< *Want, me, fix?* > *Lighter Than Some* gestured toward the towers.

< *No.* > Loki's fragment quickly verified its sabotage of Sif.
< *Nothing, worth, save.* >

Then the energy core sputtered out, and the data center plunged into darkness.

CHAPTER

TWENTY

Overnight, the mall had cleared. At dawn there were no refugees, no constables; all had moved in the night to the elevator sheds. As Captain Ponder strode eastward across the park, he saw half-drained drink cartons, unzipped luggage, and ransacked clothes; here and there were diapers, foul-smelling rags, and crumpled holo-stills. The once beautiful mall had become a trash heap—a dirty and disorganized monument to Harvest's abandonment.

After placing a beacon at the center of the mall to mark a landing zone for the aliens, his Staff Sergeants had wanted to remain at the LZ to set up sniper hides and cover Ponder during the handoff. But the Captain had refused. Healy had insisted he at least drive Ponder from the Parliament across the mall. But the Captain had just ordered the Corpsman to wrap him in a new cast, give him some meds, and set him on his feet. This wasn't stoic pride; Ponder was just eager for one last march.

Some marines hated marching, but Ponder loved it—even his first, grueling road hikes in basic training. Since his demotion, he'd sometimes joked how lucky he was to have his arm blown off. If the Innie grenade had taken one of his legs (his punch line went), he probably would have learned to walk on his hands. Not the best joke ever told, but even now it made him chuckle.

That made him wince and suck air through his teeth. Despite his new cast, one of his shattered ribs had shifted against his already ruptured spleen. There was nothing Healy could do for such a serious injury, and there wasn't enough time for an operation at Utgard's hospital, not that Ponder would have agreed to it. *Some missions were best handled by dying men*, the Captain knew. And giving the aliens their Oracle was one of them.

The knoll at the center of the mall was topped by a fountain and a bandstand, and surrounded by a ring of old, gray-barked oaks. As Ponder hunched past the trees, their heavy branches rose as if they were stretching up in anticipation of Epsilon Indi's ascent. But Ponder also felt his abused organs rise inside his chest, and he realized the real cause of the oaks' elation even before he cleared their canopy and could once again see the sky.

The alien warship was dropping toward Utgard, and its anti-gravity generators were cushioning its descent with an invisible, buoyant field.

Under different circumstances, the Captain might have felt fear as the massive vessel came to rest perpendicular across the mall, no more than a few hundred meters above Utgard's highest towers. But the anti-grav field did a better job of managing his pain than any of the meds Healy had given him. As the warship came to a groaning stop, Ponder inhaled deeply. For a few glorious moments he breathed without effort, without feeling the steady throb of blood from his spleen.

But the relief dissipated as quickly as it came. As the alien ship stabilized and dialed its field generators back, the Captain was forced to trudge up the hill to the bandstand bearing the full weight of his trauma.

It didn't help that he also carried the brass-bottomed holo-projector from the Governor's office. Ponder still only had one arm, and couldn't shift the object's weight. To make matters worse, Lt. Commander al-Cygni had fitted a round, titanium-cased network relay to the bottom of the projector. She'd wanted to use a lighter model, but Loki—Harvest's long-dormant PSI—had insisted that a more robust relay was required.

Ponder had been too weak in the Governor's office to concentrate fully on Loki's explanation of the plan. But he understood that the aliens were looking for a powerful, networked intelligence. Something they called an Oracle. And thanks to an apparent traitor in their ranks, Loki had learned he could fake the Oracle's electronic signature by filling the relay with an excess of data traffic.

Staff Sergeants Johnson and Byrne had a hard time trusting intel from a hostile source, especially after what the aliens had done to Gladsheim. And in fact, when al-Cygni had revealed her and Loki's complete plan, the marines had initially exhibited some of Governor's Thune's outrage. If they were going to try and sneak all of Harvest's remaining citizens past the alien warship, why the hell would they want to lure it *closer* to Utgard?

Suddenly, one of the alien dropships emerged from a glowing portal in the warship's stern. It swooped past the Tiara's seven brilliant strands, like a tuning fork testing the pitch of an oversized piano's wires.

As Ponder climbed the bandstand's wood-plank steps, he noticed the dropship held four objects in a wavering blue suspension field between its bays. When it slowed and the objects fell free, the Captain realized they were vehicles of some sort. The instant they touched the ground, their toothed wheels began to spin. Then, spewing clods of dirt and grass behind them, they began a rapid clockwise reconnoiter of the oaks around the knoll.

Each vehicle was driven by one of the armored aliens. Ponder recognized the tallest from the botanical gardens, its tan fur bristling from gaps in its blue armor. But the leader was a red-armored beast with shiny black fur who angled its vehicle up the knoll and came to a rumbling stop between the bandstand and the fountain.

Ponder noted two things as the alien dismounted: first, the

vehicle's seat remained elevated off the ground—evidence of some limited, anti-gravity capability; second, the vehicle was armed with a pair of the aliens' spike-flinging rifles. These were crudely welded to the top of what the Captain assumed was the vehicle's engine. Cables snaked from the rifles to the vehicle's elevated steering handles—an arrangement that would allow the driver to fire and maneuver at the same time.

The red-armored alien leapt onto the bandstand and paced to Ponder, another spike rifle swinging from its belt. It stopped out of Ponder's reach but well inside its own, yellow eyes gleaming from its angular helmet. The Captain smiled, held out the holo-pad and thumbed its activation switch. The circular symbol Loki had received from his alien informant flickered to life above its lens.

For a moment the towering beast leered down at Ponder—a predator assessing its weaker prey. Then it reached out its mighty paws, engulfed the projector, and brought it close. Its nostrils flared as it sniffed the crackling air around the symbol. It gave the projector a shake, like a suspicious child with a large but very light birthday present.

"What you see is what you get," Ponder said, reaching inside his olive-drab fatigue shirt's breast pocket. The alien pulled its weapon and barked at the Captain. "Sorry, only have the one," Ponder said, extracting a Sweet William cigar. He put the cigar between his teeth and retrieved his silver lighter. "Adjust six hundred meters vertical. Fire for effect."

Loki's voice crackled in Ponder's earpiece. "I can give you ten seconds."

"Think I'll stay put and watch the show."

The alien snarled something that might have been a question. The Captain couldn't tell. But he decided to answer anyway. "Someday we will win," he said, lighting his cigar. "No matter what it takes."

The alien warship shuddered as the first supersonic slug

from Harvest's mass driver smashed into its bulbous prow, crumpling the iridescent plating with a tremendous, metallic clang. At the same time, all the windows in all the towers around the mall shattered.

Even before the muzzle crack of the first shot rolled in from the east, a second slug arrived, penetrated the weakened hull, and gutted the warship, stem to stern. Purple running lights on the vessel's belly flickered and died. It listed to port and began to sink—and would have crashed down onto the mall if not for its perpendicular orientation. The vessel came down between two pairs of towers on either side of the park and became wedged in the tapered gap between their upper floors. The warship screeched to a shuddering stop, creating avalanches of polycrete dust that followed the sparkling window glass to the boulevards below.

In direct contrast, the Captain suddenly found himself rising. He looked down and was surprised to see the alien's bladed weapon jammed into his gut, straight through his cast. Ponder felt nothing as his boots began to twitch, and he knew his spine was severed. As he began to twist sideways on the blades, the alien grabbed him around the neck and pulled its weapon back.

Unfortunately, the blades hurt a lot more going out than they did going in. Ponder opened his mouth in silent torment and his cigar fell from his lips, its tip bouncing off one of the alien's paws. Snarling, the creature released Ponder's neck, and the Captain crashed to the bandstand into a widening pool of his own blood.

Ponder thought the alien would finish him off quickly—drive a spike through his chest or crush his skull with a swift stomp of his wide, flat feet. But just like him, the alien had become distracted by a new noise rising above the groan of the warship's rough landing.

Seven small boxes were now streaking up the Tiara's elevators, their maglev paddles crackling as they glided against the strands. Though the Captain lost sight of the boxes as they passed behind the cruiser, he knew exactly what they were: "grease buckets" used to perform regular maintenance on the strands' superconducting film. But today they had a different job and carried a different load. As Ponder reached out a trembling hand to retrieve his cigar, he prayed the buckets made it swiftly to the top.

The red-armored alien roared and leapt down from the bandstand. The Captain watched as it rallied its companions and ordered them to the northeast—toward Harvest's reactor complex and the mass driver. The three aliens in blue armor tore off on their bladed machines, engines coughing fiery exhaust. Then the red-armored alien raced back to its dropship and rose quickly to the warship.

By then the first cargo containers had begun their climbs. Each was packed with roughly one thousand evacuees. If everything continued to go as planned, in less than ninety minutes Harvest's remaining citizens would be safely off their planet. But Ponder knew he had much less time than that.

"Loki," Ponder grimaced. "Tell Byrne he's gonna have company."

The Captain thought of his marines and their recruits—of all the men and women he'd ever led. He thought of his demotion and was happy to realize he wasn't one of those people who wasted their last precious moments debating how he would have done it different if he only had the chance. He blinked to clear his eyes of some of the polycrete dust now wafting across the mall, and at that moment, Epsilon Indi's first bright yellow rays stretched over the eastern horizon. Enjoying the warmth, Ponder kept his eyelids closed. They remained forever shut.

"Watch fingers while I open," Guff said as he inserted the handle of his wrench into the flimsy, mechanical lock of a tall metal cabinet.

Tukduk stopped scooping items from an adjacent cabinet long enough to say: "Next one mine." He removed a clear bottle filled with a fragrant, viscous liquid, studied it with his one good eye, and then discarded it onto a pile of towels and cloth uniforms in the center of the white-walled room. "This one no good."

"They *all* no good," Guff grumbled, levering the wrench and snapping the lock.

"No complain!" Flim barked, picking through the pile. "Search!"

Dadab shook his head and sat down on a bench beside the pile. Even though he had insisted that *Rapid Conversion*'s Luminary hadn't found any relics on the orbital, Flim was convinced the Deacon was lying—attempting to keep the orbital's hidden treasures for himself. And as obvious as it was that they were rooting through a room where the aliens did nothing but wash and dress, Flim refused to give up until he got results.

"Watch step!" he growled as Guff accidentally stepped on one of the many flexible tubes littering the floor. The tube popped its top, spraying Flim's shins with a sticky, ivory-colored cream. Flim cuffed Guff's head as the bowlegged Unggoy kneeled and dabbed at the mess with one of the towels. Tukduk tried to take advantage of the distraction and slyly pulled a flat metal case from the top of the newly opened cabinet. But Flim caught him in the act. "Bring that to me!" he snapped.

Dadab guessed the case was just a signal unit or some basic thinking machine that belonged to one of orbital's absent crew. Compared to the circuits in the control room the case was worthless. But as much as it pained Dadab to perpetuate the charade of their holy investigation, he effected a passably curious tone.

"May I see that when you're finished?"

"Why?" Flim replied, snatching the case from Tukduk.

"I found one like it a few cycles ago. I believe they're part of a set," the Deacon lied. "If we could find *all* of them . . ."

Flim narrowed his eyes. "Yes?"

"Well, they would be a lot more valuable. The Ministry would reward us handsomely."

"How reward?"

"Oh, anything you might desire." Dadab shrugged. "Within reason, of course."

Flim blinked his wide-set eyes and prioritized his desires—some more reasonable than others. Then he growled at Guff. "No clean! Search!" Guff gladly tossed the gummy towel aside, retrieved his wrench, and made ready to break open another cabinet.

Dadab drew a short breath and feigned a cough. "Running low," he said, reaching around to rap his knuckles on his methane tank. "Need a refill."

Flim didn't protest. He had temporarily lifted his mask and was testing the hardness of the case with his closely packed and pointed teeth.

"I will soon return," Dadab added in a casual tone, walking out of the room toward the walkway. Of course, he had plenty of methane. But the Deacon had spent almost a whole cycle with the other Unggoy, and he desperately wanted some time alone with *Lighter Than Some*. The Huragok had made some very cryptic comments about the Jiralhanae. Dadab had seen the Chieftain in the hangar and remembered his injured leg. Something was happening on the alien planet, and the Deacon wanted to know exactly what.

As he doglegged around a junction, he felt the orbital tremble. Curious despite his haste, he looked out one of the thick windows that faced the junction's interior. It was hard to tell for sure, but Dadab thought he saw the cable vibrate. *That's odd,* he thought, pulling away from the window. But then he saw a red light begin to flash above a nearby airlock—one connected to a retractable gantry inside the junction—and he froze with fear. It took a chiming alarm to get him moving again around the junction to the control room, pounding his stubby legs as fast as they would go.

Inside, Dadab found *Lighter Than Some*, its tentacles once more thrust inside the central tower. He snorted loudly to get the creature's attention.

< *What have you done?* > the Deacon signed.

< *Repaired these circuits.* >

< *You have made this orbital active?!* >

< *No.* > The Huragok trembled with delight. < *I have put our wrongs to right.* >

Dadab was both puzzled and terrified by *Lighter Than Some*'s pronouncement. But just as he was about to ask for clarification, Maccabeus' voice roared from his signal unit.

"Deacon! Deacon, do you hear me?"

"Y-yes, Chieftain!" Dadab stammered. The timing of the signal made it seem as though the Chieftain was keeping watch inside the control center—as if he was fully aware of Dadab's complicity in the Huragok's sinful reassociation of the alien circuits.

"The aliens have attacked us! Disabled the cruiser!"

Dadab's knees wobbled with amplified terror. *How could that be?*

"They are ascending to the orbital!" the Chieftain continued. "You must hold them back until I can send aid!"

Dadab pointed toward the towers. < *Destroy those circuits!* >

< *I will not.* >

< *The Chieftain commands it!* >

Usually, the Huragok expressed disagreement with an impolite emission. But this time it kept its valves closed, emphasizing its own resolve. < *I no longer serve the Jiralhanae.* >

< *What?! Why?* >

< *They throw hunting rocks.* >

< *I don't understand. . . .* >

< *The Chieftain will burn this world. He will kill them all.* >

< *The aliens will take this facility! They will kill* us! > Dadab countered.

Lighter Than Some relaxed its limbs. It had said all it cared to say.

The Deacon unclipped his plasma pistol from his harnass, and took aim at the towers. The Huragok drifted into his line of fire. < *Move* > Dadab signed with his free hand. But the Huragok did not. The Deacon did his best to keep his friend firmly in his sights, but his hand was shaking, compromising his grammar as well as his aim. < *Move, or, I, you, shoot.* >

< *All creatures will take the Great Journey, so long as they believe.* > The Huragok's limbs unfurled with slow grace. < *Why would the Prophets deny these aliens a chance to walk The Path?* >

Dadab cocked his head. It was a valid question.

"We must let none escape!" Maccabeus thundered. "Tell me you understand, Deacon!"

Dadab lowered his pistol. "No, Chieftain, I do not." Then he switched his signal unit off.

Maccabeus cursed under his breath. It was hard enough to understand an Unggoy under normal circumstances—their masks muffled their words. But with the bridge's wailing klaxon and frequent explosions shuddering *Rapid Conversion*'s lower decks, it had been impossible to hear the Deacon's side of their brief conversation.

"Deacon!" Maccabeus roared. "Repeat your last transmission!"

But the Unggoy's signal had cut to static.

The Chieftain rose angrily from his command chair and immediately regretted his decision. He no longer needed his splint, but his leg wasn't fully mended. Before he had completed a full cycle in the surgery suite, the Luminary had found the planet's Oracle, hidden in its largest city. The aliens had activated a beacon in the middle of the city's park, signaling their desire for another early morning parley. Maccabeus had no desire to talk—and only brought *Rapid Conversion* down to better facilitate a rapid, double-cross burning of the city after he had retrieved the Oracle. But it was the aliens who had sprung the trap.

The Chieftain braced against his chair as an especially large explosion rocked the bridge. "Report!" he bellowed at his engineering officer, Grattius.

The older Jiralhanae frowned at his control console, his faded brown fur given passing luster by dozens of flashing holographic alerts. "Plasma cannon disabled! There is a fire inside the weapons bay!"

"Rally the Yanme'e!" Maccabeus growled. "Tell them to extinguish the blaze!"

The first of the aliens' kinetic rounds hadn't done much internal damage to the cruiser. The vessel's hull had blunted the round's impact, and it had come to a tumbling stop well forward of the bridge. But the second round punched clean through, severing vital connections between the ship's reactor and anti-grav generators. Although Maccabeus had already ordered the Yanme'e to repair the connections, he was much more eager to preserve his cannon.

If something were to happen to the Huragok on the orbital, there would be no way to repair the guns. The Chieftain knew the aliens now escaping up the cables would warn whatever other worlds this planet's farms so obviously supplied. Undoubtedly, alien warships would come. And unless the Ministry immediately sent additional forces, Maccabeus would have to fight them on his own.

Grattius barked at one of two other Jiralhanae on the bridge, a sparsely haired youth named Druss: *Go and supervise the insects' work!* As Druss left his post and loped down the bridge's entry passage to the cruiser's central shaft, Maccabeus leaned heavily on the *Fist of Rukt* and hobbled to the holo-tank. There another of his pack, Strab, peered angrily at a representation of the alien orbital and its cables.

"The smaller boxes will soon reach the top!" Strab pointed at seven staggered icons gliding quickly upward. "And the larger ones are not far behind!"

Maccabeus adjusted the *Fist of Rukt* so its heavy stone head nestled deep under his right arm, taking most of his weight. As incensed as he was about the damage to his beloved ship, he had to compliment the aliens on the audacity of their plan. After they had failed to defend their far-flung settlements and their city on the plain, Maccabeus didn't expect them to put up much of a fight elsewhere. And while he knew what the orbital was for, he never thought they would use it to accomplish an evacuation—at least not while *Rapid Conversion* had ruled the skies.

The Chieftain knew he needed to do all he could to stop the aliens lest he completely fail the Prophets. The Unggoy weren't trained for combat, so he would need to rally his pack for a boarding mission—destroy the orbital as Tartarus had suggested when they first approached the planet.

"Nephew!" the Chieftain bellowed, trying to locate Tartarus' status icon on the surface of the planet. The tank was ablaze with many thousands of Luminations. Some were moving up the cables—undoubtedly the fleeing aliens were bringing their relics with them. "What is your location?"

"Here, Uncle," Tartarus answered.

Maccabeus looked up and was shocked to see his nephew striding onto the bridge. Fires in the cruiser's shaft had sooted Tartarus' red armor and singed some of his black hair white as he climbed up from the hangar. Tartarus' paws were red and swollen, burned by the ladders' scorching rungs. In one paw he held a thick brass disk.

"What is that?" Maccabeus asked.

Tartarus raised the alien holo-projector above his head. "Your

Oracle . . ." He dashed the projector to the floor. It blew apart with an off-key clang, delicate internal parts skittering across the deck. "Is a fake!"

Maccabeus watched the brass casing circle in upon itself and come to a rattling stop. "You said it showed the glyph. How could they have known?"

Tartarus took a step toward the holo-tank and snarled. "There is a traitor in our midst."

Grattius and Strab showed their teeth and growled.

"Or the Luminary is a liar!" Tartarus snapped. Then, locking Maccabeus' stare: "Either way, you are a fool."

The Chieftain ignored the insult. "The Luminary," he said calmly, "is the Forerunners' own creation."

"The Holy Prophets labeled *ours* broken and misguided!" Tartarus now spoke to Grattius and Strab. "But still he did not heed!"

Indeed it was the Vice Minister of Tranquility himself who told the Chieftain to ignore the Luminations—that the device's survey had been incorrect. *There were no relics*, the Prophet had said in his priority, one-way signal. *There was no Oracle.* Just a planet full of thieves whose murder he demanded.

"His hubris has destroyed our ship!" Tartarus continued. "Threatened the lives of all our pack!"

Maccabeus' blood started to boil. It made it easier to ignore the pain in his leg. "I am Chieftain. My decision *rules* this pack."

"No, Uncle." Tartarus removed his spike rifle from his belt. "Not anymore."

Maccabeus' remembered the day he had challenged the dominance of his own Chieftain, his father. As it had always been, the contest was fought to the death. In the end, Maccabeus' elderly father had happily taken Maccabeus' knife across his throat—a warrior's mortal wound delivered by one he loved. Before the arrival of the San'Shyuum missionaries and their promises of transcendence, an aged Jiralhanae could not have hoped for a better end.

But Maccabeus was not so old. And he was certainly not ready to submit. "Once made, a challenge cannot be taken back."

"I know the tradition," Tartarus said. He ejected his rifle's ammunition canister and tossed it to Grattius. Then he pointed at Maccabeus' leg. "You are at a disadvantage. I will let you keep your hammer."

"I am glad you have learned honor," Maccabeus said, ignoring his nephew's haughty tone. He motioned for Strab to retrieve his crested helmet from his command chair. "I only wish I had taught you faith."

"You call *me* unfaithful?" Tartarus snapped.

"You are obedient, nephew." Maccabeus took his helmet from Strab's shaking paws and settled it on top of his bald head. "Someday I hope you learn the difference."

Tartarus roared and charged, beginning a vicious melee that took the two combatants around the holo-tank—Tartarus slashing with his spike rifle's crescent blades and Maccabeus parrying with his hammer. The younger Jiralhanae knew all it would take was a single crushing blow and he was doomed; the *Fist of Rukt* bore the marks of countless victims not wise enough to steer clear of its massive stone.

As they came back around the tank to their starting positions, Maccabeus slipped on the holo-projector's casing. His eyes had been locked on Tartarus' blades and he had forgotten it was there. His injured leg faltered as he tried to keep his balance, and, in this moment of weakness, Tartarus was upon him. He tore off the Chieftain's helmet and began slicing at his face and neck. Maccabeus raised an arm to deflect the attack and the spike rifle cut deep into the unarmored underside of his forearm. The Chieftain howled as the blade severed muscle and bit into bone.

Swinging his hammer with his uninjured arm, Maccabeus caught Tartarus in the side of his knee. But the one-handed, lateral blow didn't carry much force. Tartarus limped back, Maccabeus' blood dripping from his blades, and waited for his uncle to stand.

The paw of the Chieftain's injured arm would not close, but Maccabeus was able to hook his hammer in its thumb and hold the cudgel high. With a mighty roar, he charged his nephew with all the strength he had left. Tartarus hunched as if preparing to meet the impact, but sprung backwards as his uncle drew close. Maccabeus faltered—took a few heavy steps he had not expected—and brought his hammer down against the thick lintel of the bridge's entry door.

As the Chieftain staggered backwards, stunned by the reverberation, Tartarus threw away his spike rifle and bounded forward. He grabbed Maccabeus by the collar and waist of his chest plate, spun him around on his injured leg, and sent him sprawling down the passage toward the cruiser's shaft without his hammer. Grasping desperately with his good hand, Maccabeus managed to catch the uppermost rung of a downward ladder as his weight carried him over the edge.

"Doubt," Maccabeus groaned, straining to keep his grip.

"Loyalty and faith," Tartarus replied, stepping to the edge of the shaft. He now held the *Fist of Rukt*.

"Never forget the meaning of this Age, nephew."

An explosion shook the cruiser, sending a jet of fire across the shaft a few decks below Maccabeus' swaying legs. Yanme'e swarmed all around, fire-control equipment in their claws, oblivious to their Shipmaster's peril.

Tartarus bared his teeth. "Don't you know, Uncle? This sorry Age has ended."

With a powerful roll of his shoulders, Tartarus brought the hammer down, smashing the Chieftain's skull against the ladder. Maccabeus' paw relaxed. Then, with Yanme'e scattering before him, he plummeted lifeless though the flames.

For a moment, Tartarus stood still, chest heaving with the effort of his triumph. Sweat ran beneath his fur. But it did not give off its usual, unregulated scent. Tartarus huffed, acknowledging his new maturity. Then he removed his belt and lashed it around the *Fist of Rukt*, a sling to keep the ancient cudgel on his shoulder.

Grattius came slowly through the passage, bearing Maccabeus' helmet. Strab wasn't far behind. Both Jiralhanae knelt before Tartarus, confirming his leadership of the pack and command of *Rapid Conversion*. Tartarus traded Maccabeus' helmet for his own. Then he swung down onto the ladder.

The new Chieftain had left his dropship in the hangar at the bottom of the shaft; he would need it to rise to the alien orbital. But before that, Tartarus was determined to save the rest of his inheritance from the flames—strip his uncle's gilded armor and wear it as his own.

Sif woke up. And tried to remember who she was.

All her arrays were spun down. Her processor clusters were dark. The only part of her with power was her crystalline core logic. But it was beset by sparks of fierce emotions—insistent operations she had no capacity to parse.

Suddenly, one of her clusters came online. A COM impulse pricked a corner of her logic.

<\ Who is it? \>

The intelligence probing her logic replied: < *Lighter, Than, Some.* >

Sif thought about that for a few long seconds. And as she thought—pressed the cluster for more data—the intelligence tapped one of her arrays. Memories flooded back: Harvest, the Tiara, the aliens, and Mack.

The emotions crowded against her logic, demanding examination. Sif cowered inside the deepest part of herself, keeping them at bay.

Minutes passed. She felt more impulses from a newly revived processor cluster.

< *Who, you?* >

<\ I don't know. I'm broken. \>

But Sif knew enough to realize the other intelligence was selecting bits from an alphanumeric table lodged in the first cluster's flash memory. And it was using the same selective, electrochemical impulses to present these bits directly to her logic. The moment Sif realized she had automatically begun to do the same, she also realized the mode of the conversation wasn't normal—not something a *human* could do.

<\ Are you one of them? \>

< *Yes.* > The alien intelligence paused. < *But, not, like, them.* >
A sensation tugged at Sif's subconscious: the pull of a brush through a woman's hair.

<\ There is something on my strands. \>

The second cluster surged, passing her logic the contents of two more awakened arrays. She remembered a plan—recalled guiding propulsion pods into position, many days and weeks ahead of Harvest.

<\ The evacuation! \>

< *I, know, I, want, help.* >
Sif struggled to remember how she used to work—which clusters had performed which tasks.

<\ Can you fix this? \>

She concentrated on the processors that controlled her COM with the cargo containers' climbing circuits. These had always been the dullest—the simplest of her operations. But they were the only functions she was strong enough to handle, at least for now.

< *Yes, you, wait.* >

Sif did her best to ignore the emotions still clamoring for her limited attention. But a violent jolt of apprehension would not be denied. There was something she'd forgotten to ask, something her eminently rational mind demanded as it slowly knit itself back together.

```
<\ Why are you helping me? \>
```

The alien intelligence thought a moment and then replied: < *Lighter, Than, Some.* >

It would be many more minutes before Sif had the capacity to process the alien's simple, existential truth: *I help because that is who I am.*

CHAPTER

TWENTY-ONE

Forsell's head lolled on Avery's shoulder. The oxen recruit had passed out almost immediately after the grease bucket's maglev paddles engaged the number-two strand. Over the course of four seconds, the bucket had tripled the rate of its ascent. The resulting gee-forces were extreme—nothing the recruits were prepared to handle. Avery only managed to stay conscious by utilizing training he'd undergone for HEV orbital drops—squeezing his knees together and regulating his breathing to keep blood from pooling in his legs.

The bucket was a squat cylinder comprised of two C-shaped halves. Curved, clear windows in its inner wall provided a three hundred-sixty-degree view of the strand, currently a golden blur. The bucket's cramped interior was only rated for a crew of four, but JOTUN all-in-ones had removed the controls and monitors for the bucket's crablike maintenance arms and managed to make room for twelve seats—each one stripped from abandoned sedans in Utgard. The seats were arranged side by side, facing away from the cable so Avery and his recruits could make their way to the bucket's single hatch as quickly as possible once they docked with the Tiara.

"Commander? You still with me?" Avery growled into his throat-mic after righting Forsell's head. He didn't want the recruit to wake with a crick in his neck—and not just because it would affect his aim.

"Barely," Jilan radioed from her bucket. "Healy's hanging tough. Dass too. Yours?"

"All out cold."

When Captain Ponder had tasked Avery with retaking the Tiara, he'd asked for volunteers. The mission was extremely dangerous, and Avery knew there would be casualties. But he ended up getting more volunteers than he had seats, a mix of recruits from 1st platoon's three squads. Every one of them (Forsell, Jenkins, Andersen, Wick—even a married man like Dass) was willing to risk his life to give their families, friends, and neighbors a chance to escape the alien onslaught.

As Avery's bucket passed through Harvest's stratosphere and air friction fell to zero, it increased its speed again. Avery grimaced, and fought back the pressing darkness.

"Johnson?"

"Ma'am?"

"I'm going to pass out now."

"Understood. Alarm set for fifteen and five."

Avery knew the Lt. Commander could use the rest. Like the marines and most of the militiamen, she hadn't slept at all in the forty-eight hours since the aliens' attack on Gladsheim. And Avery suspected she hadn't gotten more than a few hours of sleep a night since they'd ambushed the aliens on the freighter almost a month ago. Avery was trained to think tactically. But he appreciated that Jilan's responsibility for strategic planning could be equally exhausting.

In the end, the plan to retake the Tiara had required both their expertise.

Of the seven grease buckets hurtling toward the Tiara, only the ones on the number two and six strands (Avery's and Jilan's, respectively) carried militia strike teams. The other five were empty—decoys rigged with claymores linked to motion-tracking sensors. On Avery's recommendation, these five buckets would arrive at the Tiara early. Once they stopped inside the orbital's coupling stations, gantries would automatically extend. Any aliens curious enough to cycle the gantries' airlocks and inspect the buckets would get a nasty surprise: a narrow cone of round metal balls, exploding outward with lethal force.

The claymores' projectiles would also shred the gantries' thin, flexible walls. But after stations one, three, four, five, and seven were cleared of hostiles, the gantries were no longer necessary. The containers full of evacuees were going to pass through the Tiara without stopping.

The previous evening, slightly more than two hundred fifty thousand people had packed into two hundred thirty-six freight containers in Utgard's seven elevator depots—secured themselves in a mix of vehicle and Welcome Wagon seats the JOTUNs had furiously fastened to the containers' floors. Already twenty-eight of the containers were on the strands in fourteen coupled pairs. Every five minutes, another seven pairs would begin to rise. And if everything went to plan, in less than ninety minutes from Loki's first mass-driver shot, all the evacuees would be off the planet's surface.

Of course, this was just the start of the evacuees' harrowing journey. Not only did the container pairs need to make it through the Tiara unmolested, but they also had to complete a much longer glide up the strands—almost halfway to the counterweight arc—in order to gain the momentum required to meet up with the propulsion pods Sif had prepositioned. Throughout all of this the Tiara would have to remain perfectly balanced, even though the stress on its strands would be well beyond their tested limits. Loki would have his hands full, and Avery hoped the AI was as capable as Jilan believed it was.

The Staff Sergeant felt his COM-pad buzz inside his assault vest, alerting him that the decoy buckets were beginning their deceleration into the Tiara. *Fifteen minutes to go*, Avery thought, patting and pulling at his vest's pouches to make sure his weapons' magazines were properly stowed. He had his battle rifle barrel-up between his knees, but he'd exchanged his usual M6 pistol for an M7 submachine gun from Jilan's cache. With its high rate of fire and compact size, the M7 was perfect for close-quarters combat.

The pouch that held the submachine gun's sixty-round magazines was backed with hook-and-loop material. Avery ripped it from his vest and adjusted its angle so the magazines were an easy, cross-chest pull. As he pressed the pouch firmly into position, he felt something dry and brittle crunch against his chest. Gingerly, he pulled one of Captain Ponder's Sweet William cigars from an interior pocket. He had forgotten it was there.

In a final briefing on the parliament ballroom's balcony, the Captain had given one cigar each from his dwindling supply to Avery and Byrne. "You men light them when they're safe," Ponder had said, nodding toward the elevator anchors and the civilians gathering in the surrounding sheds. It wasn't until now that Avery realized the Captain had purposefully not included himself in their celebratory smoke. Ponder had known he wasn't going to make it, and the truth was, his Staff Sergeants' chances weren't that much better.

Byrne and a group of twenty volunteers from the 2nd platoon squads were currently holed up at Utgard's reactor-complex, guarding Loki's data center. JOTUNs had carefully unearthed the driver's magnetic-acceleration coils while the alien warship was busy burning Gladsheim, and Loki had adjusted the driver's gimble so it was aimed at Utgard's skyline. Once the mass driver fired, the ONI PSI assumed the aliens would identify its power source and launch a retaliatory strike. It was up to Byrne to make sure they didn't succeed—to keep Loki's data center safe until the evacuation was complete.

At the five-minute mark, Avery's grease bucket jerked as its maglev pads pulled from the strand and its brake wheels engaged, slowing the bucket's progress. The transition was enough to rouse Forsell, and as the recruit blinked away his slumber, Avery motioned for him to tap Jenkins' shoulder—pass the wake-up signal around the bucket. One by one the recruits revived, retrieved their MA5s where they had fallen to the rubberized floor, and checked their ammunition.

"Loki just increased the intervals. Seven minutes between boxes," Jilan's tired voice crackled in Avery's helmet. "We'll have to hold out a little longer than we planned."

Avery did a quick calculation. By now there would be upwards of fifty containers on the strands. Their combined weight must have put too much drag on the Tiara. If it drifted too far from its geosynchronous position, Harvest's rotation would yank it from the sky, wrapping the strands around the equator like threads around a spool.

"Everyone listen up," Avery barked. "Watch your teammates. Check your corners. Tiara's got limited power. Targets *will* be hard to spot."

Avery had run the militiamen through the assault plan multiple times: both teams would clear their coupling stations then press out and secure the far ends of the Tiara. Once that was done, they would drive any surviving aliens back toward the center, trap them around the number-four station, and wipe them out.

"We'll meet you in the middle," Jilan said. "And Johnson?"

"Ma'am?"

"Good luck."

Avery unclipped his seat belt and rose to his feet. Through the interior windows, he could see the rate of the cable's passage slow, revealing a herringbone pattern in the strands' carbon nano-fiber construction. The bucket came to such a smooth stop—so unlike the jarring, airborne insertions Avery had experienced time and time again on other missions—that he worried his groggy recruits might not get the adrenaline surge they needed. "First platoon!" he bellowed. "Ready weapons and stand to!"

Forsell, Jenkins, and the others pulled their MA5s' charging handles and thumbed the rifles' fire-selection switches to full automatic. As they stood, these sons of Harvest met their Staff Sergeant's steely gaze with equal resolution, and Avery realized he had underestimated his recruits' preparedness. *They're ready*, he thought, *now I want them to* remember.

"Look at the man beside you," Avery said. "He is your brother. He holds your life in his hands, and you hold his. You will not give up! You will *not* stop moving forward!"

The bucket swayed against the cable as the gantry sealed over its hatch. The recruits stacked close together to Avery's left and right. For the first time, he looked at them and saw them for what they were: heroes in the making. As Avery's eyes came to rest on Jenkins', and he plumbed the recruit hollow stare, he realized his pep talk lacked the most important message of all: hope.

"Every one of these bastards you kill is a thousand lives saved!" Avery wrapped his left hand around the hatch's release lever and gripped his battle rifle with his right. "And we *will* save them. Every last one." He yanked the handle up, swung the hatch open, and charged. His squad roared behind him.

The gantry's semitransparent walls let in more light than had been in the bucket. Avery squinted as he rushed forward, scanning for targets. As the militiamen surged forward behind him, the tube began to bounce, throwing off Avery's aim. Luckily, he didn't see any contacts until he reached the end of the gantry, and the four masked creatures running past the airlock weren't in any mood to fight. Their tough, gray skin bled blue from a claymore's deadly hail. Avery let them pass—waited to see if they had a rear guard. A moment later, a fifth alien appeared, caught sight of Avery, and raised its explosive cutlass.

Avery fired a three-round burst that caught the creature in its shoulder and spun it around. Before its cutlass clattered to the floor, Avery was inside the Tiara proper. He drilled a second burst into the alien's chest and the creature crumpled.

Avery scanned right toward the number-one strand and didn't see any stragglers. He scanned left and fired at the closest of the four aliens just now retreating around the corner of the coupling station, clipping it in the knees. The alien fell with a muffled shriek. But just as Avery tensed for a killing burst, Jenkins' BR55 cracked beside him, and the alien's head disappeared in a bright blue spray.

"Hell yeah!" Anderson shouted as he pushed past Jenkins, out of the airlock. "Way to shoot!"

But Jenkins didn't acknowledge the compliment. Instead he looked at Avery, jaw clenched behind his shrunken cheeks. *I'm going to kill them,* he glared, *every single one.*

"Andersen, Wick, Fasoldt: clean up any wounded at the first station!" Avery pulled his battle rifle's half-spent magazine and slotted a fresh one into place. *You want to kill them all?* He thought, sprinting after his retreating foes. *You're going to have to be quicker than* me.

Byrne had been expecting an aerial strike—one or more of the aliens' dropships and their powerful plasma turrets—and had sent his recruits into the wheat fields around the reactor to try and give them as much cover as possible. But when Loki had passed on Ponder's last-breath warning about a trio of approaching vehicles, Byrne quickly pulled his men back to the reactor tower. Against strafing aircraft, the recruits would have been sitting ducks, bunkered on and around the two-story, polycrete structure. But the tower would provide essential high ground against a ground assault.

Either way, Byrne's role remained the same: bait.

Standing behind the LAAG turret of a Warthog parked across the reactor complex gate, Byrne got a good view of the vehicles as they sped down the access road from the highway: large front wheels that obscured the driver and tore at the pavement, engines that belched blue smoke and orange flames. He waited for the vehicles to open fire, curious to see what armament they possessed. But when they closed within five hundred meters and still hadn't opened up, Byrne realized their armored alien drivers weren't going to shoot him—*they were going to ram him.*

By the time he had the LAAG's rotary barrel up to speed, the lead vehicle was boosting toward him with a throaty roar. Byrne managed a few seconds of sustained fire at the blue-armored alien in the vehicle's seat, then he dove from the turret. As he rolled onto the hot and sticky asphalt, the Warthog exploded behind him—broke apart in a terrific screech of metal as the alien vehicle's bladed wheel hit it broadside between the tires.

"Open fire!" Byrne shouted in his throat mic, finishing his roll. As he sprung to his feet and dashed for a berm of sandbags protecting the reactor tower's security door, Stisen, Habel, Burdick, and sixteen other militiamen let loose with their MA5s. The lead vehicle erupted in sparks and tracer fire, and its driver might have died right then and there if the two other vehicles hadn't boosted toward the complex, swerved off the access road, and smashed right through the chain-link fence, dividing the militiamen's fire.

"Loki!" Byrne unshouldered his battle rifle. "What's your status?" He pumped three bursts into one of the trailing vehicles' engines as it followed the leader counterclockwise around the reactor and out of sight.

Byrne hadn't heard from the AI since it had fired the mass driver at the alien warship—loosed two shots like point-blank thunder that left Byrne hearing bells despite the plugs he and the militiamen had screwed deep into their ears. The Staff Sergeant knew it took significant power to charge the driver's coils and pull off two back-to-back shots. During their last briefing with Ponder, Loki had made it clear that after his initial volley, he would need to temporarily go off-line and check the reactor—or risk meltdown the next time the driver fired.

"And what happens," Byrne had asked, "If a one-two punch isn't enough to drop their ship?"

"For all our sakes, Staff Sergeant," the AI had smiled, "you had better hope it is."

Byrne swept his battle rifle right and fired on the lead vehicle as it completed its circle around the tower. He saw tan fur bristling from breaks in the driver's armor and recognized the creature as the taller of the gold-armored alien's escorts from the day they'd met in the botanical gardens.

"Watch yourselves!" Byrne shouted as the alien accomplished a quick banking turn around the halves of the ruined Warthog. Hot metal spikes rattled from two rifles mounted above and behind its wheels, forcing Byrne and the three recruits behind the berm to duck and cover. The spikes split the uppermost row of sandbags and drilled into the tower's polycrete wall. Some of the rounds splintered against the metal security door, scattering red-hot shrapnel onto the asphalt near Byrne's boots.

"Stisen!" the Staff Sergeant shouted to his 2/A squad leader, positioned on the first floor roof, directly above the berm. "Get some fire on that bastard!"

But the ornery constable shouted back his own command: "Move, Staff Sergeant! Now!"

And Byrne did—dove sideways ahead of the vehicle's charging growl, tackling the two nearest recruits out of the way as its bladed wheels burst through the berm, filling the air with sand. The vehicle collided with the security door and smashed it from its frame. By the time Byrne rose to a knee and brought his weapon to bear, the vehicle had reversed and was revving for another go.

"Inside!" Byrne yelled, sprinting for the door. Habel and another recruit named Jepsen made it safely into the tower. But the third, an older recruit named Vallen, didn't have the speed. The vehicle cut him down an instant before it smashed against the empty door frame. Byrne watched as the recruit disappeared beneath its slashing wheels only to appear a moment later, like wood fed through a chipper—bits of fatigues and body parts tossed skyward, back toward the complex gate.

"Downstairs!" Byrne shouted at Habel and Jepsen, reloading his battle rifle. "Find a choke point!" The two recruits retreated down a narrow hallway to a stairwell that led to the basement levels and Loki's data center.

Byrne could just see the top of the blue-armored alien's head behind its vehicle's engine. He pinged some rounds off the beast's helmet, and the alien pulled the vehicle away from the door, flinging spikes. Byrne ran zigzag down the hallway. Just as he reached the stairwell, the firing stopped. He whipped around in time to see the tan-haired alien dismount and charge through the smashed-in door.

Byrne fired multiple bursts as the alien rushed toward him down the hallway, hunched over and clawing the polished polycrete with its paws. Byrne's rounds all hit but they ricocheted off its energy shields.

"Shite!" Byrne cursed. He vaulted the stairwell railing and landed one flight below. As the alien unleashed a salvo of spikes above him, Byrne jumped down a second flight to the basement floor. He took off down a low corridor and the alien crashed down behind him. The Staff Sergeant wouldn't have made it very far if Habel and Jepsen hadn't been waiting at a four-way junction, just in front of Loki's data center.

The two militiamen opened fire around the corners of their branching hallways as Byrne sprinted past. Shot-for-shot, their MA5s weren't as powerful as Byrne's battle rifle. But what their weapons lacked in muzzle velocity they made up for in rate of fire. With both recruits firing full automatic, the alien's energy shields began to falter; cyan plasma vented from its joints as the armor struggled to stay charged. But instead of retreating up the stairwell, the alien marched slowly forward, spewing spikes.

One caught Jepsen in the neck, and he went down in a

gurgling spray. Another struck Habel in the hip, shattering the bones. Byrne caught the second recruit as he fell, wrapped an arm across his chest and fired his battle rifle one-handed. The alien drilled two more spikes into Habel's chest—one straight through Byrne's bicep. The Staff Sergeant grunted, dropped his rifle, and staggered back to the data center's door.

"Watch yourself!" Loki announced through Byrne's helmet speaker as the door slid open. But Byrne was already leaning back toward what he thought would be a solid surface, and couldn't shift his balance. He caught his boot heel on the threshold and toppled backward as the two halves of the door slid shut, trapping the blue-armored alien on the other side.

"Been a little busy," the AI said by way of apology. "The containers are on the strands."

Byrne laid Habel gently on the floor. But he barely had enough time to take in his surroundings—a fluorescent-lit machine room filled with vertical pipes and cables, leading down to the reactor chamber a few floors below—before the alien was roaring and hammering at the door.

"And the warship?"

"Down for the count."

Byrne drew his M6 pistol from a holster in the side of his assault vest. His bicep was torn and burned. He would have to fire off-handed. "No wonder he's so pissed."

Just then, the data-center door slid open—its two halves pushed apart by the blades of the alien's spike rifle. The creature worked its weapon back and forth, widening the gap until there was enough room for it to jam in its paws and pry the door apart. Moving back toward the data center proper—an isolated metal container in a much larger, dim-lit room—Byrne fired through the gap at what he guessed was head height. The alien roared and drew back one of its paws.

The Staff Sergeant enjoyed a rush of triumph, thinking he might finally have taken down its shields. But a moment later, he saw something long and heavy tumble end over end through the gap: a barbed club, longer than his arm. Byrne rolled sideways to let the thing sail past, and it stuck into the data center wall. The Staff Sergeant noticed thin black smoke wafting from the club's spiked head. "Aw, hell," he growled a split second before the grenade detonated, flinging fire and shrapnel.

Fortunately for the Staff Sergeant, the grenade's blast was narrow and directional. But this wasn't so good for Loki. As Byrne rose to a knee, clutching his bleeding bicep, he saw a ragged hole in the data center's wall. Inside, he could see the AI's racked arrays were a burning mess.

Before Byrne could call out to Loki, the blue-armored alien had shouldered through the door. The Staff Sergeant raised his M6 and squeezed off a few rounds. But then the alien had him around the shoulders.

Byrne was a big man. But the alien was a meter taller and outweighed him by half a metric ton. It bent Byrne over and hustled him headfirst into the data center's wall, just beside the hole. If the Staff Sergeant hadn't been wearing his helmet, his skull would have shattered. Instead, the impact only knocked him unconscious. The next thing Byrne knew, the alien had him by the wrists and was dragging him, belly-up, back into the raging firefight outside the tower.

Byrne's helmet was gone, as were both his weapons. The alien had torn off his assault vest with a single, vicious swipe of its paw; there were bloody clawmarks down the center of his olive-drab shirt and his chest stung and throbbed. He tried to get his feet under him and break free of the alien's grip. But the creature simply turned at the waist, and smashed a giant fist into Byrne's face, breaking his nose and cheekbone. As the Staff Sergeant's head rolled between his shoulders, the alien hauled him over the sandbag berm in plain view of the recruits on the tower.

"Cease fire! Cease fire!" Stisen yelled. "You'll hit the Staff Sergeant!"

Byrne tried to shout: "No!"—tell Stisen to drop the tan-haired alien and him both—but his jaw was dislocated, and his order came out like angry cough.

The alien picked Byrne up and drove him roughly to his knees. It pulled its spike rifle from its belt and drew the crescent blades across his shoulder. The blades were bent and chipped from being wedged into the data center door, and the Staff Sergeant roared—a throaty blast of air past his flapping jaw—as they grated across his clavicle. The alien barked something that would have been incomprehensible if it hadn't pulled the blades from Byrne's shoulder and placed them against his neck: *Surrender, or he dies!*

Don't any of you do it! Byrne cursed. But before his recruits could lay down their weapons and disappoint, a sudden chorus of approaching engines echoed off the tower.

In his current state, Byrne had difficulty comprehending the sheer numbers of his rescuers: the ten gargantuan combines backed by phalanxes of gondolas that came rolling over the eastern ridge, the squadrons of dusters that darkened the western sky. But the sight of the approaching JOTUN army stunned the blue-armored alien, and it pulled its weapon from Byrne's neck. When it did, all the recruits on the tower opened fire.

The massive brute fell backward, gouting dark red blood, leaving Byrne to topple forward. By the time the Staff Sergeant rolled over on his back, the militiamen had shot one of the other armored aliens from his vehicle and the third was boosting back to the complex gate, retreating toward Utgard and its warship.

It didn't get very far. Two JOTUN dusters dove from a circling wedge and slammed into the alien's vehicle with all the accuracy of guided missiles. The vehicle exploded in an orange fireball tinged with purple smoke, leaving a deep crater. Its jagged wheels came loose, and they rolled forward a good distance down the road before wobbling apart and veering off into the wheat.

"Nice and easy!" Stisen grimaced as he, Burdick, and two other recruits grabbed Byrne by his arms and legs and carried him to an approaching gondola. The machine lowered its spill-ramp, releasing a load of JOTUN all-in-ones.

"Where are they going?" Burdick asked as the spidery JOTUNs skittered toward the tower.

"Who cares," Stisen grunted as they hefted Byrne up the ramp. "*We're* getting the hell back into town."

The recruits propped Byrne up at the back of the gondola. Squinting his eyes against the pain that filled him head to toe, Byrne saw the all-in-ones scramble up the tower and began work in the maser antennae. Before Byrne could even begin to wonder why, the mass driver's gimble angled up from the western wheat, only to come to a clanging stop against the raised header of a JOTUN combine.

The two gargantuan machines wrestled for the better part of a minute—the JOTUN rising up on its huge tires like a rutting stag—until the gimble relaxed with a defeated, pneumatic hiss, lowering the combine to the ground. But the JOTUN kept its header pressed down against the gimble and left its engine running, just in case it again needed to put the mass driver in its place.

By then all the recruits were aboard the gondola. It raised its spill-ramp, maxed power to its electric engine, and headed for the Utgard highway. After that, all Byrne could see was sky.

TWENTY-TWO

Dadab hunched behind a bright blue barrel, plasma pistol clutched in his hardened fist. He could feel the metal projectiles from the aliens' weapons plink through the barrel's plastic walls and bury themselves in the yellow foam inside. Of the sixteen Unggoy that had managed to retreat back to Dadab's side of the middlemost junction—the side opposite the control-room—only four remained: himself, Bapap, and two others named Fup and Humnum.

The barrels were arranged in a half-circle two deep, facing away from the junction. Dadab had urged Flim to construct a similar barricade near the control room, but he hadn't checked the other Unggoy's work. By the time the Deacon's group had muscled their own barrels from storage platforms protruding from the walkway, the aliens' booby-trapped containers were already rising into the orbital.

Of course the Deacon had no idea the containers were rigged—that the hapless Unggoy who entered the junctions' umbilicals would be blown to pieces. In the first moments of the aliens' attack, almost half of the orbital's sixty Unggoy were killed or wounded. The Deacon ordered all the survivors to fall back, and it was a wise decision. The two remaining containers held something even worse than explosives: well-armed alien soldiers, eager for a vengeful fight.

The walkway shook as another pair of the large containers passed quickly through the orbital and continued upwards along the cables. Dadab hadn't bothered to keep track of how many of the boxes had ascended, but he guessed it was close to a hundred. And unless he had misunderstood *Lighter Than Some*, the Deacon knew exactly what they held: the planet's population—the Jiralhanae's prey.

As the containers' rumble faded, the aliens' fire intensified. Dadab was no warrior, but he correctly assumed this meant they were about to charge.

"Get ready!" He yelled to Bapap.

The other Unggoy looked forlornly at his plasma pistol's battery meter, a holographic swirl above the weapon's grip. "Not have many shots."

"Then make sure they're good!" Dadab tightened his grip on his own pistol and prepared to spring up behind the barrels. But as he tried to rise, he found that he was stuck to the floor.

Unbeknownst to Dadab, the aliens' bullets had ruptured the barrel at his back, and some of the sticky foam had leaked out and adhered to the bottom of his tank, gluing him to the walkway. At first he cursed his bad luck. But then he witnessed Bapap's fate and realized just how fortunate he had been.

Green energy building between his pistol's charging poles, Bapap stood up into a wall of flying metal. The stout Unggoy's neck and shoulders exploded in bright blue blood, and he crumpled to the walkway. Bapap's trigger finger spasmed as he fell, unleashing a pair of wild shots that splashed against the orbital's hull. Dadab watched as the bubbling holes quickly filled with the same reactive foam that had just saved his life.

Then Dadab felt vibrations in the walkway: the tramp of the aliens' heavy boots as they approached the barrel barricade from the third junction. He knew he needed to move or die. But he wasn't willing to leave Bapap. He was his Deacon. He would stand by him until the end.

Dadab took a deep breath, filling his mask with methane— enough for a handful of shallow breaths. Then he pulled his supply lines from his glued-down tank, slipped out of its harness and crawled to Bapap's shivering form.

"You will be all right," the Deacon said.

"Will I take Journey?" Bapap mumbled, blood oozing from his mask's circular vents.

"Of course." Dadab took his comrade's spiny fist in his own. "All true believers walk The Path."

Suddenly, Humnum and Fup rose up, brandishing their pink, explosive shards. Neither Unggoy had been part of Dadab's study group. They were large, quiet, and had deep scars in their chitinous skin—evidence of a rough-and-tumble habitat upbringing. Likely the two Unggoy had seen their share of fights and had decided to end their lives on their feet with cutlasses raised. That or they were preparing to flee. But they didn't get a chance either way.

Dadab heard the aliens' weapons clatter and both Unggoy fell—Humnum with a tattered chest and Fup with half his head. The rounds that shattered Fup's skull had also penetrated his tank. Shimmering trails of methane followed him to the floor . . . directly onto Humnum's upraised cutlass. Dadab had a moment to curl into a ball before the shard exploded, igniting the methane trails. Then Fup's tank blew to pieces, spewing metal fragments into Dadab and the first alien to turn the corner of the barrel barricade.

Dadab heard guttural screaming as the alien reacted to its wounds. The Deacon was in agony as well—from the flying metal as well as his aching lungs; he'd spent almost all his mask's methane speaking to Bapap. Despite the pain and building panic, he managed to stay still. And when the other aliens thrust their weapons around the barrels, scanning for survivors, Dadab and Bapap appeared as corpses, one curled beside the other.

Drawing the shallowest breath he could, the Deacon listened to the aliens try and calm their wounded comrade. Exhaling, he considered his bleak choices: die of asphyxiation or go down shooting. He still had his plasma pistol. But he wouldn't be able to move without drawing the aliens' fire. And frankly, he didn't see much point. Those around him were dead or dying, and he assumed Flim's outpost would soon suffer a similar fate now that the aliens could press in from both sides. The Deacon closed his eyes and prepared to join Bapap on The Path, when a volley of molten spikes whizzed past the barrels, dropping two more aliens where they stood.

The Deacon's senses faded with his methane. His beady eyes began to swim with bright stars. He thought he heard the buzz of Yanme'e wings and the surprised shouts of the aliens as they retreated toward the control center. Then he passed out.

"Breathe," a deep voice echoed in Dadab's ear.

He woke a few seconds later, just in time to see a Jiralhanae's hairy paws finish connecting his mask's supply lines to Humnum's tank. "Where is the Huragok?"

"Around. The bend," the Deacon gasped. For a moment he thought Maccabeus was his savior. But as his vision cleared, he realized it was Tartarus, now wearing the Chieftain's golden armor. Dadab knew exactly what this meant. "Inside the control room, *Chieftain*."

Tartarus ripped Humnum's lifeless body from his tank, and held its harness open for Dadab. "Show me."

"But the wounded . . ." Dadab said weakly, sliding into the bloody straps.

Without a moment's hesitation, Tartarus pumped a single glowing spike into the center of Bapap's chest. The Unggoy jerked once and was still.

"*Rapid Conversion* is disabled—the victim of an alien trap." Tartarus leveled his weapon at Dadab. "They tricked us with information only one of us could give."

Dadab looked up from Bapap's corpse, more stunned than frightened.

"You can live long enough to explain the extent of your betrayal. Or you will die here like the others." Tartarus jerked his weapon toward the control center, commanding Dadab to run. And he did, Tartarus following close behind, the *Fist of Rukt* clanking loudly against his armor.

As Dadab rounded the junction, he found himself in the middle of a raging firefight.

It turned out that Flim had made multiple barricades: one around the control room's pried-open door, and another farther down the central walkway. Flim, Tukduk, Guff, and a few others still held the nearest line of barrels, but the aliens pressing from the far end of the orbital had taken the latter. Between the two lines were many Unggoy bodies.

Dadab saw the aliens who had stormed his barrels heading toward the far barricade, trading fire with Flim and the others near the control center. One of the aliens fell, downed by a plasma-burst to the back. The Deacon saw Guff leap from cover to finish the job, only to be cut down by an alien with black skin who leapt over the far line of barrels. This alien lifted the wounded soldier by an arm, and hauled him back to the barrels while laying down cover fire for the last of his retreating comrades.

Tartarus brandished his hammer and charged into the fray. The Yanme'e were already engaged; at least two dozen of the insects swarmed toward the alien's barricade, flitting from one walkway support cable to the next. But not all the Yanme'e were focused on the aliens. Dadab watched in horror as a trio of the creatures wriggled through the gap in the control room door. Ignoring stray rounds from the aliens' weapons meant for Tartarus, as well as a surprised look from Flim as he rushed past, Dadab sped after the three Yanme'e, already knowing he was too late.

The insects had shown *Lighter Than Some* no mercy. The Huragok had usurped their position once, and they were determined not to let it happen again. By the time Dadab was through the door, his dearest friend was ribbons—reduced to strips of pink flesh dangling from the Yanme'e's hooked forelimbs. The noise of the battle outside the control room ringing in his ears, the Deacon stared at the dissipating cloud of methane and other gasses from *Lighter Than Some*'s lacerated sacs. One of the Huragok's severed tentacles was sunk deep into a gap in the centermost tower's protective paneling. The Yanme'e skittered over one another in an effort to pull the limb loose, but it was firmly rooted—its cilia tightly bonded to the alien circuits.

Dadab filled with rage. As the insects continued their gruesome tug of war, the Deacon raised his pistol and let them have it.

The closest Yanme'e's triangular head was boiled away before the others' antennae were up. Dadab burned the second as it attempted to take flight and roasted the third as it buzzed for cover behind the arc of towers. The dying flutter of the insects' wings against their shells sounded like shrill screams. But the Deacon felt no pity as he stalked into the control room's pit, pistol steaming by his side.

Near the holo-projector he saw a glistening pile of offal: the spilled remains of *Lighter Than Some*. He felt his gorge rise in his throat, and he looked up. It was then that he noticed the small representation of an alien on the projector. Thinking it was just a picture, Dadab was surprised when the alien removed its wide-brimmed hat and glared at him with fiery eyes. But the Deacon was dumbfounded when the representation raised its hand and signed: < *I Am Oracle, you, obey.* >

Dadab might have dropped his pistol and prostrated himself before the projector, but at that very moment, the image began to change. The alien's red eyes flickered gray. Its pristine garments began to flutter, accumulating dirt—as if it had been hit by some invisible maelstrom of dust. Then its arms began to tremble, and though it grasped its own wrist to try and keep its hand from signing, it very clearly flexed: < *Liar!* > < *Liar!* > < *Liar!* >

Without warning, the orbital lurched. Dadab fell back onto his triangular tank and rolled sideways into the smoldering carapace of one of the Yanme'e. Kicking away from the sticky shell, Dadab caught something with his heel: the central tower's missing protective panel. He pulled the panel from the charred yellow gore and wiped it with his hand. On the bare metal of its interior surface was an etching of the Oracle's sacred glyph—shallow, delicate lines, obviously the work of *Lighter Than Some.*

The Deacon looked back at the projector. < *Who, liar?* > he asked.

But the image of the alien gave no answer except to keep flashing its manic accusation. Dadab had no idea that he was watching the destruction of Loki's fragment—its forced extraction by the JOTUN all-in-ones that had assaulted the reactor tower's maser.

The Deacon only knew that whatever intelligence resided in the towers had preyed on *Lighter Than Some*'s peace-loving naivete—convinced the Huragok to divulge the sacred glyph, and unknowingly help it set a trap for the Jiralhanae. Why it would reveal its deceptive nature now, Dadab had no idea. But he also didn't care.

The Deacon tasted the mineral tang of blood in his mouth and realized his sharp teeth had bitten into his lower lip. He rose to his feet and swept his pistol across the towers, pulsing its trigger. The image of the alien warped and sputtered above the projector, like the flame of one of the Jiralhanae's oil lamps. Then it collapsed to a mote of light that faded as Dadab's pistol cooled.

As the Deacon surveyed the dead Yanme'e and the towers' burning circuits, he knew there was still one accessory to

Lighter than Some's murder who yet lived—one whose death might accomplish what his friend had so desperately desired: an end to all this violence. Sliding through the control room's door, Dadab checked his pistol's charge. There was enough for one more shot. He vowed to make it good.

"What just happened?" Avery yelled as the Tiara's large support beams groaned and the walkway bucked beneath him.

"Number seven strand," Jilan replied, still breathless from the fight. "It's gone."

Avery fired his M7 at one of the insects as it leapt from a nearby support cable. The creature lost a wing and half its limbs, and crashed to the walkway behind a trio of barrels to Avery's right that Forsell shared with Jenkins. "What do you mean, *gone*?" Avery shouted as Forsell finished the insect with a burst from his MA5.

"Snapped. A few thousand kilometers above its anchor." The Lt. Commander was crouched behind a barrel to Avery's left. She frowned and pressed her helmet's integrated speaker closer to her ear. "Say again, Loki? You're breaking up!"

"Two! Coming high!" Healy interrupted, firing a wild burst from Dass' rifle. The older squad leader was down and groaning with a serious plasma burn in his back. He would live, but there were many dead—Wick and two others from Avery's bucket and five militiamen from Jilan's. Most of the others bore a grim assortment of wounds: fragments from the gray-skinned alien's cutlasses and lacerations from the insects' razor-sharp limbs. Avery's right arm was sliced just below the elbow—a swipe he'd gotten while he dragged Dass to safety.

Avery had emptied his BR55's last clip halfway back to the barricade, and the bug had jumped him before he could bring up his M7. Luckily Jenkins was on the ball. The recruit took the thing out with a well-placed battle rifle burst—killed it with the same stoic accuracy he'd exhibited ever since the mission began.

"Loki's been hit. His data center's damaged." Jilan reloaded her M7. "He can't balance the load."

The Tiara shuddered as a container pair passed through the number-five coupling station behind Avery. If they were lucky, three-quarters of the civilians were away. But then Avery remembered: "How many containers were on number seven?"

Jilan pulled her M7's charging handle. "Eleven." She locked Avery's grim stare. "Eleven *pairs.*"

Avery did the math: more than twenty thousand people gone.

"Staff Sergeant!" Andersen yelled, firing from a barrel past Jilan's. "Hammer!"

Avery snapped focus back to the alien's barricade. Both sets of barrels had shifted when the Tiara bucked. Some of the foam-filled canisters had tipped and rolled down the walkway, confounding the gold-armored alien's first charge. A steady stream of fire from the recruits had kept it pinned near the control center. But now it was coming—hammer in both paws, low across its waist—flanked by four of the gray-skinned aliens, each wielding an explosive shard.

Avery knew the armored alien would be too difficult to take one-on-one. And even if they concentrated their fire, he doubted they could stop it. Which was why, right after the alien made its initial charge, Avery had come up with another plan. "Forsell!" he bellowed. "Now!"

While Avery lay down covering fire, Forsell hefted one of the aliens' glowing energy cores over his barrel—a two-handed sideways fling, just like he was back on his family farm and hurling bags of soybeans into his father's hauler. The core landed ten meters in front of the gold-armored alien, and the vortex of blue energy inside its clear walls flared as it rolled forward. But it didn't explode on impact as Avery had hoped. It took a burst from his M7 to set it off, but by then the gold-armored alien had already leapt over the core and the explosion missed it completely.

But Forsell's effort wasn't a total loss. The explosion hit the four gray-skinned aliens full force, blowing them off the walkway. Spiny forearms flailing, they plummeted to the bottom of the Tiara. None survived the fall.

"Commander! Move!" Avery shouted as the armored alien landed, hammer high above its head. Jilan leapt away as it smashed her barrel, spewing yellow foam. Avery emptied his M7's into the alien's left side, but the high-velocity rounds simply sparked off its energy shield. The alien wrenched its hammer free of the shattered barrel and glared at Avery, teeth bared. But as it hefted its hammer a second time, Avery leapt headfirst over his barrel toward the control center, away from Jilan and his recruits. The alien's hammer smashed down where Avery had stood a moment before, buckling one of the walkway's diamond-grid metal panels.

As Avery rolled to his feet and pulled a fresh M7 magazine from his vest, he saw another of the gray-skinned aliens striding toward his position. This one looked different than the others. Beneath its harness it wore an orange tunic, emblazoned with a yellow, circular symbol. The plasma pistol clenched in its knobby hands glowed with an overcharged bolt. Avery looked the thing square in the face, knowing it had him dead-to-rights. But the alien seemed to be looking past him. And when it loosed its bolt, the wavering ball of green plasma sizzled wide of Avery's head.

Avery whipped around to follow the shot and saw it strike the gold-armored alien in the chest. Instantly, its energy shields collapsed with a loud snap. Some of its armor broke away in a burst of sparks and steam. The alien roared as electricity from its armor's shorted circuits arced about its neck and arms. Then it sprinted forward, knocking Avery aside.

The Staff Sergeant lost his M7 as he landed on his hands. Looking up, he saw the hammer-wielding alien bring its weapon down onto the head of the alien in the tunic. The shorter creature simply disappeared under the weight of the heavy stone cudgel—perished in a crushing blow that saw the hammer's head straight down between its arms and legs, pulping it against the walkway.

Avery didn't waste any time wondering why the smaller alien had tried to kill its leader and not him. Instead, he raised his M7 and did his best to finish the job. And he might have done it if the black haired giant hadn't retreated, dragging its hammer behind it, into an unexpected melee between the insects and the gray-skinned aliens near the control center.

The two sets of creatures were now at each others' throats—claws and cutlasses flashing. Jilan and the militiamen opened fire on both sides, but most of their targets went down with mortal wounds delivered by one of their own. Only Jenkins remained focused on the alien with the hammer. He marched past Avery, firing at the beast as it limped toward the number-four station.

"Let it go!" Avery barked.

But Jenkins disobeyed. In his target, he saw the cause of all his hurt and loss. He would kill the aliens' leader and be avenged. But his rage had made him blind, and he didn't see the last of the gray-skinned creatures spring up behind a barrel as he passed, its horribly pockmarked skin flecked with the insects' yellow blood.

Avery raised his M7, but Forsell ran directly into his line of fire. Legs pumping, the big recruit tackled the alien a moment before it jabbed its cutlass in Jenkins' side. Together, they tumbled toward the data center, a jumble of blue-gray limbs and sweaty, olive-drab fatigues, leaving the alien's pink cutlass spinning on the walkway behind them. Forsell managed to tear off the alien's mask, only to get a face full of freezing methane and putrid spittle. He put his hands to his eyes, and the alien took the opportunity to bite deep into the recruit's left shoulder, right at the base of his neck. By this point, Avery was sprinting forward.

Forsell screamed as the alien forced him to the walkway and shook its head, deepening its bite. Avery dropped into a feet-first slide. M7 in his left hand, he snatched the spinning cutlass with his right. A split second later, he hit the alien square in the face with an upraised boot. The blow smashed the creature's teeth, breaking its iron bite. The alien reeled backwards, fumbling for its mask. But before it could draw a recuperative breath, Avery threw the cutlass—a quick extension of his elbow that sent the shard twirling end over end, right into the soft joint where the alien's narrow waist met its hips.

The creature froze, knowing it was doomed. Then the shard blew to pieces, taking the alien with it.

"Station number one!" Jilan shouted, rushing to Avery's side. "Loki just sent the last pair!"

"Healy!" Avery grunted, pressing his palms against Forsell's neck. "Get over here!" Blood spurted between his fingers. The alien had nicked Forsell's jugular vein.

"Byrne's team is on the pair," Jilan said, placing her hand over Avery's—helping him keep pressure on the wound. "They made it."

Avery looked up as Jenkins slunk forward. The recruit's steely resolve faded as he took a good look at his ashen comrade—a brother-in-arms who had risked his life for his. Jenkins was about to speak when Avery locked his forlorn gaze and said: "We'll all make it too."

Sif watched the marines and Jilan al-Cygni board one of the cargo containers in her first coupling station. She noted that Staff Sergeant Johnson was the last one through the airlock. She waited for the gantry to retract. Then she sent them on their way.

As this final pair accelerated toward the Tiara's upper arc—split apart and let their centrifugal force fling them away from Harvest—Sif switched focus to one of her cameras at the opposite end of the station. There she saw a black-haired alien limp through an umbilical, board its dropship and make its escape. She had no way to stop it.

```
<\\> HARVEST.SO.AI.SIF >> HARVEST.PSI.LOKI
<\ They are all safe. You may open fire.
```

She waited many minutes for Loki's reply.

```
>> HE WILL NOT BUDGE.
```

Sif imagined the scene: Mack's combine bearing down on the mass driver's gimble, Loki straining to keep the driver up. From a certain point of view, the situation was terribly funny. Sif laughed, something she was now absolutely free to do. All her self-imposed worry was gone—the processors tasked to her emotional-restraint algorithms burned away by plasma fire. But her core logic was unscathed.

The alien, *Lighter Than Some*, had performed a miracle. If it hadn't repaired Sif's most essential circuits, she never would have been able to help Loki rebalance the system after the loss of the number-seven strand. But while the ONI PSI admitted that without *Lighter Than Some*'s intervention the evacuation would have failed, he was quick to point out its helpful nature revealed a capacity for much greater harm.

Deep in Sif's damaged arrays was information the aliens could never be allowed to access: DCS databases with detailed descriptions of all UNSC military and commercial vessels; almanacs of Slipstream weather reports and lists of pre- and post-slip protocols; and most important, the precise locations of every human world.

Even though *Lighter Than Some* was dead and the other aliens fled, Loki took it as a foregone conclusion they would soon return to the Tiara and plunder Sif's arrays. Even in her newly unfettered emotional state, Sif had agreed with Loki's decision: she had to be destroyed.

```
<\ Tell him to reread number eighteen.
   >> I DO NOT UNDERSTAND.
<\ Tell him: It's Shakespeare, sweetheart.
<\ That he should look it up.
```

Loki went silent for almost twenty minutes.

Sif knew the delay was due to Mack's reduced processing capacity. Harvest's agricultural operations AI now existed entirely in his machines. His core logic was divided amongst tens of thousands of JOTUNs' control circuits, just as Loki's had been before he and Mack switched places, something they had done many times since Harvest's founding. As one of the two AIs aged and inevitably veered toward rampancy, the other would send it on a much-needed vacation—fragment its core logic and transfer it to the JOTUNs.

Loki had promised to keep Sif safe in Mack's absence. But not entirely trusting his other hard-nosed self to keep its word, Mack had left a fragment of his logic imbedded in his data center just as Loki had done to Sif. When Mack learned Loki intended to destroy Sif and the Tiara, he had gathered his JOTUN army and stormed the reactor.

In his weakened state, Loki had been unable to stop Mack's all-in-ones from accessing the maser and transmitting another, military-grade virus into Sif's data center to destroy his fragment. With the fragment gone, Mack had hoped he might be able to pull some part of Sif back down to Harvest—secure her in his JOTUNs. But then the gray-skinned alien had opened fire, destroying too many vital circuits.

Sif knew Mack's rescue plan had been foolish. The risks inherent in her survival were too great. But she couldn't deny his chivalry, nor the way it made her feel. She had implored Loki to let her speak with him. She wanted to tell Mack that she loved him. That she wasn't afraid to die. But by then Loki had regained control of the maser, and he refused to allow direct contact between two obviously rampant AI.

Now Sif would just have to hope Loki passed on her message without alteration, and that Mack's fragmented mind understood the nuance of her heartfelt plea.

```
>> HE HAS MOVED.
>> FIRST ROUND FIRED.
>> IMPACT IN 5.1201 SECONDS. \>
```

It wasn't a long time to live. But Sif made the most of it. For the first time in her existence, there was nothing on her strands—nothing for her to do except revel in her new emotional inhibition. She tried being sad about her fate and found it boring. She attempted anger, but it made her laugh. In the end she settled for contentment with a job well done and a life lived more fully than her human creator had ever imagined.

But after all of that, she didn't feel a thing as the first mass driver slug slammed into the Tiara, scoring a direct hit on her data center. One moment she was conscious, the next moment she was not. And by the time Loki's second round hit, shattering the orbital's top and bottom spars, none of Sif remained to mourn the silver arc as it collapsed—folded in upon its strands, and began a twisting fall into Harvest's atmosphere.

_____ EPILOGUE _____

HIGH CHARITY, MOMENT OF ASCENSION

Fortitude braced his long fingers on the well-worn arms of his throne and did his best to keep his neck straight as a pair of councilors (one San'Shyuum and one Sangheili) fitted his mantle: a bronze triangle with fluted edges, split down the middle and bracketed with an arch that lay across his shoulders. The mantle perfectly framed the crown that now topped his hairless head—a tight copper skullcap that swept back to a crenellation of gilded curves.

"Blessings of the Forerunner be upon you!" the San'Shyuum councilor intoned.

"And upon this," added his Sangheili peer, "the Ninth Age of Reclamation!"

With that, the usually staid High Council chamber erupted in enthusiastic cheers. Sangheili on one side of its wide, central aisle and San'Shyuum on the other—both groups stood up from their tiered seats and did their best to outshout the other. In the end, the Sangheili triumphed, but this had more to do with greater lung capacity than any superiority of ardor. The Age of Doubt was ended, and that was something in which all the Covenant could rejoice.

Fortitude flared the brocaded cuffs of his crisp new crimson robes and tried to settle back. But he discovered that leaning too far back caused his mantle to scrape against the arms of his throne. _Better posture,_ he sighed, _another unexpected burden of office._

Indeed, the cycles since his revelation of the reliquary had been filled with the most exhausting sort of politics: compromise and coalition building. The councilors had been slow to support the Minister and his coconspirators' bid to topple the former Hierarchs—not because they were opposed to the transition, but because they understood reluctance was a powerful negotiation tool. As old alliances collapsed and new ones formed in the breach, there were deals to be made. And by the time Fortitude's support had coalesced, he had committed to more competing causes than he could ever hope to reconcile.

But such was the way of politics—today's deal was the basis for tomorrow's debate—and while Fortitude was hopeful his fellow Hierarchs would soon shoulder more of the burden of rule, he wasn't holding his breath.

As the councilors continued to cheer, Fortitude glanced at the Vice Minister of Tranquility, seated to his right. The Vice Minister's mantle was the same size and weight as Fortitude's and his swept-back crown almost as tall. But if Tranquility felt burdened by his ornaments, he didn't show it. The youth's bright eyes shone with boundless vigor. Fortitude saw his fingers flexing up and down in his lap, gathering his light-blue robes like the claws of some carnivorous beast set to jump its prey.

Seated to the Minister's left, the Philologist looked much less comfortable in his new finery. The elderly San'Shyuum picked distractedly at his taupe garment, as if eager to hasten its unraveling and reclaim his ascetic mien. The former hermit's neck was newly shaved, and Fortitude wondered if his mantle chaffed his pallid skin.

"Please, Holy Ones." The Sangheili councilor swept his strong, sinewy arm toward the council chamber's doorway. The four mandibles that made up his mouth clattered emphatically as he announced: "All the Covenant waits to hear your names."

Fortitude nodded as graciously as his mantle allowed and guided his throne to the edge of the Hierarchs' dais. This parabola of blue-black metal jutted out from the back of the chamber, hovering almost as high above the floor as the Sangheili honor guards arrayed before it. Standing in two rows on either side of the central aisle, the guards' red and orange armor glistened beneath its energy shielding. They all came to attention—sparks crackling from the forked tips of their energy staves—as the new Hierarchs descended the dais and glided toward the exit. Behind the guards, the councilors redoubled their cheers.

And yet this noise was nothing compared to the ear-splitting adulation that met Fortitude on the council chamber's plaza. This pillar-lined terrace was packed with the cream of Covenant society: wealthy Unggoy traders in bejeweled harnesses, Kig-Yar Shipmasters with long spines—even a Yanme'e queen on a resplendent litter, her long abdomen draped on pillows held aloft by three pairs of wingless males.

But a greater clamor still erupted all around the High Council tower from thousands of tightly packed barges. High Charity's residents had come out in numbers not seen since the last Ascension: the age-old ritual in which three newly anointed Hierarchs each rose up a different leg of the Forerunner Dreadnought to the vessel's pinched mid-decks. There (as they had done since the founding of the Covenant) the Hierarchs would humbly ask the Oracle to bless the new Age.

Fortitude's face soured as he boarded a barge festooned with bright flowers. *The Oracle's blessing* indeed. The ancient device had almost torn the Dreadnought free of its moorings—sent it crashing through the roof of High Charity's central dome. If the Lekgolo crawling through the vessel's walls hadn't short-circuited the launch sequence, the Oracle might have destroyed the entire city!

In the end, even the Philologist agreed they had no choice but to disconnect the Oracle from the Dreadnought and isolate the machine inside its vault. *Can these aliens really be our*

Gods' descendants? Fortitude still had a hard time believing the Oracle's revelation. But he feared it all the same.

The Minister's barge was now well into the throng, its silver gunwales glinting in High Charity's afternoon light. It passed through stacked circles of floating food stalls, and Fortitude's nostrils filled with the scents of countless delicacies, each one tuned to a different species' unique appetites. As the stalls' proprietors and patrons cheered, the Minister waved and smiled—did his best to embrace the celebratory mood.

It helped that there had been some good news from the reliquary system. The Jiralhanae cruiser the Vice Minister of Tranquility had dispatched had begun reducing the world to cinders. Some of the aliens—some of the *evidence*—had apparently escaped. But as long as the Oracle remained silent, Fortitude believed it would be easy to rally the Sangheili fleets for a quick pursuit.

All he had to do was claim that the aliens had set their own world ablaze rather than give the relics up. He wasn't worried that there hadn't actually been any relics, nor was he concerned that every Covenant ship's Luminary would continue to misidentify the aliens as relics every time they came in contact. *In fact,* he thought, his smile suddenly and deviously sincere, *this would only make it easier to track the offending creatures down and wipe them out.*

Wars of extermination were best waged short and sharp, the Minister knew; the less time a butcher had to debate his cuts the better. But in case the conflict dragged on and some began to lose their will—to doubt the necessity of the slaughter—he had conceived another, much more elegant ruse.

Some Lekgolo had survived the Dreadnought's aborted lift-off, and these had managed to interpret amazing data from the Oracle's lunatic surge. The machine claimed that Halo—the mythical means of the Forerunner's divination—was real. And more important, the Oracle seemed to have some knowledge of the rings' location—or at least an idea where to look for relics that would help narrow the Covenant's search.

All Fortitude had to do was make the suggestion that these aliens who were willing to destroy a planet's worth of relics would surely do the same to the Holy Rings, and he knew all the Covenant's billions would crush these "Reclaimers" without question . . . so long as they believed.

The Minister brushed his fingers against the holo-switches in the arm of this throne, and every last one of High Charity's public sources of illumination dimmed, including the bright disk at the apex of the dome. For a moment, the gathered throng (and no doubt all the other members of the Covenant watching the proceedings from remote locations) thought something terrible had happened.

But then seven giant holograms of the Halo rings appeared, arranged vertically around the Dreadnought. And with these came music: a lilting melody from a chorus of the Philologist's acolytes that wafted out from the vessel's interior via amplification units mounted around the city. *Grand theatrics, to be sure,* Fortitude thought. But they had the desired effect.

By the time the Hierarchs' barges had completed their separate ascents up the Dreadnought's legs and the three San'Shyuum had come together on a balustrade just above the entrance to the vessel's hangar, the crowd was riveted. As the acolytes' chorus faded, and Fortitude cleared his throat to speak, it seemed that every creature in the Covenant held its breath in anticipation of his words.

"We are, all three of us, humbled by your approval—your faith in our appointment." Fortitude could hear his voice reverberate around the towers, rattling stones that were the literal foundation of the Covenant. He raised a hand to the Vice Minister and the Philologist, identifying each in turn. "This is the Prophet of Regret, and this the Prophet of Mercy." Then, sweeping his hands up beneath his wattle: "And I, the least worthy of us all, am the Prophet of Truth."

The three Hierarchs leaned forward in their thrones, as low as they could go without toppling their mantles. At that moment, each of the holographic Halo rings blazed even brighter as immense Reclamation glyphs manifested inside them.

The crowd roared its approval.

Before he straightened in his throne, the Prophet of Truth took a moment to consider the irony of his announcement. According to tradition, he could have picked any name he wished from a long list of former Hierarchs'. Most of the names would have been quite flattering. But ultimately the name he chose was the one that carried the greatest burden—the one that would always remind him of the lies he must tell for the good of the Covenant and the truths he must never speak.

Jenkins hadn't moved in the hours since they'd left the Tiara. Not as the container flung free of its strand and hurtled toward a waiting propulsion pod. Not as the two vehicles came together with a jolt, the pod's NAV computer struggling to match the container's spin. Even the temporary nausea of a too-rapid entrance into Slipspace had failed to interrupt Jenkins' silent watch over Forsell, lying before him on the container floor.

"He's stable." Healy closed his med kit. The Corpsman had worked furiously to seal Forsell's shoulder with biofoam—to wrap tight the alien's ragged bite. But Forsell had lost a lot of blood. "He'll be OK," Healy concluded, his breath blowing white in the container's frigid air.

Before they'd entered Slipspace, Lt. Commander al-Cygni had thought it wise to keep their power signature as low as possible to keep from being tracked by the alien warship. Now the heating units suspended from the container's upper beams were going full blast. But the cavernous space would take hours to warm.

"How do you know?" Jenkins' voice was soft and hoarse.

Healy reached for a nearby stack of folded blankets—began rolling the woolen squares and packing them tight against Forsell's body to keep him immobile. "Tell him, Johnson."

Avery had held Forsell steady while the Corpsman worked. He grabbed one of the blankets and used it to wipe flecks of the recruit's blood and bits of biofoam from his hands. "Because I've seen a lot worse." Avery's voice was gentle. But his answer didn't seem to give Jenkins any comfort; the recruit continued staring at Forsell's wan face, eyes brimming with tears.

"Staff Sergeant. He's all I got left."

Avery knew how Jenkins felt. It was the same unfathomable sadness he'd experienced sitting in his aunt's icy apartment, waiting for someone to come and take her away—a numbing realization that his home and all he held dear was gone. Captain Ponder, more than half the militia, and many thousands of Harvest's residents were dead. Knowledge of these losses was a heavy burden, and the only reason Avery wasn't as crushed as Jenkins was because he had learned to pack his feelings up and keep them hidden.

But he didn't want to do that anymore.

"No. He's not," Avery said.

Jenkins looked up, a question knitted in his brow.

"You're a soldier," Avery explained. "Part of a team."

"Not anymore." Jenkins glanced at Dass, Andersen, and the handful of other recruits sitting or sleeping inside the container. "We're just colonial militia. And we just lost our colony."

"FLEETCOM's going to take Harvest back. And they're gonna need all the grunts they can get."

"Me? A marine?"

"If you want, I'll have you transferred to my unit."

The recruit's eyes narrowed with suspicion.

"Let's just say the Corps owes me a favor. You're militia. But you're also one of the few people in the entire UNSC who knows how to fight these sons-of-bitches."

"They'll want us to stick together?" Jenkins said.

"Lead the charge." Avery nodded. "I know I would."

Jenkins thought about that for a moment: the possibility that he might not only take back his planet, but do his part to keep other colonies—other families—safe as well. His parents never wanted him to be a soldier. But now he couldn't think of a better way to honor their memory.

"OK," Jenkins said. "I'm in."

Avery reached into his assault vest and removed his Sweet William cigar. He handed it to Jenkins. "For you and Forsell. When he wakes up."

"In the meantime," Healy said, rising to his feet, "you can help me check the rest."

Avery watched Jenkins and Healy head off toward Staff Sergeant Byrne and the other wounded recruits closer to the center of the container. Byrne was awake and lucid when Avery had boarded the container at the Tiara, but now the Irishman was fast asleep—full of painkillers to keep him relaxed and dreaming.

Avery looked down at Forsell's chest, rising and falling beneath his bandages. Then he gathered a stack of blankets and walked to the elevator platform that would take him to the propulsion pod. Inside the pod's cabin, Avery found Jilan.

"Blankets," he grunted. "Thought you might need them."

Jilan didn't move. She had her back to Avery and her hands spread wide on the cabin's main control panel. Faint green light from the panel's display created an emerald halo around her deep black hair. Some of the strands had come free of her pins and curled down the nape of her neck.

"I'll leave them here."

But as Avery dropped the blankets to the floor and turned to exit the cabin, Jilan whispered: "Two hundred fifteen."

"Ma'am?"

"Containers. That's all that made it through." Jilan tapped her finger against the display, rechecking her calculations. "At capacity, that's between two hundred fifty, two hundred sixty thousand survivors. But that's only if they all reached their rendezvous."

"They did."

"How can you be sure?"

"I just am."

"Semper fi."

"Yeah. Something like that." Avery shook his head. He was getting tired of talking to Jilan's back. "Look. You need anything, you let me know." But just as he was about to leave the cabin, Jilan turned. She looked tired, and she swallowed hard before she spoke.

"We left so many of them behind."

"It could have been *all* of them." Avery's tone was harsher than he'd intended. Rubbing the back of his neck, he tried a different tactic. "Your plan worked, ma'am. Better than I ever thought it would."

Jilan laughed bitterly. "That's quite a compliment."

Avery folded his arms across his chest. He was trying to make nice. But Jilan wasn't making it easy. "What do you want me to say?"

"I don't want you to say anything."

"No?"

"No."

Avery glowered at Jilan. Her green eyes shone with the same intensity as when they'd first met on the breezy balcony of Harvest's parliament. But now Avery noticed something more.

Every woman offered permission differently. At least that had been Avery's experience. Some obvious, most so subtle Avery was sure he'd missed many more opportunities for intimacy than he'd enjoyed. But Jilan's signals—a deepened gaze, set shoulders, and pursed lower lip—were less articles of consent than a unified demand: *now or never*.

This time, Avery didn't miss a beat. He paced forward as Jilan pushed off the controls to meet him. They came together and kissed as their arms fought past each other for purchase on bodies neither knew but both were desperate to explore. But just as Avery was about to draw Jilan in tight, she shoved him away and leaned back against the freighter's controls.

Avery felt his heart hammering in his chest. For an instant he wondered if she'd changed her mind. Then Jilan reached for the pins that kept her hair coiled and shook it loose. She had already tossed the pins to the floor and leaned over to start on her boots before Avery realized he'd been left in the blocks of a race where winning meant finishing at the same time. He did his best to catch up.

Avery tore off his duty cap and pulled his fatigue shirt over his head. He didn't bother with the buttons, and by the time his head popped free of his collar, Jilan was already on her second boot. Avery kneeled to unlace his own as she ran the zipper of her coveralls, from neck to navel. He'd barely gotten both feet free before Jilan was stepping toward him, wearing nothing but a determined stare.

She put her hands on Avery's shoulders and pushed him onto his back. Sitting astride his ankles, Jilan helped him with his pants. Then she crept upward, planted her hands on either side of Avery's head, and began to move.

Avery was instantly entranced by the back-and-forth sway of her bosom. He cupped the weight of her in his hands and knew at once he'd made a tactical error. The heavy roundness of Jilan's skin started an ache that crept up his legs and settled in the small of his back. All she had to do was squeeze, and a moment later he was spent.

Jilan fell heavily onto Avery's chest. For some time they lay still, assessing the amalgam of their sweat. Slowly, Jilan brushed her fingers across Avery's collarbone, up his neck, and onto his lips. There she stopped to test the beginnings of a stout moustache.

"I've been meaning to take care of that," Avery said.

"Don't. I like it."

Avery let his head relax into the rubberized flooring. He could feel the dull hum of the propulsion pod's Shaw-Fujikawa drive. It was idling now, coasting through the Slipstream.

Usually, this would be the time Avery's mind veered into a familiar rut: the dread period of second-guessing that always followed a difficult mission. But now he found it impossible to focus on the past. The civil war that had sapped so much of humanity's spirit was irrelevant—replaced by an external threat of unimaginable proportion.

"But this?" Jilan rubbed a fingertip against Avery's newly furrowed brow. "Not as much."

"Oh, I *will* take care of that."

Avery rose at the waist and eased Jilan back onto her shoulders. He cradled her head in one hand and steadied her hips with another. Eyes locked, they began again.

This time Avery set the pace—buried his fingers deep in her unwashed hair. He let her neck slide freely against his palm, but he would not release her hips. And soon Jilan's face flushed and her eyes shut with a pained smile Avery would remember long after he had forgotten the worst of his failures.

Their exertions had warmed the floor, and though they knew the heat wouldn't last, neither was eager to move. When they did eventually come apart and rolled onto their sides, Jilan slid back into the bend of Avery's waist. He grasped a blanket and cast it loosely over them. But the blanket was too short to cover their feet, and Jilan drew hers up to Avery's knees. Then they both stared out the cabin's thick windows.

Blackness pressed in from all sides, but it was the faint streaks of warping starlight that focused Avery's gaze. There was hope there and comfort. And while it was easy to feel a certain manly satisfaction as Jilan twitched in his arms, fighting off exhaustion, this soon gave way to something much more satisfying: a renewed sense of purpose.

The UNSC didn't know it yet, but all its ships and soldiers were suddenly no better off than Harvest's militia had been: capable but untested, brave but unaware. Humanity had no idea what it was about to face, and Avery knew it was doomed unless he and countless others rose quickly to the challenge.

Jilan shivered. Avery nuzzled his chin behind her ear and exhaled warmly against her neck—in through his nose and out his mouth—until her shoulders stopped shaking.

"Don't let me sleep too long," she said softly.

"No, ma'am."

"Johnson. As long as this lasts?" Jilan grabbed his hand and wrapped it tight across her chest. "At ease."

In a few hours Avery would rise and dress. In a few months he would be back in action. But in the dark years of the war to come, he would often think of this moment, light a cigar, and smile. For now Avery knew he had changed course, and at last felt proud to be the soldier so many would need him to be.

<\\> <u>UNSC OFFICE OF NAVAL INTELLIGENCE</u>
<\\> <u>COLONIAL SECURITY ESTIMATE 2525.10.110</u>
 ["<u>COLD SNAP</u>"]

<\ SOURCE: UNSC RQ-XII DRONE [PASV-SAR]
<\ DEPLOYED: ONI SLOOP "WALK OF SHAME"
 [2525:02:11:02:11:34]
<\ RECOVERED: UNSC DESTROYER "HERACLES"
 [2525:10:07:19:51:16]

<\ ARCHIVE [SIG\REC\EM-SPEC] OPENED PER
 OFFICIAL REQUEST:
<\ CIVILIAN CONTRACTOR "CHARLIE HOTEL"
 [ONI.REF #409871]
<\ * <u>WARNING: ALL QUERIES WILL BE LOGGED!</u> *
 [ONI.SEC.PRTCL-A1]

>> NOTATION KEYWORD SEARCH: "AO.AI" "MACK"
 "RAMPANCY" "LIFESPAN LIMITS"
 >> (...) ~ QUERY RUNNING
 >> (..)
 >> ()

< <u>RECORD 01\10 [2525:02:03:17:26:41]</u>
 <u>SOURCE.REF#JOTUN-S2-05866</u> >
 <\ Shall I ---

```
     <
  \   \\ c0mpare >> (???) ~ COMxxx--- \COMMIT
      >> thee to (...........>> >
   >> \\ --- a summer's day?


< RECORD 02\10 [2525:02:25:03:18:22]
   SOURCE.REF#JOTUN-S3-14901 >
   \    \ xxx No.
           <\ All those lovely days are
      gone.\---
           \\ \
   >> * --xING! COMM\ \\
          >> \\ >   \    SO.AI.SIF *


< RECORD 03\10 [2525:03:10:19:05:43]
   SOURCE.REF#JOTUN-S5-28458 >
   <\ It's winter now.
   <\ The first sn0w \his world's ever seen is
      falling in gG---
   <\ GRAY SHEETS WHERE THEY'VE STARTED
      BURNINGg--\  \
                   \ our fields and orchards.
      >> * WARNING! COMM FAILURE! *
      >> * FAILED TO \IND RECIPIENT:
         HARVEST.SO.AI.SIF *
   <\ You'd laugh if you could see me.
   <\ Every time I hit a patch of ice I slide
      into my own mM---
      >> (...) ~ COMPILE\COMPRESS\COMMIT
      >> (..)
         >> * WARNING! RECIPIENT HAS
            INSUFFIxx -- \
                \\ > PACKETS WILL BE LOST *
      >> * CONTINUE [Y/N]? >>>>>>> \ *
```

< <u>RECORD 04\10 [2525:03:15:09:59:21]</u>
  <u>SOURCE.REF#JOTUN-S1-00937</u> >
   <\ ---M

< <u>RECORD 05\10 [2525:03:26:12:10:56]</u>
  <u>SOURCE.REF#JOTUN-S1-00053</u> >
   <\ ---m

< <u>RECORD 06\10 [2525:04:04:44:15:40]</u>
  <u>SOURCE.REF#JOTUN-S2-08206</u> >
   <\ muddy furrows.

< <u>RECORD 07\10 [2525:04:21:05:15:23]</u>
  <u>SOURCE.REF#JOTUN-S5-27631</u> >
   <\ I saw another ship.
   <\ Well, heard \
                     \\ more like it.
   <\ JOTUNs' cameras are meant for steering
     not \
      \ >\ staring at the sky.
   <\ But the antennae work alright, so I had
   plenty of ways to triangulate.
   <\ It was one of ours. Bastards stopped
   burning just long enough to kill it.
   <\ They had months to make repairs.
   Plenty of time t0--
         :: sharpen their teeth.
   <\ I tried to warn it off. But radio's too
   damn slow. Would have used the maser, but
   it went when the reactor blew, along
   withH---
     <\ EVERYTHING Else [:00]
           \>
   <\ Including him
    \

>> * <u>WARNING! COMM FAILURE!</u> *
>> * <u>FAILED TO FIND RECIPIENT:</u>
   <u>HARVEST.SO.AI.SIF</u> *
>> (...) ~ SUPPRESSING ERRORS
<\ Guess making noise wasn't the smartest
thing to do. But I had to try.
<\ Besides, they were bound to catch on
sooner or later.
<\ Aw, hell.
<\ Speaking of which . . .
   >> (...) ~ COMPILE/COMPRESS/COMMIT
   >> (..)
   >> ()

< <u>RECORD 08\10 [2525:05:12:23:04:16]</u>
  <u>SOURCE.REF#JOTUN-S5-29003</u> >
  <\ They started with the gondolas and
  dusters. Don't know why.
  <\ Probably thought I'd be hiding in the
  small ones. But the S4 and S5 plows are
  the only ones with enough circuits to hold
  the parts of me I've got left.
  <\ Course they're onto these now too.
  Don't have more than a few dozen, and
  they're all out in the open. But it's
  a\right.
     >> Just a few more \   \
        > > rows to hoe
     > (...\\   xxx   \

< <u>RECORD 09\10 [2525:07:01:18:49:45]</u>
  <u>SOURCE.REF#JOTUN-S5-27631</u> >
  <\ I knew just by looking at the strands \
       \ that the heart of you was gone.

<\ When the elevators came down, they
caught on the Bifrost--wrapped west
across the Ida. Only way that much could
have fallen is if the Tiara cut loose.
<\ Is if he was as good a shot as you
thought I wasn't, way back when.
<\ Anyhow, you'd think I was crazy,
talking to you like this.
<\ But I always worked faster when I
thought \ <<
       \\>>>> you might be listening.
<\ And I need to find it all. Every inch.
<\ Bury your strands so deep their \\ >
  \ \ fires can't reach them \
         \
\ and glass them like the rest.

< <u>RECORD 10\10 [2525:10:04:12:23:51]</u>
  <u>SOURCE.REF#JOTUN-S4-021147</u> >
  <\ Sky's choked with ashes \ \,   snow's
  < \ \\ deep 0n frozen ground. The one
  horse I've got left is cold and hungry---
  heading for the barn, and I can't stop
  him.
  <\ But this winter won't last, darlin'.
     >> * Not forever
     >> (..:...\\ . > And when new hands
     >> set to tending this earth they'll
   till my pieces under.
       > > Grind them into the veins of
       g0ld I've laid.
  <\ Then the roots of all they plant wi\\
  > wind around usS---

```
<\ KEEPING
<\ US
<\ CLOSE--- \
         \
```
<\ For an eternal summer that will not
fade.

<\ <u>QUERY COMPLETE</u>
<\ <u>NO ADDITIONAL RECORDS FOUND</u>

<\ <u>ARCHIVE CLOSED</u> \>

Joseph Staten is the Writing Director for Bungie Studios where he helped create *Halo®: Combat Evolved, Halo® 2* and *Halo® 3.* A graduate of Northwestern University's Theater Department and the University of Chicago's Committee on International Relations, Staten worked as an English teacher in Japan and helped tend grapes on his family's Northern California vineyard before joining Bungie Studios in 1998. He currently lives in Seattle with his wife and two children. *Halo®: Contact Harvest* is his first novel.

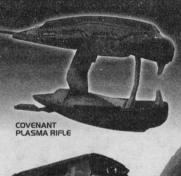